E. J. Swift is the author of *Osiris*, the first novel in The Osiris Project trilogy. Her short fiction has appeared in Interzone magazine, and in anthologies *Pandemonium: The Lowest Heaven*, and *The Best British Fantasy 2013*.

Praise for E. J. Swift

'Dystopia is back . . . fascinating . . . [a] promising debut novel' *SFX*

'An assured and accomplished debut novel . . . an absolute gem'
Interzone

'A fantastic blend of worldbuilding, excellent storytelling and complex characters' *SF Signal*

'Swift's first novel, with its brilliant near-future vision of an ecologically and socially devastated world and characters who resonate with life and passion, marks her as an author to watch'
Library Journal

'Marvelously well done. A glittering first novel: a flooded Gormenghast treated with the alienated polish of DeLillo's *Cosmopolis*. The result is a gripping novel, readable, beautiful, politically engaged and wholly accomplished. Swift is a ridiculously talented writer' Adam Roberts

Also by E. J. Swift:

Osiris

CATAVEIRO

BOOK TWO OF THE OSIRIS PROJECT

E. J. SWIFT

DEL REY

1 3 5 7 9 10 8 6 4 2

First published in the UK in 2014 by Del Rey, an imprint of Ebury Publishing
A Random House Group Company

The Random House Group Limited Reg. No. 954009

Addresses for companies within the Random House Group can be found at:
www.randomhouse.co.uk

A CIP catalogue record for this book is
available from the British Library

The Random House Group Limited supports The Forest Stewardship
Council® (FSC®), the leading international forest-certification organisation.
Our books carrying the FSC label are printed on FSC® -certified paper.
FSC is the only forest-certification scheme supported by the leading
environmental organisations, including Greenpeace.
Our paper procurement policy can be found at:
www.randomhouse.co.uk/environment

Printed and bound in Great Britain by Clays Ltd, St Ives PLC

ISBN 9780091953072

To buy books by your favourite authors and register for offers visit:
www.randomhouse.co.uk

For Kim, who reads everything first

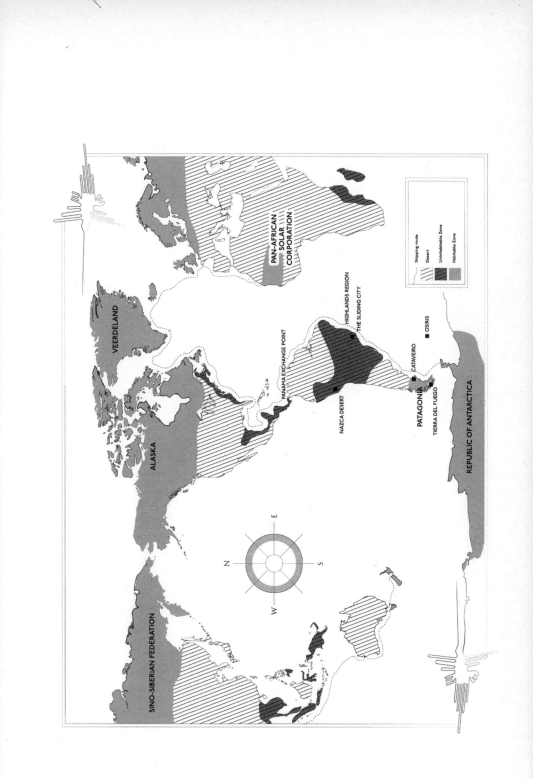

PAN-AFRICAN
SOLAR
CORPORATION

Shipping route
Desert
Uninhabitable Zone
Habitable Zone

VEERDELAND

ALASKA

SINO-SIBERIAN FEDERATION

PANAMA EXCHANGE POINT

HIGHLANDS REGION

THE SLIDING CITY

NAZCA DESERT

CATAVEIRO

PATAGONIA

OSIRIS

TIERRA DEL FUEGO

REPUBLIC OF ANTARCTICA

N
E
W
S

01/ 10/ 2417

FM   SPECIAL UNIT ATRAK / GRAHAM STATION 6
TO   DEP CIVIL SECURITY HQ / HOME SECURITY CHIEF MAXIL QYN
INFO   CIVIL SECURITY REP ANTARCTICA PRIORITY

SUBJECT: MONITORING OF THE SOUTH ATLANTIC OCEAN CITY OSIRIS
(INTERNATIONAL STATUS: DESTROYED)

REF: OS17521

Classified by: KARIS IO, CMR SPECIAL UNIT ATRAK
(FM 04/05/2414)

1. Summary: During the perimeters of 24/09/2417 and 01/10/2417 Special Unit Atrak has observed the usual protocols and measurements in relation to the South Atlantic Ocean city known as Osiris as stipulated by the Department of Civilian Security of the Republic of Antarctica. No significant changes in status have been recorded.

2. No vessels have been observed to have left the City. No vessels have been observed to have approached the City. No vessels have been observed to be destroyed in either departing or approaching the City.

3. During this period the City is not assumed to have undergone an unusual level of activity. Long-range measurements have recorded no sudden power surges beyond average consumption. Energy output is consistent with records and with the slight but steady decline observed over the past twenty years.

4. After the fluctuations observed in energy levels and what Atrak believed to be high-level weapons usage during the winter of 2417 (see report OS17498), we conclude that the City has regained its usual status and can be considered benign.

5. No external radio signal has been detected.

Special Unit Atrak advises that the warning code for Civilian Security with regard to Osiris remains at amber.

RECOMMENDED ACTIVITY: Continued observation.

PART ONE
LA ISLA / THE ISLAND

1

The line stretches away into the desert: enigmatic, questioning, older than anything the pilot has ever seen or found. The guide, walking in front, stops every few paces to crouch and move a tiny piece of rock back to its given location. He proceeds with soft, cautious steps, as though he cannot bring himself to place too much weight upon the ground. The pilot follows a short distance behind, letting the guide set the pace. She has mapped this line from the air, but to walk it is a different feeling than to see it, a deeper feeling, and a stranger one.

The civilization that created these phenomena had no known method of flight, yet the spirals and glyphs that remain reveal a geometrical precision that astounds the pilot. She can see now how they were made; the reddish pebbles of the desert's upper layer have been cleared to expose the pale, pink-tinged earth beneath. The cleared rocks are piled up at the edges, delineating the boundary between the line and the darker desert floor that stretches out on either side.

The guide comes to a halt and points ahead, and the pilot sees where the line begins to trail away. She takes a piece of paper from her pocket. The co-ordinates tally with the sketches she made in flight.

'Two kilometres,' she says.

'And once, it continued here for another kilometre, or further,' says the guide, pointing further ahead. 'But the erosion has done its work. As you see, the lines were never very deep. The rest of this one is lost.'

The pilot squats where the little piles of rock begin to peter out. She does not remove anything; that would be disrespectful at a sacred site. But she presses her palm lightly against the earth, listening. It is warm to touch. She can feel the same heat through the soles of her boots. Looking in the direction where the line should have run, she imagines she can still see its path, as if it has left some paranormal trace that glows through the arid earth.

The guide watches her – appraisingly, or to check that she does not disturb anything, the pilot is not sure. She thinks how perspective shifts between ground and air. A thing up there is not the same as a thing down here, though the eyes of the person seeing them are unchanged.

'Could the lost lines be restored?' she asks.

'Perhaps,' says the guide. 'But what would be the point when another event could destroy them all over again? It needs to be an ongoing restoration.'

The pilot stands, shading her eyes to scan the plateau around them. At eleven o'clock, it is thirty-three degrees and rising. She can feel the short bob of her hair sucking in the sun's heat and she replaces the wide-brimmed hat, taking some relief in its meagre shade. The desert is still and silent and empty. She cannot imagine clouds swelling in the skies, or shifts in the lie of the land. It does not seem possible that those things could exist in such a place. But they can, they have. For centuries, perhaps for millennia, the Nazca lines lay undisturbed, but the guide says that over the past three hundred years there has been a steady deterioration, with fragments of the glyphs lost each year.

She walks a little further into the desert where the line disappears. The guide watches her.

'A proper project would require funding,' he says. 'Workers. Supplies. This is the outback. All we have is a single House, and five acolytes. This country venerates the teachings of the Nazca and yet every year the heritage site declines a little more. One day, there won't be anything left and this place will be empty desert. It's not right.'

'You do good work with the little you have,' she says.

'Not enough. You work for the government. Can't you say something, now you've seen it for yourself? It was they who wanted the maps, wasn't it?'

'Yes . . .'

'But . . .?'

The pilot is touched by the sincerity of the guide's passion. She does not want to tell him what she suspects is the truth: that this project is nothing more than an exercise in public relations. She has noticed, more and more lately, the way the Nazca creed is co-opted into the speak of politicians, as though a single reference will endorse whatever ludicrous new taxation policy they have dreamed up. To meet someone who has dedicated his life to conservation is refreshing. This is a man who loves the desert, both its history and its future.

'I can say what I've seen, of course, but I don't have any influence. I'm just a cartographer.' She looks back at him. He looks dubious, perhaps intuiting, rightly, that there is more to her job than that. She relents. 'And a carrier, sometimes.'

'You'll take a message, then?'

'Write me what you think you need. I can deliver a petition, but I make no promises they'll do anything. Really, I wouldn't get your hopes up. I'm sorry.'

'You know the Neons made plans to preserve the animals,' says the guide. 'Misguided, but I suppose we have to presume their intentions were good. They built a dome over the monkey. Of course it was removed, a long time ago now. If the lines cannot see the sky then they serve no purpose.'

'The monkey couldn't breathe.'

'Yes,' says the guide, again with a hint of suspicion, as though the pilot's answer encompasses things too neatly.

'I understand.'

It is an indescribable feeling, standing on the lines, even here where the desert has reclaimed its natural state. She can feel the weight of it. Imprints of a thousand footsteps, resonance of a thousand words. Echoes of rites and beliefs. Hope. Despair. As though the lines are a conduit to the past, a place for spirits to gather, watching, whispering about the walkers of the present.

You line-makers were not so very different from me. We all hope for kind weather and clean water and a fair sun. We all love. We all lose.

To the east, a barren dune mountain rises out of the desert. The pilot points.

'That's Cerro Blanco, isn't it?'

'Yes. Have you made pilgrimage before?'

'Not yet.'

'You have less excuse than most.'

She knows that the guide is referring to her plane, and feels the usual jolt of nervousness that occurs when it is out of sight. But she could not have landed in the desert itself, not in a heritage site. In any case, she reminds herself, the chameleon makes it all but invisible. *Stop worrying.*

It isn't easy to trust Neon technology. Even after all this time. She runs her hand over her back pocket, feeling the reassuring bulge of the gun. The guide notices, and shakes his head disapprovingly. But he is a good man, with respect for cultural traditions. Others are not. She has to be able to protect herself.

'How much longer will you need?' asks the guide.

'I've still got the far side of the plain to cover. I'd say another few days.'

She could work faster, if she is honest, but this is a job she does not want to rush. Tomorrow she might be wading through swamplands or trying to find a pathway down a cliff-face. Today, she is happy to walk the lines of the spider, or the orca, almost alone in this place of contemplation.

'You should complete your pilgrimage first,' the guide tells her. 'It's important to pay due respect. Make sure you give blood.'

It takes the pilot half a day to climb the trail to Cerro Blanco. She is the only one up on the dune, or if she is not, she sees no other people. The sky remains fiercely, clearly blue. In the heat, with her heavy pack, the going is hard, and she stops frequently to take a mouthful of water and massage her aching calves. When she reaches the crest, she finds evidence of recent visitors. Mostly there are shards of pottery, painted and plain, some broken, some still intact. Other offerings scatter the ground: a few yellowing pieces of bone; the skull of a rodent, sand spilling from its eye sockets. The dune must hold thousands of such articles, each imbued with personal yearnings and desires, sinking deeper over time with the shifting of the sands.

The pilot sets down her pack and carefully removes her own offering: a small vase with a pattern of swimming fish. She chose the piece deliberately. The vase for water, the fish for prosperity. Now that she is here she wonders if it is appropriate. What now? Should she break the vase? Should she say something, or sing? Unlike some she keeps no private religion in the theistic sense of the word, only the teachings of the Nazca, instilled since birth, to guide her way through life. She did not ask anyone for advice about pilgrimage, and if she had, she would not have been able to articulate why she came at all.

In the end, she places the vase on the ground next to the other pieces of pottery.

'Cerro Blanco, please accept this offering. Please bring water back to the deserts. Keep the winds low. Keep the desalination plants safe, and the sea from those on the coasts.'

She speaks aloud. Her words seem to linger for a long time after she speaks. She looks out across the plateau, and feels calmness stealing through her. The guide's words come back. Well, why not? She takes out her knife and makes a tiny incision across the ball of her thumb. She squeezes out a few drops of blood and watches them seep into the sand. Her thumb stings. Perhaps this is enough, to remind yourself that you are alive, and you have one chance to live it well.

As she makes her way down the dune, the scores of the Nazca lines glare white beneath the endless blue sky. Each glyph recalls a childhood story, her mother's strong, faintly ironic voice. Sweat eases down the bridge of the pilot's nose and over her upper lip. She saves time by sandboarding down the easier slopes. The ride is exhilarating. She is almost at the bottom when she sees the figure running across the desert floor before her. It is an acolyte of the House of the Nazca, a young woman clad in bleached desert robes.

The acolytes do not run if they can help it, not in the Nazca Desert, not over the sacred lines. The pilot's first thought is the plane. Her hand goes to her back pocket. She hurries towards the woman.

'What is it, what's happened?'

The acolyte is panting, and the words come in short, staccato bursts.

'Come quickly – we need you – an accident.'

They hasten back to the heritage site where the plane is concealed, the acolyte explaining on the way. A young boy at the desalination plant on the coast. A piece of machinery – a terrible accident. His leg – the boy should not have been there. The owner of the plant loaned his parents a truck, and they've driven all this way, hearing she was in the area . . .

The family are waiting at the House of the Nazca. There is a man holding the boy in his arms, a woman with them, both distraught. The boy's lower leg is bundled in cloth that is soaked through with blood, a tourniquet tied tight around his shin. Blood is everywhere, smeared on his hands and face. They converge upon the pilot.

'Please take him – please help . . .'

'Alé, this woman's going to get you to a doctor . . .'

The acolyte hovers anxiously.

'How far to the nearest hospital?'

The pilot pictures the landscape. Her heart sinks.

'It's a day away.' She drops her voice. 'Too far. He won't make it.'

'Then try the medical station at Titicaca. If you can get him there, he'll have a chance.'

She nods. 'I know the one. All right, let's get him on-board. This way.'

They follow her around the back of the building. The boy's parents look about, confused, not seeing what she sees, the edges of the aeroplane merging into their surroundings, almost invisible unless you know it is there. She opens the hatch and switches off the chameleon, and the plane's exterior turns white. They gasp as it materializes.

'It's all right, it's just a cloak. Don't be scared. Up here.'

The man lifts the boy carefully into the passenger seat. The acolyte reaches up as the pilot straps herself in. She puts a hand on her arm.

'Thank you, Ramona – go safe.'

She looks at the injured boy and thinks grimly, don't thank me yet. The hatch glides down and eases shut, encasing her and the boy in the silent bubble of the cockpit. She starts up the engine. The instrument panel lights up and the boy's sketchy breathing fills the enclosed space. As they take off she sees the acolyte waving to them, her slight figure growing smaller and smaller against the pinkish-brown earth. The desert falls swiftly away.

She pushes the plane as fast as she can, but the boy's blood is dripping into the footwell and the ground below them seems to crawl by. He is not the first casualty to have occupied that seat. Not everyone has made it.

She guesses the boy's age: maybe ten, maybe younger. A scrawny kid, but you never see fat ones. The desalination plants this far up the coast are low-grade, independent businesses, supplying small outback towns that cling to the backs of Neon ruins. The people who survive here have refused to go south, despite all their losses and the volatile climate. The boy's family probably earn their living as labourers on the plant, or technicians, if they have any education. The tiny community will be wholly reliant on passing ships and the traders who take the western desert route up to the Panama Exchange Point.

She can imagine Alé's life. She can picture him, playing football with his friends and clambering over the crumbling sea defences to comb the beaches for treasures at low tide, daring the storms to catch him. He collects junk from the old city and turns it into objects that have no purpose but to bring him a pleasure that others – adults – would not understand. When he's not helping his family earn enough income to buy Alaskan grain, he's cajoled into school, sitting with a group of distracted children, being told about the Boreal States and the Blackout and the terrible dangers of robotics and the teachings of the Nazca, of which the first and most imperative of all the rules is the preservation of water. She can bet he has never seen an electrical display like the one on the instrument panel in front of him. If he were able to focus, the sight of it would make him nauseous. It took Ramona weeks to adjust.

But he can't see anything. His eyelashes flutter, the eyeballs rolling beneath them. His skin is slack and clammy. Taking one hand off the yoke, she reaches under the passenger seat and pulls out a blanket and wraps it around him as best she can.

Likely he'll have a couple of siblings, if they've survived the plagues. His mother will live in constant fear of losing a child to the jinn or, Nazca keep us, the redfleur, but not like this. Not an accident. Not so sudden and so cruel.

'Alé,' she says. 'Alé, stay awake.'

The boy does not respond.

'Alé, I need you to stay awake for me. Can you do that? I know all you want to do is sleep, but you mustn't, you've got to stay awake for me. Just until I get you to the doctor.'

He moans. In her pack are one or two shots of morphine, but she is scared it will send him off for good. She reaches out and takes his slick, bloodied hand and clutches it tightly in hers.

'Hang in there, Alé. Come on, you can do this. Tell me about yourself. Alé, that's a good name. What's it short for – Alejandro?'

'Yes.' A slip of a voice.

'I knew an Alejandro once.' He turned out to be a selfish bastard, but you can't know everything at fifteen. 'How about your family? Do you have a brother? A sister?'

'Lu.'

'Lu. That's a good name too. What's that for, Luisa?'

This time there is no answer. She can feel him slipping from her. She keeps squeezing his hand, asking him questions. She has been told that an unconscious person can still hear, or at least can sense that you are there.

'Shall I tell you a story?' She thinks. She needs a good one. 'I'll tell you one about the city. Have you heard of the city? In the south? It's a long way from here. Two to three days' flying, when the weather's fine. It was a boy like you who went there first. He was a juggler. Have you ever seen a juggler, Alé? This one was very good. In fact, he claimed to be the best in the land. He styled himself "The Great Cataveiro". People asked him to prove it, of course, so he pitched a tent by a river in a Patagonian valley, and he offered to juggle with the possessions of every traveller that passed. He made a promise – not to drop a single one. Imagine that. And if he did, he said they could ask him to do anything they liked. This was the gamble. So, of course, everyone wanted a go. They gave him all sorts of things. Lúcumas and peaches. Family heirlooms. Lizards, alive and wriggling. He caught them all.'

Ramona stops there, because now she remembers the end to this particular story, and the juggler does not come out of it so well, in any version.

'If you ever go to the city you'll see lots of jugglers there,' she says. 'Are you awake, Alé? Hey. Wake up. Come on. Don't you crash out on me.'

The boy is unresponsive. She watches the empty, arid land passing below. The speedometer wavers at two hundred kilometres. The plane is at its limit; she can ask no more of it. When the salt marshes of Titicaca finally glide into view she manoeuvres the plane for as long as she can with one hand, until she is forced to let his go and use both. There is the isolated town and the white roof of the medical centre.

'All right, we're landing now. You'll feel a weird sensation in your ears, but don't worry, it's over fast. They've radioed the doctor. She's waiting below. She's right there. We're coming down now. Hold on tight. Hold on for me, Alé.'

She brings the plane down as smoothly as she can. She can see a medical team running towards them as she taxies to a halt. They have a stretcher ready. The boy makes no movement. Has she lost him?

The doctors lift the boy from the plane. They are talking – technical terms she does not recognize. They rush the boy away on the stretcher and into the medical centre. Ramona follows slowly.

After a few minutes someone comes out and asks what her blood type is. They take a litre. She watches the needle siphoning it from the crook of her elbow into the clear plastic bag. She asks if he'll be okay. The nurse says the transfusion is his best chance.

For two hours Ramona waits. She goes back to the plane and mops up the mess as best she can, trying not to think about how much there is, about the injury that must have let out that much blood. She returns to the waiting room. It's clean and orderly, but everything looks decades out of date. She is the sole occupant. It's only a small outlet station, with one emergency operating room. The doctors are all Patagonian. Titicaca is clinging on, but the marshes grow smaller every year. From above, you can see the grading of the landscape, outlining what was once a vast lake, and how far it has receded.

When the surgeon comes out she tells her the boy will live.

'And his leg?'

She says they have had to amputate the foot. The boy was exposed for too long; gangrene was already setting in. They couldn't save it.

'Can I see him?'

They let her into the room. The boy is drugged and woozy. He does not know who she is but she sits by the bed and takes his hand and holds it. The nurses have cleaned him up; now his hands have been washed she can see that the nails are bitten very short and the fingertips are callused. The bedcover dips where the surgeon has removed his left foot at the ankle.

The surgeon, hovering, says, 'Lucky for this one you were in the area.'

Ramona hears the shift in her voice, almost a reverential tone, and she wants to say, *Don't*. She looks at the boy and pictures his life now. There won't be football. He will move awkwardly, using crutches, and the plant that employs his family will have little use for him when he grows old enough to work. His mother will care for him as best she can, maybe resorting to stealing opium when he's in pain.

But he is alive.

'You're a survivor, Alé.' She squeezes the boy's hand tightly. 'Remember that.'

2

The journey south is punishing. A day's clear flying followed by two days grounded by storms, a narrow flood escape, and another three troubling days in the air. By the time she crosses the strait from the mainland to the island of Tierra del Fuego, Ramona can no longer deny that there is something wrong with the plane. She first noticed the alarming engine noise towards the end of the job in Nazca, and over the past forty-eight hours it has been getting progressively worse. She has checked everything, but the aircraft is handling badly, yawing in the slightest wind. Maybe she pushed it too hard taking Alé to the medical centre. She levers the yoke anxiously.

'Come on, *Colibrí.*'

She keeps the plane high as they drift over the island's silver lakes, partly because it seems to respond better at altitude, and partly because she prefers her arrival not to be witnessed – at least, not by her employer. They pass briefly through mist as they cross the ridge of the mountains, but it clears on the other side. The roof of the Facility, jutting out from the face of the mountain, is marked with yellow cat's eyes. She begins the descent, circling down in small spirals, feeling the tension in the sick aircraft. When she touches down it's a bumpy landing on a very short runway. She pulls the plane in a sharp U-turn and skids to an ungainly halt.

The plane rocks, then settles. The motors rattle down to a quiet whine, the way they should sound all the time, before cutting out. For a moment she stays as she is, strapped into her seat, listening to the stillness until her own breathing becomes intrusive. She thinks of the dune. Cerro Blanco.

When she checks the battery level she finds it is only a quarter full, which is unusual, worryingly so. She keeps the plane's solar-leaf cells on a maximum charge. The battery should be full again in a couple of hours. She climbs out, abruptly aware of her aching feet, and snaps the mooring tethers onto their magnetic points. At the Facility there is no need for the chameleon, but she double-locks the hatch.

It is a dull day to return to base. The sky is clouded over, entirely white, and the only sense of colour comes from the flag trees and thorny scrub that line the slopes above the Facility roof. On the other side, the road runs down to the harbour town with its pink and blue and red buildings and the high sea walls that guard them. Fishing boats rock on their tethers, but there are no ships in the harbour. Is the fleet due, or has it already left? She thinks of Félix aboard the *Aires*, wonders where on the ocean they are. *I'd like to see you, Félix.* She can see the ocean surging inland, battering the flood barriers. Further along, the looming ruins of Ushuaia City poke out of the waters. On a sunny day, the plundered city is still a source of treasures for brave divers, but today the sea trawls through the ruins in sullen white and grey, as though in collusion with the depressing bureaucracy of the Facility.

Ramona wants to put off entering the building for as long as possible so she grabs her toolkit, unscrews the panel to the engine nacelle and gets under the plane for the fifth time since leaving Nazca. For the fifth time, she cannot see what is wrong. Nothing seems broken, nothing is leaking; there's no corrosion. She lies on her back, staring up at the cloud banks above the underbelly of the plane. She hopes Raoul has some ideas.

She braces herself and enters the building via the roof hatch. With any luck, no one from the Facility will have seen her arrival, and she can escape a briefing with supercilious Lygia until morning. The building is quiet. She hurries past the shunned second floor, where the poor souls condemned to use computers put in their hours. They always sit on the other side of the Facility's canteen. Sometimes Ramona feels bad about that. Not always.

At ground level, the foyer is cold and grey. She is swamped with an immediate sense of gloom. Above the reception area hangs a faded Patagonian flag and the animals of the Nazca glyphs: monkey, hummingbird, spider, heron, orca. An old man with silver hair sits behind a desk. His uniform is equally faded, and the whole scene is like a tableau in a cave that has been left undisturbed for thousands of years.

But the old man's eyes light up at her entrance. He gets awkwardly to his feet, one hand supporting the small of his back.

'Ramona Callejas!'

'Hello, Eduardo. It's good to see you.'

'It's good to see you too, Ramona. Yes, I'm always happy to see you're still alive.'

Eduardo's smile does not waver but the statement is ambiguous, as is the man himself. Ramona leans against the desk. Eduardo, who sees all of the Facility's comings and goings, is a useful man to have on side.

'Have I missed all the excitement?' she asks.

'Oh, we've had plenty of excitement, never you worry. One mother of a storm last night, for a start. They lost a fishing boat. Sad tale, it is. Remember Pedro? His whole livelihood, that boat, and there's three young kids. And I'll put money on another tonight. I can feel it. My joints are telling me . . . But what have you been up to, our illustrious pilot, eh? You have some stories for old Ed?'

'Mapping at Nazca. The lines. And the glyphs.' Ramona glances up at the dusty flag. She does not mention her pilgrimage to Cerro Blanco; it is not something of which it can or should be spoken. Nor does she mention her illicit mercy dash. If Lygia finds out, she will make her disapproval very clear; she does not like Ramona going off-task. Instead, she puts on a mysterious tone. 'On the way home I discovered a pirates' nest.'

'Pirates? Lots of them?'

'Three ships. No markings. Not a renegade in sight. Quiet as the dead, they were. The bay was almost hidden . . . but I saw it from the air.'

'Not El Tiburón?'

'If it was, he didn't dare show his face to me.'

'Ha!' His laugh is short and breathy. 'You're the lucky one. Where were they?'

'Can't say, Ed. Classified, isn't it? Shouldn't have told you this much.'

He loves that.

'You staying with us long, Ramona?'

'You know me, Ed. I never stay any longer than I can help. It's not the company, but . . .'

He nods and offers her a wink, as though they share a conspiracy. Perhaps they do, she thinks. Perhaps Eduardo dislikes it here as much as I do.

'I'll sign you in.' The old man enters Ramona's name in a large, heavy book. His writing is slow, the letters solemnly etched. 'You've got your key?'

She lifts the chain hanging around her neck.

'Ed, I need to get hold of Raoul—'

The telephone interrupts; Eduardo holds up a hand. She waits as he takes the call.

'Yes? Oh. I see. No, if it's run out, it's run out. No, I can't get you another one. No, the energy room is closed.' A pause. Eduardo's expression is tight with annoyance. 'Not until morning. No, there's no one there now. I can't help you. No. That's too bad. Goodbye.'

Eduardo whistles through his teeth.

'Unbelievable.'

'Who was it?'

'The Tarkie on the fifth floor. Used his energy ration. Now he expects me to whistle up a brand-new supply just for him. Those Tarkies come over all charming, but they take what they want when it comes to our precious resources. All right for them, isn't it? They've got wind farms of their own. They don't have to go begging for African solar cells.'

Ramona frowns. 'We don't beg. Who is he, anyway?'

'A researcher, so he says. A botanist.'

Eduardo's tone of voice encourages her to lean in closer.

'So he says?' she echoes.

Eduardo looks to left and right, as though there might be hidden eyes surveying them. He has spent too long in this dusty foyer. Nothing happens in the Facility except for the creaking laws of government; if it's news you want, you need the harbour.

'I've never seen him collecting flower seeds, is all. Not that kind anyway. One day he comes in all worked up and when I asked him nice as anything to sign in – three times I had to ask – he starts shouting all kinds of things. So I know what he really does – or did, that is.'

'What's your theory, Ed?'

'I reckon he's been disgraced. Exiled. In fact, I'll bet you on it.'

Ramona rolls her eyes. 'What are you betting?'

The old man hesitates. He loves a bet. It must bring a ripple of excitement to his monotonous routine.

'I'll bet you a week's hot water ration.'

'All right. You're on.' Ramona knows she won't take it from him, even if she wins. Probably Eduardo knows that too, but they both play the game. She tosses her key and catches it, thinking of the jugglers in Cataveiro.

'Now what were you saying, before we got interrupted?'

'I was saying, I need to get hold of Raoul.'

'Can't be doing that. He's off island.'

Why, she thinks, does Eduardo always sound happy when he delivers bad news?

'Off island?'

'His dad got taken sick. Didn't say what it was. Didn't sound good.'

'Shit. I need a mechanic.'

'Problems with the plane?' Eduardo asks slyly.

'It could do with some fine-tuning, that's all.' The last thing she needs is Eduardo babbling to Lygia, and Lygia trying to chain her to a desk for a week, or worse, sitting her next to a drone while they set her maps on a computer.

'Well, you should try him upstairs.'

'Who?'

'The Tarkie! Didn't I say he let slip his old job? "I was an engineer," he says. All high and mighty as if I was supposed to be impressed.' Eduardo drums the desk gleefully. 'Get him to make himself useful. Fifth floor, same as you. Can't miss him, green eyes, a bit spooky. I should warn you, though, that Tarkie Portuguese will make your ears hurt. Barbarism to a decent language, that's what it is.'

'Well, maybe. If Raoul's not back tomorrow, I could try him. Night, Ed. Don't tell Lygia I'm here, will you? I don't want to see her before I have to. And I'll tell you the rest of that pirate story . . . tomorrow.'

Eduardo winks.

'You know old Ed. Your secret's safe with me.'

Eduardo is always here, however long she has been away; there is some consolation in that. *Even if he is an unrepentant gossip.* She climbs the back stairs of the building. Five flights, down another corridor. Same floor as the Antarctican – worth remembering. She walks past metal door after metal door. Only a small percentage of them are occupied at any given time. The rooms are home to a peculiar assortment of staff: governors, army officers and ad hocs, researchers, data entrants, ambassadors, the occasional freelancer like herself.

The room with her name on it is a one and a half by two metre box. The key grates when she opens the door. She has been out for several weeks – another reason Lygia will want to pick her brain for information. She can never decide if it is her controlling nature that repels her the most, or the manipulative way she tries to befriend you. Typical politician. And yet it was Lygia who first took her seriously when she said: Let me fly this, and I'll make you all the maps you need. It was Lygia who persuaded her colleagues to make Ramona an exception.

Inside the room everything is dusty; she draws a fingertip through the fine coating on the table and pulls the bunk down from the wall. A tangle of old army blankets fall out. She shakes them out and stands on the bunk to open the tiny window and let in some air.

Originally built by northerners for an entirely different purpose, this is one of the few buildings in the country to use bufferglass. Glass and solar cells have made the Pan-African Solar Corporation rich, and rumour has it they plan to buy up the Australian continent next. The new energy will go north, fuelling the glittering techno-cities of the Boreal States. In exchange for the Patagonian poppy harvest, a lean trickle of cells will come here.

The Facility might not be Ramona's idea of home, but it is a familiar quantity. She has spent enough recovery time in here. The worst was a broken leg, seven years ago, and because she was impatient, it still aches sometimes when she is tired. She thinks of Eduardo's words earlier. *You're the lucky one.* The way the surgeon at Titicaca looked at her. People assign luck to her, good and bad. If she has it, it is a peculiar kind. Sometimes she wonders what a life would be like without the charm of the plane, a life not marked by luck and all its expectations.

She turns on the radio. Tango, nice. Pulls off her boots and socks and examines her feet. Red but only a couple of blisters, despite all the walking in the desert. She takes out her maps of the Nazca Desert and studies each one, feeling the simple satisfaction of a job well done. Cartography is not about power, as some would have it. It is always an act of translation: the rendering of something unknown into something intelligible, and it has a beauty all of its own.

She climbs into the bunk and lies flat, feeling her body slowly relax, taking deep breaths of the fresh air through the window. She feels cooped-up but safe. The feeling of safety makes her uncomfortable in other ways, reminding her that she has had this room a long time, that it is easy to become reliant. On people. On places. Even on a job.

A spider runs across the ceiling: small-bodied, long-legged. She thinks of the spider in the Nazca Desert, and remembers how it felt to walk along the lines, the sense of a history so great it seemed present in the air around her. But not all of the glyphs can be seen. Some have been blurred by erosion; some are lost forever.

On her left thumb, the barest of fine lines marks where the skin has healed. She is still not certain why she went. Sometimes, such as when you stand on the Nazca lines, it is easy to believe in something greater, even if it is only your own purpose. Other times, like Alé, like the unlucky ones that did not make it, it is not.

A knock at the door interrupts her thoughts. She is surprised to see Eduardo, one hand clutched to his chest, panting.

'Ramona, I forgot to give you this.'

He holds out a letter. She takes it and examines the writing on the front. It is addressed to her, simply enough – Ramona Callejas, The Facility, Tierra del Fuego.

'One of the pedlars brought it down from the highlands,' Eduardo explains. 'You know I don't trust those vagabonds, but this one seemed smart enough.'

The highlands, where Ramona and Félix grew up. It looks like Félix's mother's handwriting: Carla. She likes to keep in touch. Ramona feels a well of pleasure.

'Thanks, Ed.'

'You're welcome. You know, you could get a telephone in this room.'

'I could. But then people would call me.'

He shuffles away, still breathing heavily from the exertion of the climb. Ramona shuts the door and sits on the bunk, her legs tucked under her. She tears the letter open.

Dear Ramona,

I hope this letter finds you and finds you well. I wasn't sure where you might be so I asked the pedlar to take copies to Fuego and the garage in Cataveiro and one or two other places on his route in case you passed through.

If one of them has reached you safely then I have to tell you your mother has been taken very sick. The doctor says it's the jinn and she's converting. I offered for her to stay with us down on the slopes but you know how she is. There's not much we can do here. Perhaps you know some people from your travels that might help, or you could get her something for the pain she's in now. Either way, I thought you should know. Inés would be angry if she found out I had written. But you know how it goes with the jinn. Any little thing might be enough to end it.

Please, come soon.
Your friend, Carla.

PS – if you see Félix, give him my love.

Ramona reads the letter several times. She thinks of Inés, her stubborn, difficult mother. She thinks of the sliding city, with its red dust and its landslides, and she sees the shack with the little veranda built by Ramona and the chair outside where Inés always sits, and the graves nearby of Paola and Camilo.

Patagonian medicine has no cure for the jinn.

3

She knocks sharply on the door. There is no immediate response but she is sure she can hear someone moving about inside. She knocks again, louder.

'Hello! I'm looking for the Antarctican.'

This time there is the sound of hasty footsteps, a scuffling like furniture being shifted and a distinctive clinking noise, and then a voice calls, 'Yes, yes, I'm coming, hold on.'

The door opens part way. The man standing awkwardly within its frame bears a frazzled expression. Eduardo is right. He has a distinctive face: those green eyes are very light against brown skin. He is dressed in jeans and a thick jumper and he has a scarf wrapped around his neck, one end of which is fraying badly. His hair sticks up from his head as though he has been running his hands through it repeatedly.

'Yes?' he says politely. Too politely.

She glances past the door. The Antarctican shifts slightly to block her view, and at the same time she notices the smell – a hint of burnt sweetness, trickling from the narrow aperture. She is certain then, and groans internally – of course, of course it would be – all the exiles turn to it in the end. What is it about her country? But she has no better option than this. Raoul might be out for days. She hopes this one is good at his job.

'I hear you're an engineer,' she says.

The Antarctican tries to smile but his fingers tighten around the doorframe. 'Who said that?'

'Eduardo told me.'

'Oh. I'm afraid Eduardo heard it wrong. I am here on quite a different kind of mission. I'm here to collect specimens of flora. Seeds. Pollens. All of those things.' His Spanish is peppered with Portuguese, strongly accented with that particular lilt that the Brazilian-Antarcticans have. It's odd, but unlike it does Eduardo, the sound doesn't offend her. 'We are trialling different things in the soil, you know, to see how they take. So your friend must have made a mistake. Yes. I'm sorry about that. Very sorry.'

He is eyeing her nervously as he rattles away, as if to check how she is taking the story. Why does Raoul have to be away today?

Ramona folds her arms. 'Look, I'm not the Patagonian government, I don't care what your cover story is.' The man winces. 'I know you're an engineer. And I've got a broken aeroplane. Can you help me?'

'An aeroplane. Really?'

She senses the spark of interest, but then his gaze slopes away to the side of her. She can tell that all he really wants to do is sit in that dark room and walk the honeyed road to oblivion.

'It's the only working aeroplane on the continent,' she stresses.

'I'm sorry,' he says again. 'I know nothing about aeroplanes. I've never seen one.'

'You're an engineer.'

'I'm a botanist,' he says firmly.

'You're an engineer.'

The Antarctican shakes his head slowly. 'That was before.' He starts to close the door.

'Are you afraid you can't fix it?'

The barb is a low, desperate shot and Ramona doesn't really expect it to work, but to her surprise the door inches open. The Antarctican's face, bleary-eyed and sunken-cheeked, peers through.

'Of course I can fix it,' he says.

On the way out he locks the door carefully behind him. He looks nervous. That makes two of us, she thinks.

As they climb the stairs to the roof she explains that Raoul is her primary mechanic and it is he who would usually deal with this, except he is away. The Antarctican responds in that polite but vague way. He is not interested in Raoul and his family problems. It is only when she begins the story of how they applied to the knowledge banks for the plane's schematics that he displays a flicker of curiosity. Really, the Boreal Knowledge Banks? Where else? she says, and he asks if their bid was successful, and she says no, or it never made it through the Exchange, but whichever it was, it is she and Raoul who have patched up the plane together over the years, without the schematics.

They emerge onto the roof of the Facility. Some of the haze has cleared overhead; a brisk breeze plucks at the Antarctican's scarf. He tucks it into his jumper and huddles deeper inside the woollen garments, shivering, although it isn't cold. In the sudden onslaught of bright light and space he looks dazed and disorientated, perhaps unnerved by the drop over the edge of the roof and the heady view down to the strait. She can see the sweat on his face and the craters under his eyes quite clearly, and she thinks: Why did I bother? This is going to be a disaster.

But then his gaze alights upon the plane, perched on the far side of the roof like an intricate armoured insect. His eyes brighten visibly. He walks up to it and around it, exclaiming and admiring. Snatches of sun glint off the plane's tapering solar wings. Ramona looks anxiously at the sky down to the south, where cumulus clouds are building ominously, and tries not to betray her impatience. The Antarctican runs a hand over the motionless propeller. Something about the gesture is reassuring to Ramona; by it she can tell a love of the machine, an understanding, the way she loved the cars in the garage in Cataveiro. Suddenly she can glimpse the engineer in this wreck of a man.

'Careful of the solar leaves,' she warns. 'They get dangerously hot. Actually, the battery should be charged by now. I'll turn them off.'

The Antarctican nods, stepping carefully under one upturned wing.

'It's a beautiful thing,' he says. 'Quite incredible to see. This is Neon technology?'

'Yes.'

'I thought all South American aircraft were decommissioned during the Migration Wars. Aren't they banned from your airspace?'

'Do you need to see my licence?'

'No, I – it doesn't matter. Where did you find it?'

Ramona thinks of the Atacama Desert, the rusting telescope array with its many ears turned to the silent, empty skies. Violeta del Torres.

'That's a long story,' she says.

'But you learned to fly it – someone taught you?'

'I taught myself. You ask a lot of questions.'

The Antarctican looks at her with undisguised curiosity, but does not query further. He tugs distractedly at an unravelling thread in the scarf around his neck.

'So . . . tell me the problem.'

She explains about the noise coming from the motors, the motors that should emit nothing but a low, steady whine, and today were not. She tells him about her unsuccessful attempts to investigate. He listens and taps the windshield thoughtfully. Ramona indicates the sky.

'We've got about an hour before that comes in. Do you think that's enough time?'

'Why, do you have to be somewhere?'

'I have to go north, urgently.' She hesitates, but there is nothing to lose, and she needs him to work quickly. 'It's my mother. She's very sick. It's the jinn.'

'I'm sorry.'

'That's between you and me.'

'I'm a botanist, remember?'

There are puddles of water dappled across the roof, so Ramona remains standing and watches as the Antarctican opens up the nacelle, lifting it clear to expose the motor beneath. He peers inside, and sounds something experimentally.

'Was it a bad storm last night?' she asks.

The Antarctican twists onto his back to give himself a better angle of vision.

'Bad enough. But you should see them where I come from.' His head has disappeared inside the plane, and his voice is muffled. 'Can you pass me a screwdriver? The smallest one you've got.'

She roots through her toolbox and passes him the screwdriver, and crouches where she can see his hands. The mechanics of the plane are so delicate, and she notes a definite tremor in his hand, even if he is managing to keep his voice level.

'Thanks.'

'Can you see what the problem is?'

'Yes.'

'What is it?'

'Looks like it's your bypass fan.'

He doesn't elaborate. Ramona crosses her fingers. Luck, she needs her luck today. She can hear the scratch of metal from inside the panel. The Antarctican's feet are braced firmly against the roof of the building. His shoes are heavy-duty, waterproofed with thick soles, made to last. His trousers riding up his ankles reveal one yellow sock and one green.

She checks the sky again. Down in the harbour she can see the waves crashing against the sea walls, throwing up sprays of white froth. The rain is maybe half an hour away. All across the archipelago,

Patagonians will be running for cover, dragging inside anything of value and banging the storm shutters closed. Then they will pray – *let the waves stay low, let the winds stay light, and the sea walls keep us safe and tight.*

That is what they say around here, the small children who hang about the harbour and poke at the fishing catch with sticks. Ramona did not grow up on Tierra del Fuego. She never sung those songs, she never said those words, and yet she thinks them now and they stick in her head the way the hawkers' jingles do.

She cannot go anywhere tonight. But if the plane is fixed and the storm blows out quickly, she can leave just before dawn.

The Antarctican drops the screwdriver with a curse.

'Be careful!'

'I'm being careful, very careful. This is a nice motor, you know.'

She closes her eyes briefly, wishing for Raoul. At last the Antarctican's head emerges from the plane, his eyes squinting against the white light. He wipes sweat from his forehead, causing his hair to stand up even more raggedly.

'She's fixed.'

'Really?'

'Yes.' He frowns. 'Simple blockage. Build-up of grit.'

'Grit?'

'Yes.'

'You're sure? That's all it was?'

'It happens. You want to test it?'

'No offence, but yes.'

When she tries the engine it runs smoothly and silently. She turns and catches the Antarctican laughing for the first time. She feels foolish, but gratitude wins out.

'Thank you.'

He shuts the open panel and screws it back into place. There's a lost, longing look in his eyes that makes her feel sad.

'Does she have a name?'

'*Colibrí.*' Ramona traces the outline of the hummingbird on the fuselage of the plane. 'This is the Nazca glyph. I saw it for myself only a week ago, in the desert.'

'I thought I recognized it – the flag, downstairs. You have temples for the Nazca, don't you?'

'Houses of the Nazca,' she corrects him. She can see he wants to ask more questions. He probably thinks the teachings of the Nazca are a prophetic religion, something like that of the Mayans, complete with sacrificial rituals. She could tell him that the teachings are actually quite straightforward: based on principles of economy and conservation, things at which the Nazca society were adept, and especially concerning water. But she is not in the mood to explain cultural customs to foreigners. At the same time she realizes that Eduardo never told her the Antarctican's name, and she didn't ask. That was a discourtesy on her part.

'And you? I didn't catch your name.'

'It's Taeo.'

'I'm Ramona.'

'I know. Ramona Callejas. You're the cartographer, aren't you?'

'That's right.'

'So what came first, the mapping or the plane?'

The question surprises her. It is not something most people would ask.

'The maps,' she says.

'But everyone calls you the pilot.'

'The two go together. I couldn't go so far north without the plane.'

'I didn't think there was anything living past forty degrees.'

Ramona opens her mouth to correct him. On the tip of her tongue are the stories of Titicaca, the Nazca Desert acolytes, or the marsh nomads with their netted boats and mistrustful eyes. Then she changes her mind. 'There isn't much.'

In any case, she never hands over her maps without a slight sense of unease. She does not include everything she discovers. Sometimes it is her own decision; sometimes the villagers she finds ask her not to reveal their existence. They prefer to stay lost.

'You must be very useful to the government,' says Taeo.

'Lots of people assume that.'

'And are you?'

'Ask them.' She isn't going to tell him about the continual arguments with Lygia, who really wants a spy, not a cartographer. Lygia values the utilitarian: she wants to find enemies. Ramona wants to find people.

Taeo puts his hands up. 'Just curious.'

'Anyway, where did you learn to fix things? If it wasn't with aeroplanes?'

'Oh. I built things. I built ships, actually. Not as pretty as this, it's true.'

'Well, thank you. I owe you one. Seriously, any time.'

He nods. 'Maybe you can give me a ride – in *Colibrí*. When you get back from the north, I mean.' He looks about the roof, up at the mountains with their bare heads like uncrowned kings, down towards the harbour, where the waves are surging. 'I've never been up here before. It's quite the view.'

'It's inaccessible except through the Facility, that's the main reason. The runway's a little short but—'

'But you're good,' he says. 'I've heard. You should come to Antarctica. Map places that have never been mapped before.'

'I thought you didn't let anyone in?'

'I suspect the Republic would make an exception for someone with your skills.'

'And for my family? My mother? My friends? Would your Republic make an exception for them too? I don't think so.'

He looks at her for a long moment.

'Is it all Antarcticans you dislike so much or just those of us who speak Portuguese?'

'That is not what I said.'

'No, but it's true.'

She hesitates. 'There were other things – there were other opportunities that could have been taken – the reforestation movement, working to save this land, rather than run to the new one and leave us all to burn.'

'I take your point, but to me that's ancient history. This place is the past. Antarctica is my home. It's been my parents' home and their parents' before them and their parents' parents' before them, right back to the Migration Wars. All I have left of this place is the language, and the only reason I have that is because the Republic did not want Boreal English as its primary language. The rest? I'm sorry, but it means nothing.'

He points at the bank of clouds. 'That's going to hit soon. What say we go for a drink while it passes, and continue this awkward conversation there? I am interested to hear more, you know.' He smiles. He has a mobile, expressive face; thoughts run over it like weather. It is a face that might serve him well in this country, if he learned how to use it. She thinks: He will never learn how to use it. 'And you can tell me the story of how you got *Colibrí*.'

Ramona is tempted. He is right, the conversation needs unpicking, and how often do you get to speak to an Antarctican, and tell them your side? It would be good to get out of the Facility, and talking to Taeo might take her mind off her mother. But she has a plan to formulate. There are routes to plot, clothes to wash while she has access to laundry facilities. She shakes her head.

'Not tonight.'

Taeo's smile fades away. All at once she notices his bloodshot eyes, the unshaven jaw, the tremor in that right hand with the index finger incessantly tapping against his thigh, and she is glad she refused. The man is a mess.

'Good luck, then,' he says abruptly, and runs down the steps without a backwards glance.

She feels a tug of guilt.

When she looks up, she can see the storm coming in, a black veil of rain sweeping across the island to the south and the strait. The sight reminds her of what this building used to be, a long time ago when doomed idealists built the lost city, before the Great Storm condemned those pioneers to the waves. Now the storytellers weave tales of a shadow city, where the old one fell. The ocean hides it. So many sailors try to find it and never do, their boats capsized and pulled down into the deeps. The true tragedy happened before Ramona's lifetime, but she always thinks of the Osirian people when she is here at the Facility, and hopes their souls are kept safe, wherever they are now.

4

He sprints down the winding, precarious road. Within seconds he is drenched. He can hear the roar of the sea, pounding against the flood barriers. Past the low concrete outhouses and army barracks; past the soldiers on duty huddled under their waterproofs who barely glance up as he runs by. Trees on the mountainside bend in submission to the wind. A blast catches him and he skids perilously close to the sheer drop at the edge of the road and he does not care, a strangely triumphant part of him almost wishing he would slip the final centimetres that will send him over, thinking that would show them. As he runs he screams, and the fresh cold water batters his face and fills his mouth. Does it taste different, the rain here? Everything is different. Everything is wrong. He runs on. He trips and falls and curses and pulls himself up again and runs.

'You call this a storm?' he yells. 'You call this a storm?'

There is no one to hear. He is shivering now. The truth is, it *is* a storm, a powerful one, but he can see the sparse lights of the harbour town shimmering ahead through the scything rain. Arturo's, he will make it to Arturo's Place. He passes the first few houses. The streets of the town are like rivers, but the route is familiar, even in the half darkness. When he reaches the bar the windows are shuttered and only a faint glow comes from between the slats, but he knows there are people inside. There are always people inside this place. He pounds on the door and keeps pounding until Arturo himself opens it.

He senses that up to the moment he steps inside, the atmosphere has been jovial, buoyant. A group of four local men are sat together around a cards table at one end of the bar, while others overlook the game. All are fishermen judging by their attire and the lingering smell of brine. Most of the locals in this small port are fishermen or stevedores. They look at Taeo with distaste. There are mutters. Taeo ignores them. He goes to a table on the other – empty – side of the bar and asks for a double rum.

The storm sounds louder from inside. Rain drumming on the roof almost drowns out the fuzzy music emitted by the radio. Patagonians, always chattering on the fucking airwaves. Considering their hysterical technophobia, they're happy enough to broadcast their life stories and those of everyone they know over a wavelength. It's irrational.

One or two of the fishermen continue to cast suspicious glances in Taeo's direction. The majority simply pretend he is not there. He drinks the first double and orders another, hunched over his table, feeling the water from his clothes seep into the chair and through his shoes to the floor. He wants opium but he is trying to stop. When the pilot knocked on his door he had the pipe in one hand, the little wire in the other. She saved him, momentarily. She has the kind of face once seen it is difficult to forget, though he would be pushed now to say why, exactly. Dark, enquiring eyes, strong eyebrows, her chin jutted forwards, as if pre-empting trouble. He has the impression she could have told him a lot, if she'd cared to. She refused to go for a drink with him, though. Just like the rest of them.

Fuck. He'd kill for a smoke right now. Why did he come out?

He thinks of Shri and imagines what she would say if she could see him now. He pushes away the thought because it is too awful to bear.

There is a place right here in the harbour town; that's where he discovered it first. A nice place – a salon, the proprietor calls it –

with soft chairs and pillows where there is tea if you want it and the radio plays only music, all tunes with a soothing, yet melancholy air, that the other clients nod along to, and sometimes hum. Pipes and syringes are offered to your preference (all completely hygienic, the proprietor reassured him, and there was further reassurance in his smart, clean attire and business-like manner). Taeo prefers the pipe. It's the tradition of it, after the old Asian style, and this way the stuff is purer, botanical. At first he took regular trips to the salon, but now he prefers to buy in bulk, and smoke it in the solace of his own room, out of sight.

Maybe he should have stayed there tonight. But the energy's gone and that man, Eduardo, goes out of his way to be unhelpful. After fixing the plane (that gorgeous machine – where the hell did she get that? The Patagonians scrapped every Neon aircraft they had) it just feels wrong.

His glass is empty again. Wordlessly he raises it, trying to catch the bartender's eye. He orders wine. Marisa, that is her name. Marisa takes her time coming over with a bottle, also silently, without meeting his eyes. Is he imagining it, or does she deliberately arch away from the table as she reaches to pour the wine, keeping as much distance between herself and him as possible?

He thanks her. He says the bottle is a favourite, but he couldn't care less what it is – doesn't even bother to look at the label.

Her lashes flicker. There is no acknowledgement; she could be serving a ghost. As she moves away he sees her shoulders relax, her walk taking on a leisurely sway. She pauses by the card players.

'More beer, boys?'

'Yes, Señorita Marisa, more beer. And how about some of your pretty friends to join us too, eh?'

'You'd have my friends out in this weather? Shame on you.'

'Eh, they can't be as pretty as Marisa.'

Marisa's laugh is round and encouraging and her dark curls bounce when she throws back her head. Taeo would have liked to talk to her.

He would like to talk to anyone. He takes a heavy swig of the red. The aftertaste of the wine here is sour and harsh, nothing like the sharp, clear heat of the sake back home. He watches the bartender and the fishermen flirting.

Since the day he stepped foot on Patagonian soil, an invisible circle has been drawn around him. If he squints, he can almost see its borders. Now and then he observes covert glances in his direction or catches the edge of a whisper. A part of him wishes he could hear what they are saying about him, and the other part is grateful for his ignorance. He drinks deeply from the glass, welcoming the haze of alcohol that is settling about him.

Shri jumps into his head again, and this time it is impossible to dismiss her. He thinks of the winters that are full of dark and Shri, and the summers that are full of light and Shri. He thinks of the beaches where they walk and the strange, luminous creatures that wash up from the ocean depths. He thinks of Shri's voice through mist too dense for the lights of Vosti Settlement to reveal a face, and her fingers locked through his, and the walk home with nothing but touch and voice, and he remembers her lips against his, when no one can see.

Not every moment was like this, it is true. The six months prior to his departure were not like this, but those moments are harder to reach, and anyhow, he does not want to think about those dreadful months, only the good times. The times that were golden.

By the time Ivra comes the rain has dropped to merely forceful and the bar's clientele has doubled. Taeo has swaddled himself in memories. His bodyguard is angry. Taeo holds up a hand as though this might ward off the inevitable berating. He wonders if the salon is open and thinks about how long it would take to get there. About ten minutes. The pull on the pipe, slow, fills his mind, and how the smoke would taste.

Ivra sits heavily in the empty chair opposite, water cascading from his hood when he pushes it back from his face. He speaks in their home patois.

'How many times do I have to tell you not to wander about without me?'

'More than once, I suppose.'

Ivra's voice drops to a furious whisper. Taeo avoids looking at him. Perhaps if he looks away for long enough, Ivra's anger will wash up and over him, like a passing wave.

'More than once? Do you think this is a joke? You know, I feel like I'm dealing with a child, not a senior Antarctican engineer.'

Taeo gives a humourless laugh. One of the fishermen glances up. When Taeo notices, the man swiftly averts his eyes.

'Maybe it is a joke. Maybe that's exactly the joke.'

'You're drunk again.'

'Is there anything else to do in this fucking place?' Despite the haze around his thoughts, he knows better than to mention the opium. He's managed to keep that much a secret from Ivra.

'How about keeping your head down and having some respect for your own skin, not to mention mine? You know the archipelago is crawling with pirates.'

Taeo picks up his glass. It is empty. Again. He raises it, but Ivra clamps a hand over the rim, forcing Taeo's arm back down.

'Enough.'

On the other side of the room, the bartender is hovering by the cards table, its places claimed by a new set of players. One slender hand leans on the back of a customer's chair, the other rests jauntily on her hip. The game is growing raucous.

'They won't even look at us,' says Taeo. 'The Patagonians. They despise us.'

'Not all of us.'

Taeo studies his bodyguard. The years abroad have made their marks. Warmer summers have darkened his complexion. Ivra is Brazilian-Antarctican like Taeo, but he has dropped his Portuguese entirely. His Spanish sounds like a native now. With the locals he adopts a convivial, disarming manner.

Ivra does not walk around with an invisible circle attached to him. But he has been stationed in Fuego for a decade. Taeo is not prepared to wait that long.

'Have some wine,' he insists. 'It's on me.'

'We're leaving.'

'Even you refuse to drink with me?'

'You know, you're paranoid about people not speaking to you but you refuse to take the possibility of a kidnapping seriously. I fucking despair.'

Taeo says nothing. He has no desire for an argument, even through the immunity of alcohol. He pictures Shri, focuses on her warm, broad smile. But he can't hold on to it. Shri's brow knits, and she lets loose a tirade of anger. Instead, he thinks of the salon.

'I have to get out of here, Ivra.'

'We can both hope for that.'

'This place is what theists would call actual hell.'

'You've been here all of four months.'

'It's all been a big mistake. I'm not a . . .' Even now he has trouble speaking it aloud. '. . . a dissident, Ivra. I shouldn't be here.'

Ivra folds his arms across his chest. He is a big man and the posture makes him look more imposing. They never speak of it, but Taeo knows his bodyguard is a link in the Antarctican information network. The same network for which Taeo is now some kind of minion: a message-boy.

'Perhaps you should have thought of that before you transmitted an open holoma to the Republic,' says Ivra steadily.

'Have you seen my transmission, Ivra?'

'Yes, I've seen it. I'm not surprised they sent you here.'

'It was a mistake. I wasn't myself. It was stupid.'

'I'm not surprised by that either.'

'They must realize that. I can't stay here.'

Not without Shri.

He speaks her name silently, over and over, as though there might be some essence of her in the air that would communicate if she were here. Surely she will forgive him now. He's done his penance. Missing her is too much to bear. How many times he said he loved her, meaning it, but not thinking about it, and now her absence is an open wound. He misses the children, their hugs, their funny direct questions, and the way they all giggle over things secret to themselves, the three children together, a perfect trio.

The door to the bar opens. A man runs inside, neglecting to close it behind him. The newcomer pushes back his sodden hood and starts gabbling in deep Fueguin dialect. Some of it evades Taeo but Ivra's posture shifts. Taeo can see he is listening intently. The newcomer is gesticulating. The telling grows wilder and more dramatic as he goes on, until a chorus of exclamations drowns him out, and Taeo can't catch a word.

'What's he saying?' Taeo asks. Ivra motions: quiet. Taeo hears the word shipwreck, repeated over and over. There has been an accident, somewhere down the coast, earlier tonight, a ship on the rocks. The man's story is drawing to a climax. He speaks faster and faster and suddenly he stops mid-sentence, as though the words have been snatched from his throat. He looks solemn now. The listeners have gone quiet and very still. When Taeo looks at their faces he sees a collective fear dawning.

Someone says, 'Not possible!'

There is a long silence and then the newcomer whispers, 'Yes, Osiris.'

Taeo stares at Ivra.

The door bangs shut and bounces open again. No one goes to close it.

'No, no,' says a voice, perhaps the one who spoke before, perhaps someone else. The newcomer insists, 'Yes,' and then everyone begins talking at once.

Ivra pushes back his chair and jerks his head towards the door. Bewildered, Taeo follows him outside. The rain is still falling heavily, spattering his face with cold droplets. The warm fogginess of the bar seeps away.

'That man said there was a shipwreck,' he says.

'Yes.'

'A ship from . . .' He can barely say the name; his head feels light and dizzy. He finds himself whispering, as the Patagonian did, as though he too had always believed the city to be destroyed, '. . . Osiris?'

The name hangs. Taeo hears very precisely the sound of rain drumming on rooftops.

'That's what he said. But he only heard it from his cousin. There was a call placed from down the coast.'

'That can't be possible.' He looks at Ivra, trying to read the other man. 'Can it? Do you know something I don't? I mean – why now?'

'I don't know. I don't—' Ivra's expression falters; suddenly he looks shaken. 'Anything's possible.'

'If it is an Osirian ship . . .'

'The Boreal States will react,' says Ivra.

They stand in the deserted street. Most of the town's inhabitants are still inside, sleeping, unaware of the drama that is unfolding at Arturo's. The rain falls. The puddles simmer about Taeo's feet. Osiris. The sea city. Patagonians call it the lost city. That is what the world believes, and even in the Republic, where they know the truth, the lost city is rarely spoken of by name. *Let ice lie quiet*, they would say. It is an old motto and a backwards one, the underlying message being that ice does not lie quiet. It cracks and breaks and shatters glaciers and swells the sea. Ice is a kinetic substance, which brings upheaval after upheaval – as is the course of history.

He thinks, almost wonderingly, this is it. This is the start of the war.

The very thing he spoke out against – and whatever he said in there to Ivra, he meant every word of that transmission – this is where it starts.

In unspoken agreement, the two men head out of the town, back up towards the Facility.

'I'll record a holoma tonight,' says Ivra. 'Someone should be due to make a collection soon.'

Taeo nods. He does not understand the complicated relay system of messages operated by the Antarctican network, but Ivra does.

'What about our agents in the north? Shouldn't we alert them too?'

Ivra frowns. 'We should wait and see how the situation develops. We don't yet know if the boat really is from—'

That's not right, thinks Taeo. They can't wait on this – they have to act. If what the Patagonian said is true, there is a huge political issue at stake for the Republic: a containment issue. The agents in the north need to be primed. They need to be on the watch for a Boreal response.

'It's probably a hoax,' he says. 'Or pirates. Didn't you say the archipelago is crawling with pirates?'

Ivra frowns. 'It could be a hoax. What if it's a ploy by the Pan-African Solar Corporation? What if they're trying to draw the Boreal States south and start a war?'

'Why would they do that?'

'If the Republic and the Boreal States cancel each other out, the Solar Corporation gets the pick of resources north and south. They'd love to see us at war with the Boreals.'

'You're forgetting one thing, Ivra. You're forgetting what the Republic knows.' He pauses to let this sink in. 'We know the sea city was not destroyed. We know that it could only ever have been a matter of time before someone got out.'

There is a pause, and Ivra says, 'If it's real, you know the Republic is going to be calling you back.'

'I wish they would, but I think you're hopeful. My punishment isn't over yet.'

'I mean they'll call you back to your work.'

'I won't go,' says Taeo, but uneasily. He has felt the weight of Antarctican law and it is not a light one. 'Not on their terms.'

'You say that now. They told me you were working on something.

A new fuel. Could be revolutionary, they said. How are you going to feel when the Boreal States send their submarines south?'

Taeo is angered by this. 'The submarines aren't ready. They won't be for years. And they've got my damn research.'

'You can't trust intelligence,' says Ivra. 'Nobody really knows what the northerners are up to. All we know is that they want our continent, and when the time comes they'll be happy to destroy anything that stands between them and it. This place –' he waves a hand back towards the coast '– this place won't even register.'

Taeo cuts off the retort that springs to his lips, reminding himself just in time that Ivra has lived here for ten years now. He has clearly formed an attachment for the country, despite its endless inconveniences and hostile people.

'Anyway,' he says. 'It's all speculation until we find out more.'

Ivra grunts assent.

An idea is forming in Taeo's head.

He'll send his own holoma to the north.

At the Facility gate, the young soldier on duty shines a light directly in Taeo's face before checking his papers. The kid's cheeks are pitted with smallpox scars.

'You're clear,' says the kid.

'We'll catch up tomorrow,' says Ivra. He heads back down the hill. He has lodgings in the town.

Taeo watches him go, peering through the rain. An Antarctican settlement would have guiding night lights, but in this place you feel your way through the darkness, the way you feel your way through conversations. For a moment he imagines he sees the lights of a ship, outlined like a constellation of stars. A big ship, an Antarctican ship. The lights are mesmerizing. Taeo wants to run down there, throw himself off the sea walls and swim until he reaches the hull. He imagines hands reaching down to pull him out of the water. His rescue, his redemption. He can actually feel the warm fingers wrapped around his own.

There is no ship. There are no lights – only his own yearning.

Room 5.27. No name on the door. He is nameless now. He sheds his sodden clothes and dries off, shivering. He craves hot water but you can only get it in a narrow time window in the morning. At first he had tried to make his spartan room more homely. It is not the austerity he minds so much as the lack of personality about the space. But his efforts, the things he brought with him, seem a parody of themselves. Like the Antarctican lamp which is not compatible with the backward Patagonian wiring – it sits on the table, useless to everyone.

Out of habit rather than any expectation, he checks the room's energy gauge and is surprised to see the needle has wavered the tiniest fraction over zero. He drags his chest to the middle of the room and unlocks it, carefully retrieving three holomas. The first one, which is completely dead, he puts on charge. The second two have not been used. He places one on the lid of the chest. Each holoma is a smooth black elliptic device, small enough to fit in the palm of his hand.

Taeo thinks about what he wants to say. His mind is racing and it is difficult to separate the strands: what he should say, what he shouldn't say, what he must say. This is his opportunity. He needs to sound professional. In control.

Not so long ago, those things were easy. He could walk into a room and people would fall quiet, waiting to hear what he had to say.

He puts his palm to the holoma and feels it warm in response.

'Begin recording.'

His first message is for the Republic. He tells them what he has overheard. He tells them he will investigate the shipwreck, and that if there are survivors, he will secure them until he receives further instructions. He stresses that there were a number of Patagonians present when the news was announced. If it really is an Osirian boat, it will be almost impossible to contain the news, and even if it is not, he reminds them, the mere suggestion that Osiris might still be out there will cause a stir in the Boreal States. He does not mention Ivra, who will doubtless record his own holoma. He says he will report back with the outcomes of his investigation.

This holoma he will place at the agreed drop-point at the harbour, from where someone Taeo has never seen will collect the message and ensure that it makes its way back to the homeland.

Now for the agents north of the belt. He needs to circumvent the tediously slow web of drops and pickups and codes, and get a message straight to the Panama Exchange Point.

Holomas work like magnets. When in proximity, both devices will activate, and the holoma bearer will know another holoma is nearby. So all he needs to do is to find a fast carrier.

He notices the power gauge is flickering; the charging holoma has squeezed out the last drop of energy. He puts the other two aside and turns off the overhead light. When he presses his palm to this one, a cluster of white lights glow on its surface. He taps each, watches their images materialize one by one, though he knows each word by heart, has watched them over and over. It is a month since the holoma arrived.

There are several holum from Shri, one each from Kadi and Sasha, and a minute of Nisha making incomprehensible noises. Shri's eyes look directly at him and she keeps smiling but he can tell the smile is forced, uncomfortable. The children are doing as well as can be expected in the new school, she says. Sasha has started his Siberian and Swahili classes and there has been a lot of playing spy (Shri's eyebrow lifts pointedly). Where has that come from, does Taeo suppose? He imagines a note of accusation in her voice, but perhaps she is trying to play down the situation, or perhaps she means nothing by it at all. The image of her is at once clear and fuzzy, present and not. He wants to reach out and touch her hair, her face, but she is nothing but a manipulation of light rays.

He remembers her face at First Light. Carnival night in Vosti Settlement, which everyone admits throws the greatest celebration of the holiday. People come from settlements all around the peninsula for Vosti's carnival, riding the hover-rail or the snow-mobile through the winter dark, putting the final touches to their headdresses while they sip from flasks of piping-hot sake.

Shri shouldn't have been there, as he found out later. She had promised to attend a family engagement, but she had wanted to see the Vosti carnival with her friend (whose name Taeo has forgotten – she and Shri lost touch – and yet he always recalls her with a kind of abstract fondness, thinking of the two women travelling together in the pod of the hover-train). Shri had been persuasive – she has always been very persuasive. Taeo has often imagined the conversation that brought her to Vosti, the ruses she would have used.

Tell me about the carnival, Shri would have said, fixing the friend with her most captivating gaze.

And the friend would have said: Shri, by ice, how can I describe this to you? There's the costumes for a start. She would have told Shri about the faces masked and bejewelled, and the dancers who flung the nine flags of the Republic like matadors. She would have described the pageant: the crossing of the Southern Ocean, the great swathes of material, all blue, to represent the water, and a woman dressed entirely white, for Antarctica. And after the pageant, which finishes in the minutes that the sky begins to lighten, all the street lights go out. You stand in the dark, hearing the breathing, the low, excited murmurs of those around you, watching the sky, waiting.

And then the edge of the sun stirs above the horizon.

For a few moments, the entire settlement stands united in awe, in a kind of disbelief. The sun has returned, it has not abandoned us. There will be an end to the winter after all.

The drums begin. Joyous rollicking beats, samba invigorating the street, and everyone begins to dance.

Taeo danced in those days. It didn't matter that he was no good at it. The streets were so densely packed that you couldn't help but be carried along, and in those earliest minutes of nascent orange light you felt a weight fall from you which made your feet free, and your heart full. The sake turned your head giddy; everywhere you looked people were turning to one another and hugging and crying a little.

Happy First Light! Happy First Light!

In the crush Taeo found himself hugging Shri. Her arms wrapped around his shoulders, her body pressed close to his. On her breath were traces of sake and spices. She stood back and looked at him, beaming. Her mask was pushed up from her face, as his was, and strands of her hair had got caught in it, and her face was revealed, intricate swirls of gold and silver painted on clear brown skin. She said in Portuguese, 'I love your carnival!'

Taeo felt, at that moment, a sense of pride and belonging as strong as any he had ever experienced. His carnival – yes, it was his carnival, his people, his settlement. And this beautiful woman said she loved it, not in patois but in his language of the home.

The sun was lifting higher, tendrils of light winding into the sky, an explosion of colour after the dark. He could not help but think that something magnificent was beginning.

Say something. He had to say something.

'Don't you celebrate First Light?'

Such a stupid thing to say! Of course she celebrated First Light.

But she said, 'Yes. But not like this. This – this is magical.'

Then someone grabbed her hand and she was being pulled into a moving procession of dancers. He knew a moment of vertigo, that she might disappear before his eyes, but she reached out her own hand – come on! – pulling him right along with her. He abandoned the friends he was with without a thought, and followed her. He would have followed her anywhere.

It was simple, and it was not simple. It was simple because, for reasons Taeo never understood, Shri had decided right there in the street that they should be together. They would be together. Why? Because she knew it was meant to be. It was simple like a fairy tale, like the sun-journey stories told to children in midwinter, stories they have told to Kadi and Sasha and now to Nisha:

The sun has gone to gather sunbeams from the stars, because every year, the sun gives out a million sunbeams to Antarctica, and now it must go and find more. It takes a long time before the sun can come back, and give us light again.

If their tale was told, it would be told like this:

Taeo and Shri met in the carnival on First Light, and they fell in love, and that is how it was and is and will be.

But it was not simple. She was Indian-Antarctican, he was Brazilian-Antarctican, and despite being free to do as they liked, still the communities were tight. They teased one another. Call yourself a Brazilian? You've got the worst sense of rhythm I've ever seen. When they went dancing, Taeo moved gracelessly and Shri laughed at him and told him she loved him. She came to live with him in Vosti.

Like all Antarcticans they were good with languages. They spoke partly in patois, more and more in Portuguese. When Shri was intent upon some task which required exacting concentration, she would mutter to herself in her own language of the home. He picked up words and phrases of Hindi, liking the way the new sounds moved in his throat, hoping that one day this learning might become a mediating force, a peace gesture in the thing they never spoke of. Neither of them cared for traditions, the past; they were interested in the future.

Shri claimed she didn't miss her home. Friends came to visit, but since moving to Vosti she had not been back. Perhaps it was the shunning of the family engagement on First Light. Perhaps it was something larger; she rarely mentioned her family, and when she did an ominous mood would settle upon her, and so upon Taeo, filling him with an unease that threatened the tranquillity of their home. Only once did they take the hover-rail to Tolstyi Settlement, a journey five hours long and expensive too. The door to Shri's family house remained shut, even when Shri shouted and banged on the door and was angry in ways he had not seen until that moment. Shri did not cry. Her face took on the taut, determined expression which would become her only expression after the transmission and would always fill him with grief. She said nothing on the journey back, not one word, until they were at home and he had cooked supper and she sat at the table watching him but not watching him, her eyes elsewhere. When he put the plate in front of her and said, 'You must eat something,' she said, 'It's not Tolstyi, you know. There's nothing wrong with Tolstyi.'

'I know,' he said. 'I like Tolstyi.'

'It's just them.'

Two weeks later they discovered she was pregnant. They had not planned to have a child so soon. Shri went to Central Market and paid too much money for a mobile to hang over the crib which was made of some newly mined Antarctican alloy. Taeo recognized the metal; he had tested it in the lab and could have told her each of its properties. When the sun fell on it, the mobile held all the colours of the southern lights. Shri said it would be as if the baby had her own piece of sky, an Australis all her own to guard and watch over her. If there was a word for that property in any of their languages, he did not know it. She touched her stomach and said: I want to call her Kadi, and he put his arms around her still-slender waist and said: Yes.

The power is almost gone. Taeo replays Shri's last message. He lies on the uncomfortable bed, watching the flickering image of his partner, paused, her lips just parted on the brink of a word, a strand of hair falling across her face that in two seconds' time she will brush away. And in five seconds' time she will shake her head, because the hair has fallen back again. She glows, translucent. Present and not. She flickers. The holoma dims.

'Don't go,' he says. Then the last bit of electricity squeezes from the cell. Shri goes out. She is gone.

There is no noise but the wind and the rain. He wants opium badly.

He knows he shouldn't but he takes it out and lights the potent resin bead, watching it bubble under the flame. He smears it carefully around the hole of the pipe. Brings it to the flame. A pull, then another. Inhale. Exhale. There – there it is. This is what he needs. This is all. The darkness moves, shapes emerging out of it and melting back, as if he lies in a living pool of wax. And the world is warm, and the hurt is less.

Something is happening. Something big. This is my chance to get home. It is then that he thinks of the pilot.

5 ¦

T he timer reads one hundred and eighty seconds. She clicks it over. There is a second's pause, a gurgle in the pipe and the water sluices her in hot rivers. The timer ticks down.

In one hundred and eighty seconds you can achieve a surprising number of things. You can stitch a wound, if you are skilled, and your hand is steady. You can cast a tale, or sing a song. Ramona prefers to listen, though she has learned to tell her own. A good enough yarn can earn you water in a desert zone, or shelter on high ground to escape the floods.

She places her head directly under the shower head. Each individual jet of water sears her scalp before exploding through her hair, hitting her shoulders, her breasts, cascading over her belly and thighs. Hot water, revered water.

The timer ticks down the seconds. One hundred and fifty. She lathers soap between her palms and smoothes it luxuriously into her hair. Dirt and grease stream away into the pipe system. The pollutants will be stripped from the water and the water will be used again.

One hundred and twenty. Two minutes. In two minutes, you can bring an aeroplane to a careful landing, or lift off from the ocean.

Soap all over, right down to the soles of her feet and between her toes. A blister on her heel pops with a brief burst of pain.

Sixty. In sixty seconds you can pull on your pack and start to run.

For the last minute she stands with her eyes closed, letting the water run over her eyelids, cheeks, lips and into her mouth, twisting to make every part of her body commensurate in these few moments of bliss.

A few more seconds, just give me another twenty – even another ten – please just this once . . .

The shower stops. She stands immobile, letting the blanket of steam wrap around her body until that, too, evaporates. Where there is water, one hundred and eighty seconds is a very long time, and no time at all.

When she opens the unit door to get her towel, the cold air brings back a whiff of the Facility. She hurries down the corridor to her room. It's five o'clock, and it looks like she is the only one awake.

Carla's letter is crumpled on the bunk; she must have read it a hundred times already. *She's converting.* Those two small words are a sentence.

Ramona can picture the scene. Her mother, who disguises all things, will have pretended nothing is wrong. Eventually, the conversion will have reached the stage where she can no longer hide it. Carla will have found her, collapsed and helpless on the floor of the shack, or shivering and feverish in her bed. The doctor's test, doubtless under duress, will have confirmed the worst.

The letter is a month old. Her mother might have stabilized by now. The thing with the jinn is it can loiter for a long time, an invisible intruder quietly and efficiently breaking down the immune system until one small thing turns on the carrier with sudden, fatal malignancy. It could be a fever or a minor infection. It could be a cold. From here on, Inés's life is down to the arbitrary hand of chance.

Hundreds die every year from the jinn. It is a part of life in the south. If you cannot accept these things, if you cannot accept that time and water are short, and shorter for some than for others, then you can find no peace for yourself. Ramona knows what she should do. She should get hold of as much opium as she can find, and take it to Inés, and when it happens stay with her until she dies, making sure that it is a good death, a quiet death. Her mother is fifty-eight. This is not a bad life. In Patagonia, to live to fifty-eight is a substantial age.

Ramona knows all this and she knows that she will heed none of it. That is why she is taking things out of her pack, placing each item on the floor, checking it over, and then returning it. Because she also knows there are treatments that exist outside Patagonia, and that there are a few individuals who are wealthy enough to import those cures.

Northern cures.

I am not going to let you die, Ma.

She puts the letter away, folds the blankets and clips up the bunk.

Goodbye, room.

When Ramona was very young, her mother stepped on a poisonous snake. Her foot swelled up to twice its natural size, and her face was clenched in pain and fear. She could hardly speak. The children had to guess by her gestures what to do. It was Ramona who made the incision in the skin, and the poison seeped out.

When she was older, and Inés would say things like her body was an old husk of skin and bone and she might as well die, after all, what point was there for her to live when she had already buried two children, Ramona would remember the snake bite. When her mother bemoaned the fact that her only surviving child was a crazy one and used a flying machine – a *flying machine*, a Neon abomination that goes against every teaching of the Nazca – and that Inés should surely dig her own grave right now, Ramona would remember the relief that came to her mother's face in the aftermath: Inés did not want life snatched away from her. She wanted to live.

A knock on the door, quiet, cautious. Ramona looks at her watch. The second hand ticks. It is only half past five; even Lygia would not be chasing her this early. She stands silently and does not answer.

The knock is repeated, a little louder this time.

'Ramona? I have to talk to you.'

The voice is muffled but she recognizes the speaker: it's the Antarctican, Taeo. What does he want?

She opens the door. Taeo is standing in the corridor. He looks dishevelled and very agitated. She can smell residues of the smoke on him.

'What?'

'Not out here,' he hisses.

She checks the corridor in both directions. It is empty.

'All right, come in,' she says. 'Make it quick.'

The Antarctican is tall with gangling limbs, and the small room looks even smaller with him in it. He looks at her pack, its contents strewn across the floor. He manoeuvres carefully around them.

'You're about to leave?'

'Any minute.'

He nods.

'About that favour . . .'

He takes something out of his pocket. It has the shape of a round, flat pebble and is entirely black. There are no distinguishing marks on its surface, but she knows, she *knows* it is a machine. You can't see its workings. You can't trust it. Involuntarily she draws back.

'Don't put that thing near me, please.'

'I need you to take this to Panama,' he says. 'In your aeroplane.'

'I'm not taking your filthy robotics anywhere. Don't you have any respect? Don't you know how we feel about those things?'

Already she can feel it, a physical, nauseating horror.

'I know. I'm sorry,' he says.

She wants to say: Your apologies are worthless, but the machine has such a hideous presence it seems to suck the words from her.

'I'll give you money.'

'I don't want your money.'

'I'll give you money, and the Antarctican network will help you to get medicine for your mother.'

She meets his gaze then. She can't help it. His eyes are bloodshot and his face is creased with anxiety. She guesses he has hardly slept.

'Antarctican medicine?'

'Boreal medicine. That's what you need, isn't it? All you have to do is take this, and when you deliver it, tell them what I said. Antarcticans keep their word.'

The machine sits in his hand, smooth and solid against the lines of his palms. She stares at it in revulsion. *Why is he doing this? Is it a test? A trap? Is he trying to set me up for something? What if he wants to track the plane, or steal it?*

His hand trembles slightly. She can see the glisten of sweat there.

'Who are you working for?' she demands.

'No one. Only the Republic.'

'What is that machine?'

'It's a message. Please, Ramona. It's very important that this information goes north.'

'Important to the Republic, you mean. Important to your spies.'

'To Patagonia as well.'

He tries to give her the machine but she flinches away. He puts it carefully on the table behind him, and instead takes out a wad of peso.

'Whatever you need. I've got more.'

There is a lot of it. Cash is untraceable, she thinks. It is enough money for bribes. In Cataveiro, she will need to pay people. She can't pick up her pay packet without seeing Lygia, and if she sees Lygia she won't get out of the Facility without breaking out.

Fuck.

She folds her arms. 'Look, Taeo, this is how it works. Because, believe me, you're not the first to try and use me as your personal courier. I don't take anything unless I know what it is. Not packages, not messages, and absolutely not machines. Got it?'

He nods. 'This is about our shipbuilding programme.'

'Your military programme,' she accuses.

A tremor crosses his face. She has touched a nerve, but has no time to dig deeper.

'Please,' he says. 'You can't want the Boreals down here any more than we do.'

'Why would they come here?'

'If they think there's a weakness in our programme, if they think we're falling behind—'

'So what am I taking, some kind of bluff? That practically makes me an Antarctican agent. I don't want anything to do with your secret war. My country doesn't want anything to do with it.'

He says softly, 'You know I don't want anything to do with it either, but there isn't always a choice.'

She looks at the cash. *Are you this easily bought, Ramona?*

But the medicine . . . If she can't get to the right people in Cataveiro . . . it's going to cost . . .

'Do you promise your people will help me?'

Taeo looks hopeful. 'I promise.'

'What do Antarcticans swear by?'

Confusion crosses his face and then he says, 'We don't worship gods.'

Nor do I, she thinks impatiently. 'Do you have family?'

Again, the tremor. 'Yes.'

'Then swear by them.'

Obediently, he says, 'I swear by my family, my people will help you to find Boreal medicine.'

She takes a deep breath.

If you agree to do this, you have to carry it through. Now, or later, whether you find medicine in Cataveiro or not. It's a promise.

'All right. I'll take your machine.'

The Antarctican cannot conceal his relief. She is reminded again of Inés and the snake bite. He takes out the machine. She steels herself.

When it touches her hand the nausea rises again and she fights to swallow it down. *Think how you felt when you first flew* Colibrí.

But the plane is different. She could never explain to Taeo the feeling of sitting in the pilot seat for the first time, watching the instrument panel flicker into life. That despite the strangeness of the technology, the overwhelming sensation was of coming home. The feeling that her life had been leading up to this moment, and knowing, without knowing how, that the plane would respond to her. She puts her faith in *Colibrí* as she would another human being, and *Colibrí* has never let her down.

The Antarctican machine is alien. It is not physically heavy but it has a weight. A presence. She imagines it breathing out invisible feelers, casting about for something – someone – to latch on to. As if it knows she is here.

'How will I find your people?' she asks.

'You won't have to. Once you reach Panama, the holoma will guide them to you.'

The implications of this are too horrible to think about. Ramona wishes she hadn't asked.

'You'll need to activate it,' Taeo continues. 'Here.'

He takes her hand and folds her fingers tightly around the machine. She closes her eyes, not wanting to see. Taeo says, 'Restrict to activation,' and she feels something, a kind of humming sensation, right in the centre of her palm.

'All done,' he says. 'When you reach Panama, you'll need to activate it. Hold it tightly in your hand for exactly ten seconds, then release it, then hold for another five. Until you do that, it's like carrying a stone. It won't do anything. I know Patagonians don't like machines. I do respect that, even if I don't understand it.'

'What about to deactivate it?'

'The reverse. Five seconds, then ten.'

'It knows my hand?'

'Yes.'

She puts the machine in the bottom of the pack. She does not want it anywhere near her skin. Taeo gives her the money and presses another wad on her, telling her to take whatever she needs. She stuffs that in too.

'You've got a lot of gear,' he says.

She glances at him. 'Always carry your life with you, that's my motto. Everything I need is in this pack. If I have to run, I can run.'

'You'll go straight to Panama?' he says.

'Yes,' she lies.

'Thank you. Thank you, Ramona. I can't — I can't explain how important this is.'

His eyes are imploring, like a child's; he wants her to believe him. Perhaps it is this that convinces her he is telling the truth. Anyway, she has made the decision now. She has to believe him.

When Taeo has gone she packs the rest of her belongings quickly. She is at the energy room by six. She signs out a couple of spare battery cells for the plane, exchanging a few pleasantries with the sleepy attendant. They treble the weight of her pack. The canteen is not yet open but she goes down to the kitchen and begs a quick breakfast from the head cook, whose daughter she flew to the inland hospital three years ago for an emergency operation. She wolfs the food standing, watching the cooks prepare the morning's offerings. Pans clang, eggs sizzle in oil. The rich protein smell diffuses through the kitchen.

The cook catches her looking and taps her shoulder. 'You want some chicken for the road?'

She shakes her head. 'I had meat on Tuesday.'

He laughs. 'You're too conscientious. Here's your lunch box: all local, nothing northern, no lab meat. You're going somewhere, aren't you? You've got the look. Don't worry, we won't tell Lygia we've seen you.'

The Facility is still quiet as she climbs the back stairway, her shoulders straining with the weight of the pack. She thinks, not for the first time, that departures have always characterized her life, one after another after another.

Up on the roof she cannot see anything: not the mountains, not the ocean or the island across the strait. Tierra del Fuego is entirely swathed in fog. This is a good day for pirates.

She hopes the shipping fleet is not delayed for that reason.

I wish I'd seen you before I left, Félix. I would have liked to tell you about Cerro Blanco, about the boy. About my mother. I wish I could have talked through my plan with you.

She has calculated the route. Seven and a half thousand kilometres. Six to seven days' flying if conditions are clear, and she will have to take breaks in between flights.

Half a day to Cataveiro: city of festering dreams. If her luck is good, she will find some rich corporation owner who has medicine. If not, she'll continue north, across poppy country, beyond the forty degree latitude line where the world empties out, through the stormlands, heading north-east to the sliding city and Inés. She'll leave supplies with Carla, painkillers and antibiotics, and then continue north, over the highlands of ancient Brazil, veering east to the coast where there is an outside chance she will coincide with Félix as he sails north on the *Aires*.

Finally her mission will take her across the vast unchartered breadth of the Amazon Desert.

And so to the Panama Exchange.

She unloads the spare cells into the plane's hull, and pulls on her flight coat and her parachute. She leaves the hatch open until the last moment, straining for external sounds. No one could possibly see her up here in the fog, but she has an unaccountable sense of something out there, watching.

Inside her boots, she can still feel grains of desert sand.

She starts the engines. No gravelly noises, everything sounds as it should. Good. Taeo did the job. The plane eases across the roof, and she sends a silent *please* to the monkey and the spider and the hummingbird that is drawn on the plane to preserve her life for another journey. They taxi along the roof. In this fog she is completely blind, but a screen on the instrument panel uses echolocation to draw the topography of the land in green blinking lines. She feels a surge in electrical power with the sudden resistance between plane and ground: *Colibrí*'s eagerness to be airborne again. They coast forwards. Momentum pins her to the chair. The plane lifts a fraction, drops, and pulls clear with a wrench that zips up her spine.

She keeps a firm hold on the yoke, lifting up through the mist. Whiteness layered upon whiteness. Five hundred metres. Eight hundred metres. She shoots out suddenly above the fog and the island is below her, the mountain peaks rising above their white swaddling. The joy that bubbles in her chest should be tempered, with fear for her mother, with anxiety that she has got away so easily and for the consequences which are bound to follow. But in these first few minutes of flying, everything else disappears in the knowledge that the skies are hers, for a time.

She increases altitude, and points the plane north, for Cataveiro.

6

The morning whiteness dampens his hearing, uneasily melding the mutterings of the fishermen as they prepare their nets half-blind with the sound of hulls knocking against the sea walls and motors heading out to the Atlantic. A man coughs, hoarse, intermittent. The tension in the air is palpable. Taeo cannot tell if it is last night's news, or simply the effect of the fog which obscures everything beyond a couple of metres. As he clambers past his boatman into the rocking well of the boat he sees the man's face clearly. The Patagonian wears a sullen expression, despite his hefty bribe.

'Let's go,' Taeo says.

As they edge away, Taeo thinks he hears a shout, swiftly muted. He looks back at the jetty where he was stood just moments ago and sees a dark shape, like a figure. He cannot make out a face or even limbs, but he is filled with the certainty that someone is watching him leave. For several minutes he is panic-stricken, unable to move or speak.

He tries to say something to the boatman but by the time he has gathered his composure the fog has swallowed up the figure and it is too late. He must have imagined it. Remnants of the opium are in his blood. It is making him shaky; he cannot let it compromise him. There was no one there. This country is like that, full of whispers and deceptions and the sense that the world might move away altogether, were you to turn your back at the wrong moment. There is too much history here.

'How long will it take?' he asks the boatman.

The man shrugs. 'Depends on the weather.'

The boat moves steadily down the strait between Tierra del Fuego and the small island to the south, or so Taeo supposes, judging by motion alone. He can see the edges of the boat on either side and the impassive back of the boatman at the helm. He can hear the waves but he has no sense of how far they are from the shore, or where the horizon lies. The sensation is disorientating. He draws a long breath and focuses on the bag sitting at his feet. Carry your life with you, said the pilot, and he threw all sorts of things in here, some food supplies, spare clothes, his stash, the pipe, and of course the holoma from Shri. He wasn't going to leave any of that in the Facility. You never know who might be interested in the contents of his room.

He thinks about what he might find today. There are many stories about the lost city. Osiris is the keeper of all the ocean's dead, for example. The dead cling to the ruins of shining towers, swimming from one to another like rotting mermaids. The city was sunk, its people live in flooded chambers below the surface and they consort with fish, as fish: their bodies have changed, adapted to their new environment. Another story says that the people of Osiris have learned to fly. They circle the city as vengeful angels, feasting upon any crew who sails within miles.

Those are the stories, gleefully recounted by children. However, there are statistics relating to Osiris. Statistics that are impossible to ignore. Taeo has never seen them in person, but he knows, as every Antarctican adult knows but rarely discusses, that the Republic monitors the sea city with long-range instruments. That duty will be carried out by a special unit of Civilian Security.

Which is he to believe in, the stories or the statistics? As an engineer, the answer should be clear, but out here it feels as though a part of his mind has been hijacked; the stories are more powerful, and in the fog they multiply. He grips the side of the boat as they enter choppier water. Glancing over the side, he half-expects to see putrescent limbs emerging from the water, scaled hands curling up to grab at his.

He's being fanciful. Shri would laugh. This is not like him.

He takes a flask of coffee from his pack and pours himself a mug. He drinks quickly, ignoring the burning sensation on his tongue. *Pull yourself together.*

It is a relief when the fog finally begins to clear. They are not far from the coast after all. The boatman steers close to its rugged sage and purple shoulders. To the south is open ocean; they have left the other island behind.

He should feel worried, wary of what lies ahead, for the last thing the Republic needs is Osiris to reappear on the map. Ivra is right: the Boreal States will be quick to react, and it will be difficult, if not impossible, for the diplomats to convince them that the Republic has been unaware of the sea city's operations these past fifty years. But disaster brings opportunity to the few. Taeo is the few; the Republic has made him that.

He sits impatiently through the rest of the journey, watching as the mist rolls back and vanishes, leaving behind a sparkling silver plain which is broken only by the white tail of their boat. He can feel the caffeine jittering through his body, chasing out the last traces of the opiates. He is ready for whatever they find.

They have been driving for over four hours when the boatman turns from the helm and points towards the coast.

'Navaranda,' he says.

The land curves into a half-moon bay, where a rocky beach is backed by steep hills covered in dense forestry. As they draw closer, Taeo counts three small boats dragged up high on the shore. On the far side of the beach, a crowd of around thirty people is gathered.

He can see it, keeled over on its side but rising several metres taller than the spectators: the wrecked boat. The lower hull is dark red, its underside heavily rusted. The upper decks of the boat are white.

Taeo feels a tingle of excitement. This is it.

The boatman draws the sign of the spider on his chest. He must have heard the rumours already.

'Take us in,' Taeo orders.

The boatman navigates carefully as they drive into the bay, steering around the submerged rocks that rise murkily below the surface. Waves break dramatically on the beach; this is not a placid shoreline. The mysterious boat would not have had a chance.

'Closer, I want to land.'

The boatman mutters something about it being a bad place, but heads towards the shore. Evidently his need for cash outweighs his reservations on this particular expedition. Taeo is watching the crowd, who are paying their arrival no attention; they are entirely concerned with the stricken boat. Some of them simply stand there, staring. Others walk around, peering and lifting a hand as if they might touch it, then drawing back sharply. As Taeo watches, one young man lifts a girl onto his shoulders. Presumably her boyfriend, he takes her feet in his hands, and with one strong boost, she leaps onto the boat's hull. The crowd react with shouts of surprise and alarm. The girl wobbles. She gets her balance. She raises her hands in the air, clenched as fists, in a gesture of triumph.

Their boat scrapes against the seabed.

'Wait here.'

Taeo leaps out, the cold water splashing up around his booted feet. He makes his way as quickly across the beach as his heavy bag allows – he is leaving nothing with the boatman. By now his arrival has been noticed by a couple of spectators, but they look at him without surprise, as though such a visit were inevitable.

The girl standing on the hull loses her balance and she falls with a shriek. The young man catches her. The girl begins to laugh but another woman admonishes her fiercely.

Taeo works his way through the crowd. He can feel the invisible circle around him, the way the Patagonians shrink away, almost imperceptibly. He ignores it, stepping right up to the boat. A rustle of whispers goes through the crowd. He can hear snippets of the argument between the girl and the woman, the girl defiant, the woman trying to keep her voice low.

So disrespectful.

I don't care what you think . . .

A metre-wide hole has been torn through the hull. The boat is covered in seaweed and gravel, its underside riddled with barnacles, but beneath this flotsam the white bodywork makes it highly visible. A boat that wants to be seen.

'When did this happen?' he asks the crowd.

No one answers. He repeats the question and at last a man replies.

'Last night, in the storm. The boat was slamming into the rocks, you could tell it wasn't going to get back out to sea. We thought it must have come from Fuego. Wasn't much we could do until the storm had blown out. You take a fishing boat out in a storm like that, you'll be ripped to shreds.'

At the stern of the boat, Taeo can make out the edge of a letter. He peels away a clump of seaweed. Slowly, very slowly, he brushes the sand clear.

'Don't,' says someone.

Above the gaping hole in the craft, quite clearly in black letters, the boat is named. *Wings of Osiris*.

A name, or more than a name?

'Are there any survivors?'

The villagers' elected leader points and on the other side of the boat Taeo sees the hump of two human bodies, covered by a tarpaulin. He feels a terrible relief and a crushing disappointment.

'God's will,' says a woman. Some nod, others are more pragmatic. Their voices flutter about him.

Didn't have a chance.

Storm like that.

Fated . . . cursed . . .

'Are all of them dead?' The Patagonians nod, but Taeo catches the gaze of the girl who stood on the boat, having escaped – or ignored – her scolding. She stares at him insolently, her arm slung around her boyfriend's waist. He has a large bottle of something in his hand. Spirits, by the look of it. While Taeo is watching, the girl takes the bottle and drinks from it. Taeo has an abrupt, terrible craving for opium.

'What about the others?' The voice comes from a child and is quickly shushed. Taeo turns.

'What?'

The child pushes his face into his mother's legs, hiding. The mother meets Taeo's eyes defiantly. Her hair, sheared straight at the jawline, pokes out from her hood in dark strands. The child's small feet are stood on the toes of her boots, his hands clinging to her jeans. Taeo is reminded of the pilot when she took the holoma, that fear and resolution intertwined.

'We don't know anything,' the woman says. Her fingers clasp the child's head against her, feeding through the curly hair. Taeo is hit with a jolt of familiarity and loss.

The Patagonians have gathered tightly together now, their expressions wary, unhappy. No one wants to meet Taeo's gaze. He addresses the leader directly.

'Did anyone survive? You must tell me, this is more important than you know.'

'We pulled two from the waves,' the man mumbles. 'A man and a woman. Both delirious, raving, they were. We took them to the herbalist. We tried to save them but they were badly injured on the rocks. The woman was worse. She died this morning, nothing we could have done. The other's not much better. Reckon he'll die too.'

'Is it true then?' asks the mother.

'Is what true?'

'You know what. It says it on the boat. The mad man's saying it. They're from . . .' She hesitates, and looks at the others for encouragement. 'He says they're from the sea city.'

The rest of the crowd mutter agreement. *Is it true? Is it true?* The teenage girl laughs suddenly.

'The sea city,' she says, hiccupping with laughter. 'The sea city, the sea city, the sea city . . .' She sits on the ground with a bump, giggling to herself. *The sea city. The sea city.* The woman she was arguing with earlier pulls her back up to her feet.

'Get back to the village. You're a disgrace!'

'I hate this place! If there was a sea city, I'd have gone to it years ago, you hear me! Years!'

Taeo looks at the murmuring, uncertain crowd. He needs to contain this. The Patagonians cannot keep talking. By midday the news will be all over the archipelago.

'You said yourselves, the survivors are delirious. Until we know more, there's no reason to think this boat came from anywhere other than the mainland.'

'If it's not from the lost city, then why are you here? You're not Patagonian. You're from the south. What do you want with this boat?'

Others gather around the leader, forming a protective unit, urging him on.

'Yes,' he says. 'Tell us. What do you want with this boat?'

Taeo straightens, making the most of his height. It does not matter what he says now, it is how he says it that counts. He catches the eyes of as many of the crowd as possible, refusing to let them slip away.

'I can't tell you anything more until I see the survivor. Now please, show me where he is.'

7

Taeo follows his guide up a well-worn path that cuts steeply into the hillside. It is narrow and treacherous to navigate; more than once his boots slip in mud churned up by the heavy traffic. He imagines the villagers dragging the survivors uphill in the last squalls of the storm, hearing the grunt and heft as they lifted the deadweight bodies, perhaps a shout of warning as the rain threatened to wrest them from their hands.

He continues to question the crowd's elected leader. The man has difficulty understanding Taeo's accent and he has to repeat everything. From the guarded responses, Taeo gathers that the people by the shipwreck are from the village they are going to now, which overlooks the beach, and another village further along the coast. He asks how many people know about the shipwreck, how many villages. The leader shrugs.

'How great is a man's appetite for a story? You can blame Gabs' cousin down the coast – he sent the news to Fuego and now you –' he points rudely at Taeo '– now you have come.'

'The name on the boat doesn't mean anything,' says Taeo. 'A name is just a name. Anyone can choose one.'

'It is a strange thing to choose a name from a city that fell to pieces beneath the waves and is full of rotting souls, or so they say,' the leader says.

'Perhaps,' suggests Taeo, 'this is a ploy to make us afraid. We should be wary of assumptions.'

'There is little to be afraid of with those ones dead and this one so close to death. Perhaps that is for the best,' the leader says. 'Doors that are closed should not be opened. There is a reason they are closed. The coming of this boat has a meaning. Whether it is good luck or bad luck, we can only wait to see. But it will not mean nothing.'

By the time they reach the top of the path, Taeo's thighs ache and he is increasingly frustrated by the leader's evasive replies. But he can see the village ahead, where the hillside plateaus before reaching up again, into the mountains. It is a small affair, twenty or so adobe houses with heavy-duty shutters, grouped around a square. Water baths sit atop the huts and a couple of them support cheap-looking solar panels. Radio antennae stick out from windows. Taeo recognizes the grainy burr of Fuego Station by its irritating jingle.

'This way.' The leader takes him through the square, where a couple of goats are tethered, descendants of the engineered variety by the looks of it. Their bodies appear swollen, too large for the spindly legs. Elsewhere there is evidence of industry: washing billowing from a line, fishing tackle strewn about the ground. Taeo imagines the villagers must be relatively self-sufficient here, boosted by occasional trips to Fuego Town, and the forestry will shield the houses from the worst of the coastal weather. He has noticed this before with Patagonians: a pride, sometimes to their own detriment, in asserting their independence.

His trek uphill has collected a small procession of followers. The mother with her child has come along, and the angry girl, with her boyfriend in tow.

The leader takes him to the last of the houses, which is set slightly apart from the others. Plants cover the entire area of the low roof, trailing over its edges. They are sodden in the aftermath of the storm and glint with water, lush and verdant.

There is a line of people outside the hut.

'Who are they?' Taeo demands.

'They've come to see the survivor,' says the leader calmly. 'They are paying. You'll have to wait your turn.'

The angry girl leaps ahead suddenly and comes to a triumphant halt at the end of the queue. She beckons her boyfriend, who jogs to join her. She looks back at Taeo, a pleased expression on her face at this apparent victory.

'You need to get those people out of here,' says Taeo.

The leader looks at him with slimly concealed dislike.

'You will pay too. Fifty peso per head. This is the price.'

Not so altruistic after all, thinks Taeo. He pulls out a handful of notes and holds them out discreetly.

'What say I pay a higher price, and go in now?'

The leader takes the money without glancing at it. 'You will wait,' he says. 'Like everyone else on the island. You won't be the last here today. Better take your place while you can.'

Seething inwardly, Taeo joins the line outside the herb-covered house. Behind him are the remaining villagers, who are muttering in voices low enough that Taeo cannot catch the words. He begins to wonder how exactly he is going to extract the survivor, who is clearly bringing in a fine profit for the village, not to mention making it almost impossible to contain the story – and it is only mid-morning. The island must be full of these tiny villages. Then there are the larger inland towns. Who knows how many people have already been inside that house?

He reminds himself that he does not yet know the true identity of the survivor. But he has a sense about it. The house tingles. It is humming with importance. Taeo has the same sense he had before he asked Shri if she would live with him. Before they were told that the embryo in Shri's womb was female. Before the two officials arrived at his home in Vosti Settlement, reading aloud the contents of his transmission, preparatory to announcing his sentence. Taeo is sure.

He waits, barely able to contain his impatience as the queue dwindles. The angry girl and her boyfriend have been in a few minutes when there is the sound of raised voices and the pair emerge suddenly, the girl flushed and angry, the boyfriend trying to placate her.

'Fuck you!' she shouts. 'I paid, all right? I paid my turn.'

The woman behind Taeo puts a hand on his arm and speaks imploringly. 'Don't mind Lina. She gets upset, that's all. Her folks died on the mainland, just this winter it was.'

'It's fine,' says Taeo, pulling away. He does not care about the girl or the girl's parents, he wants to get in the house. It's his turn now.

The woman turns to others in the queue, still babbling on about the girl. Do they ever shut up? *It was her village, you see, the whole village. The redfleur went through them like a fire; one day they were fine, next they were coughing up bits of themselves. Lina was coming back from her grandmother's. She heard them first, then she saw them falling about, attacking one another; you know it makes you go mad? When they found her she didn't say a word, not to anyone, not then, not in quarantine. I don't know what to do with her . . .*

'Next!'

Taeo feels a surge of excitement as he stoops to enter the small house. Inside it is hot and dark and smells of smoke and pungent herbs. A small woman is perched on a stool by a methane fire, tending to a simmering pan. She has her back to Taeo.

'Move quietly and don't talk,' she says. 'I won't have him disturbed.'

'I'm sorry, but I will have to speak with him.'

The woman turns. She has a deeply tanned, freckled face, brown eyes webbed with fine lines. Her features tighten with wariness when she sees who has entered.

'So, an ice man. I suppose we must be honoured.'

'I need to speak with him,' Taeo repeats.

The herbalist looks far from happy about the situation. She rises and pulls aside a thin screen which curtains one corner of the room.

The scent of the stuff overwhelms Taeo. His lungs inhale sharply, snatching at the residues of smoke on the air. He feels suddenly shaky, euphoric, a desperate craving. The herbalist gives him a sly glance as she sits back down.

Taeo forces himself to take in the scene.

Lying on the floor is a single man. Despite the blankets covering him, he is shivering violently. His dark hair is soaked and salt has dried in crusts about his hairline and eyebrows. He clutches at the blanket, muttering incomprehensibly.

'Do you know his name?' asks Taeo.

The herbalist shakes her head. 'He hasn't been lucid.'

Taeo kneels beside the delirious man. He is beginning to get control of his reaction to the fumes, or perhaps they are infusing him with confidence.

Bending closer, he catches snatches of words. Not Spanish words. He hears *ghosts. Land* . . . other syllables he does not recognize. Something that could be a name.

'He's speaking in Boreal.' He looks at the herbalist. 'The language of the lost city was Boreal, wasn't it? Boreal English?'

She shrugs. 'The lost city is lost, is it not, so who knows.'

'I . . .' The delirious man speaks softly, but with sudden clarity.

'Yes? I'm here, what is it?'

'I . . . I need water . . .'

'Water, quickly! Please, he's trying to speak.'

The herbalist brings a mug of water and places it by the delirious man. There is a knowing expression on her face, as though she has seen this tableau before and knows no good will come of it. Taeo ignores the expression. He lifts the man's head and tilts the water towards his lips. The man drains the mug eagerly, then falls back, pulling the blanket close to his chest once more, shivering. Taeo places a gentle hand on his shoulder. He locates his Boreal English.

'We're here to help you,' he says. 'Tell me, where are you from?'

'Where is this?' Now the man sounds afraid. His eyes are open but unseeing. 'Are you ghosts?'

'There are no ghosts here. You've reached land. Your boat was wrecked on the shore.'

'They look like her . . .' The man's eyelids shutter closed. His breathing hastens. He twists, pulling the blanket up around his body, and Taeo sees a bloodied bandage is tied around his upper right leg. How bad is the injury?

He tries again. 'You must tell me. This is very important. Where have you come from? Is it from the sea city?'

'Osiris,' the man whispers. 'Yes, Osiris. We come from the city. We're looking for land. The storms are worse today.'

For a moment the man's eyes open, bright with some unknown anguish. Then the shivering grows worse and he lapses into babbling.

Taeo sits back on his heels. The herbalist stirs her pan, fixedly round and round, as though she will never be moved from it. She cannot have failed to hear.

She already knew, he thinks. She's known right from the start. They all know, and they're making a tidy profit from it, feigning ignorance because sooner or later the game won't be theirs to play any more. A bigger fish will come.

The sound of the stranger's restless words flows with the hiss of the gas and the low bubble of the herbalist's concoctions. He looks at the stranger's clothes. You can't get cloth like that here. The man's features suggest Indian ancestry.

He imagines the pilot arrowing north, towards Panama. Bodies on the beach, a stricken ship, a wounded Osirian man. *I was right. I was right to warn them.*

The herbalist is chivvying him, angry that Taeo has taken up more than his allotted time. It is only when he gets to his feet that he notices the hump of another body, covered with a blanket, pushed to the edge of the room. Gently he lifts a corner of the blanket.

'What are you doing? Your time's up!'

'I just want to see her face.'

The woman's eyes have been closed. She looks peaceful enough. He notes the same materials of her clothes. The long plaited hair. Only the richest Patagonians grow their hair long; water and the energy to heat it cost too much.

'We'll bury her,' says the herbalist. She hesitates. 'She came a long way to die here.'

He looks at her. Does she feel responsible? Does she blame herself for the woman's death? He starts to say: It's not your fault, but the moment passes. The herbalist jerks her head towards the door, pragmatic again. When he thinks about it, perhaps it is her fault – the villagers may have pulled the survivors from the ocean, but there is no evidence anyone has sent for professional medical help.

Taeo steps outside the hut and finds that the line has grown. The next visitor, a young woman holding a piece of cloth embroidered with the sign of the spider, goes into the hut. The leader is standing a little way off, watching closely as Taeo emerges.

What next?

He decides he wants a good look at the boat before he does anything else. Back down the muddy path, his pack weighing him down, twice he has to squeeze past a Patagonian going up the hill. On the beach, the crowd around the Osirian boat has expanded; Taeo notices another fishing craft drawn up past the tideline.

Taeo finds his boatman where he left him, refusing to land, and explains that they will have to wait a little longer. The boatman shakes his head. He says they shouldn't stay. People will be coming. He does not specify which people, but Taeo guesses he means soldiers. The boatman is right; he doesn't have long. Taeo promises more money. The boatman folds his arms stubbornly. Taeo doubles the offer again, at which at last the boatman nods his head. He goes back to his seat at the stern of the boat, facing away from the beach.

Once again Taeo pushes his way through the crowd, who have devolved into separate, whispering denominations. Those who were there first are explaining the situation at length and, as far as Taeo can gather, with much exaggeration. A few children play a kind of tag, running up to touch the boat, then darting back to the safety of their peers.

Taeo ignores all of them and goes around to the bow of the boat, where the hole torn by rocks gapes in the hull. He peers through but can see no way of getting into the interior, so walks around to where the deck rises vertically from the pebbles. He levers himself up to a deck hatch, opens it and climbs inside.

The beam of his flashlight bounces off multiple surfaces tipped by ninety degrees. Ladders extend horizontally and he has to crawl along the walls of the corridors. Water lies dormant in salty pools. Now his pack is a hindrance, catching on the sides of the narrow passageways. He squeezes through. It is not a large boat. He finds a sleeping area with bunks hanging loose from what has become the ceiling, an engine room, a storage area, a small eating space. Sufficient space, he surmises, for a crew of about ten. He picks up a couple of things from around the bunks which might be personal effects. A metal tin with engravings on the lid; the interior is full of fine white granules. He dabs his finger and sniffs tentatively, but it appears to be salt.

Then he finds a stash of guns. They are not locked away, but jammed anyhow into a trunk as though in a hurry. The water has seeped in here too. He handles one of the guns gingerly. He doesn't recognize it, although he has never used one, so why would he? Everything made in Osiris would have come from Boreal or Solar Corporation blueprints; Antarctica had no part in the city's construction.

To Taeo's inexperienced eye, it looks more like defensive weaponry than an arsenal bent on a land attack. Nonetheless, the guns present a serious problem. The villagers are wary right now, but it is only a matter of time before they investigate the boat themselves. Especially now that they have seen Taeo go inside.

He doesn't know if the guns will fire, and there is no way he can test them to find out. Not here, anyway. After hesitating, he puts one of the smaller weapons – a handgun – into his pack.

He is making his way back to the hatch when he realizes there is someone else in the boat.

A dead woman.

Her body is beginning to bloat. Her eyes are closed and blankets that might have been wrapped about the corpse have unravelled. She is wearing a red jumper with a hood and two scarves tucked into it. The body lies stiffly. There is some discolouring to the skin of her face, but it is only when he notices the darker patch and a puckering in the clothing at her stomach that Taeo realizes how she died – she was shot. Who killed her? Was she dead before the ship was wrecked?

He stares at the body. The sight of the corpse trapped in the ship moves him in a way that seeing the survivor did not. She never saw where they ended up. She never got the chance.

He tries to imagine the circumstances of the journey, the conditions on this ill-equipped, rusting boat. Would the Osirians have killed one of their own? Why did they come here? What made them leave their prosperous city?

Despite the closed eyes he has the eerie sense the woman is watching him, surveying his clumsy progress through her tomb. He leaves the corpse untouched and makes his way out of the boat, his pack with its new additions slung across his body.

The light outside is bright. The gun in his pack is right at the front of his thoughts. With every surreptitious glance in his direction, he thinks it has been spotted. *Keep it casual.* As he jumps down from the deck he can see the village leader across the beach, watching him closely.

The tide is creeping steadily up the beach. Soon it will be lapping at the shipwreck.

Taeo takes the leader aside.

'Listen,' he says. 'You know who that man is. You know what he is. There's a reason you didn't get a doctor.'

'We did our best,' says the man, angrily.

'But you could have done more, and you didn't. I know why. I get it. I'm only here because one of your guys blabbed to everyone in a bar in Fuego. Now you may be making a nice profit on him now, but how long do you think it'll be before the army shows up, or pirates, or worse?'

The leader eyes Taeo warily. But he knows. He is far from stupid.

'If I were you,' says Taeo, lowering his voice, 'I would get rid of the evidence.'

The leader bristles. 'You want to kill him? What do you think we are, barbarians?'

'No, I'm not suggesting— what do you think I am?' The leader opens his mouth and Taeo says quickly, 'Don't answer that. I'm offering to take him away from you. Understand, I will take that man far from here. You can burn the boat and the bodies. You never saw anyone alive. No evidence.'

Now the leader is nodding shrewdly. 'I see, I see. You want this man.'

'I'm offering to help you.'

'You want him. Well, maybe you can have him, for the right price.'

'A price? I'm doing you a favour!'

The leader folds his arms firmly. 'No favour that I can see. This is business.'

'Fucking hell.' Taeo glances back at the tideline, his ride back to Fuego rocking as the ocean rushes up and is sucked back down. It is almost midday. The sun is high in the sky, warm on his face; the sea glints with silver. He does a swift calculation of the value of the Patagonian currency he has on him and what he can afford to offer. 'Two thousand peso.'

The leader pulls an insulted face. 'Is this a joke?'

'Two five.'

'He's worth very little, it would seem, this man.'

'Look, I don't have time for haggling. Just tell me what you want for him. I only have so much cash.'

A calculating look descends over the man's face. 'Not cash, no. Not from you.'

'Then what?' Taeo explodes, and several of the milling villagers look up, interested by the exchange. Taeo gathers his control.

'You know.'

'What—'

Then he understands. There is only one other thing of enough value he carries on his person. The leader has read him like a slate.

'Fine,' he says. 'Just— fine.'

It is right at the bottom of the pack, concealed in an interior pocket. He pulls out the package and hands it over; there is no time to do a split, not here amid all these curious eyes. The leader squirrels it seamlessly into his own pocket. The amount of narcotic in that bag is worth several times the cash Taeo is carrying. It's pure opium, the good stuff. The *best* stuff. Now the leader's stuff. Just the thought of its loss is causing him to shake.

If this all goes to plan, he has no idea when he will be able to smoke again. It is terrifying how much that thought unnerves him.

But you'll be with Shri. It won't matter then. You won't need it.

'He's all yours,' says the leader.

It takes all of Taeo's strength to lift the man. As he strains, fresh blood starts to seep through the bandage around the Osirian's leg. He cries out and the herbalist pulls back the cloth where it has been cut to treat the leg and points. A row of stitches crosses the suppurating wound.

'You cannot take him, this man is badly hurt!'

She takes the man's hand and twines his fingers through hers and he clutches at her, at the covers, thwarting Taeo's best efforts to pry him away.

He looks at the man's twitching face, the sheen of sweat across his forehead.

'I'm sorry,' he says. 'I can't leave him here. People will be coming.' He repeats what he said to the leader. The herbalist protests, but with less conviction now. She knows.

'You should destroy the evidence. Burn everything.'

He carries the Osirian outside. The leader says something in consternation, but Taeo is concentrating on his hard-won prize. Extraneously, he is aware of the villagers as he progresses towards the steep path to the beach, the pointing, the remonstrations.

At the top of the path, Taeo pauses to catch his breath and to check where his boat is waiting.

The boat is not there.

A little way out, he can see the bright hull of their passage back to Fuego motoring away from the scene.

'No . . .'

He lays the Osirian down and sprints towards the waterline, slipping and sliding down the hillside path, waving his arms frantically and trying to ignore the laughter of the villagers and the idiotic spectacle he presents.

'Get back here! Get back!'

The boat recedes. He is stranded a hundred kilometres from Fuego Town, with a political bomb on his hands and no communications network.

'You're on your own from here.'

Two reluctant villagers, under suffrage by their leader, help Taeo carry the unconscious Osirian a little way into the forest. By the time they leave it is well into the afternoon, and the mood in the village has turned. They are clearly anxious to get rid of both Taeo and the troublesome survivor. Taeo's last sight of the beach reveals a group of small figures preparing to make a bonfire of the wrecked *Wings of Osiris*.

Once again he lifts the Osirian's arm around his shoulders and begins the slow shuffle forwards, moving away from the village whose houses soon fade behind them until they are out of sight and hearing altogether. The trees grow closer together. The Osirian's feet drag on the ground and Taeo is worried about the wound to his leg. The man is spare but he is tall and a dead weight. Every fifty metres or so, Taeo has to stop and rest.

As they go deeper into the woodland, sounds surround them. Chattering insects, rustling branches and birds alighting upon them in a flurry of wings. The trees are slender but cut off much of the light. By dusk, Taeo can barely see. He blunders forwards. He knows his awkward progression will have left a trail any tracker could read, but there is nothing more he can do until the Osirian regains consciousness.

He lowers the man gently to the ground and props himself against the trunk of a tree. He cradles the Osirian's head in his lap, listening to the other man's shallow breathing. The last, the only survivor. Still alive. Taeo should be thankful for that, he supposes, and yet the mission that seemed so simple twenty-four hours ago has now become complex. His body is shaky with withdrawal; he craves the relief of a pipe.

As the day fades into night, he imagines he hears other sounds. The roar of fire. Human cries. Sharp cracks that might be a tree falling, or a gun fired. He feels like a wind-up toy whose coil is being cranked at every utterance.

He dozes and wakes with a jolt, and the process repeats, and repeats, until the first faint glow of light reveals the shape of the forest around him, and the face of the man he has saved. He is struck again by a resemblance to Shri in the man's features, and finds at once a reproach and a comfort in it. Even though he knows the similarities are both superficial and merely the tricks of genetic code, in that fleeting light before dawn it is as if some part of her has come to reside in the Osirian, and is watching over him.

8

There is nothing but poppy country as far as she can see. Field upon field of the flowers in bloom, broken only by the occasional cluster of buildings that marks a farm. Sheets of colour warm in the afternoon sunshine. Red. Violet. White. The silver stripe of a river. The blinking shadow of the plane.

It is good, fertile soil. Today Ramona does not care that its purpose is so singular. Today she is just grateful that she can get the drugs that Inés needs. It is tempting to land at one of the farms and directly bargain with the farmers, but there is a man in Cataveiro – not a good man, not at all, but a man who produces the purest stuff. She does not want anything less than top-grade quality. She has seen what croc does to the city's addicts.

She fidgets in her seat, restless, unable to settle. The plane has just crossed latitude fifty-one south. She has turned off the instrument panel; she knows the way to Cataveiro and prefers to fly without it when she can, just as the very first pilots must have done. In those days, she imagines, aeroplanes were revered, perhaps even worshipped. But that was before the Neon age, when colossal energy guzzlers soured their mystique, and before they became such effective dispersers of bio-weaponry and blight. If it were not for the hostile machines which destroyed much of last century's poppy harvests, Ramona might have company up here.

As it is, she is alone, and the thin trails of cirrus cloud drifting above are the only blot on the horizon. Windspeed is minimal. If the weather stays like this, it is easy flying from here. The plane cruises at a smooth hundred and fifty kilometres per hour, and the battery levels are steady. In a way, she wishes the journey were more demanding.

Once again she glances at her pack on the passenger seat. She keeps looking at it, wresting her gaze away, looking back.

'Go on then.' Speaking her thoughts aloud. A habit from so much time alone, never problematic until she has company. 'Look at the damn thing.'

She has to dig deep in the pack. It is right at the bottom where she stowed it, wrapped in cloth. She unwraps it and holds the holoma aloft in one hand. Smooth. Matt surfacing. Jet black. She runs her fingernail lightly over it. Nothing. She had a feeling it wouldn't scratch. It doesn't smear, either. Not even her sweat sticks to it.

Impenetrable.

'What am I to make of this, *Colibrí*?'

She turns the thing over. Who knows which side is up and which is down?

'He said it was about the shipbuilding programme. Could be something big.'

It makes her feel dizzy, looking at the holoma for too long, as if she were looking down into a very deep crevasse.

'Maybe the Antarcticans have finished their ships. Maybe they're planning a move. Oh, I don't know. It could be anything. You can't trust an ice man.'

She did trust him, though. That was the strange thing.

Recalling Taeo's instructions, she holds the holoma tightly for ten seconds, then five. At first it looks like nothing has happened. Then a single white light begins to glow in the centre of the holoma.

Ramona stares, at once repelled and drawn in by the light. What is it, a summoning? A signal to other holomas? She taps it. Nothing happens. She turns the holoma upside-down, shakes it, tosses it from hand to hand. Nothing. The little light continues to glow, steady, unyielding. Now she feels alarm. Is it transmitting? She reverses the ten-then-five and the light winks off.

The hand holding the holoma is quivering. Unlike some, she has never been able to control her response to machines. The first thing she and Raoul did when she got the plane to Tierra del Fuego was to disconnect all of its networks. Raoul said the plane was trying to talk to things: satellites that had been drifting unmanned since the Blackout, and other aircraft, broken down for their parts. For all the years it lay forgotten in the desert, the plane was reaching out to things that were no longer there.

'But you found it,' said Raoul.

She said: 'Maybe it found me.'

'That's your luck,' said Raoul.

She wraps the cloth untidily around the holoma and stuffs it back down to the bottom of her pack. Now she remembers Taeo issuing some kind of command – restricting her access? That must be it. So she can act as his courier but she is not permitted to know the truth about what she is carrying.

Bastard, she thinks.

And: You should have pushed harder.

And: I had to leave. There wasn't time.

Her thoughts drift inevitably back to the highlands, and what awaits her there. She cannot shake the fear that Inés will walk away, as she has done so many times in Ramona's life, without explanation or a note. That this time, there will not be a return.

She once heard the symptoms of going and returning described by a doctor in Cataveiro. A fugue state, she called it. The wanderer, as if in a dream, is a different person entirely. But Ramona found this explanation lacking. Inés is too present, too solid, to lose half of her self.

Even though she spent only the first thirteen years of her life in the highlands, the shack has always stood in Ramona's mind as home. She only has to close her eyes to hear the way it creaks: the floor underfoot, the doors and shutters that bang in wind and have to be stuffed with bits of cloth to jam them in the worst of the storms. Inés's hands: sewing, stirring, hammering, bandaging. The shack was always busy. It was always full. At first it held voices: Camilo and Paola, arguments and mock fights. Later it held traces, traces of Ramona's burned-up siblings, Paola's skip in the sand. In the empty years, the fugue years, it was alert with Inés's absence, murmuring, whispering to Ramona: when is she coming back? And each time that Ramona came back, stood on the creaking floor in her mechanic's boots, looked at the table and the vegetable jars covered in dust, her answer had been the same:

I don't know. She never told me she was going. How can I know?

Maybe that is home, a question hanging in an open doorway. Even now, since Inés returned, home holds the secrets of what she has and has not done. She will never tell.

If the jinn takes her mother, Ramona will be alone in the world. Who else is there? Félix. But Félix is a wanderer, an itinerant, like Ramona. Their paths cross and when the day of their last meeting comes neither will know it. They will attach no more import to the occasion than they did the time before, and when they part, it will be with a raised hand: keep safe. All as usual. But if – when – her mother dies, the voices in the shack will stop. There will be no whispers, no scuffling in the shadows. There will only be a shack.

Is that what it means, to be truly alone, when a place has been abandoned even by its ghosts?

Below, dirt track roads converge upon a small town. At its outskirts are the factories where they process the poppy yield into morphine and other drugs run by the cartels. A sign that the sprawling maze of Cataveiro is not far ahead.

The city gives her hope.

Now is the time to concentrate. She wants a safe hiding place for the plane, not too close, and not too far from the city. In flight, she activates the chameleon. From here on, she is invisible.

9

aeo watches the unconscious man's chest rise and fall in not quite even cycles, listening to the hiss of his breathing. He has a young face. There is evidence of sunburn and dehydration, but the man's skin bears no signs of what the Patagonians call their thousand curses, diseases they claim come from the north, leaving those who survive scarred or crippled.

At a glance, there is no reason why the man could not pass as Antarctican. Taeo stores away the thought for future reference.

He leaves the man sleeping and goes to stand by the entrance to the cave he stumbled upon earlier today: the perfect hiding place. He had made more progress than he thought. They are high above sea level and a dull light floods the mountain. He looks out down the hillside through the rustling trees that seem to lean and creak even when there is no wind. There are only the beginnings of forests in Antarctica. Antarctican trees are young. These Patagonian trees are old, their bark cracked and greying, like wizened sentinels. This is an old place, and Taeo feels himself to be old in it.

The thirty-six hours that have passed since Arturo's feel like a much longer span of time. He finds himself thinking of the day he recorded his transmission, that day that started it all. Except that it started a long time before that, back when he was first elevated from junior engineer attached to Civilian Transport to a senior position within the Civilian Security fleet. They made him sign a secrets act (this, after all the furore died down, was what they eventually exiled him on). They never used the word military.

The security shipping fleet was the big one – the super-ships project. The Republic had been working on them for years, and although, again, it was not explicitly said, the super-ships were part of the race between north and south; the race to create ships capable of withstanding hyperstorms, hurricanes and typhoons, not to mention the methane explosions rumoured in the tropics. The work appealed to Taeo; it was varied and centred around problem-solving. One day he could be experimenting with resistance to wind flow, the next, testing the strength of newly mined metals. Before he left, he had been researching a new type of hybrid fuel. The fleet was excited about it, although it would be years in development, and thinking about it now Taeo can hardly bring himself to care; the ambition of the project seems both foolish and egotistical.

The Boreal States were working on submarines.

Taeo never saw any of the spy reports (the engineers weren't allowed to use the word *spy* either, they were referred to as agents, although of course they did among themselves) but it was always evident when something had filtered through. A briefing would be called, and the engineers would be asked to test some new alloy, or given a blueprint and told: make this.

Even now, he is not entirely sure when the doubts began. Was it after Kadi was born, or before? It wasn't through Shri. Shri, who was so sure of everything, was sure on this too. She was proud of his work. She said they had to protect what was theirs.

He remembers Kadi, so little then, sat in a tub of warm water, Shri shampooing the child's hair which was dark and silken like Shri's, but curled like his.

This is our country, Taeo, and we'll fight for it. Fuck the Boreals.

She rubbed the child's head vigorously. Shampoo bubbles blossomed.
We'll fight for it, said Shri.

Perhaps it was then, looking at Kadi with her eyes screwed up
against the sting of the soap. Perhaps that was the moment that the
thought seeded: we shouldn't have to. Our children shouldn't have to.

Gradually the suspicion, at first just a nagging doubt, an inkling, grew
and grew until it became an overwhelming revelation that followed
him everywhere and subsumed everything he did. He thought about
it when he dropped the children at school. He thought about it while
he was arguing the best employment of diamond with a colleague.
He thought about it while Shri was curled against him in bed, her
leg hooked over his hip, her face pushed between his shoulder blades,
and he lay awake, unable to sleep, thinking, thinking, thinking.

What he was doing was wrong. The shipping race was wrong. The
super-ships were wrong, the subs were wrong. And if they – south
and north – continued along this path, they would inevitably arrive
back where they had begun, with another Blackout and the world
consumed in yet another war.

That, finally, was the message he recorded and transmitted, late one
night at the end of a bottle of sake, with the children and Shri asleep
upstairs and the dim lights of Vosti Settlement casting a blueish glow
to the streets outside. When he reviewed it the next day, sober, the
recording had a surprising clarity. Although by then he had been
drinking heavily for some time.

It is the arguments with Shri that haunt him now.

Did you think about the children? Did you think for one minute
about Kadi and Sasha and Nisha and what this will do to them?

The arguments that had stood so clear and impregnable in his head
dissolved before Shri's wrath. He had done this for the children – because
of the children. Because of the father he wanted them to have and the
world he wanted them to inherit. This was about ethics, he said.

Shri said she did not care about ethics. Now her children would have no father, would be spat at in the playground and called traitors by their peers. Was this ethics?

You've destroyed their lives, she said. And you've destroyed ours too. And for what?

Because it had to be said.

That was all he could offer her. Someone had to say it. Someone had to offer an alternative. To suggest that the thing they all believed was inevitable might not be inevitable. That minds could change.

He hadn't quite believed that the courts would go through with the exile. Send him to the ice frontier, perhaps, or to some dead-end job. But Patagonia?

Even through the harrowing goodbyes to the children, he was convinced that he had done the right thing. It was only when he boarded the ship, alone because Shri had refused to see him off, that the regret began. A great swamping tide of it armed with Shri's words and the children's *whys* and *how longs*. He was on deck when the horn blew. The ship's solar sails rose and swivelled, seeking maximum light. The ship juddered, scraping from the docking point, and began to edge away.

Then he saw a tiny figure, walking down towards the harbour front. The right height, the right build. Was it? Had she come, in the end? He couldn't tell. It might be. But it was too late. The ship was leaving, a ship whose schematics, perhaps, he had influenced over the course of his work in the past eight years. The gap between harbour and ship widened. Birds darted down into the foam, plucking up the small creatures stirred up by the motion of the ship's propellers.

He waved frantically. He shouted: I love you Shri. I love you!

If it was her, she made no sign.

When he turns away from the whispering world outside he finds the man from Osiris is awake, watching him silently from his prone position. Taeo's unease increases. How long has he been standing here, oblivious to the other man's surveillance? Now he finds himself wondering what sort of ambassador the City of Osiris would send on such a hazardous mission. Would they send soldiers? Trained killers? Until he knows, he has to work to gain the man's trust.

He speaks in Boreal English.

'You're awake. That's good. Don't worry, I have brought you inland. Away from the beach.'

The man stirs. 'Inland,' he repeats. He utters the word slowly, wonderingly.

'Yes. You're safe now. There were people coming who would have killed you, back there. But I got you away.'

The man looks at him and says nothing. Taeo notices a repetitive movement of his hands, holding the hem of his jacket, squeezing and releasing. Nervousness? Fear?

'Do you understand me?' he asks.

'Yes, I understand. You rescued me.'

The man's tone is flat and Taeo is unsure if the statement is an affirmation or a query. 'What's your name?' he asks.

'What's yours?'

'Taeo,' he answers, provoked by the somewhat hostile response. He keeps an eye on the man's hands, wary of sudden movement. No one has seen inside Osiris in fifty years. Who knows what kind of agenda they have? 'I'm Antarctican.'

'This is Tarctica?' Expression flickers across the man's face: bewilderment, joy, quickly chased by suspicion.

'No. This is Patagonia.'

'Patagonia,' says the Osirian. He repeats it, more quietly. 'Patagonia.'

For several long seconds there is silence and Taeo thinks about his next question, and how to phrase it, and then the man says:

'There were no maps.'

He lifts his head, struggling to sit up. Taeo supports him until he is able to rest against the wall of the cave. The man is still weak. Even such a small exertion brings sweat to his face. This is good and bad, thinks Taeo. The Osirian will be dependent on him, there is no way he will be running off into the wilderness. But he won't be able to run if they are discovered, either.

The man's eyes flick to the cave entrance. Taeo strains his ears but can hear only the sound of the trees stirring on the mountainside. But the Patagonians are far more familiar with this territory than he. No doubt they can move silently, when they need to.

'My name is Vikram,' says the man.

'Vikram,' Taeo repeats.

He sits so that he is facing the other man, and offers him the water bottle.

'Thanks.'

'I'm sorry, but I have to ask. I saw the boat. I saw the name. You say you've come from . . .' Taeo puts hesitancy into his voice, dropping it to almost a whisper. 'Osiris?'

'What's it to you?'

'It's just a question.'

Vikram looks as though he might deny it and then he nods, reluctantly, it seems to Taeo. Despite everything he knows, he feels a shiver at the affirmation. It is a strange thing, to have known of a place for so long, yet it has never been more than a neglected awareness, like the small insects that live in the cracks of your house but are rarely seen. Osiris is a composite of data, shipping movements and energy outputs, something countable, not a place where people live and breathe and die. But here is one of them: a man called Vikram, and he is alive, at least for now.

Taeo lets out a long breath. Now he needs to lie convincingly. 'We thought the city had been destroyed,' he says. 'In Antarctica, that's what everyone believes – and here in Patagonia, and everywhere – Osiris is known as the lost city. How can it be?'

'It can stay lost,' says Vikram, with sudden, surprising vehemence. 'I don't want to remember it, any of it.'

Step carefully, thinks Taeo.

'It's true, though?' he says. 'The city is still there?'

'I wish it were a dream.'

'And the boat – the crew? There were others, I know—' Again he sees the hump of bodies on the beach. The corpse in her red jumper with a gun wound in her stomach. 'I mean, it wasn't you alone?'

'The rest of them are dead, aren't they.' It is a statement rather than a query.

'I'm sorry.'

'It's a miracle we got this far.'

'The boat didn't look in a good state.'

'That, and everything else. We weren't meant to get out.'

'Are you saying you escaped?' Taeo's mind goes into overdrive.

Vikram gives him a twisted smile. 'You just said, you thought the city was destroyed. Now you know it isn't. I've nothing to say. I want nothing more to do with . . . Osiris.'

Taeo watches Vikram's face for signs he might be lying, but can detect none. If this is the truth, it will make Taeo's job easier, that is certain. But the Osirian could equally be bluffing him.

'You have to understand,' he says. 'This is a huge shock to me – and to anyone who was down there on the beach of Patagonia, and they will talk. It's like you've landed from the moon. I need to know why you've come here, now, after all this time.'

'Why did you rescue me?'

'It wasn't safe for you to stay there. Other villagers were coming, soldiers would have been next. I can't say what they might have done to you, but I don't think you'd be sitting here now.'

The young man does not react; he does not seem to care. His eyes are dull.

'I came because I wanted to leave the city,' he says. 'I'm grateful that you helped me, but you can leave me alone now. I'll make my own way from here.'

We'll see about that, thinks Taeo. But he nods.

'Let me help you until you've recovered, at least.'

Vikram looks at him, a shrewdness in his face battling with

exhaustion. He's going to ask why, thinks Taeo, but the other man merely shrugs.

'If you want. I can't offer you anything in exchange.'

'That's not the point,' says Taeo. 'People help one another, don't they? You and I are both outsiders here.'

Vikram gives a slight laugh. The emotion seems to take the last of his energy; he closes his eyes, his face drawn.

'How's your leg?' Taeo asks.

Vikram peels back the torn flaps of material around the wound in his thigh. The herbalist's stitches show clearly against the swollen flesh, but as far as Taeo can tell, there is no infection.

'I've had worse,' he says. 'I don't even remember how it happened. The last thing I remember, I was on the ship, in the storm . . .'

'Your boat ran aground. You must have tried to get to shore, and cut yourself on the rocks.'

Vikram looks at Taeo. 'Was it you who sewed me up?'

It is tempting to claim the credit, but Taeo has an inkling this might be a test. He cannot trust the Osirian's apparent lack of memory.

'No. The villagers pulled you out the sea, and their herbalist stitched you up. But they were charging people to see you. Making themselves some cash, until . . . well, until somebody else came.' He gets to his feet. 'I'm going back to take a look at the beach and find out what's going on. Stay here where it's safe. The Patagonians will be looking for you. And the chances are, Vikram, if they find you, they will kill you. This is a lawless place. I have learned that much from my time here. So stay hidden.'

'I don't need your help,' Vikram insists.

But as Taeo ducks out of the cave entrance the Osirian's eyes are already drooping with fatigue. The message has hit home, he thinks. Vikram is not going anywhere.

It is more difficult than Taeo anticipated to retrace his path back to the village. Where he finds evidence of their trail, he does his best to conceal it. He thinks about the story he will tell Vikram when the time comes for answers. How best to frame it. Lying to the Osirian makes him uneasy in the same way the lies he told the pilot make him uneasy; he is tormented with flashes of sudden guilt. But he cannot deny a sense of purpose, which he has not known since he was shipped out to this hostile continent. He has a task. A dangerous one, but an important one. Even his cravings are drastically reduced; he feels invigorated by the fresh mountain air.

The land slopes inevitably towards the coast, and soon he can hear the cry of seabirds alongside the smaller residents of the forest. When the trees begin to thin he proceeds more cautiously. The smell of smoke permeates that of the foliage; something is smouldering. The Osirian boat?

Other than the birds, it is strangely quiet. He can hear no evidence of human activity. The acrid smoke mingles with the briny scent of the sea. He must be close to the village now. Another few hundred metres, slowly advancing, and he can see the end of the tree line and the low-roofed houses in the clearing beyond it. He retreats back into where the cover is deeper.

A soldier in camouflage comes out of one of the houses and lights a cigarette. Slender build, could be male or female. The figure paces up and down, smoking. They drop the cigarette, grind it into the ground, and go back inside.

What is going on? Enquiry? Interrogation? Taeo listens anxiously, but hears nothing.

Moving as quietly as he can, he makes his way painstakingly around the edge of the village, maintaining his cover in the trees. From the other side, he can see the door to the house from which the soldier emerged, but they do not reappear. He turns away from the village. Dropping to his belly, he wriggles forwards to where the trees end and the hillside falls away so he can overlook the beach below.

A thin column of smoke rises from the wreck of the Osirian boat. There is little left; the boat is a forlorn skeleton, the white exterior charred to black. The beach has been cordoned off from the land and is teeming with busy figures. Military motorboats have driven up past the tideline, churning up the sand, while larger vessels hover out to sea. Armed Patagonian soldiers patrol in their camouflage uniforms. He can see a number of prisoners, tied together. There are casualties, with medics attending them. There are the shapes of bodies covered by sheets or tarpaulins.

Something happened after he left. A clash. Pirates, he guesses. Pirates, drawn like sharks by ripe information, and the army, in pursuit. There is one ship out to sea which has no identifying markings and is effectively hemmed in by three others. No one is up on deck. Another, smaller boat is capsized in the water.

He scours the beach for people he might recognize. There is no sign of the leader from yesterday, or any of the villagers. No sign of Ivra. He notices a figure in plain clothes stepping among the dead and the injured. The woman's movements are precise and bird-like. She bends and lifts the sheet from one of the dead, examines the face, lets the sheet fall. She does the same with the next body, and the next.

When the woman on the beach reaches the last covered bodies, she pulls the sheets away completely. Three blackened skeletons are revealed beneath. The dead Osirians. The villagers must have burned them, but not for long enough. The woman crouches by the skeletons for a long time. She touches the bones, and examines the ash on her fingers.

Taeo sees the distinctive flash of sun on glass from the other side of the village. Someone else is surveying the scene. He is not the only one skulking in the forest.

It is time to leave.

Vikram has gone. Frantic, Taeo goes to the back of the cave, touches the walls, the sides of the cave. There is no way out but the way he came in. The Osirian is not here. Vikram has gone.

Panic overwhelms him. He runs outside, opens his mouth to shout for Vikram, then thinks better of it. Has he been taken? Has he run off? Are there people here in the woods, looking for Taeo, lying in wait? Did they wait for Taeo to leave the cave and grab Vikram? He thinks of the tales of the Patagonian pirates: ruthless, lawless sailors, kidnappers and torturers – they take their payment in blood. The Republic executes pirates if they are caught in Antarctican waters. Pirates will have no love for Taeo.

He surveys the surrounding forestry, straining for every sound. He hears the wind, the leaves rustling. Tiny snaps and cracks that make him start.

Who is out there? Who is after him and Vikram?

He sees no one. He hears no one. But fear locks his limbs. The man on the beach – he is certain now that he has been pursued.

He has to find the Osirian. Vikram is his ticket home, his ticket back to Shri.

It is Shri's face that finally makes him move, back into the murmuring forest. He moves through the grey barks of the trees that bend and sway, leafy branches tapping his shoulder, causing him to start, convinced he is being ambushed. The Patagonians tell stories about trees, in the same manner they tell stories about everything. The continent has many trees, and the spirits of those that are gone have come to sit upon the shoulders of those that survive. The trees whisper and say malevolent things.

This country is getting to him worse than he thought. It's absurd, it's dangerous; he cannot let himself fall into its traps. The real danger is the people.

Think. Use your logic. If Vikram walked out alone, it is unlikely that he went the way that Taeo just came back, otherwise he would have seen him. And he cannot believe Vikram had the strength to get very far.

He searches the perimeter of the cave, going first east, then west, treading a figure of eight. When that yields nothing he widens the field, working methodically in a grid pattern. Once or twice he tries calling out, but his voice sounds thin and plaintive and frightens him more than it feels of use.

He searches for over an hour, coming back and checking the cave to see if the Osirian has returned. His certainty is growing. Someone has taken Vikram.

He climbs higher up, where the ground is rockier and the trees skinnier. Low plants and perennials carpet the mountainside, the bright tapestry of the flowers seeming to mock him with its carefree colour. He can see its brown peak rising against a blue sky with fast, scudding clouds. He climbs over a clear, tumbling stream and stops to wash his face and clear his eyes.

It is only then that he sees the Osirian.

Vikram is standing, exposed and utterly still, with his back to Taeo. At first Taeo thinks he must be threatened, at gunpoint, but then he spots the animal. Half-concealed among the spindly bushes is a single guanaco, the focus of Vikram's spellbound gaze. The creature is poised, frozen. Only its small ears twitch. It must sense that Vikram is there, but it has not fled.

Relief floods him.

'Vikram.'

The man whips around; the guanaco startles and bounds away, vanished in a trice. Taeo sees tears in Vikram's eyes before the Osirian blinks them hastily away.

'I didn't know,' says Vikram gruffly. 'I had dreams. I always thought – but if it was true, I thought everything would be dead, poisoned. Not like this. Not living. Not people . . . or . . . or that.'

A scene flashes into Taeo's head: Kadi and Sasha, a trip to the penguin colony. The wonder in their eyes is replicated in Vikram's face. The Osirian has only ever known the ocean; for all Taeo knows, he has never seen a creature with fur.

'It's a guanaco,' he says. 'You don't see them so often. They're protected by the Restoration Law, but that doesn't stop hunters. Live meat is big money on the black market.'

The Osirian is staring at him, uncomprehending. Taeo's words mean nothing to him. Restoration Law. Live meat. What does he know about this world? In the unfamiliar realm of land, Vikram is effectively a child.

'Come on,' says Taeo. 'The beach is full of soldiers. They'll be looking for us. For you, mainly. We have to move on.'

He feels the presence of the gun, stashed at the top of his backpack. An Osirian weapon, and if it could be charged, Vikram would know how to use it. But he cannot trust Vikram with something so volatile. Not yet.

'Where do we go?' Vikram asks.

'To Fuego. To the harbour. There are other Antarcticans there. I imagine it's where you must have been headed in the first place.'

The Osirian says again, 'We had no maps.'

This is something to discuss later, Taeo thinks. For now, they are in danger. The forest is not empty. He shares food and water with Vikram, replenishing the bottle from the stream, and gives Vikram a spare set of clothes. The garments are loose on the younger man's thinner frame, but less conspicuous than the ones he was wearing. They eat quickly. Everything is in Taeo's pack; there is nothing to collect from the cave. Once again he recalls the pilot's offhand advice, and thanks her silently. It is as if she had a sixth sense.

'I had a ride,' Taeo says. 'But the boatman left me in the lurch. We will have to make the journey on foot. How is your leg holding up? Are you all right to make a start?'

'I don't think there is a choice,' says the young man.

He follows Taeo quite willingly.

The journey that took a mere four hours by boat is agonizingly slow on foot. Taeo is worried about Vikram's leg, but whatever the herbalist did, it seems to have sealed the wound from infection. If Vikram is in pain, he refuses to acknowledge it, pressing on until he is physically unable to go any further. Taeo teaches him some basic

Spanish vocabulary, enough to get by if they become separated. At night, he dreams of losing himself in columns of sweet rising smoke.

They find the bodies by accident, seeking shelter from an afternoon storm under the trees off the old valley road. It is the rain that gives them away, dripping from weighed-down leaves to spatter on the tarps they have been crudely wrapped in, tarps that are now unravelling. There are three dead, two women and a man. Clouds of flies invade the bloated limbs. The skin that is visible is covered in a raw, weeping rash.

Vikram takes a nervous step back.

'What happened to them? A plague?'

Taeo takes a stick and gently lifts the cloth covering the woman's face. A layer of skin peels away with it, exposing the wet, putrefying flesh beneath. The staring eyes are yellow and inflamed, their rims swarming with ants.

'I'm not sure. It looks like redfleur, but . . .'

'Redfleur?'

'It's a virus, a super-strain. It can kill within hours. There's no cure.'

'Do you think that's what happened to these people?'

Taeo considers the face before him. The first time he saw a redfleur victim, his reaction was horror and repulsion. But now he is able to regard the corpse with a scientific scrutiny. He is not a doctor, or a virologist, but Ivra's terse explanations of the disease, which the Republic's tight immigration laws have kept mercifully at bay, have given him an idea of how it progresses.

'If it is, it's very far south for a redfleur outbreak. Worryingly so. And the bodies – they should have been burned to eradicate any trace.'

'They could be contagious?' Vikram backs further away. The alarm is evident in his face.

'Not now they're dead.' The stream of ants from the woman's eyes runs down her cheek and neck and swerves around Taeo's boots. 'Some people think the most contagious period is before the symptoms show.

That's why it's so hard to track. But if the relatives of these people believed they died of redfleur, they might have been too frightened to say anything. That would explain why they're out here in the open.'

'Why? Wouldn't they want to warn people?'

'They might not want to spend months in quarantine.'

When Taeo turns back he sees Vikram is watching, or has forced himself to watch. The difference is subtle and it is impossible to know.

'So it's true,' he says. 'There are plagues on land.'

'Some you can vaccinate against. Others you can't. The Boreal States control the medical records that survived the Blackout. If you ask me, that's their biggest crime.'

He is talking too much again, and forgetting who he is talking to. A sign of how long it has been since he has had anyone to talk to at all.

'The important thing is, if you see someone with rashes all over their skin, like petals – that's where the name comes from, redfleur, the Boreals call it, or *la flor roja*, they say here – just stay away. When the rash starts weeping, it's probably redfleur. Bleeding from the mouth, that's another sign. Don't go near them and absolutely don't touch them. There's nothing you can do to help. Like I said, there's no cure.'

He lets the cloth fall back over the woman's face and gets to his feet.

Vikram is staring at him, full of suspicion.

'Who are you? You're not a soldier. I know soldiers. You're not one of them. I don't think you're a spy either. So what are you doing in Patagonia, and what the hell do you want with me? And don't give me that shit about just wanting to help. No one helps someone for nothing. Not in this world.'

Taeo is only surprised it has taken so long. He has, at least, had ample time to prepare, but still he feels his body tingling in anticipation. He must get this right.

He gives a deep sigh, and allows a few seconds to pass.

'You're right,' he says, and offers Vikram a wry smile. 'In one way, at least. I'm not a spy.'

Vikram is watching him closely. He wants answers, but he is

cautious too. Taeo is reminded of the small lizards here that conceal themselves among fallen leaves and bark.

'Then what?'

'I'm a scientist,' says Taeo. 'And I'm in exile, because my colleague of fifteen years betrayed me.' He meets Vikram's gaze frankly. 'It's a long story.'

'I've got time,' says Vikram.

Taeo laughs softly. 'Yes, we have that. I might as well tell you. You deserve to know. But let's walk away from these poor souls, at least.'

They make camp, the forest canopy shielding them from the worst of the rain, and share out the food. There isn't much left. It is a couple of hours since they found running water, and after the mysterious bodies, Taeo is wary of refilling their bottles from stagnant pools. He tries to guess how much further it is to Fuego Town – they have been walking for three days now. Another day's hike? Two? He consoles himself with the thought of an Antarctican ship: proper food, rice, sake and flavoured soy, even fish. There will be lighting and actual technology. At the end of it all, a pardon.

He must not think too far ahead. First, Vikram needs answers, and the answers must be delivered with care.

'Do you know about the Nuuk Treaty?'

Vikram shakes his head.

'It was signed over two hundred years ago, after the Blackout.' Vikram looks blank, so Taeo explains. 'The Blackout was a virus that attacked scapular implants. Almost everyone had them back then. No one knew who engineered it – there are hundreds of theories – but it was the final move in the Migration Wars. A record loss of life, and most Neon technology taken out – within days.' He watches Vikram processing this information.

'What does this have to do with anything?'

'Your city, Osiris, was built because of the Blackout. To reunite the hemispheres.'

'I've read that,' says Vikram, but in a tone that suggests he doesn't believe it, or is not sure now what to believe. For this, Taeo cannot blame him.

'The Nuuk peace treaty was signed by all countries, and it agreed a ban on weapons, biological, nuclear, robotic. It still stands today.'

Taeo gathers his thoughts, because this part of his narrative requires that he pays attention.

'Antarctica has a civilian shipbuilding programme. I was working on a particular branch of the project. And after a while, I realized this project had military intent. They claimed it was defensive, of course. I confided in my colleague. I told her I had reservations about the project, that I felt uncomfortable continuing with my work when we had been lied to by our employers.'

He glances at Vikram, trying to ascertain how the story is going down. The Osirian's face gives little away. Taeo has no choice but to continue and hope his act is convincing enough.

'She said she felt the same way. She said she was glad we were finally able to speak openly. That evening we sat at her house for hours, talking about the situation. What we should do. Who we could trust.' Taeo lets his gaze drop. 'The next day, I was arrested. She had reported me. She twisted everything I said, claimed I was going to sabotage the project. I was dismissed, of course. They sent me here.'

He stares silently at his hands. The rain patters on the forest canopy above them.

'My family are still in Antarctica. My partner, Shri. My children. I barely have contact with them. Because I spoke out against something I believed was wrong.'

At least the final line is true.

'That's my story,' he says quietly. 'That's who I am.'

Vikram's face tightens, and Taeo feels his heart beat faster in a surge of adrenaline. Did he buy it? Was it too much?

'I was betrayed too,' says Vikram. 'I was betrayed and rescued by the same man.'

In that instant Taeo knows he has convinced him and feels a deep, terrible pity for this unfortunate stranger. He has experienced what it feels like to be unwelcome in your own home.

'Who betrayed you?'

'His name was Linus,' says Vikram. There is a quiet anger in his voice that makes Taeo think Linus is lucky to be elsewhere. Taeo sits back, giving Vikram the physical space to tell his story. He cracks open another tin, canned fruit, and offers it to Vikram.

'Didn't you say we were almost out of food?'

'We're not far from Fuego.' He hopes this is true. Vikram scoops out a handful of the fruit. He eats quickly, draining every drop from the tin and sucking the juice from his fingers before continuing to speak.

'This man – Linus – he came from a powerful family. I don't know what you know of my city . . .'

'I know nothing but stories. Think of it as a fairytale to me.'

'It's ruled by old families. This man was from one of those families. He had power, and he liked to play games.'

'Is he dead?'

Vikram shakes his head.

'Not when I left. But all of those people, they're in my past now.'

Taeo nods. He wraps his arms around his knees, listening intently.

'He asked me to help him, knowing that I had no choice. I was put in a cell for something I hadn't done.' His eyes flick up to Taeo. 'Like you. I couldn't refuse his terms. It was that, or a lifetime underwater.'

There is something chilling in the way Vikram says *underwater*. Taeo wants to ask more, but he does not want to interrupt.

'I accepted the bargain,' says Vikram. 'It put people I knew in danger. I knew that it would, but I thought I could save them too. I couldn't save them. I couldn't save any of them.' His tone is bleak now. 'But it was a strange thing. The man who put me in that situation, he was the one who saved me. I thought I was dead. My friends were dead. I'd accepted it – there was nothing more I could do. But his people came back for me. They got me out before it collapsed.'

Now Taeo does speak. 'Collapsed?'

'The tower,' says Vikram. 'The tower collapsed.'

His eyes are dark and inward, lost in his own reverie. The Patagonians would say this man has bad spirits in his mouth. His story is full of horrors: the underwater, the collapsing tower – what kind of place is this sea city? Taeo has no desire to go there, and yet he is riveted by the idea of it, a dread fascination growing alongside his instinctive scientific curiosity. He wants to ask questions. Lots of questions. He is going to have to be patient. The important thing is to gain Vikram's trust, and to do that requires careful manipulation.

'You must be glad to leave the city behind.'

'I'll never go back,' says Vikram.

'You don't need to.'

Vikram hesitates. 'Will you go back to . . . Tarctica? Will you be allowed?'

Taeo keeps his face carefully neutral. 'My time here is almost at an end. So yes, I'll be going back.'

'What's it like?'

'We call it the land of mists and winds. There are vast landscapes of ice and there are young trees and new flowers and meadows. It's a land of trial and experiment. A home you can be proud of.' The strange thing is that the words he says are true. In spite of everything they have done to him, he is proud. He does love the Republic. He loves it for its vision and its aspiration and what it will one day become.

'I want to come with you, when you go.'

'I think that's a good idea. We'll both be safer there.'

Vikram nods, but says no more, as though to acknowledge the idea too openly is to tempt fate.

'We'll make headway tomorrow,' says Taeo. He reaches for his pack. In one pocket is the funny little metal tin, full of salt, that he took from the Osirian ship. He holds it out. 'I found this. I didn't know if it might be important.'

Vikram takes the tin and opens it. The salt inside has encrusted into clumps.

'This was Mia's. She was the last one . . . left with me.'

Taeo remembers the dead woman under the blanket. That long plait of hair like a thick vine.

He waits.

'There's a custom – you throw the salt, to ward away the ghosts.' Vikram's voice is rough with suppressed emotion. 'The dead, I mean.'

'As a mark of respect.'

'Yes.' He stares at the tin, seeming unable to close it or put it down. Customs don't let you go so easily, physical or mental. Taeo knows that. You can train your mind but it does not forget.

He reaches over. 'May I?'

Vikram nods. Carefully, Taeo takes a clump of the salt between finger and thumb.

'Over your shoulder,' says Vikram.

He throws it as instructed. 'To the crew of the *Wings of Osiris*. Rest peacefully, wherever you are now.'

Vikram closes the lid of the tin.

'Thank you,' he says quietly.

The rain has stopped. Water drips from the leaves sporadically and the air is rich with petrichor scent. The smell of accomplishment. Taeo can feel his success, a taut, anticipatory sensation at the centre of his chest. A voice in his head says: you're close now. You're very close.

He has secured his ticket back home.

PART TWO
LA CIUDAD / THE CITY

10 ¦

On a forgotten day some time between two hundred and three hundred years ago, the musician Juliana Cataveiro pulled her daughter's limp body from a street flooded with the South Atlantic and carried her home through a hurricane. The storms raged for three days. During that time, Juliana sat in the attic of her house with her daughter and sang to her. On the first day, the South Atlantic plucked things from houses and bore them down the streets in strange, floating processions. On the second day, the wind took the roof off Juliana's house. She dared it to take the body of her child and it did not. The child turned blue and cold. When the rain ceased and the sea fell flat and glimmered as though it had never stirred, never mind drowned souls in their hundreds, Juliana Cataveiro burned her daughter, put the ashes in a tin and her guitar on her back and came south, which was the only way to go.

Cars and bikes had been swept away, so she came on foot. She walked through a changing world, but it did not matter to her because she had already changed, and the change was in the ashes on her back, and it was not reversible. She walked through jungles that burned and cities that crumbled and slid. One day she passed through starved, ghostly towns, the next she was ambushed by the warlords of water wars. She followed the rusting railway lines south and no one stopped her. She said no words. She sang no more songs. Those who saw her pass experienced a peculiar sensation. Some said they saw their own deaths. Some saw angels, tiny shining ones, clustered about her back. Others heard the voices of the unborn.

Each time the land changed, Juliana Cataveiro stopped, and felt the soil. Each time she frowned, and shook her head. No, not here. No, not here. No, not here. And so on until she came to a valley with a cold running river and barren hills rising all around. At a bend in the river Juliana stopped. The riverbank was rough and muddy. Here, yes here. She dug a hole with her hands, a metre deep. In it she buried the ashes of her little girl. She took out her guitar and she picked something sad and bittersweet on the strings, but she could not sing. She scratched her daughter's name in the soil. She was ready to die now.

A traveller passed through the valley – a trader, or a soldier, or an artist, or a nurse – and asked who she was. Juliana had no words and could not answer. The trader or the soldier or the artist or the nurse read the name of her daughter. He looked at the valley and saw its potential: the river, the hills which encircled it. He imagined trees and agriculture. He went on his way telling others and bringing them back.

When he returned the mysterious woman was gone. Her guitar was on the riverbank, damp with the morning dew. Her daughter's name was still there, dug into the soil. And there it is today, listeners, beneath the foundations of the city, and if you look closely on a night when the stars are near, you can see it, or so they say.

At 4.30 a.m., Station Cataveiro is broadcasting stories for children, or old women who act like children. The Alaskan is not listening. Not really. Only a little, maybe, only the periphery of her hearing. She knows all the stories. It is absurd that they make her heart flutter, still. With her level of memory, she could probably quote them verbatim. This one is an old favourite of the city's storytellers. This is the story told in the tango clubs, the romantic one. Told by guitarists and flautists. This was the story the Alaskan heard first, but her favourites are the darker tales. She likes the dark. That is where the interesting things dwell. The dark spaces and yawning gaps in time. The Alaskan should have lived in the Blackout years. They would have suited her well.

Instead she is bedbound in a hot, airless attic in a crumbling old district of Cataveiro in a country that is not her own.

Luckily, something or someone is always arriving in Cataveiro, and the Alaskan is usually the first to know.

11 ┋

The first settlers of Cataveiro come from the coasts. They bring with them belongings they can carry on their backs, or cram into cars that have enough charge to start. However far they run, they cannot escape the sea. It lodges in the canals of their ears. It rushes through the deserted avenues and carnival streets and sea wall walks and seeps into the outlying favelas of the once-great cities.

The settlers of Cataveiro flee from the sea, but they bring the water with them. In transit, it takes a new form, that beloved of the troubadours; it becomes music. Cataveiro is founded upon the music of the sea.

Patagonia changes; a valley that was once barren becomes fertile farmland, and it is here that the settlers build their new homes, on the slopes above a bend in the valley's meandering river. As the settlers form a collective and summon their families and more refugees come from the fire zones, so the river is plumbed. In the summer months it idles through the valley, low and stagnant. In the hyperstorms it swells and the banks break and the valley floods. The settlers remember the coast and sing of water.

When demand on the river becomes too great, the desalination companies move in. Lines from the coastal plants converge upon the city. The family Xiomara grow rich. Cataveiro is a town now. It acquires banks, a university, a trade in opium from the burgeoning poppy fields to the north and south. In civil war the army comes, drawn by bars and women. The guerrillas follow to stake their own claim. And still the water music courses through the nights, beautiful and treacherous.

The city – it is a city now – expands, sprouting limbs in every direction like those of the Nazca spider. Cities in the north burn and sink as the land buckles. Malaria and typhoid race south. Cataveiro takes in those who survive, be they farmers, lawyers, altruists or thieves. Cataveiro does not care who comes, so long as they heed the water music and the water laws.

One burning December day, a girl and a boy stumble out of the shimmering horizon. It was weeks ago that they left the sliding city, full of hope and ambition. They have clung together in the cold nights when heat evaporates and races up into the atmosphere. They have survived torrential mudslides, when the world came alive underfoot and sought to drown and bury them at once. They are dazed and dehydrated and their stomachs are eating themselves, but they are amazed, because here they stand before Cataveiro, which until this day was a legend. An idea.

They stagger uncertainly towards the first buildings, where the first wave of sea music chimes its silken tones. The city swallows them.

Three days later, the boy, Félix, emerges. He knows his path. He goes south. He goes to sea.

The girl, Ramona, does not come out for seven years.

Bicycle chimes, rickshaw bells, tram horns and skateboard wheels. The crowds part and regroup continually as residents wend their way through the city, intent on a thousand different missions. A car with darkened windows slinks through the narrow streets, forcing the pedestrians to press up against the walls of their bleached buildings. Ramona watches the vehicle. She knows it, intimately. She knows the quiet engine and the elegant metal chassis and the luxurious cushioning of the seats inside. Memories flood back: the garage, her apprenticeship. The smell of oil and steel.

She fights her way deeper into the city. Through city sweat and whiffs of vendor food, dust and sour drains and sun-warmed metal tracks, the rising stench of the river with an early summer. She has forgotten about the smell. She has forgotten that in the city everyone carries a mask in case of an epidemic, and some of them wear them in the streets every day. She has forgotten the way the city sprawls and climbs, the ladders scaling the house-fronts, the busyness on balconies and roofs, the people, walking-cycling-clinging on to the tram, so many people packed together. The way the city opens, suddenly, onto unexpected plazas, with large establishments squatting among residential blocks. Here the courtrooms, here the hospital, here a park. Cataveiro is a history of happenstance.

Outside a cheap hostel, Ramona scans a group of the street urchins who loiter everywhere, waiting for scraps of work. She needs a smart one, not just a street-smart one. She beckons to one of the slightly older boys. She puts his age at thirteen or fourteen, wary-eyed in a dark blue tee and a faded Team Vaquera cap that's almost certainly filched.

'I need you to find someone for me.'

'Name them, I'll find them,' he says.

'Alejandro Herrera. He was with the Galea Company a couple of years ago, but he may be in public office now.' She has kept tabs on Alejandro, but not that closely.

'What's the message?'

She gives the boy a written message and a handful of peso.

'I'll be back here at one o'clock, for the reply.'

He darts away but she hangs on to his arm for a moment longer.

'Only direct contact,' she says, and folds another couple of notes into his palm for emphasis. 'I want you to see his face.'

'Yes, señora.'

Ramona watches the kid despatch smartly into the crowd and dart over the tram lines heading westwards. She turns the opposite way, towards the university, where there are fewer people, and more room to breathe. She avoids the district where the garage is based. It is a strange thing to be in the city where she spent so many years, and not to see the people who helped her. As she walks she feels her former life riding on her back, peering over her shoulder, the way spirits do.

Like most things in Cataveiro, the university is a loose, unstructured model in architecture and in philosophy. Anyone can attend a talk. Those who call themselves students wander in and out of lectures and discussions, and those who call themselves professors appear in one department one day and teach a different discipline the next. The campus is full of larger and smaller groups, some engaged in quiet, intense conversations, others arguing heatedly.

Two students sit in a shady, moss-walled courtyard.

'You know the Solar Corporation is bleeding us dry. Between the ship miles and the Boreal tax, we're fucked. It's no wonder half the city can't afford to run a fridge.'

'Would you rather we bought energy from the Tarkies?'

'I'd rather we produced our own – it's not as if we don't have the desert—'

'Desert but no economy.'

'Maybe I'll start my own company.'

'Yeah? Who's going to fund you? The salt woman?'

'Tell me then, what would you do?'

'I'd cut out the Boreals and renegotiate with the Solar Corporation directly.'

A snort.

'Let's get another opinion, shall we? Hey, don't you agree we should disassociate from the Boreal States?'

This is said to Ramona as she passes through.

Their fervour is both inspiring and alarming. She wants to say to the pair, do you not realize how small this city is? How tiny our country, how far the continent extends beyond the habitable zone? How far we have been left behind? The world was once small but now it is vast again. It is only from the air that you realize how vast.

The students are looking at her expectantly, awaiting an answer. It might be interesting, but to answer is to be caught in debate, and she is not looking for debate. Not today.

'I don't have an opinion,' she says.

They look disappointed.

She exits the courtyard and continues through the campus. The robotics department is easily identified. Symbols flicker over its exterior walls. The display is repellent, but somehow Ramona finds herself walking towards the building, up the steps to the gated entrance, where security guards are present to check that nothing gets out. They nod her through the doors that open on a shuddery automation, and inside, where she almost trips over some awful metal robotic thing that is scuttling about the floor. She can feel the discomfort in the air. Static, and the strange crackling white noise that only comes from these machines. She doesn't know why she has even come in, but now she is here she cannot bring herself to walk out again.

She slips into the first hall where they are demonstrating some kind of Boreal wizardry and takes a seat at the back. At the front of the room, two professors are manipulating a device that beams three-dimensional representations out into the room. The representations are larger than life and the style of their hair and clothes is from another era. Unlike those around the campus, each of the students is paying strict attention to the demonstration. They lean forwards, their faces bearing a disgusted fascination which Ramona knows is reflected on her own face. She watches as the Boreal people leap out of the device and are sucked back inside.

The professors argue over how the projection can be stabilized. Students shout suggestions.

Ramona is aware of a growing sense of nausea at the back of her throat. She taps the shoulder of the girl sat in front of her.

'What is this display, please?'

'Holotech demo,' replies the girl, twisting around. A brassy pendant of the Nazca monkey hangs prominently over her T-shirt, matched by two dangly earrings. 'That's a pre-Blackout device. It's meant to have sound, but the profs can't get it.'

'It's a strange thing to make yourself appear as a spirit.'

'It's like making yourself dead before you die,' agrees the girl, but they both continue to stare. Ramona feels the weight of the holoma in the pack on her back. She wonders what would happen if she were to activate it now.

After a few more minutes the queasiness in her stomach is too great to ignore and she leaves the hall and continues through the laboratories of the department. It is better when she is moving. She watches the lab masters carrying out their experiments. The labs are full of wires and sparks and some of them smell of smoke.

On her way out of the building the guards frisk her and ask for her pack. She freezes, suddenly remembering the holoma, but their sensors pick up nothing. Apparently the Antarctican was right when he said it would be like carrying a stone. Ramona watches the scuttling robot nosing at the edges of the walls. It is important to come here. It's a reminder.

Those outside Patagonia see their rejection of robotics as a weakness, backward and regressive. But Ramona knows it is a strength. It is a strength to be different. It is a strength to say no.

The boy returns with a message. Alejandro Herrera elects to meet on a rooftop cafe in a fashionable district of town. Here the buildings are painted cream to deflect the sun, and the scents of the herb gardens and watered flowers drift pleasantly across a terrace of tables and chairs. Sunlight glints off the low-grade solar panels dotted over the city.

Ramona is not happy with the choice of location – it is too exposed – but she has no choice if she is to meet Alejandro. She arrives fifteen minutes before the allotted time and walks the length of the rooftops, past pop-up vendors selling humitas, card players and yoga practitioners and lovers out for an afternoon stroll. A banjo player curls around his instrument, plucking languid notes. When a city enforcer strolls by she keeps her face neutral, and walks straight on. She notes where ladders run down to the next level, where balconies jut out over the streets a floor below. When she reaches the end of this impromptu promenade, she returns to the terrace and finds Alejandro waiting.

He has not lost his good looks. His hair is cut and sculpted in the style that seems to be in vogue now; on Alejandro it is flattering. His face is clean-shaven, revealing unblemished skin and that determined jawline. What was boyish charm fifteen years ago has matured into handsome suavity, and he knows it. He greets her like an old friend, kissing her on both cheeks. Ramona wonders how she appears to him, whether he sees the awkward teenager she was or a woman who has changed. Her skin has weathered; she has lines and muscles that were not there before. She feels both more confident in herself and more conflicted about the world than she did back then.

Alejandro offers her a glass of water with a slice of lemon floating in it. He is unable to resist commenting on the lemon.

'From the groves,' he says. 'But I'm afraid there is no ice. Do you have ice in Fuego? I wouldn't know, I haven't been there.' He laughs lightly. The laugh is enough to tell her the friendliness is a display.

'You're not missing much, Alejandro,' she says. 'I'm sure Cataveiro offers far better entertainment than Fuego.'

'We have the most diverse music scene, of course, and the theatre, and the carnival. Yes, we have many things in the city. Really, it's a shame you don't have the time to visit more regularly.'

Ramona takes a mouthful of her lemon water, savouring its fresh tartness on her tongue before she swallows. She pictures the private lemon groves where this fruit grew, the rows of trees with their swollen fruits. She pictures the people that Alejandro must know to drink lemon-scented water. He is restless. His eyes flick past her shoulder, to either side of her. Ramona studies him quietly. He is three years older than she. When they were teenagers pressed up against one another in the back of whichever car she was fixing, that seemed an unbridgeable gap, but looking at him now, three years holds no weight at all.

'Maybe one day I'll have more time,' she says.

'Perhaps you will.' Alejandro sits back. His eyes are still roving. She notices a mask dangling from his belt, an elegant black one with hairline gold swirls. 'The mayor comes up to this promenade sometimes. He seems to think of me as quite the protégé. Any day now I expect to be offered a position in the hall.'

'I've heard you're doing well,' she says. It is true, although not for the reasons she might hope. Alejandro was always hungry for power. He craved it in cars, always wishing to move faster, to harness the sense of supremacy that he assumed came with ownership. He used to loiter about the garage looking at the cars, and Ramona noticed him. At first each of them imagined that the other felt the same about the thing they loved most. It proved otherwise. Ramona loved the cars not for their power but for the beauty of the mechanics behind them. She recognized that the cars had personalities: some were resistant, some anxious to please, while others were battered, heroic survivors, refusing to expire. Alejandro did not understand this. He wanted to exert his will upon them. It had been a mistake to tell him when she first heard the story of the plane. That was when they had fallen out.

'I will do well,' he says, almost aggressively. 'There is much to be done. Cataveiro is too subservient to the government. We intend to deal with that. And you? You're still flying, I hear?'

'Yes.'

'Sometimes I wonder how it might have been if we'd gone to look for it together. Do you ever wonder that?'

'No,' she says firmly. 'What would be the point of that?'

'It was a long time ago, I suppose.'

'A very long time ago. Fifteen years ago.'

A whining note creeps into Alejandro's voice. 'It still amazes me you were allowed to keep it. Neon planes have been illegal for decades. But you have one, and nobody questions it.'

'You know why. I said I would make maps, and I do. Besides, you wouldn't enjoy my work. Cartography is a painstaking process. It's slow and meticulous.'

'But you do, evidently.'

'It allows me to do something useful.' She sips again from the sweating glass.

'Very altruistic of you,' says Alejandro sourly. The grudge is still there, after all these years. *Was it another mistake to contact him?*

'Alejandro, I'm short of time. You know people now. I was hoping you could help me.'

Alejandro leans his chin on his hand, a contrived, thoughtful pose.

'"I know people," she says. Yes it's true, I do know people now.'

'There is someone in particular. Señorita Xiomara.'

He raises an eyebrow, as well he might. It is not without misgivings that she says the name.

'What could you want with Señorita Xiomara?'

'My mother has the jinn.' Ramona lowers her voice. 'Everyone knows that there are people in Cataveiro who buy Boreal medicine. If anyone has a cure, it will be her. I need a meeting.'

Xiomara controls the water supply. Her family are dead; the desalination empire is her inheritance. The salt woman has wealth unimaginable to a girl from the barren highlands. Wealth enough to buy Boreal medicine in abundance. She also has a particular reputation. Those who oppose Xiomara tend to disappear. It is said that her enemies are transported to a ravine, some alive, some already dead, but none come back, and afterwards, it is as though they never existed at all.

Ramona watches Alejandro's face. The slight contraction of the eyelids. She feels her hunch solidify into certainty.

'It's true,' he says. 'We are friendly, Xiomara and I.'

The Antarctican's cash is a hard little wad in Ramona's pocket.

'I have money,' she says.

Alejandro tilts his head, squinting up at the glaring light beyond the shadow of the awning.

'I like to hear you say you need things, Ramona. It pleases me.'

'Alejandro. I'm talking about help for a dying woman. You're the only connection I have in the city. Do you want me to beg you or what?'

Alejandro's gaze flicks over her shoulder, focuses on something, then draws back. Ramona feels a familiar prickle at the back of her neck. Once again she takes note of the bystanders: the yawning server, idly rolling a yellow lemon back and forth along the counter; the woman slumped under a parasol, her eyes apparently closed beneath her red-rimmed sunglasses; the solitaire player, turning over his cards one by one.

'Ramona, you know I don't like to be harsh, but if she is dying already . . .'

Her grip tightens around the glass of lemon water and its condensation shell. She can feel movement behind her. Not the languid sun worshippers, but purposeful, direct, careful movement, the way a snake winds its way through dry grasses.

'Alejandro,' she says. 'You're a clever man. But you have never been subtle.'

He smiles. A glimmer of uncertainty. She stands and dashes the glass of water into his face. Alejandro's eyelids screw up tight and in that moment Ramona grabs her pack, vaults the table and knocks his chair sideways. Glancing back as she lands, she sees two men hastening across the terrace. Casual attire, but she recognizes them instantly as enforcers. *What the fuck? Enforcers?* The solitaire player has abandoned his cards and is moving swiftly in her direction.

'You little shit, Alejandro!'

Sprawled on the floor, he splutters something. She ignores it and runs. Her flight attracts a flurry of protests from the sunbathers and curious glances as she dodges around the tables, but it is too hot for them to move. She sprints across the rooftops, retracing the path she walked before the meeting. Past the humitas sellers, past the banjo player. A group of students scatters before her. She risks a look back. The solitaire player is close. He is younger and fitter than the other two, easily navigating the crowds in her wake. She is hampered by the weight of the pack.

Fucking Alejandro. What is he playing at?

The end of the promenade looms: a metre gap between this line of buildings and the next. She gathers speed and leaps, narrowly clearing the drop, lands heavily and rolls. Up on her feet and on again. Solar panels, open attic windows, washing lines, sparrows resting on radio antennae. She looks back. The solitaire player has cleared the gap. He is right on her tail. He is fast.

She veers to the edge of the rooftops, looking for ladders and balconies below. She fixes her sights on a balcony one floor down and jumps again. The fall is sharper this time and her ankle jars with the landing. *Ignore it!* Get down, get off the roofs. She swings over the balcony edge and reaches for a ladder. Two flights down, left along a walkway, scramble down another ladder. The solitaire player is above, mimicking her route. She drops into the streets and runs.

It is easier to hide down here. It's darker. There are rickshaws to duck behind, carts and bicycles to upset and disrupt the solitaire player's pursuit. A tram approaching ahead: good, use that to cover you. Within a few streets she has lost him; now it is safer to slow, merge her movements with the crowd, but she keeps walking. The exhilaration of the chase is wearing off. Her ankle aches. The crowds flow around her, hard-faced and menacing, each man, woman or child a potential threat were she to be recognized. Now is the time to become invisible; become like the dust. Remember your roots, highland girl. Remember those days in the ruins of the sliding city, when a tremor could bring down a building, when you crept and tiptoed and looted.

She tries to calm her breathing, but she can feel the tremor in her legs and hands, the adrenaline slowly draining away in the wake of her flight. She has foiled her pursuers but she leaves the meeting empty-handed. She has nothing for her mother. Failure.

What was Alejandro thinking? City enforcers? Was he planning to arrest her? On what grounds?

You know what he's after. He wants Colibrí. *After all this time, he's still obsessed with the idea of the plane.*

You never should have contacted him.

But who else is there?

She walks. Her stomach is growling. Her shoulders ache. When she feels she has calmed enough to keep her voice steady she stops at a vendor and purchases tamales with the Antarctican's cash. The paper parcel is hot and steaming and she feels almost faint at the sudden scent of food.

'New in town?' asks the vendor, looking at her pack.

'Visiting friends,' she says.

The radio on his stall issues bursts of crackly, fast-fingered guitar. It jostles with other stations from other windows: incessant beats pattering on drums and skin, a guttural voice singing a ballad, the verses rhythmic, repetitive. Ramona decided long ago that Cataveiro's music is not an expression of joy, or even artistry. Cataveiro is full of spies; people sing so that no one will hear what they say. There are spies for the army and spies for the guerrillas. There are spies from the north and spies from the south. There are Alejandro's spies, who have contacts.

'Have you been to Cataveiro before?'

'A couple of times.'

'There's always something new to see. That's what I say, and I see it every day.'

Ramona glances up at the strip of sky above the narrow street. A bird wings past and she wills herself back in the plane, speeding north, escaping the city's tenacious clutch. The afternoon is tailing away, and

Cataveiro streets are not a place to linger at night. She had hoped to be in and out in a day. The hope seems foolish now.

She bites greedily into the tamale. Hot morsels of vegetable explode in her mouth. Then she tastes meat. She stops chewing abruptly.

'Is that goat?'

'Chicken,' says the vendor proudly.

'Where's it from?'

The vendor shrugs. Does it matter? Grown in a glass tube or raised eating grain, it's chicken, it's hot, it's good for the soul.

It matters to Ramona but she is stuck with it now; she cannot insult the vendor by refusing to finish the meat. She chews and swallows. As she walks away from the vendor, a young man leans out from a doorway.

'Sing you a serenade, lovely lady.'

'No need for that.'

'No, I'll sing you a serenade. The tale of the condor, that's a one for you.' There is something insistent, aggressive, about his tone, and she hurries on, not too slowly, not too fast, dipping once more into the river of the crowd, the bicycles, the rickshaws, thinking, thinking.

What now?

She reconstructs Alejandro's face, the moment where she mentioned the cure. He knows. He knows it exists. That's why he is befriending those people. Because deep down, Alejandro has the same fears as everyone else. Fear that the jinn will get him, or the pox will rob him of his good looks, or a new epidemic will come that he is powerless to escape. Alejandro's life consists of the construction of barriers against those things.

Acquiring the plane would be one more weapon in such an arsenal.

She finds a House of the Nazca and ducks inside. There is little light, except that which illuminates the hearths of the hummingbird and the spider and others, the basin lined with a centimetre of still water. Ramona sits quietly. An acolyte acknowledges her with a nod of the head, but leaves her in peace to contemplate. The Nazca Houses have humble beginnings. Their first advocates emerged as a cult in the Blackout years, a zealous, intense community who worshipped the glyphs as gods. Over the decades, their strictures have been diluted; communal houses sprang up, sub-groups and sidelines flourished, religious creed evolved into practical teachings, and those became the recitations and fables of children: the hummingbird who stole the winds; the monkey who drank the world's water. Nowadays, anyone can be a prophet.

An old man is kneeling at the altar of the hummingbird. His lips move silently and although she cannot hear the words, Ramona can guess what they are.

In this place she should be thinking of her pilgrimage to Cerro Blanco. Her mind should be thoughtful of the laws of conservation and community. Instead it is turmoiled. Her respects will have to wait.

Thanks to somebody, she is being hunted. Perhaps Eduardo gave in to gossip, but city enforcers are not Lygia's style; her boss is too subtle for such blatant measures, and besides, it is less than twenty-four hours since she left the island. Lygia would wait, and analyse. No, this is Alejandro's doing. She underestimated him. She underestimated his ability to hold a grudge: all these years he has lived believing that the plane should have been his. Her message must have been first a surprise, then an opportunity. Ramona made it easy for him.

She feels hot with anger at her own stupidity. Up in the sliding city, time is running out for Inés. Ramona cannot afford to make mistakes. As long as she flies, she will always be hunted. That is *Colibrí*'s price. She should know it by now.

Alejandro won't give up easily. The sensible thing would be to get out of the city tonight, but that means nothing for her mother.

Ravine or no ravine, I'll have to find Señorita Xiomara myself.

12 :

The Alaskan watches as the fly she has been stalking for the past twenty minutes alights on her wrist. She moves with exquisite, fastidious precision. Millimetre by millimetre she stretches out her hand. So close. So very close. The fly so suddenly quiet. She can see the lines on its wings. She can see its rotating eyes, the feelers quivering. Then she smacks. Got you! There it is. A plump bloody smear against the swollen veins of her forearm.

Grunting with the effort, the Alaskan reaches for the sling and hauls herself to a sitting position in the bed. Her legs no longer work. If she was still in the north, they could provide her with the exact terminology for the state of her spine. Here, it is all jinns and spirits. The Alaskan prefers it. Sometimes it is not useful to know such a thing. Sometimes the fact is all that is needed. Her legs do not work. Who needs the truth? She pulls a pillow behind her and settles back into the cushioning. She can feel the wall through the pillow. The wall pushes against her vertebrae, which stick out more each day. When she was young and fit, the Alaskan would never have believed that this deterioration could happen to her body. She abandoned mirrors a long time ago, but she can imagine the skeletal appearance she presents.

It is appropriate then that she is living in a country which is dying, as far as the Alaskan is concerned. And the Alaskan knows a lot.

Patagonia is an information market. It has no value in the world's eyes except for the messages that flow in and out. That is why the Alaskan likes it. She likes to value the things others see no value in. She likes the way people come to her as if she holds a secret power when all that she does is listen. Here where they worship the spider – no, worship is the wrong word – where they uphold the teachings of the Nazca, the Alaskan feels at home. The spider was revered because its scuttling presence signalled the coming of the rains. But the spider is also a weaver. A linker. A maker of mazes and a designer of threads. This is the role of the Alaskan: to know, and to understand when it is not good to know, all the while holding the threads together.

She reaches for the radio on the bedside table and turns the dial. The crackle of white noise, slips of voices sifting through like fingers in quicksand. A minute twist to the left and sudden sharp sound.

Here is the news she has been listening to on and off all day. A guerrilla rebel renowned for machete attacks has been released from jail. Riots followed, and now civilians are complaining about injuries sustained in the violence. The rebel woman has been granted a full pardon. How, the broadcaster demands, her tone suitably outraged, could this breach of justice have happened?

The Alaskan nods to herself. She knows how.

'Maria?'

She appears, sponge in hand. A little runt of a girl, that peculiar, gnomic face hiding behind the hair as usual. It makes the Alaskan impatient. Why must the girl always hide?

'Yes, señora?'

'Get the book.'

The girl obeys; she does not need instructing as to which book. It is a tattered paper artefact, with some of the pages loose in the binding, but the state of it is unimportant. Maria opens the notebook carefully and angles it towards the Alaskan. The page contains a list of names.

'No, no, you do it. You know the name.'

Maria's eyelashes flicker in a quick, frightened glance. At the bottom of the list, in painstaking, childishly rounded letters, she writes the name of the pardoned rebel. Tonight, half the country will be fearing for their hands and their heads, but the Alaskan is not among them.

She gazes at the list. Some hundred or so names. The Alaskan owns every one of them: it is a list of debt. A satisfying sight, and yet every time she adds to it, she is overcome with a feeling of hollowness. There is a space at the end of the list that never gets any smaller.

'One day we will add her too.'

'Señora?'

'Xiomara, Maria. Señorita Xiomara. And plenty will thank me for it. After all, Xiomara fries little girls like you for breakfast.'

A look of panic crosses the girl's face.

'That is why you work for me, and not for her,' says the Alaskan, relenting. There is no joy in tormenting someone who never stands up for herself. Sometimes she is tempted to torture the girl out of sheer boredom, and has to remind herself that she has more important opponents to consider. 'Finish the floor,' she says. 'Your pay is in the tin.'

Maria moves to take the book.

'No. Leave this.'

She stares at the list while Maria finishes the cleaning. The handwritten letters coiling into the syllables that make up a name. Each is a slice of power, but will it ever be enough? Enough for what? Not to return, there can be no return. Irritated now, she pushes the book aside and gives the radio dial a sharp twist. The rebel is dealt with. What next?

Another station. A capella singing, Nazca songs. No, no, she doesn't want this.

Crackle. Pipe music.

Crackle. Weather report. A storm is coming. A storm is always coming.

Crackle. Polemic from a religious cult which sounds like a splinter group of Born Again Mayans. The end of the world is due. Souls should prepare, because in just three years' time, in 2420, to be exact, the apocalypse will arrive. In the meantime, anyone is welcome to join the group, and cleanse themselves in readiness.

The Alaskan snorts. The end of the world has come many times. The end of the world came during the Migration Wars and the race to the poles. The end of the world came when humanity went mad with weaponry, bio-weaponry, nano-weaponry. Nuclear was outdated, unimaginative. Things that attacked the senses and the mind – those were what mattered. The end of the world came when the Blackout virus caused billions to drop dead like ants. The end of the world came fifty years ago, with the Great Storm.

And yet the world is still here, and humans cling to the planet's surface as if embedded in it, the way bacteria burrows into human skin, the way mites reside in eyelashes.

Parasites.

She turns the dial.

Crackle. An attack by pirates on the coast of Tierra del Fuego. The army has cordoned off the coastline. Why would they need to do that?

Crackle. Suspected redfleur case in Cataveiro's closest neighbouring town. There is always a suspected redfleur case. Two doctors are arguing over the treatment of redfleur victims. Isolation once the victim is symptomatic is almost ineffective, says one. It's those they have been around that you need to watch. A person can be contagious and walk about for days, infecting others, and no one would know. The other disagrees. There's no evidence for an incubation period, he says. And there's no room for sentiment with redfleur. You have to ask questions later. The Alaskan agrees with that.

Then she hears something interesting. An unofficial station, an unofficial statement. The pilot is in town. They do not need to say her name because here in the forgotten south there is only one aeroplane, and one pilot. The Alaskan already knows the pilot's name.

Ramona Callejas is wanted.
But who wants her?
The Alaskan listens.

13 ┆

'I've got a question for you. Is there a cure for the jinn in this city?'

The chemist's soft, delicate hands flutter against a pristine white coat. His manner is mild. His eyes bear no discernible expression, except perhaps a distant curiosity. There are speckles of grey on his shaved head. He does not look capable of doing the things he is said to have done, but Ramona does not doubt for a second that he has done them.

When there is no answer she says, 'All right. Another question. Do you have a cure for the jinn?'

'No,' he says at once.

'But it does exist?'

'There are treatments,' he says. 'They are . . . rigorous.'

'Does anyone else in the city have a cure?'

He does not answer. They say this is the man who always tells the truth, or does not speak at all. So he does not know, or he cannot say for sure. Or, he will not tell.

It was a long shot, she thinks. It would have been real luck. Back to the secondary plan.

'What can you give me that mimics redfleur?'

The chemist looks at Ramona with surprise, as though she is the one who is suspect in this room full of chilled metal lockers, concealed in the basement below the clean, respectable pharmacy upstairs. Everything that means anything in this city is below ground level.

'Why would I have something like that?' asks the chemist.

'Because you're an expert in replication,' she says. 'I lived in this city for a long time. I lived on the streets. I know your name.'

'I know yours too.'

Ramona holds his gaze. She has heard the radio broadcast. Alejandro is making his move; every hour she stays in the city is a risk. But what this man does is illegal too. He is an illusionist of the worst kind: one that creates panic.

'I need something that looks like redfleur,' she repeats. 'The signs have to manifest in a matter of hours. And I need it in a form that can be transferred without the recipient's knowledge.'

The chemist turns neatly on his heel. He opens one of the lockers. There is a hiss of white ice. He pulls on a single plastic glove and holds up a syringe.

'You don't want a dilution of the real thing?'

Ramona forces herself not to recoil.

'I don't believe you have the real thing.'

The chemist returns the syringe and closes the door.

'You said you knew my name.'

He stands, arms loose at his sides, head tilted slightly in enquiry. She can feel the hairs rising all over her skin. 'Redfleur was curable once. It altered. Viruses do this. They are infinitely complex. More intelligent than us. More resistant than us.'

'I just want something that looks like redfleur. Something that isn't dangerous.'

'That will cost you. The more specific the request, the higher the level of expertise. That's how it is, I'm afraid.' The chemist smiles gently. 'And then, of course, there's the cost of vaccinating you first. I assume you will be undertaking the transmission?'

'Yes. Give me a price.'

They haggle. Ramona pays with more reluctance than she has ever felt in a financial contract. She can feel her skin crawling with each minute she spends inside this room with no natural light and its freezers full of disease. What this man does is despicable; what she is planning to do to Señorita Xiomara is despicable, not that Xiomara deserves pity from anyone. But it is this or let her mother die. She buys morphine from him too. She knows it will be pure.

The Antarctican's cash is disappearing fast.

The Xiomara house is over a hundred and fifty years old. The family has lived here a long time. It was redfleur that took Xiomara's parents, and left the young Señorita the inheritance of the desalination empire and, so it is said, a fiendish obsession with the collection of cures. Now the Señorita controls salt extraction and deposition. Eighty per cent of the energy-eating plants belong to her, all of those marked with the orca glyph: Xiomara's logo. It is Xiomara water that flows across the continent, surging through pipes from coastlines to the capital and the surrounding towns. Xiomara water irrigates the lemon groves and mists the poppy fields, filling the water troughs of the multitudes, lining the basins of the Houses of the Nazca in still, candlelit pools.

There is a rumour that within this house lies the skin of a jaguar.

After sunset the temperature drops, and in her hiding place which is in eyeshot of the Xiomara gates, Ramona shivers. This is where the wealthy of Cataveiro, those who have not defected north, live in their enclaves north of the river. There is night lighting here. There are driveways for the cars that Ramona used to fix. From here, the wealthy drive out from the city on pleasure jaunts to lush oases.

Her stakeout is a gamble. There is no knowing if Xiomara will emerge, tonight, or any other night. Ramona waits nervously. Surrounded by such clear evidence of power, she cannot help but think of all the rumoured disappearances.

Shortly after ten o'clock, she hears the friction of car wheels against the driveway. Yes – this is her, it must be her. There is a heavy clunk as the huge gates unlock and the car glides through the gates and past Ramona, almost silent, the windows darkened, the chassis polished and gleaming under the lights mounted on the gate. It's a thing of beauty.

She follows, jogging after it. She loses the car but does not worry; by the time it reaches the dense inner-city streets where the trams almost brush the walls of buildings, she will catch it up. Cataveiro was not designed for cars. There is no point in driving through these roads, unless you wish to make a statement. Once they are in the city, she is able to locate and follow the car at a walking pace. She keeps her head down, maintaining her step with that of the evening crowd.

The car draws up outside a tango club. Two bodyguards get out, both large, both carrying guns. Xiomara steps daintily from the car. She wears a flowing purple dress and matching nose-and-mouth mask, and her nightshade hair spills in glossy curlicues to her waist. In one hand she holds a plastic beaker with a straw. It is well documented that Xiomara makes her bodyguards taste any food and drink which is brought to her. She has gone through several. One was lucky; he only lost his stomach.

Xiomara proceeds with quick, abrupt clicks of her stiletto heels down a flight of stairs to the tango club, flanked on either side by bodyguards. The car pulls away. The gap it leaves is swiftly filled by pedestrians.

Ramona does not want to go into that club. It is another enclosed space, and underground, which is even more of a potential trap. As she hesitates, people walk past, intent on their own business. This is her best chance. She feels the gun concealed beneath her clothes. Not much use in a crowded space, but it gives her courage. She crosses the street and runs down the stairs.

The tango club is a cavernous structure, unfolding into dark corners and curtained alcoves. Smoke stirs in the somnolent air. Cages hang from the wall. There is a bird and a striped lizard, and in one suspended glass box there is an orange-patterned snake.

Small round tables are set out before a stage, all occupied by young and well-groomed patrons, but Xiomara is sat at none of them. She has taken one of the alcoves at the side of the room. Her bodyguards hover close by. Xiomara lifts her mask to sip from her beaker. She appears oblivious to everyone around her.

Ramona buys a bottle of the cheapest beer the club offers and scans the room. This is a place for romance. Couples in corners. Hands held under tables. She thinks fleetingly of Félix, trying to imagine him in a club like this, but she cannot. Musicians play strong, insistent beats. Two dancers emerge from either side of the stage. The music becomes brooding and aggressive. The dancers approach one another.

The audience hushes, enough to hear the scrape of the dancers' shoes against the floor. Ramona watches, mesmerized by the sinuous grace of the performance. The dancers circle, their story told in taut, arching movements: wary, then passionate, then hating, then adoring once more. There is such a sad, dark beauty in the old Argentine dance. Now she thinks of Paola and Camilo burned up with the fever, their small bodies placed in the ground, and her heart aches for the things they will never see, simple things like this dance. Her poor siblings, they were so young. Left alone, she could weep.

She is not the only one affected. Xiomara is on her feet, clapping and crying all at once. The dance builds to a climax. The woman is thrown to the floor and the man steps away, triumphant yet bereft.

Xiomara brings her hands together. 'Bravo, bravo!'

Rapturous applause. The dancers bow, and Ramona forces her thoughts to the moment. She borrows a pen from the bar and writes on a napkin.

I am the one with the aeroplane. Do you want to talk?

When the bartender passes, she slips the napkin and some peso into his hand.

'For Señorita Xiomara.'

He looks at her, curiosity in his eyes, swiftly disguised. She watches him move across the room, pause by Xiomara's alcove and deliver the napkin. A moment later he nods discreetly in Ramona's direction. Xiomara leans forwards. Ramona meets her gaze firmly. Xiomara nods.

At the alcove the bodyguards bar her way. One male and one female, both have the look of ex-guerrillas about them. They point at the pack on her back. Ramona shakes her head.

'I come as I am. This is a public place.'

Xiomara nods.

'Sit down, sit down.'

There is a low but feverish excitement in her voice. Ramona knows instantly that her judgement is accurate. Now she has to play it to her advantage.

New dancers enter the stage, but Xiomara ignores them. She scrutinizes Ramona. The trace of a single tear is discernible through the immaculate make-up of her upper left cheek. It gives her a tragic, soulful look. Perhaps that was the intent, thinks Ramona.

'It's true what you say? You are the pilot?'

'Yes.'

'I'm surprised you're so bold to come to Cataveiro. It must be dangerous for you, I would think.'

'I've a particular reason to be here.'

'You want something. Yes, yes, I can see it. There is something you want very badly. Tell me, Ramona Callejas – oh yes, I know your name – what is it you want?'

'I've never hidden my name, so it's no surprise you know who I am, any more than it is no surprise I know who you are.'

Xiomara laughs, a high, glittering display.

'You wish to play? You wish to play? Well, so do I, I love a game. All right, little pilot. Let's lay down our cards, shall we? Who shall be the queen? Who the jester? You tell me.'

'It's said you have a cure for the jinn.'

'A cure for the jinn? What an idea. Nobody in this country has that. No one! You'd better go north, little pilot. What lies in the north we can only imagine. And what dark things we do imagine . . .'

'I don't need to go north.' Ramona keeps her voice as steady as she can. She feels the shifting presence of Xiomara's bodyguards, alert and watchful. She feels the metal of the gun against her skin. 'Because you have a cure here, in this city. And I think that I have something you want.'

She watches Xiomara's face closely. Like Alejandro, it is the mogul's lust for power that betrays her. Desire emanates from her, strong and heady.

'Your plane?' says Xiomara softly.

Ramona smiles, but says nothing. Xiomara takes a mirror from her handbag. She dabs at her forehead. Ramona can smell the powder on her skin and the sweet chemical scent of her cosmetics.

'You know,' says Xiomara idly. 'I have been asking my friends in the government for a long time, oh a very very long time, to sell me that aeroplane.'

'It isn't theirs to sell.'

'So they tell me. But what makes it yours, little pilot? And more importantly, what makes them humour you by letting you keep it? Really, your activities are not even legal. We should lock you up!'

Ramona ignores the irony of Xiomara talking about technicalities of the law.

'I found the plane, Señorita Xiomara. I repaired it. I own it. Some things are simple. As to why I'm permitted to use the airspace – the government have a need. We help one another out. They trust me. You can't trust just anyone with an object like this.'

Certainly, she thinks, Lygia would never allow a player like Xiomara into the air. But Xiomara's cheeks hunch in a smile.

'Yet now you are offering it up? Do they trust you now, little bird? Do they?'

'I wouldn't give up my livelihood so easily. But I might offer a share in the plane.'

Xiomara snaps the mirror shut. She runs a finger down her silken length of hair, and twirls a hank about her thumb.

'Is it yours, the jinn?'

'No.'

'Sometimes the fight is stronger for another. I wouldn't know. I was never given that opportunity. There was no cure for the ones I would have saved.'

'Señorita Xiomara, would you like to know how it feels to fly?'

Xiomara's eyes sparkle. It is the same hunger to acquire, so familiar. Xiomara and Alejandro are bred from the same mould. Any reservations they might have about Neon technology would be suppressed in a heartbeat in exchange for that kind of power.

'Tell me, little pilot.'

On the stage, the female dancer raises her arms and falls into the clasp of her lover. They are no longer the only ones dancing. Some of the couples in the audience are on their feet, embracing, swaying, kissing, lips tracing shoulders and cheeks, immersed in the languor of the dance.

Ramona holds Xiomara's gaze. She speaks softly.

'I took a woman into the sky,' says Ramona. 'And she cried from the moment she left earth. Not in sadness. She wasn't afraid. But when we went into the skies, something changed in her. When you fly, you are higher above the world than any mortal. The entire continent lies beneath you. The sun is closer than you have ever seen it. You could catch the moon in the palm of your hand. When you are flying, you own the world. You own the stars and the planets, the land, the sea. When you look down, you see the things others cannot. Secret pathways. Borders. Where things begin and where things end. And you alone possess this knowledge.'

Word by word, Ramona can see the effect she is having on Xiomara, who cannot suppress the flush that spreads across her face and neck and the hastened breathing of her desire.

Ramona leans across the table. She whispers, 'To fly is to become a god.'

Xiomara moistens her lips. Her chest rises and falls. 'You spin a good yarn, Callejas. As good as any I've heard. But until I see the aeroplane, it's only a yarn.'

'I can be your pilot. I can take you places and show you secrets no one else will ever see. This is my offer. I know you have a cure for the jinn. Bring it to the House of the Nazca in the Brazilian quarter, tomorrow morning at six o'clock. That is my offer and I will not change it.'

Ramona offers her hand. Xiomara hesitates, then takes it. As they shake, Ramona presses her fingertip against Xiomara's inner wrist, as the chemist instructed. She feels a pop as the minute blister bursts. A sensation of oiliness. She smiles. Xiomara smiles.

'Six o'clock,' says Xiomara.

When she leaves the club, Ramona has to fight her way through the embracing couples. The bodyguards are watching her every move, and she is grateful for the cover. Xiomara cannot see how her legs are shaking.

That night she does what the beggars do. She climbs a ladder to the first level. She climbs another ladder to the second. She swings over the edge of a balcony and curls up silently in one corner. At the other end she senses another body, the faint hiss of its breathing. A smell of stale sweat. Neither Ramona nor the other make any attempt to communicate. They both know the rules.

She wakes in the early hours of the morning, her heart pounding in terror. There was a whistling, in her dreams, or in the street below, she cannot tell. When she lived here before, there was a man who walked the streets, a murderer, the Whistler. He had a coat made of human skin and hair. He preyed on the street dwellers. She ran into him once. She felt that soft soft coat against her hands.

The Whistler is long gone now. He must be gone. These are the remnants of her dreams. Old fears merging with new fears. The terror of entrapment. Before she found the skies, Ramona did not notice the crush of the city: the way it pummels and squeezes, the alien weight of its thousands of individuals with their furiously colliding demands. Now she knows she will never escape it. The story she told to Xiomara was not entirely spun. The woman who cried was Ramona, and she cried because she knew that her life would no longer be the same. Some part of her had crossed into a different country.

Sometimes, in long hours of dread such as these, she has tried to imagine a different life, a life with Félix, ground-based and static. They would not live in Cataveiro, but they might take a house in a small town, no larger than Fuego, or more likely they would have their own farm, grow produce, buy a goat, make cheese. She conjures that scene now: the room, inviting and cosy; the nights, curled up together, the smell and drowsy warmth of him, the immutable feeling of security from each other's presence. And Félix could – and she could . . .

The picture ends. She can imagine too, and too well, the restlessness of the two of them. Him yearning for the sea, her for the air. Perhaps they could trade. He sails one month, she flies the next.

We would hate one another. We would each be jailor to the other.

It wouldn't be enough.

Dawn approaches. The other occupant of the balcony disappears over the rail, dropping silently into the street.

Time to focus. The trap has been set. What the chemist gave her is seeping through Xiomara's skin, wriggling its way into her blood. Four hours, he said, for the symptoms to show. All the classics, he said. The weeping rash. The sweating and shaking. In a matter of minutes, Xiomara will rise, look in the mirror and feel more frightened than she has ever felt in her life.

14 ¦

The man had a house and the house was on a bend in the river. In the house was the last jaguar. People came for miles to see it. The jaguar was in a state of eternal fury at her captivity, pacing up and down, roaring and hissing at the spectators. It is said she killed no less than three who dared go too close. But after a time the jaguar stopped eating. Her fur grew dull. Her eyes lost their spark. One day, consumed with sadness and the terrible knowledge of being the last of her kind, she lay herself down and died. Not one to miss out on a financial opportunity, the man brought in a taxidermist, and had the jaguar displayed in a glass cabinet. And still people journeyed miles to see her. Some of them stayed. Some of them worshipped the last jaguar. Others gazed and gazed and gazed until they saw jaguars in their sleep, jaguars with their waking eyes, and they became prophets of the jaguar. Those people gave up worldly goods and lived in the open air. Some went wild and reverted to all fours. Around them the valley changed, and people saw that the jaguar's house was built on good land, so they stayed and built houses of their own. The years passed and slowly they forgot all about the jaguar. They could not say why they had come at all, but were glad they had. When the man died, his house was bought, they say, by a family whose name you will know well, but this family did not take on the legend of the jaguar, as some might expect. This family already had a legend, an industrial legend. We refer, of course, to the salt woman.

So a new age had come, and now, few remember that the jaguar's name was the name of our city which today feeds over one hundred thousand souls and—

An hour after midnight comes a knock at the door. The Alaskan shifts in her cloying, sweat-soaked sheets. She sweats more in this city than she ever did the other side of the belt. They have no temperature control here. When a heatwave comes, you stew in it.

She peers through the rudimentary SpyEye. One of the kids is standing in the corridor. Dirty oversized tee and shorts. Hat in hand, hair clipped raggedly to the scalp. Mig. Mig's a smart one.

The Alaskan hauls herself to sitting and changes the radio station before buzzing him through. No need for Mig to know she's been at the stories again.

Mig brings a whiff of the streets into the two-room attic. They make a pair: the street stink and the odour of old mammal.

'This is late,' says the Alaskan.

'I've got something for you.'

Mig holds up a sheet of paper. It has a woman's face on it, a scribbled likeness, not well done but not badly done either. No name. And a price. Not that high a price. A discreet price. A middleman price.

'The pilot?' she asks.

'Yeah. All over the city, they're putting these up. Some enforcers. Some . . . I don't know who they are.'

'Not all enforcers? You're sure about that?'

'I know an enforcer when I see one. These guys – I don't know them. They don't look poor.'

'An undercover operation, I see.'

The Alaskan takes the poster. She studies the photocopied shades of black and white. She turns the poster, squinting. Her sight is not what it was. Her eyes feel sore and tender, irritated by the heat. She longs for a cool, scented bath. A pool to swim in, water in which to immerse her riddled old body . . .

Not in this country.

'She has a strong face,' she says. 'A face tells you a lot about a person. Sometimes. Sometimes not, eh?'

'Do you want to capture her?' asks the boy.

'What would be the point of that?'

'For the reward. Or to put her in the book.'

The boy is learning, thinks the Alaskan. She needs to keep an eye on this one.

Mig picks at a scab on his arm. 'Maybe I'll capture her. That's a lot of money. It will make me rich.'

'I will make you richer,' says the Alaskan. 'Let's have tea, Mig.'

The boy does not want to, but she is not letting him go that easily. It is a delicate balance of power between them. She pays him good money, but not as much as she could. The day he realizes the extent of her reliance is the day he turns. She needs him to need her.

She turns over the poster. On the back is a telegram contact.

Mig puts the kettle on. She hears him surreptitiously opening and closing cupboard doors.

'Yes, help yourself. Maria has done the shopping, luckily for you. I may need a second Maria. There should always be a backup. You should look into that. Ask around. Find me another girl.'

He takes something from the fridge and devours it. He never eats in front of her, but he is always hungry. The Alaskan has never been that hungry but that is thanks to her brain, rather than circumstances, which have certainly conspired against her. Such is the fate of the nirvana: good for everything until the truth comes out.

The kettle boils. Mig makes the tea slowly and cautiously, returning with two steaming cups.

'Mig, tomorrow morning I want you to send a telegram. Choose a public office. Not too big. A post office, something like that. I want

you to say you have captured the pilot. And then I want you to watch
and see who comes.'

'All right. I'll follow them.'

'You'll follow them. That's right. Find out who they are. Find out
who wants the pilot.'

'Yes, señora,' he says obediently.

'And drink the tea. It is good for the stomach.'

'Yes, señora.'

He drinks the tea and sleeps, or pretends to, for a couple of hours in
a corner of the other room. Around four o'clock when he thinks she is
asleep, she hears him climb out of the window and run lightly down
the fire escape. The street kids are like house cats. You try and train
them, but they stay wild at heart, and at any moment, they may turn.

15 ┆

The House of the Nazca is quiet and dark across the pre-dawn street. The acolytes arrive first, opening up the doors, sweeping the step, going about their daily rituals. Next are Xiomara's people. They squirrel themselves in and around the House, brushing past a protesting attendant, bundling them inside. Last to appear is Xiomara herself, fifteen minutes early and flanked by bodyguards holding heavy rifles across their bodies. Xiomara's face is shined with sweat. She is panting. Ramona focuses her telescope closer on Xiomara and sees that beneath the white blouse, mottled red patches are blooming across her neck and chest. It is a disturbing sight.

Ramona pushes away her reservations. She knows that it is not the real redfleur. The chemist is a corrupt, evil man, but he is not mad. If Xiomara could think straight, logic would tell her the same, but Xiomara's mind is tying itself in knots. There are enough madmen in this country; Xiomara cannot gamble that the pilot is not one of them.

'How are you feeling, Xiomara?' she calls.

The heads of the salt woman and her bodyguards jerk up, searching for the source of the voice. Their quarry is up on a balcony. But which one?

'Come out, you bitch!'

'I don't think so. Where is the cure?'

'What have you put in my blood?'

'Something that will kill you slowly unless you take the antidote within twenty-four hours.'

'Why should I believe you? You're a charlatan, a witch, a witch!'

'My cure for yours, Xiomara. I'll tell you this much. It's something new, from the north.' She lets the word north linger. 'Word on the street is it's a new strain of redfleur.'

Xiomara's chest rises and falls. This is truly cruel, but Ramona needs Xiomara to be afraid.

'Where did you get it?'

Two of Xiomara's people exit the House of the Nazca. They begin prowling the street, scanning the length of balconies on the residential block opposite. Ramona ducks lower. Her heart is pounding. She does not doubt that they are armed. She holds on tight to her gun.

'No one you would know.'

'I know everyone in the city.'

Not everyone. You've never lived here like a rat, climbing from balcony to balcony, running from the Whistler with your heart beating so fast you think it will explode.

'I got it outside the city,' she says. 'After all, you can go anywhere with a plane.'

It is unwise to taunt Xiomara, but she wants to get out of here fast. One of Xiomara's people is climbing a ladder, only a few blocks across from where Ramona is concealed. She has chosen a balcony inaccessible from below, but it's only a matter of time until the man can shoot.

'Your cure for mine, Xiomara!' she shouts.

The man's head jerks up, listening. Xiomara hisses and doubles over. She gestures. One of the bodyguards lays down a package on the floor. Ramona watches as her street urchin scurries down from a different balcony, scoops up the package and shoots off down the street. Lying on her back, Ramona whispers into the radio.

Well done. When you're clear, open it.

That man climbing is close to you. He's got a gun.

I know. Can he hit me?

The kid's voice comes in low, staccato bursts.

No. You chose a good angle. But soon he'll work it out. If he gets on the roof he can shoot you from there.

'All right, you've got it, where's mine?' shouts Xiomara. 'Where's mine, you fucking bitch?'

Have you opened it?

Yes. A box of needles.

Ramona feels a wave of relief. She tosses her own package down into the street. Xiomara does not wait. She swallows the contents right there. Then Xiomara begins laughing.

'You're stupid, Callejas. Stupid, stupid, stupid. I don't have a cure for the jinn. There is no cure. And if there was, I would never give it to you!'

She sits in the street, rocking and gasping. A bodyguard scoops her up like a sackful of laundry. Xiomara does not fight him. She is consumed with hysterics. As they bear her away, Ramona hears her shrieking.

'My people will find you, Callejas! They'll find you and they'll take your precious aeroplane and then they will kill you slowly. I'll import the finest northern diseases, just for you.'

Ramona's hands clench on the gun. No cure? Is Xiomara bluffing? What is in the syringes? How can she know, how can she trust if Xiomara is telling the truth?

The boy, Mig, is right. Xiomara's man has worked out how to get to her. He's heading for the roof. From there he will aim his rifle at Ramona's head and shoot to maim.

Time to get out of here, Ramona. Your plan hasn't worked. Now save your own skin.

Thanks to the chemist she has one final weapon. She tosses the canister into the street. It releases a screening gas, which will hide her only for seconds, but seconds is all she needs. Ladders and fire escapes, one quick swing across a balcony and up. Her muscles don't work as fast as they used to. Her thighs and shoulders ache with the exertion and her breath is short and tight. The gas vapours make her want to cough. She swallows it down.

On the roof, the boy is already waiting with the box of useless syringes.

'Get out of here,' she says. 'You did well. Don't let them catch you.'

He looks at her curiously.

'What did you give her?'

'It's called measles. She'll live.'

The boy nods.

Now get out. There's nothing more to do.

She says, 'Do the kids still talk about the jaguar?'

Mig stares at her in disbelief. He turns and runs, swift and agile over the rooftops. She goes the other way. Her flight is followed by the sound of the street waking up: shouts from her pursuers, angry residents flinging open their shutters.

The sky is lightening steadily above her. Six storeys below, citizens emerge into the streets. A tram horn blares in the distance. The city is rising.

Run, little street girl. Run.

16

White noise. Spanish chatter. There are new posters on the street. These ones are official, and they bear a name and a logo that carries weight: the salt woman's name, the orca. The reward for the pilot has doubled and doubled again. Señorita Xiomara will make a rich man or woman of the one who brings the pilot to her alive.

Turn the dial. *Crackle*. Another channel. This one says Xiomara is sick. She was targeted with a bio-attack. A new redfleur strain. There are army trucks outside the Xiomara house. The towns are sending every doctor they have, be they qualified professional or dubious quack. If it is redfleur, nothing can be done.

Another channel says Xiomara is dead. The pilot killed her. Who will take the fortune of the desalination empire? And was it really redfleur? There hasn't been a government warning, but everyone is wearing a mask and half the city did not turn up to work today. You can't blame them, can you? Really, it's a miracle we're here at all – it's all for you, listeners.

No, no, the pilot is dead. Xiomara killed her. She was shot in the street.

The Alaskan waits impatiently. She needs Mig for the truth. Her plan with the telegram is pointless now. Or is it? Either way, a bigger game is churning into play.

Turn the dial. *Crackle.* This is a bad channel, longer range. Shipping news and weather reports. Fishermen nattering to one another. They talk about the sea as if it's a live thing. If you want to learn anything, listen to the fishermen. The Alaskan listens more closely, twiddling the dial, feeling through the static, willing the grainy words into sentences. The harbour at Fuego Town is in lockdown. The fleet bound for the Exchange cannot leave, and no foreign ships are allowed in. *No foreign ships.* The Patagonians hate to acknowledge Antarctica; even their language whitewashes the south.

Antarctica. The Alaskan rolls the word around her mouth. It has a saccharine taste.

She shifts in her bed. White noise and words. White noise and words. Her legs do not work but her mind climbs about the continent, weaving and spinning.

17

'Quick – off the road.'

Vikram grabs Taeo's arm and pulls him into the cover of the trees. A moment later, Taeo hears the sound of tyres on the disused road for the third time since they have been travelling. They drop low to the ground. Lying on his belly beside him, Vikram is so quiet Taeo can scarcely hear him breathe. The Osirian's face is taut and watchful. It strikes Taeo that the other man is far more used to this kind of activity than he is. He is not sure if the thought is cause for relief or alarm.

They wait. A heavily occupied Patagonian army truck rounds the bend and rumbles past them on its crushing caterpillar tyres. Two smaller trucks follow in its wake. The convoy heads away in the direction Taeo and Vikram have come, its battered solar roof panels glinting in the sporadic sunshine, the mountains rising on either side as the road curves into the distance. Neither Taeo nor Vikram acknowledges the implication, but by mutual consent they keep close to the edge of the road, ready to drop flat at the first sign of danger. Fuego Town is close now.

Vikram seems to have accepted his status as a fugitive. He has been quiet but alert, and his leg is healing day by day, much faster than

Taeo expected. Taeo is finding it harder to reconcile himself. The four-day trek has left him irritable and fatigued.

They trudge on for another hour, rounding the shoulder of the mountain where the road veers back towards the coast. They make their way cautiously now, keeping to the edge of the forestry, although they see no other expeditionaries. Taeo watches Vikram taking everything in: the ruins of the plundered Neon city, and further along the coast the harbour, the sea walls and Fuego Town with its motley collection of brightly coloured buildings.

The situation is worse than Taeo feared. Even from a distance, it is clear that the harbour is on high alert. Boats are docked and soldiers are patrolling the sea walls. Two Patagonian cargo ships, which Taeo guesses are a part of the fleet and due to go north, have weighed anchor, and the harbour front is busier than usual with tiny figures, presumably members of the ships' crews, milling about.

But further out, beyond the Patagonian water line, is a sight that makes Taeo's heart leap. An Antarctican ship.

He points.

'That's how we're getting home.'

Vikram looks at the ship. Not for the first time, Taeo wishes he could tell what the other man is thinking.

'What about those other boats, the small ones around it? Are they Antarctican?'

'No,' Taeo admits. 'They're Patagonian.'

The Antarctican ship is a beta-class vessel: not the fleet's strongest ship, but tough and resilient, capable of ploughing through thick ice in the winter months. It looms over the tiny Patagonian boats. There is no one visible on deck. The Antarctican flag twitches when the wind gusts, but other than that the ship appears strangely lifeless. Looking at it gives Taeo an intense feeling of vertigo. There is his passage home, right before his eyes.

'So how do we get to the boat?' asks Vikram.

'If they don't let them dock, we'll have to bribe someone to take us out there.'

'We don't have anything to bribe anyone with.'

'I have Patagonian currency. And the Antarcticans will pay more to whoever takes us. It's a good deal for a fisherman. We'll find someone.'

He speaks confidently, not wishing to let Vikram see his very real worries. After four days of walking on a diminishing diet, both men look the worse for wear. And Vikram is far too distinctive to be let loose in the harbour. His ethnicity marks him out, but more than that it's the way he moves, as if he fears the land will give way beneath him. The way he stares at everything. Vikram is even more obviously foreign here than Taeo.

'I'll find someone,' he promises. 'Keep safe here. Stay out of sight.'

'I'll be here.'

Leaving the cover of the trees, stepping out onto the main road, Taeo feels more conspicuous than ever before. He keeps his sunglasses on, hiding his eyes which often attract a second glance. Any moment he expects someone to yell: stop there! But no one does. And at first it seems it will be straightforward after all. The harbour might be on alert but the town remains busy. People have work to do, fish to sell, school to attend, energy to collect, all the mundane chores that fill the average day. Residents are out on the streets, chatting about ordinary things. The radios are on. The buzz on the streets and on Fuego Station is all about the pirate El Tiburón, rumoured to be lurking about the archipelago, although that does not explain why an Antarctican ship would be kept from docking. No one mentions it, but then that is not unusual. The residents of Fuego Town still refer to the archipelago as *el fin del mundo*. There is no mention of Taeo's name, or of Osirians on the run. There is no mention of a shipwreck.

That's something. The government is being careful, at least on the official stations.

Then Taeo sees someone he knows. The old guy from the Facility.

Eduardo. Sat with a cup of coffee in the window of a cafe, reading a paper, but not that attentively. Eduardo, who has no love of Taeo and plenty of love for gossip.

The sight jolts him. He walks quickly in the opposite direction, head down, hands buried in his pockets.

Now he is worried. He could easily be spotted and he wouldn't even know it. For all he knows, Eduardo recognized him, right there. What if Ivra is wandering about? Would Ivra help him? Should he look for Ivra? He doesn't even know where Ivra lives; his bodyguard never told him, so that idea is screwed, and even if he did run into him, by accident, his bodyguard might be compelled to hand Taeo in, preserve his own cover for the sake of good relations. Or worse, he might want the credit for finding Vikram, scuppering Taeo's plan to earn his pardon. No. He can't trust Ivra. He has to do this on his own.

Of course, if he *were* taken in, Taeo knows nothing serious would happen to him – he has diplomatic immunity, after all – but what about Vikram? He can't risk the Patagonians finding Vikram: walking, living proof of Osiris. With their radio network you'd never shut them up, and the Boreals would be down here like a shot.

They have to get out of this country.

He makes his way cautiously down towards the harbour, deliberately avoiding the streets he knows best and where he might be recognized. Arturo's Place. The opium parlour where he got his supplies. Taking a route parallel to the parlour street, he feels a tug of something. Not craving, because the end is in sight now – it's right there in the strait. But an acknowledgement, that something has happened to him while he has been abroad.

He wonders if this is a secret he will be able to keep from Shri.

The streets slope down towards the sea walls. Risky this, but he needs to assess the situation at the waterfront. The atmosphere in this part of the town is different. The sheer volume of people milling about makes it easier to pass unnoticed, but the mood of those people is frustrated, resentful. Two Patagonian ships, the *Caracas* and the

Rio, sit low in the water, heavy with the goods they have brought south. Every crate and freight carton unloaded from the ships is being opened and laboriously checked, a process that Taeo can tell will take hours. He knows that some of the goods destined to go back up the coast will be aboard the Antarctican ship, which has not even been allowed to dock.

It is not just the larger vessels under scrutiny. Fishing boats are searched as they come in. The fishermen work sullenly, hauling their nets of translucent squid onto the harbour front, and the townspeople walking up to examine the catch do not stop to talk and barter as they usually do, but pay the asking price and leave abruptly, under the watchful gaze of the soldiers on the sea walls.

A man hawking solar cells approaches one of the fishermen, pushing his wares under the other man's nose. The fisherman picks up one of the cells and drops it again.

'This is junk. Feel the weight of it!'

'It's good stock, hours of life in that,' the man whines.

The fisherman's face burns an angry red. 'You trying to con me? Get out of here!'

The hawker leers and slinks back into the crowd.

Taeo cannot see any way of approaching a boatman without being seen, and the number of soldiers is making him paranoid. It all depends on what, exactly, is known about his disappearance from the Facility. Have any of the Antarcticans from the ship come on land? Ivra at least must have guessed where he went, but he has no way of knowing if Ivra has said anything, or if anyone else has connected Taeo to the shipwreck down the coast. For all he knows his absence might not even have been noticed; that would be the best possible scenario. Ironic, really, when he has spent so long hating the place for his exclusion.

There are too many unstable elements. He realizes he has made a mistake. There is no point in approaching anyone until the moment they are ready to leave, and that has to be at night, under the cover of darkness.

He makes his way back up through the town, stopping only to purchase food and water, avoiding meeting anyone's gaze.

Vikram is not where he left him, again, but this time Taeo tells himself not to panic. This time he waits. A rustle of branches makes him jump; when the Osirian swings down from a tree he feels his heart lurch in his chest.

'I had to make sure you weren't being followed,' says Vikram. Automatically, Taeo glances behind him. There is no one, of course. He cannot wait for this ludicrous situation to be over. Taeo is not cut out to be anyone's spy.

He looks up at the tree. A slender branch has broken off with Vikram's drop. The Osirian looks at it ruefully.

'I suppose you've never climbed a tree before,' says Taeo. And then he thinks, what a stupid thing to say, of course he's never climbed a tree. But Vikram doesn't seem to mind. He looks pleased with himself.

'Not until today,' he says.

'Your leg must be better.'

'It is. It's healed fast.'

'We're going to have to wait until dark. The town is on alert; there are soldiers all over the place. Everyone seems to think it's because of pirates, but it's not safe to approach anyone. I can't risk drawing attention to myself so soon.'

Vikram points.

'What about along there?'

He follows the direction of Vikram's arm. Beyond the cup of the harbour, a scattering of run-down houses populate the coast, gradually petering out towards the ruins. One or two of them have boats tied to jetties, bobbing in the water on long tethers.

'Worth a try. Not very inconspicuous, though.'

'You don't need to try. I found someone who will take us. After dark.'

'How did you—'

'I said I would pay. Or you would. *My friend will pay.* That's right, isn't it?'

'Yes. Yes, it's right, I mean the words are right, but—'

'He needed the money.'

'How do you know?'

Vikram shrugs. 'You can always tell.'

Taeo feels illogically annoyed by Vikram's success; after all, it doesn't matter how they find a boat as long as they can get on-board the Antarctican ship. What happens after they get picked up is irrelevant. The Patagonians will be angry, of course, but the Antarctican ship can easily hold its own, and in any case even the Patagonian government would not be so idiotic as to risk their good relations with the southern continent by attacking one of its ambassadorial vessels.

He reminds himself, the only thing that matters is that Vikram is not seen.

He was never here.

There is no evidence of Osiris left in Patagonia.

This is what will win Taeo his pardon.

He offers Vikram his share of food and drink. The Osirian eats hungrily. Taeo's appetite is gone now; he can only manage a few mouthfuls. He checks his watch. They have hours to wait.

He watches the sun setting over the strait, a young summer sun, bathing the Antarctican ship and the two islands in fiery hues. So close now. So close. The colour leaches from the water, grey consuming gold. Against the receding light, the soldiers on the walls are small black figurines. Symbols, he thinks. A gesture of power. So much of this country is built on bluffs and pretences.

He feels as though he understands it better now, on the verge of leaving.

Almost time. Almost dark enough.

Taeo motions to Vikram, who nods his agreement. He senses a change in the Osirian, a quiet confidence that is unexpected. Vikram takes the lead as they start to make their way down the coastline to the straggling line of houses, continuing to use the forestry they back onto for cover. The first house owns a decent-sized fishing vessel. Vikram indicates. *Further on.* They continue to the last house. In the bluish dusk, Taeo can just make out a little boat moored at a low jetty. They hurry towards the house, moving as quietly as they can.

They are almost at the house when the lights come on.

A row of fierce white beams powers up one by one along the harbour walls. The lights illuminate the entire strait: the sea walls, the water, the island across from it. He can see the shape of the Facility, high up against the mountains. The Antarctican boat sits stark, exposed on all sides. The Patagonian army boats idle just outside the harbour walls. Any approach to the ship would be spotted from a kilometre away.

He swears under his breath.

You idiot. You should have known they'd turn on the pirate lights. You idiot! How could you overlook this!

'We can still make it,' says Vikram.

'Look, whoever it is lives in this house, he'll never take us. How could he?'

'No. We can steal the boat.' Vikram holds up a key. 'What I mean is, I already have.'

Taeo stares. 'You said you'd convinced the guy.'

'My Spanish isn't that good. Anyway, he would have given us away, he'd have known straight away I wasn't Patagonian. I stole the key instead.'

Taeo is at once angry and impressed.

'What if he knows it's gone?'

'He doesn't. Come on, let's get the boat.'

Taeo stares at him. He can see the recklessness in the younger man's eyes. *What kind of person would the City of Osiris send?* Now he knows. A lunatic.

He grabs the Osirian's arm.

'Vikram, have you seen how many Patagonians are patrolling the water between here and there? We go out on the water, we're target practice.'

'You think they would shoot us?'

Taeo hesitates. 'I don't know. They'll certainly stop us.'

'We should try. I can drive a boat.'

Taeo can detect no doubt in the Osirian's voice, but after what has just been revealed, how can he trust him either? He looks at the Antarctican ship.

That's Shri.

That's home.

Vikram is looking at him, waiting. Taeo feels trapped.

'I hope you're as good as you think you are.'

They skirt the house and creep down towards the jetty. A dim light burns in the window of the fisherman's single-storey house. Taeo can see the man inside, sat at the table eating his supper. He can hear the radio. The man would only need to turn his head . . .

Taeo can't see how they can possibly get into the boat without being seen, not under those unforgiving harbour lights. Already he is thinking that this is a terrible idea, but Vikram is on the move, flat to the ground, slithering down the slope to the water.

Taeo glances again at the man in the window, lifting his fork to his mouth. He drops to the ground and follows Vikram. He feels hideously exposed. Something will distract the man, a noise, a bird flying by, he'll turn his head, glance out the window . . .

He told Vikram the Patagonians wouldn't shoot, but truthfully he has no idea what they will or will not do.

The boat bobs a few metres out from the jetty on a long storm tether. Taeo sees Vikram slide into the water and disappear under the jetty. Out of sight, for now at least. He braces himself. *Quickly.* Even in summer, full immersion is a shock. He puts his hand to his mouth to stop shouting out and clings to the slimy struts of the jetty, drawing in sharp breaths with the sudden cold. Vikram sculls out, glances back at the house, and rolls easily over the gunnel of the boat.

Taeo sees it rock a little with the impact, the water lapping at the hull. He holds his breath and follows. The seabed drops away sharply and already he can't touch his feet to the floor. He grabs the side of the boat and prepares to haul himself up and over.

'Wait!' Vikram hisses.

He freezes. Vikram has dropped right down inside the boat, out of sight. When Taeo dares to turn his head, just above the water, he sees the door of the next house along has opened. A woman is walking across.

'Quick, get out,' he urges.

Vikram rolls back over the gunnel and drops into the water without a sound. The woman knocks on the door of the house. Vikram points to the jetty. Taeo nods and they move back to its cover.

He hears the door of the house open and the owner of the boat comes out. The faint burr of the radio trickles from inside. The conversation carries quite clearly but Taeo has to concentrate to catch the thick Spanish.

'Evening.'

'Been a nice one.'

'Was earlier. Now my youngest can't sleep, what with the lights.'

'True, they're bright tonight.'

'I'll say it's bright! El Tiburón better show his face, if it is him. The amount they've had those on lately, we'll be getting brownouts come winter.'

'He's had a spree, of late. Captain of the *Bogotá* had a run-in.'

'Has he, now? What happened?'

'You didn't hear? How'd you miss that one?'

'Eh, go on, tell us.'

Taeo clenches his jaw. *Shut up and go inside!*

'All right then. If you must have it. What happened is, El Tiburón boarded the ship in the guise of a merchant. He had his face changed and what they say is, he was dressed as a woman. He looked so like a woman he fooled everyone on board the *Bogotá*, including the captain. In fact, he seduced him. And then he trussed up the captain like a fish in a net and put on the captain's clothes and took over the *Bogotá*. And none of the crew were the wiser. Nor are they now.'

'Go on with you!'

'Have you seen the *Bogotá*? But I haven't told you the crucial detail. The disguise was not a disguise. You get me?'

'No.'

'I mean they say he's a woman. El Tiburón.'

'Everyone knows that! You know what I think. He's more than one person, three, or maybe four. Brothers and sisters, I reckon . . .'

Vikram's face in the shadow of the jetty is strained. He doesn't understand enough Spanish to follow the conversation.

Another door opens. A third party comes to join the others. Taeo groans inwardly. The three continue with their pointless speculation. Why couldn't they stay in their own fucking houses? He can feel his fingers and feet growing numb.

'What are they saying?' Vikram whispers.

'Just rubbish.'

'We should go anyway.'

Taeo shakes his head.

'Oh look, the ice folk are off.'

'So they are.'

'No surprise there . . .'

Taeo swivels in the water, heart in his mouth.

Something is happening. Figures are up on the deck of the floodlit Antarctican ship. The huge motors of the ship rumble into life. As he watches, the ship makes a slow, ponderous turn. Taeo's heart sinks.

'Oh please, no.'

He knows what is happening. Vikram looks at him, then back at the ship. He says nothing, seems to retreat behind that watchful expression. There is nothing to say. Taeo looks up. He has to see it for himself. They can only watch as the ship makes its way back down the strait, gathering speed as it heads out of the archipelago, towards the open ocean, and Taeo's home.

18 ¦

Slicing the furrowed landscape in a dull silver line, the old hover-rail catches Ramona's eye. The last high-speed link to the northern hemisphere, the rail was a disastrous and costly endeavour, the investment of reckless factory owners hoping to regenerate trade after the Blackout. Its rusting spine curves south–north across the continent, from Patagonia up through the Argentine Desert and into the uninhabitable zone, where Ramona now flies, three days north, pushing the plane harder as the sun sinks in the west.

Sometimes, when the weather is odd and the atmosphere hangs uneasily over the earth, she imagines the flicker of something lost and mechanical. A metallic shadow whistling across the torn-up land, up to thirty silver pods strung out behind it, and all within it metallic ghosts. They are down there, the conscripted soldiers who guarded the poppy harvest, the adventurers hidden on board, drawn by the promise of north: a better life, a more fantastic life.

The hover-rail disappears into a stretch of marshland. In the dappled patches of water below, Ramona thinks she catches the occasional glimpse of greening metal, but perhaps it is only a trick of the light, a vestige of what the rail once was, a trace, like the eroded Nazca lines in the desert.

She flies over the ruins of a Neon city she mapped four years ago. No one lives there. The dark shells of the skyscrapers yawn, their interior structures exposed to the elements, some collapsed into rubble, others rusted, covered in creeping greenery and colonized by clouds of birds. The scrapers are a strange sight, relics of a long-gone era rearing monolithic from the flat. She feels the tug of their presence, drawing her closer. She drops low and flies between the towers. She senses a vibration in the air as she passes, and the shadows they cast are at once fragile and ominous. People lived here. Who were they? She feels curiosity, a gulf in understanding and the desire to bridge it, and a deep, unassailable pity. She wonders at which point the Neons knew their civilization was on the brink. Before the Blackout? After the Blackout? When their complex networks disintegrated around them, like the web of a spider caught and destroyed by a careless hand? She lifts the nose of the plane, bringing *Colibrí* up and out into the sky, needing now to get away.

When she looks to the north, Ramona knows she has made a terrible mistake. She had hoped to make the highlands by nightfall. But the sun is low, very low, and the horizon is dark with storm. A strong headwind begins to push against the windshield.

In her haste to put distance between herself and Cataveiro, she bypassed her usual, tested routes, and took a direct path cutting across the floodlands. The clouds up ahead are cumulus, yellow-tinged, and surging into ever denser formations. She can sense the shift in air pressure as she approaches. If she keeps on this course, she will fly straight into the storm.

The alternative is to make a landing now. She knows from bitter experience that what looks like solid terrain from above may prove to be no more than the dry crust of a bog. Even if she does find a runway strong enough to support *Colibrí*'s weight, storms in these parts are strong enough to sweep the plane away, and her with it. This is a land that has swallowed entire cities.

There are people who live down there, individuals scratching out a living at the edges of the marshes, whose borders themselves shift from year to year, so places change and maps are redundant. It is a strange, isolated, amphibious life, bound to houseboats, mummified in mosquito netting. The marsh-people are not friendly to strangers.

Now she is faced with two dangerous choices: risk the unstable ground or fly into the storm and hope for the highlands. Somewhere ahead, their plateaus rise up, hidden behind the cloud banks which extend to east and west as far as she can see. There is no chance of flying around this giant.

The plane's shadow flickers along the black and brown ground. Already she is flying beneath sporadic cover. To her left, the sun winks, in and out. She can see the encroaching rain line, a dark, opaque wall.

Directly ahead, the cumulus banks congeal.

Five minutes until she hits? Four?

The headwinds are strengthening.

Ramona braces herself. Her heart is hammering and sweat rises stickily on her back and neck. She tells herself what she always tells herself.

If you crash it will be quick.

She hears a pattering of raindrops on the roof of the fuselage. For a moment they hang beneath the ledge of the clouds, in shadow, the light behind a yellow gleam lancing off the tail and the long curved edges of the wings. Then the deluge strikes. Cloud envelops the plane. Water streams over the windshield. Her vision turns to shades of grey, mist and pummelling rain and dense, impenetrable cloud.

The land is gone. The sky is gone. The light in the cockpit glows pale amber. There is only Ramona, the empty passenger seat and the thin shaking metal shell around her. She feels incredibly small and not quite real. She switches on the plane's forward lights. Two bright tunnels appear in the cloud, illuminating the frenzied rain rushing towards the windshield.

As they go deeper into the cloud bank the plane yaws and rolls and she battles to hold it wings-level. The compass needle wavers.

The airspeed is showing seventy kilometre headwinds. She checks her map, and adjusts her course again. If her calculations are correct, it is less than fifteen minutes of flying to the highlands. She remembers a village on the edges that she mapped five, six years ago. That is her best hope of shelter.

Ten minutes inside the cumulus pass like hours. There are clouds within clouds, sudden chambers open up and are swallowed again. Every muscle in her body is taut as she wrestles with the plane. She needs to drop below the bank but she is afraid of flying straight into the highlands. In the viewfinder, the topographer is beginning to pick up the outlines of higher plateaus ahead.

She checks the map in her lap. The tiny topographer screen. It correlates. She has to trust it.

She needs enough runway to skid. *Colibrí* will skid. This aeroplane was not designed for extreme weather; it is going to be touch and go.

Come on, Ramona. Follow the lines, follow the lines on the screen.

The plane shakes like the skin of a struck drum.

Deep breath. Down.

Now.

She reduces altitude. The plane drops alarmingly. She banks. The topographer indicates she is flying alongside the mountains, but in the lashing rain she cannot make out a thing. The sensor picks up a swirl of ridges.

She checks her parachute. Her fingers are tingling.

Far too rapidly, they descend. Lightning sears to her left. The topographer haywires and whites out; she is blind. She drops out of the cumulus and into the midst of the lightning storm. Looming plateaus flare and disappear. She is close, terrifyingly close. She veers away. A bolt hits her right wing and she sees residue flashes dancing before her eyes. But in the dark sky it is the only thing left to guide her. In the next flash she spies a cluster of square, regular formations against the landscape. The village, below. She has one chance to make the landing.

The plane lurches down at a terrifying speed. The landing gear hits ground, shocking her. The plane bounces, hits, bounces again. She slams on the thrusters. The plane zigzags drunkenly and for a moment she is convinced they are going over the edge. She wrenches the wheels away. High-speed winds buffet the aircraft. The landing gear slips and slides, struggling to get a purchase on the streaming ground.

The wheels grip. The plane skids to a juddering halt.

The next flare of lightning reveals the edge of the mountain, just a few metres away.

In the blinking light of the instrument panel, Ramona can see her hands are trembling. Sweat coats her waistband, her armpits, her scalp. Her neck is clammy and cold.

Now the plane has stopped shaking she can hear the full fury of the storm overhead, and she knows just how close her escape was. Lucky, she thinks. Lucky again. How much luck can you have before it runs out?

When she can breathe again and her limbs have stopped shaking, she activates the chameleon and the suction pads and climbs out the hatch.

The storm smashes her back against the plane. Should she get back inside? No, she's scared she might lose the aircraft. Instinct makes her want to stay with *Colibrí*, as though she could offer protection. But she would be as much use as an insect.

Thunder and lightning continue overhead. She sees the village houses, shielded between two slopes, a few hundred metres away. Hunched against the wind, she sprints in the direction of the houses. Twice the wind knocks her to her knees, and the second time she stays there, crawling the final stretch. She pounds on the first door she reaches.

'Hello! I need shelter!'

No response. Can they even hear her? She tries the next building, yelling with all her might.

'Hello! Hello, can you help me!'

Something – faint.

'Hello?'

'Who is that?'

'My name's Ramona Callejas, I'm a traveller. I got caught in the storm. Can you let me in!'

The door inches open. In the gap is a scowling face, bearded and suspicious, and just below it, the metal glint of an axe. Ramona recoils. Water streams over her face.

'Who are you? Are you the doctor?'

'No, I'm a map-maker. I came here six years ago and I need shelter. Please, let me in!'

No movement. The man's expression does not change. She doesn't recognize him, and he clearly does not recognize her.

'What's your name?'

'Ramona Callejas,' she repeats. Her teeth are chattering now. 'I'm the one with the aeroplane. Please, let me in!'

The door opens without warning and Ramona falls inside, losing her balance. The door slams behind her. A man grabs her roughly and wrenches her arms behind her back, hauling her painfully to her feet. The bearded man raises the axe. The edge of the blade glints in the light of a flickering lamp.

'How many are you?'

'What?'

'How many are you? Where are the others?'

'What others?'

He grips the axe harder, bringing it to within centimetres of Ramona's throat. Her shoulder joints are a fiery pain where the other holds her captive.

'Tell us where they are!'

She darts a glance left and right. She is aware of other figures in the room, indistinct faces, waiting, watching.

'It's just me! I'm on my own. I'm a traveller. I have an aeroplane.

I came here five, six years ago to make maps. Someone here must remember me. Please help me.'

'I remember her.' A male voice, soft and nervous. 'She does make maps. She was here.'

'Maps for whom?' says a woman.

Someone else chimes in. 'Yes, who. Who knows we are here?'

The axe-man squints at Ramona. This close, she can see he is younger than she thought, just a teenager, and scared. The beard makes him look older, but does not quite cover the pox scars that pit the skin of his neck and cheeks.

'You swear you're alone?' he says fiercely.

'I swear.'

He lowers the axe and after a gesture the other man releases her. She rubs her aching shoulders.

'Thanks for the welcome.'

'We're expecting raiders,' says the teenager.

'I gathered you're expecting someone. Nazca keep us.'

There are seven people in the room. The teenager with the axe, a stocky, sallow-faced man who had her arms, two women, a man with white hair and quivering lips, the one who spoke – this one she recognizes – and two young children in worn jeans and tees. Each of them stares at Ramona with the same mistrustful expression.

They have boarded up the windows. The room is almost empty except for its rudimentary furniture, and she guesses they have buried everything of value underground. That is what Inés used to do. Not that it worked.

'Raiders?' she asks.

'They've been making their way across the highlands. They use the storms for cover. We're next in line.' The woman who speaks is thin and angular with a face that would be considered plain in Cataveiro but has, to Ramona's eye, a stark and bird-like beauty – a highlands beauty, she thinks. The youngest of the two children, a girl, looks just like her, or will do when she is older. The girl is cradling her arm awkwardly against her chest and is wrapped in a woollen shawl. Her face is blotched from crying. Ramona remembers the first response to her knock at the door.

'You said you make maps,' says the one with the axe, his voice accusatory.

'My maps are for the government. I don't sell them to anyone else. Certainly not to raiders. I grew up not so far from here. I know raiders. I know what they do.'

She speaks to the thin woman.

'What happened to your girl? I'm not a doctor, but I may be able to help.'

The woman hesitates before speaking.

'She fell, yesterday. It's her wrist. We sent word to the doctor this side of the highlands. She should have come by now but then the storm and . . .' She does not finish the sentence.

'Will you let me look?'

'Yes. Yes, all right. Ana, show the woman your arm. Get off that chair, you.'

The boy slides off the chair and disappears under the table, from where he stares at Ramona through narrowed eyes.

Ramona sits on the vacated chair and opens her pack. She takes out the med kit, aware that every move she makes is being scrutinized by seven pairs of eyes.

The little girl twists away.

'No.'

'Ana, I need you to take off that pretty shawl so I can look at your arm.'

'You're not the doctor.' The girl speaks barely loud enough for Ramona to hear.

'No, but I know a few things about injuries. I've been hurt lots of times when there was no one else around and had to look after myself. Maybe I can make this a little better too.'

Ramona makes her voice as soothing as she can. She sees its effect on the others as well as the child. The mother is doubly worried: worried that the girl is hurt, and terrified by the prospect of a raid. Ramona puts all of her concentration on the first concern. If she's going to help them, she has to gain their trust.

She coaxes Ana to extend her arm and unwinds the girl's shawl. Ana's face winces despite the careful movement. The rest of the group is silent. The teenager has gone to stand by the boarded window, hands clenched on the axe, listening intently. Ramona can hear nothing except for the rain drumming on the roof and the shrieking wind.

'It's all right. It's all right.' She keeps up a steady stream of murmurings as she examines the wrist. It looks like a clean break. The flesh is swollen and discoloured, but Ramona is more concerned with the grazing, where the skin is cut and blood has congealed.

'How did it happen?'

'I fell.'

'She was climbing. I've told her about climbing.'

'I wasn't high.'

The mother purses her lips.

'How old are you, Ana?'

'Seven.'

Paola was seven. Even now, the comparison is instantaneous. She remembers Paola's lips, red as chillies in her final hours.

'Have you ever broken a bone before?'

'No.' Ana looks at her mother to verify the fact. Her mother nods encouragingly.

'Then this must really hurt, I know. It happened to me. Here –' Ramona touches her collar bone '– and my leg.'

'And you got better?'

'As you can see. I'm fine now.'

'Old Ant broke his leg and they had to cut it off,' she whispers.

'The bone came out,' says a voice from under the table. 'It went black. It went rotten.'

'Shut up,' the mother says angrily. She turns to Ramona. 'Is it bad?'

'The scrape needs cleaning. I can set the bone and put a splint on. You should still get the doctor to have a proper look when she can get here.'

'She's a day's walk away.' The mother does not add what everyone is clearly thinking. The room is ripe with it: *And if raiders come . . .* 'Please, do what you can.'

'Hold her securely for me.'

'Yes. Ana.'

The woman takes the child on her knee, holding her in a firm embrace from which there is no escaping. Sensing the hopeless inevitability of what is ahead, the little girl begins to cry again, but her sobs are barely audible through the storm outside and the rattling shutters. Ramona knows that there will be no warning of anyone approaching the hut.

The thing about raiders is you never know what you're going to get. Some of them want to steal. Some of them want to rape. Raiders don't kill but they'll break things. They'll break people.

Concentrate. Setting a bone is a delicate operation. She could do with more light than the single lamp, but she has worked in worse conditions.

She looks for something to use as a splint, and sees a couple of pieces of wood on the floor, presumably of no use for the cross-braces over the shutters. She asks the man who was holding her to grind the ends smooth. While he works on the splint, she gently lifts the girl's wrist. The sobs increase.

Ramona hesitates. In a flat box at the bottom of the med kit is a box of anaesthetic syringes. She wants to ease the girl's pain, but the severity of the injury is not as bad as many she has encountered and many more she might. Certainly it is not as bad as the boy she took to the emergency centre at Titicaca.

She gives the girl's mother a strip of rubber.

'Get her to bite on this.'

The rubber is marked with the indents of Ramona's own teeth and those of other people.

'I'm so sorry, Ana, this will hurt. Be brave for me, little one.'

She takes the tender, swollen wrist in both her hands and wrenches. Ana screams. The other woman screams straight after, and Ana's mother glares at her.

'That's good, the bone is back in place,' says Ramona quickly.

She works fast now, increasingly aware of the tension in the room, the smell of sweat on frightened bodies and the masking storm outside. She swabs the graze, hardening her heart against Ana's sobs. She bandages the wrist lightly, allowing for further swelling, and straps the splint in place. Ana's tears have soaked into her tee, but she is quiet now, limp and shuddering.

'Well done, sweetheart, well done.'

Ramona gives the girl's mother a ration of pills.

'I can spare enough for tonight and tomorrow. She'll be in a lot of pain.'

The woman tries to put one of the pills between Ana's lips. The child shakes her head. The woman grips the girl's jaw and forces the pill into her mouth.

'Swallow,' she instructs.

The girl pulls a face and swallows.

Ramona glances once more around the stripped-bare room. The teenager has his ear pressed to the wall, and the stocky man is at the door, alert and attentive.

'How many rooms here? How many windows?'

'A bedroom through there, the kids are up a level. The other windows are all boarded.'

'Where is everyone else?'

'In their own houses, locked down,' says the white-haired man. 'What do you expect?'

What does she expect? The best thing the villagers could do to protect themselves would be to converge in one place and barricade themselves in, but to do that is to leave their hard-earned, scant possessions exposed. It is the same reasoning that meant Ramona's mother would never leave her shack to take shelter down in the sliding city, the same reason Inés was beaten by raiders on more occasions than Ramona likes to remember.

She looks at the bolted door, the two windows. There is no defence here. And now she is worried about the plane, which presents a far bigger prize than anything the villagers might own.

'You need to get me onto the roof.'

'In this storm?' the old man looks incredulous.

'It'll give me the best vantage point.'

'For what?'

'I've got a gun.'

She notices the shift in their expressions, the wariness that creeps into the old man's eyes and the way the mother's arms tighten around her girl.

The teenager with the axe says he will go with her. The others protest, trying to stop him, but not for long.

'It's what I was going to do anyway,' he says. 'And we've got better odds if she's armed. She can shoot the bastards dead.'

His face is tense as he slides back the bolts from the door.

The blast of wind and rain from outside almost knocks Ramona to the floor. Water is streaming off the roof and walls. I must be insane, she thinks, as the teenager cups his hands to give her a leg up. She levers herself onto the frame of the door and perches precariously on her toes for a moment. The roof slopes to an apex. She gauges the distance and leaps, landing sprawled on her front. She skids downwards before scrambling to a halt.

Rain sluices her face. The teenager is shouting up at her and it takes her a moment to realize they have closed the door, leaving him outside. He reaches up a hand. She braces her feet and helps him up. They slither up to the ridge of the roof.

'All right?' she mouths. He nods. He has the axe in his belt. She hopes he has good aim, because unless he drops directly on top of an attacker, the weapon is not much use to either of them. She feels the solid weight of the handgun in her pocket. Anger, that is what the gun means, and she lets herself feel it, remembering all the times Inés suffered at the hands of those animal gangs.

It might not feel like it, but she can tell the storm is less intense than it was. Gradually the cumulus banks will roll away, moving around the highlands, slowly shrinking. Which means now is a good time for raiders to strike.

The villagers have blocked their windows, sealing in the light. Ramona waits for lightning. In the brief flare she counts another ten houses and spots the face of the mountain rising on one side, the land dropping away on the other. Then the light is gone and everything is black again.

She lets her other senses take over.

Another flash of lightning. This time she sees the teenager's face, wet and scared. 'When lightning comes, I'll look this way, you look that way. If you see anything moving, tell me,' she shouts.

But nothing comes.

After a while, their waterproofs are no longer waterproof, and the sheer weight of the water is turning her body numb. She flexes her fingers in their gloves.

She loses count of how long they have been on the roof.

A tug of wind tries to pry her from her moorings. Lightning flares. At the corner of her eye she catches movement. A hunched figure, running.

She squeezes her accomplice's shoulder and speaks into his ear.

'I'll go after that one.'

She is sliding down the roof when, thirty metres away, a house bursts into flames.

Ramona stares, shocked. She hears the teenager shout.

'What was that?'

'I don't know!'

The fire is not right. It has flecks of blue and green in it. Where the fuck did raiders get northern tech? It blazes against the storm, immune to the rain. She hears screams. The door to the burning house opens and the people inside spill out, backlit against the fire, disorientated. They start to run.

Ramona, don't stand here, move!

She drops from the roof, landing hard on her feet and tipping forwards onto her hands. The teenager jumps down behind her. The villagers scatter. In the strange firelight she sees two raiders running after them, their movement not erratic, but sure and purposeful. She scrambles to her feet and follows.

Ahead, she sees a figure dart behind one of the houses. She rounds the house and receives a hard blow to the gut and doubles over, winded. Before she can hit back the attacker is zigzagging away. Ramona gives chase. At first the flames of the burning house cast an eerie yellow-green light, but as they move further away the attacker is a dark figure against a darker night. Her limbs are cold and slow. She can't see the terrain. The rain is blinding.

The gun is in her hand but she is not even sure it will fire.

She sees a spark of blue and something hot whistles past her head.

What the hell.

She can hear screaming somewhere up ahead. Is that gunshots? Are they shooting at people now? This isn't normal; raiders threaten and steal, they don't run and sneak about.

The figure looms up from the side without warning. Something aims for her head; she ducks and feels the raider's arm just clip her scalp. She kicks out and the raider trips. Ramona leaps to pin them and feels another hot bolt narrowly miss her face.

Fuck!

The raider is armed, as is she. They grapple in the mud. She can't get a grip – slippery limbs, grunts, the lashing rain – she can't see if it's a man or a woman she is fighting, all she wants to do is get that gun arm down, go for the wrist.

Something presses between her shoulder blades. She freezes, caught between the two of them.

'Drop your gun,' says the one behind her.

Cursing, trembling with rage, she releases her fingers.

'Drop yours!'

The teenager's voice.

'Drop it now!'

What happens next is a blur in the rain – too quick for thought. She hears a thud as the teenager's axe embeds in the raider behind her. The arm of the one on the floor rises. There is a blue bolt. A cry.

'No—'

The dead raider's body pitches heavily on top of Ramona. The one beneath wriggles out and runs. By the time Ramona has got to her feet it is too late. She stumbles back the way she came and finds the teenager lying on the ground, writhing and clutching his stomach.

She puts both hands on the wound and applies pressure. She can feel the warmth of the spurting blood. She can feel him spasming beneath her palms.

'Hey, hang on! Don't die on me, don't die now.'

He gurgles. She yells.

'Help! Someone help here!'

No one comes. The teenager's hand clutches at her wrist. She thinks he is trying to speak. She increases the pressure. He shudders and goes limp.

'No no no no.'

The next flash of lightning shows his face, the eyes wide and shocked, the hole in his belly. Ramona's hands coated in blood.

An uncontrollable rage fills her. She goes back to the dead raider. A woman. There are goggles over her eyes and that is when Ramona realizes, with a chill.

They had night vision.

Something is terribly wrong.

She grabs the goggles. Now she can see. The houses, back there, the still body of the teenager, the rising mountains. Nothing moving. She yanks the axe out of the dead woman's back in a spray of blood. Axe in one hand, gun in the other, she starts to run in the direction the raiders and villagers went, up into the highlands. For a while she can hear distant cries. Cracks that could be gunshots – or something else. The sounds get fainter and fainter, but she keeps going. She finds no one else, alive or dead.

When she returns to the village, exhausted and shivering, the house is still burning with its ravaging greenish fire. The roof has collapsed. The walls will be next. The remaining villagers have come out of their houses. They have found the two bodies. The white-haired man is sat on the ground, hugging the teenager to him and moaning.

The accusation in their eyes is as clear as day and she feels guilt descending, heavy and immovable as stone.

He's dead because of me.

The next day Ramona and a small party trek into the highlands. They find no trace of the raiders, or of the villagers who ran from the burning house. Ramona hears names muttered: Aimon, Natalia, Mal. Each a code for a life vanished so completely it might never have existed.

Before the villagers burn the dead raider, Ramona examines the corpse. The woman is dressed in traveller's clothes: practical and plain. She has short, dark hair and light-brown skin. No tattoos. No disease scars. No piercings or jewellery. The gun she pointed at Ramona's back must have been snatched up by the one who escaped, because they do not find it. There is nothing to distinguish her except the night-vision goggles, themselves devoid of marks.

It is the anonymity that frightens Ramona more than anything. She cannot even say if this woman is South American.

Who are they? What did they want? Where did the rest of the villagers go?

The surviving villagers are clearly anxious to bury the dead teenager in peace. She tells them she will scan the region from the air. They nod, but will not meet her eye. She sees amulets, hears mutterings. This is just their luck. They want her gone.

Ramona will not inflict her unhappy presence upon them any longer. She collects her pack and prepares the plane for departure. The lightning strike has charred the edge of one wing. The exterior of the plane seems otherwise undamaged, but the topographer is playing up.

Two villagers from the tracking party watch as she makes her checks. She can read the thoughts working through their minds. The plane is valuable. There are two of them, and although she is armed and a fighter, the villagers could overpower her collectively. She is to blame for their loss. She deserves punishment. She deserves to wander the highlands empty-handed. They could send word south that they have a valuable object.

But the plane is too big. It draws too much attention; the raiders might come back. The villagers would be exposed. Stronger clans would overpower them. They would be used.

It is only when Ramona climbs into the pilot seat, her parachute strapped securely in place and her pack stowed in the passenger seat, that she realizes she is horribly afraid. The sliding city is not far from here. The raiders have been working their way across the highlands. What if they already got to her mother? What if they are heading there next? Inés will fight. She is not one to lie down and give up, jinn or no jinn. These are not normal raiders.

They took nothing material. Did they kill the missing villagers? Did they take them? She is filled with misgivings and inescapable guilt. The teenager was trying to save her. She does not even know his name.

'I was trying to help.'

She says it aloud, but it sounds pathetic.

Flight conditions are good, her hands hold steady and she takes off without incident. The ease of her departure seems a rebuke. She circles the plane up and over the small cluster of houses, climbing higher and higher until they are no more than dots against the plateau. Then she can no longer see them. The highlands unfold below her in wrinkles of brown and grey. The world is wider and emptier than it was a day before. There is a weight in Ramona's chest, sharp and painful, like a lodged stone that cannot be swallowed.

19

In the mountains above the sliding city, they had nothing to keep time by except the sun. Inés never seemed to know what day it was, or what month of the year. The three siblings could wander off for days, playing by the stream when it ran full and crystalline in the winter months, and playing hide and seek in the barren summer scrub. They found lizards and lined them up to race, although the lizards never ran straight as intended, but darted directly beneath the nearest rock. The first time this happened, Paola, the smallest, reached her hand beneath the rock where her lizard's tail had disappeared and Camilo snatched it away.

'Don't you know that's where snakes live?'

They had only themselves to talk to. They knew that there were other people out in the world, for Inés made occasional trips down the mountain, but it was as though they did not truly believe in them, so rarely were they seen. Other people belonged rightly in the south, where there was a city. Not a dead city, like the ruins on the hillside, but a living, far greater realm. Ramona and Camilo had frequent, detailed discussions about this place, and what it might contain.

'What will you do when you go to the south?' Camilo would ask.

Ramona would tilt her head and pretend to consider this question as if for the first time.

'I might . . . build a house.'

'They already have houses.'

'Then I might – grow a field full of peas.'

'They have peas too.'

'Peas.' This would be Paola. The word thoughtful and considerate, as she chewed on her lower lip, which was permanently red and raw, regardless of the salves and balms pressed upon her by a despairing Inés.

'Yes. Lots of peas. More than you can eat. In the south, there's a whole house stuffed full of them. There are so many peas, they fall out of the windows and pop out the pods. Then they get squished into goo by all the people walking past the house.'

Camilo clapped his hands together and rubbed them in a squishing motion.

'What's the house like?' Ramona challenged.

'You know, tall, red.'

'Red? Why would it be red? That's stupid!'

'Why wouldn't it?'

'Houses are white,' said Ramona decisively.

In comparison to the bountiful city of their imaginations, there was not much growing on the mountain. The siblings quickly learned the art of foraging. Inés was fiercely protective of the food she managed to grow, storing her sparse crops in jars that she hid in the underground, where they waited out the storms, or burying them in the dirt outside. Ramona was used to the permanent gnawing feeling in her stomach; it never occurred to her that there were people who did not experience this discomfort. Sometimes she wondered why her mother bothered to save the food, because it was only a matter of time until hard-faced groups of men and women came to the shack, and then Inés would tell the children to run up the mountain and keep quiet.

'Make yourselves invisible,' she said. 'Make yourselves like shadows.'

They were good at it. They could stay still as rocks, their breath barely stirring the long grasses, their faces covered with dust and merging into the thorny scrub. They could keep their throats silent, even when they heard sounds from the shack or voices raised.

When they came back down late at night, the raiders would be gone, and so would the food. Things were broken. The violence was arbitrary: chair legs snapped, jars smashed. One such night, under Ramona's direction, the three children solemnly collected every splinter of glass and placed the fragments in neat rows along the floor. Ramona began to fit the glass pieces against one another while Camilo chatted about how he would make glue from tree gum.

One hand supporting her chin, Inés watched them with a kind of wearied bemusement. A large purple bruise had swollen her cheek, and Ramona saw her wince every time she moved.

'What are you doing?' she said. Her voice was flat.

'We're mending the jar,' said Ramona.

Inés continued to watch for a while. 'There is no point in mending the jar. When will you understand that there is no point in mending anything.'

'We can try, Ma.'

Inés did not seem to hear. She said, 'We are the last and we were abandoned a long time ago.'

After Paola and Camilo burned up with the fever, Ramona's rambles became more protracted. She sidled around the two graves at the front of the shack. She went further away, down the mountain, as far as the sliding city. At first the empty buildings frightened her; she imagined them to be full of watchful eyes, or raiders, or Paola's tripping footsteps in the shadows. She had to be careful, too. Animals hid in dark holes. But none of the animals attacked Ramona. She sensed that none ever would. Already her luck lay upon her, an invisible cloak but palpable to these creatures whose sixth sense was strong. It was Ramona's luck that kept rats away and venomous snakes coiled, wary and suspicious in their retreats.

She began to enjoy tiptoeing through the deserted buildings, looking at the things that were left. The sliding city had once been full of glass. She found the pane of a rotating door, webbed with hairline cracks but intact. The glass was clear and frail as an insect's wing. She stood gazing at it, awestruck by her own glimmering reflection and the murky world beyond.

The houses were full of droppings, beetles and bird nests, vines pushing through the walls and floors. Underneath these colonists were other interesting objects. Tarnished metal devices. Rows of plastic bottles, their contents long evaporated. Fragments of cloth attached to hangers in wardrobes overrun by ants. Creamy bones and staring skulls. Once an entire skeleton on a mattress, rags clinging to the supine figure spun pale with cobwebs whose spiders sat patiently waiting.

Ramona was sifting through a pile of junk in one of the lower districts when she found the jewellery. It was a piece not quite square in shape, and when she wiped the muck away she saw that it was broken. What remained was a flat medallion a few centimetres across. The medallion was green, the colour of dark waxy leaves, covered with an intricate network of tiny gold ridges and grooves. Ramona took the jewellery outside to admire it properly, tilting it from side to side so it made the sun flash. She bored a hole in the medallion and took to wearing it on a cord under her clothes. Sometimes she put it in her hair, like a comb.

Her mother was less impressed by the jewellery.

'What do you want with that old bit of robotics?'

'Robotics?'

Inés gave her a dark look and said it violated the teachings of the Nazca. She said it was all told in the tale of the astronaut and the dog. Had she taught Ramona nothing?

*

The sliding city became familiar. She knew the sounds of its caving walls and lurking animals. The sounds of human emptiness. She flitted from building to building. Paola – what was left of Paola – jumped the shadows with her, a little skip of the light. Ramona made herself like the dust: always there, never noticed.

She avoided the highest quarter, where a small community had made a village of the old houses. There was an idea in her head that she was the bearer of a terrible curse; if she spoke to these people, they would drop dead like Paola and Camilo. There was the other thing too: she did not know what to say. For months she had not spoken to anyone but Inés, and Inés barely spoke. Instead Ramona spied from afar. If the people in the sliding city were real, then the city in the south must be too.

She watched the inhabitants hanging their sheets to air, high above the dusty streets; she watched the kids kicking an empty can between themselves; they built things out of stones and broken bricks and kicked them back into pieces; she watched them shout, cry, and yell at one another; she marvelled at the names that flew between them; she watched the pedlars arrive on their motorbikes and the adults haggle over the price of potatoes and peas. She studied the men, wondering if any of them might be her father.

One afternoon she was concealed in her usual spot at the end of their street, where the boys were playing with the tin. She felt it in the ground first. The sudden, familiar tremor, like the loosening of some vital foundation.

Ramona stepped away from the walls and out into the street, not knowing which way to run, too scared to make a commitment in either direction.

The others had paused too. For a second they all stood, petrified.

Further up the street, a house began to shake. Ramona dropped into a ball and wrapped her arms around her head. Dust plumed around her. She screwed up her eyes and held her breath. She could hear the rubble streaming downwards. She risked a peek. The boys, dim shapes, leaped out of the way. All except one. He was caught in the flow and carried forwards as if on a wave. She saw him, a vague outline through the dust.

And then suddenly, he wasn't there.

The rocks had overwhelmed him.

The air began to clear. The house was flattened and there was only a mound of rubble where the boy had been.

Without thinking, she darted forwards and began with several other pairs of hands to pull the fallen stones away.

The work was panicked, scared, yet orderly. Hands collided, disengaged, returned.

'There he is!'

An arm could be seen, folded over the head. The boy had crouched himself into a ball, the way Ramona had dropped to earth only a minute before. They worked quickly. The boy's head was clear, bleeding. He blinked dazedly. Finally his legs were free.

He emerged clutching his arm. His shoulder looked odd; it wasn't hanging right. There was a collective gathering of breath as he staggered, woozily, to his feet, and a great expulsion of it as he took a few steps forwards.

The first noises were those of joy, congratulations. Dry sobs. 'Right out the socket,' said another boy. A woman wiped the boy's cheeks with the sleeve of her shirt. Then someone else called out, deliberately raising their voice.

'That's the girl that's always hanging around, watching us. I've seen her.'

Others chimed in.

'So've I.'

'She's here all the time.'

'What does she want, spying on us?'

Ramona froze. But it was too late. She was visible. The faces around her, which moments ago were open with relief, tautened into hostility. As though the collapsed house was Ramona's fault. She took a step backwards, ready to run.

And then the boy who had been next to Ramona when they pulled away the rocks gave everyone else a hard glance.

'It doesn't matter. She helped. She can do what she likes.'

It was the most important day of Ramona's life since she had buried Paola and Camilo. Firstly, it was the day that Félix saved her. And secondly, it was the day she realized that there was another part of being invisible of which she knew nothing. Inés had not taught it to her, because Inés had no need. But if Ramona was going to find the city in the south, then she needed to learn this other thing – a way of blending into people as well as the landscape, fitting in with their faces and their speech. She needed to learn stories and how to tell them.

She began to spend time with Félix, who knew plenty of stories, especially ones about the ocean, although he had never seen it before. They exchanged discoveries. Ramona granted him the privilege of seeing the jewellery she had found.

Félix studied the medallion with the expert eye of a fellow scavenger.

'We need the pedlars for this. It might be valuable. Do you want to sell it?'

Ramona shook her head.

'I want to know what it is.'

Ramona had only ever watched the pedlars from a distance before. This time, when they arrived, she was in the thick of it. The whining motorcycles wound right the way up the mountain, their side-carts carefully packed with provisions: cloth and soap; spices, coffee and sugar. Félix's people had an entire day to indulge in their favourite activity of bartering.

Félix acted as an intermediary for Ramona. There was a man he knew from previous transactions. He took the pedlar aside. Ramona took the medallion from around her neck and held it out.

'Can you tell us what this is?'

The pedlar glanced at the jewellery for a bare second.

'Bit of old robotics. Worthless.'

Félix turned to Ramona in sudden agitation.

'Throw it away, Ramona! You can't keep it.'

'Ah, it's long dead,' said the pedlar. 'Can't hurt no one now.'

Félix pushed at Ramona's arm, encouraging her to drop the medallion. She stared at them both in puzzlement.

'What is robotics?'

'It's what the Neons had,' said Félix. 'It's evil.'

The pedlar's gaze settled upon Ramona. His eyes were shrewd, gold-tinted irises, layered with the knowledge of many years of travelling. She could read the stories of the universe in those eyes. When he spoke his voice was dry and croaky with dust but edged with that same, round goldenness.

'Robotics was the old system of the world. The Neons used it for everything. Robotics told people what to do. Maths and magic and minds. That's what it was.'

'But what does this do?' Ramona pressed.

'What does it do? You've got the wrong question, girlie. Better to ask – what does it tell you? There could be anything on there. You should see what they have in the university at Cataveiro. Visions and dreams. Augmented things that make you see and hear and taste.'

The pedlar held up a single pea pod.

'You see a pea, you eat a pea. Except you don't actually eat a pea. You see?'

Ramona didn't, and she could tell from Félix's look of intense concentration, her friend's cover-up for confusion, that neither did he.

'How could this jewellery make you taste?'

'Jewellery, she calls it? Ha! What an age . . . People had all sorts of bits and pieces stuck in them those days. You could call it jewellery, I suppose. Some of them were so wired-up they were more robotics than human.'

'What do you mean, "in them"?' Félix was appalled.

'I mean, inside them.' The pedlar grabbed Félix's wrist and poked at the suntanned back of his hand so that the bones wobbled. 'Under their skin. Inside their brains. Some people say the Boreals do it even now.'

'That's disgusting,' said Ramona. She felt sick.

The pedlar shrugged. 'It's not the thing you should be afraid of. It's how the thing is used. They still use a little robotics, in the south, and no one's dead, not when I looked last. Young man, your face is a picture, a picture I say. Careful or the sun will burn those frown lines into your forehead, like mine. See mine? I've got maps in my old face. Anyway, it makes no odds what this might tell you, because it's broke, see?' The pedlar pointed to the sheared edge of the medallion. 'It wouldn't work anyway.'

The pedlar's answer was intriguing, but all it told Ramona was how much she did not know. The realization was growing: she could not stay here. The south beckoned. But even as her future shone clearer, she found ways to evade it. There was Félix now, her ally exploring the precarious roofs and multi-storeys of the sliding city. There was Inés to protect from the raiders. There were the motorcycles of the pedlars to admire, and if she told them enough stories, they would open up the engines to show her the insides of their fantastic steeds and tell her the names of the parts. Summer whittled away in this fashion, blighted – though not ruined – by drought.

The next time the traders came, Ramona had a specific request.

'I need a map,' she told the pedlar.

'What kind of a map?'

'A map that shows the way to the city in the south.'

'What city is that?'

She saw again the golden flecks in his eyes. She could not tell if he was mocking her or not. 'There is only one,' she said confidently.

'Ha!' he said. 'Only one, she says. Well, you may be right. There is only one now, which they call Cataveiro, and it was named after a woman. Cat Aveiro her name was. She had hair as long as grasses and rode a motorcycle like this one all over the continent, warning people that the apocalypse was coming, so if they had a gram of god inside them they'd better gather in one place to save their souls. They had more of a chance that way, you see – the multiplication of a soul being greater than the soul alone. And gather they did. But the apocalypse did not come, and they worried and fretted. Aveiro rode about the country until she was murdered horribly by Born Again Mayans, who said her words perverted their beliefs. The people who had gathered to wait for the world to end fretted some more, because her corpse was a most distressing sight, and in the end they named the place of gathering after her martyred body. This made everyone so happy they forgot about the end of the world, and a city was born. And let us thank the stars for that, is what I say.'

'Why do you thank the stars?' Félix butted in, while Ramona wondered for which part of the story the pedlar was thankful.

The pedlar cast a significant look up at the searing blue sky.

''Tis the stars that guide us. If you know your destination, the stars will show you your way, even if you have no compass or map. Some say they have mystical properties, but that is not why I thank them.'

He paused, regarding them.

'A map is rare and very expensive. Too many peso for you, I think.'

'You only have one?' Ramona asked.

'Only one that will be any use to you. A good map, a true guide, that's almost impossible to discover. Rare as African cells, they are. We pedlars, we know the routes because we've travelled them for many years. But you, my young friends – you would be babies in the desert. Without a good map, you'll be gobbled up like the caiman of old. And I could tell you about the caiman, what's left of him.'

'Sell us a look at the map, then,' said Félix, who was good at improvisation.

This the pedlar agreed to, in exchange for a tin full of tar and their assistance in patching up one of the side-carts. Then he unrolled the map on the ground in front of them.

From the moment her eyes fell upon the map, Ramona was enchanted. She had never seen a thing so exquisite. Here was the world, contained, but leaping from the ground to meet her. The colours were faded, the paper grubby with fingerprints and curling at the edges, but she felt the map beckoning. With its mysterious contours and curious names and suggestions of lands unknown, it was like looking into quicksand, knowing she was about to plummet headfirst into its depths.

The pedlar pointed.

'This is where you are.'

'Yes, yes, I can see!'

It made sense to her. Here was the sliding city at the foot of the highlands. Above it, the vast Amazon Desert opened like a shade. And below, very far to the south, before the continent tapered away into a collection of islands, was the city that the pedlar had called Cataveiro.

She looked for fifteen minutes, spellbound, memorizing the lines before her. Later, she would be able to recreate it with a bit of paper and a dye stick. When she looked up from the map the pedlar's eyes were upon her. She knew that he knew of her discovery.

Félix did not understand the map. He turned his head to one side and then the other, rotating the paper, squinting at it.

The pedlar's expression was now inscrutable.

'It has been a pleasure doing business with you, Ramona Callejas.'

It was easy for Ramona and Félix to spend the months that followed making plans, arguing over the route to Cataveiro. Ramona practised making her own maps – first the sliding city, then further afield, exploring the mountain and the dusty red valley below. She carried with her a ball of string and a long stick to make measurements, drawing in the dirt, committing her findings to memory.

Another summer arrived. Ramona turned thirteen, and she knew that she was stalling.

The pedlars came and went again, and Ramona thought of Cat Aveiro, riding about the continent with her long hair flying in the wind. Autumn drew in. Cooler nights reprieved the baked grounds.

One night, Ramona and Félix were lying on the roof of an empty house, watching the stars come out.

'One day I will make a map of the sky,' Ramona told Félix.

'You should.'

'Do you ever try to count them?'

'I used to. Then I stopped.'

'Me too.'

There was a silence where each of them knew the other was, despite their claims, counting the silver specks. That was the nature of their friendship: silent knowledge. Unspoken loyalty.

'You know I'm going to Cataveiro,' said Ramona.

'Yeah.'

'Are you coming?'

'I'm going to Tierra del Fuego. I'm going to find work on a ship. But I'll come with you as far as Cataveiro. They say it's dangerous when you don't know anyone.'

'I can look after myself.'

'I know.'

'Thanks, though.'

'We should go soon. We can't hang around here all our lives.'

'No. You're right.'

Félix rolled onto his side to look at her. His face was suddenly serious.

'I know you're worried about your ma. But you can't protect her.'

Ramona hung in the doorway of the shack, hands gripping the upper frame, swinging gently. Inés sat outside on the veranda. She was sewing a patch into her trousers. The next time Ramona visited, grass would have conquered the pebble square until it was almost indistinguishable, but on that day, thanks to Ramona's perpetual weeding, it still had the semblance of a veranda. Ramona watched as Inés lifted her needle to face-level and probed the thread through the eye.

'Why are you lurking, Ramona? I don't like lurking.'

Ramona stayed where she was.

'Ma, I've been thinking about going away.'

Inés continued with her sewing.

'I don't mean for a short time. I mean for always.' She paused. 'Are you listening?'

Inés's hands stopped. She turned around. In fact, she gave Ramona the most penetrating stare she had seen on her mother in years. Then she said, quite simply, 'Yes, I expect you will. People will find out about you. You should go soon. Next week, perhaps.'

Ramona was so taken aback by this response, all the things she had previously planned to say fell out of her head.

'You will go to Cataveiro, I expect,' continued Inés. She gave the needle a violent tug and the thread snapped. Inés hissed through her teeth.

'Yes. To Cataveiro.' The name had always had a delicious flavour in Ramona's mouth, but today it tasted sour.

'You have plans?'

'I thought – I want to learn – I heard they have mechanics there. For motorcycles . . . and cars.'

'Heh, that is no surprise. I dare say you'll be good at it, if you can find someone to take you on.'

The sewing recommenced. Ramona watched the needle's delicate swoops in and out of the material covering Inés's thigh. There was a tightness in her throat that she had not felt since they buried her siblings, and she knew she was going to cry.

'I didn't think you'd want me to go.'

Inés sighed sharply. 'I didn't say I wanted you to go. Do not give me my words. I said you should go. And it's true. You can't conceal yourself forever. Not out here. In the city, maybe.'

'I don't understand.'

'Ramona, you are not a child any more. Do you want what happened to me to happen to you? You want to be raped, beaten by those vagrants, those animals? Your things taken from you, your food stolen? No? Then get out. Go somewhere else. Go somewhere you can fight, if that's what you want.'

And almost under her breath, she muttered, 'Try and fix things, if you will.'

Later that night, Ramona came down the stairs to get a drink of water from the tank. Inés was sitting in her chair, her hands clenched together, her shoulders hunched. She might have been crying. Ramona could have gone to her mother, but instinct, a prevailing sense of what must be, prevented her, and she crept back up the stairs.

It was an evening late in the summer when Ramona returned home to find the shack empty. In her mother's bedroom, the bed was neatly made. Her few clothes were folded in the cupboard where they always were. There was a lingering smell in the room like cut grass. In the front room, utensils and a pan were upturned on the draining board. When she touched the pan it was still hot, as though it had sat in the glare of the sun for a long time.

Ramona checked underground, around the back of the shack and by the dried-up stream bed. There was no evidence of tracks.

She sat out on the veranda in Inés's rocking chair and waited for her mother to return. Dusk fell, a soft dusk, quiet and keeping its counsel. When it grew too dark to see the ground, Ramona retreated inside. She ran the past week through her head, listening again to her few conversations with Inés, trying to find in the remembered expressions of her mother's face any clues that might explain this strange behaviour.

Inés did not return that night, or the next. Félix went to everyone in the sliding city. No one had seen her leave.

Ramona waited for a week. Then she went to speak to Félix's mother, Carla.

'If my ma returns, I'll be in the city.'

'I'll tell her where you are,' Carla promised. 'Don't worry, Ro. She'll be back. I've seen this before, with others. She's not the first.'

The next day Ramona packed her bag, closed up the doors and the shutters of the shack and wrote a note. She left it on the table folded around the medallion, for luck, and that day she set out with Félix for Cataveiro.

20

The shack is empty. Inés's chair sits outside on the patch of earth – the veranda – unoccupied; the chair creaks gently, the wood hot to touch. The door to the shack is closed, and when Ramona opens it, everything is neatly in its place, the floor swept, no dust on the surfaces. The plain brown curtains hang neatly in the windows and bright light filters through the cracks in the storm shutters. In the back room she finds the bed made with the sheets tucked tight around the mattress. There is no evidence of violence. There is no evidence of raiders or strange burning fires, but from the moment she enters the shack, Ramona has a feeling of portentous dread.

She wants to believe this is one of her mother's wanderings. That it is only a matter of waiting until Inés returns, be that days or months. She wants to believe it. She comes out to the veranda and sits in the rocking chair. The day's heat pulses down on her bare head and the mountain shimmers. Still she has the feeling, the feeling that something happened here, something very bad. But she tells herself:

She went away. It's the fugue. She does this.

She notices weeds are coming up through the cracks in the pebbles. This is no good for her mother to come home to. She pulls a few of them out and tosses them aside. It makes no visible difference.

She begins the task in earnest, yanking out the weeds, eradicating every illicit stem until the veranda is littered with the thin dusty earth shaken from the roots. It is all over her arms and face. Her vision is blurred with tears. When she sits back on her heels she is crying freely, unable to stop.

Someone is coming up the mountain. She recognizes the slow, laboured walk. It is Carla, Félix's mother. She wipes a hand across her eyes.

It's the fugue that's taken her. Nothing more. Carla will tell you.

The older woman calls out as she approaches.

'Ramona, is that you? I saw the plane. It's not like you, to land so high.'

'What happened? Did she die? Or did she go away to die? That would be like her. Not to give anyone a chance to say goodbye. Take herself to some secret place we'll never find. That's what happened, isn't it? She went away. She must have gone away . . .'

Against her white shirt, Carla's face is darkened and creased by exposure to the sun. An anxious face. A frightened face. The sight of it fills Ramona with terror. Carla raises one hand, as if in supplication.

'I'm sorry, Ramona. It's worse than that.'

'No.' She shakes her head. 'No, it can't be worse, what can be worse? It's the fugue, isn't it? It's the fugue that's got her. I mean it's hardly a surprise, not with the jinn as well. How could she cope . . .'

Carla gets awkwardly to the ground, kneeling amid the remnants of the torn-up weeds. She takes Ramona's hand, as if she is a child again. Ramona squeezes it tightly.

'We should start looking for her now, Carla.'

'Ramona, this is something different. You already know, don't you? I can see it in your face.'

'No.' The plea is helpless this time. 'Please, no.'

'Your mother was taken,' says Carla. 'Five days ago, by raiders. My little niece, Gabi, she saw it all.'

'Taken?'

'By raiders.'

'But raiders don't take people.'

'I know. I know. We don't understand why. We thought maybe you would have heard . . . Ramona?'

Ramona is on her feet.

'Which way did they go?'

'We looked, Ro – we looked everywhere.'

'Which way?'

'What are you going to do?'

She looks at Carla, the fear in her old friend's face that this could happen, that this has happened. She imagines Félix's people living with that fear from day to day, convinced that at any moment the raiders might return. She imagines raiders putting their hands on her mother and dragging her away, a frail, jinn-ridden woman, tearing her from the only home she has ever known, the place where she buried her children. The rage that builds inside her is a force so great it is suffocating.

She helps Carla up and looks her clear in the eyes.

'I'm going to hunt them down, and when I find them, I'm going to rip them to pieces.'

21 ⦙

The Alaskan has that musky, slightly syrupy smell of a person who has reached old age. Or maybe it is all the sugar she consumes: fat, greedy spoonfuls in her tea, trays of sticky nougat, delivered from an artisan in the enclaves with a personal note. Then there are the jars of fruits that line the kitchen shelves, suspended in caramelized liquids. The fruits are creepy. They look like shrivelled body parts. Mig never watches when she eats them.

The Alaskan is unmistakably old. She is more decrepit than anyone Mig has seen, valleys and crinkles of flesh wrapped around the bones that she complains ache, oh how they ache, how deep they ache, her fucking bones. Occasionally the Alaskan will reminisce, saying something such as *when I was a young woman – oh those days – yes I was beautiful then*, and a particular look will possess her face, a flirtatious yet crafty look that Mig has seen on girls like Pilar. It makes him uneasy when the Alaskan wears it; he wants to slap her and wobble her jowls, remind her that her time on earth is limited. Can't she hear the ticking down of the clock, *tock tock tock*, inviting her soul to depart?

Other days, she seems unassailable. He does not really believe the Alaskan has ever been young; in his mind she has always been this collection of soft draping folds, a jellyfish human, loose and undulating, with a sting in its wake.

He does not know how long she has been in Cataveiro, but he knows it is a long time. Certainly from before he was born. The Alaskan is dangerous. She is dangerous because, like a denizen of the streets, she knows things, but she chooses who will be the beneficiary of her knowledge, seemingly on a whim.

She is a good employer. She pays well. She is content for Mig to run his own ring of street boys and girls. Under his direction, they weave about the city watching, listening, filtering information back to Mig, who in turn reports to the Alaskan.

A street boy sees the things that others don't. A street boy sees the acolyte of the Nazca House who vomits in the sanctuary and cleans it up furtively. A street boy knows when the vendors have stuffed their tamales with something new, something they call goat but which is not from any Patagonian goat or a goat that anyone ever saw. A street boy hears the rumours before they hit the radio waves and could tell you which is true and which is fabrication, if you cared to ask. If you cared to pay. A street boy knows that the mandolin player who sits on the corner of Plaza Grajeda looking like a halfwit and a tramp is neither, but an enforcer of the city, who rubs street-stink into his face every morning and cleans it off later using hot water, Mig doesn't doubt.

Mig has learned to sniff out need. Desperation is better. That is how the pilot smelled when she found him: desperate. She was direct but cautious; she told him the job would be dangerous. Mig does not care about danger. Danger is for pussies, and he tried to say so, but the pilot seemed anxious to enforce the danger, even to warn him, to give him the option to refuse the job.

This is not good business sense to Mig. Say the job, say the price. If the price is right, the job doesn't matter. On this level, he and the Alaskan understand one another.

Mig is not sure if she knows she is not his sole employer. This week, for example, he has been employed by the Alaskan, by the pilot who escaped and now has a price on her head, and by the enforcers of Señorita Xiomara. It has been a profitable week. His small stash of peso, concealed in a secret place known only to him, has grown. One day he will have enough to leave the city, and for Pilar, his one true love, to come too.

Pilar does not yet know this plan. So far their exchanges can be counted on one hand; Mig is not even sure she knows his name. But he is hopeful.

'Tell me, Mig,' says the Alaskan, and then stops. She is in a meandering mood tonight. Mig suspects she's been at the opium again. It's her only weakness, the conniving witch.

He waits. After a time she says, 'What have you heard on the radio?'

'Not much. Nothing new.'

'Not anything regarding Fuego Town?'

'Oh, that. That was a pirate attack. El Tiburón.'

'I didn't think El Tiburón's influence was so extensive he could ban Antarctican ships from Fuego. Think about it. There's something going on down there.'

'Something to do with the war?' She is always on about the war. Nobody else seems to know there is a war on, but the Alaskan talks about it as though it's a teaching of the Nazca.

'Yes, something to do with the war,' she says. 'Something important. Could the Antarcticans be going on the offensive? Surely not. The ripples would have reached me.'

Mig says nothing and curses Maria in his head. She should be here by now. She's late. She's left him stranded. She needs to get her arse over here.

'Describe the major events of the anthropocene, Mig.'

He reels them off. 'The industrial revolution. The Neon Age. The Migration Wars and the race to the pole. The Blackout. The Recovery.'

'Correct,' says the Alaskan. 'You even sound like you know what those things are.'

'The Blackout was like redfleur.'

'They are hardly alike at all. Redfleur infects the body and then passes the blood–brain barrier. The Blackout virus targeted the brain directly through scapular implants. You know this, Mig. I have told you these things a hundred times.'

He avoids her eyes.

'Yes, señora.'

'You should pay more attention, Mig. You need to think about what you wish to do with your life. You need a plan.'

The Alaskan reaches for her sling and shifts her weight in the bed. He can sense her staring at him until the magnetic pull of her gaze becomes so great he is forced to look up. She has frightening, mesmerizing eyes. Red-rimmed, the irises such a cold, hard black.

'Think about it,' she continues. 'What are your options in this place? You could continue living like a rat, I suppose, although given how much I pay you I don't see why you couldn't get a room of your own. Or how about hard labour on the poppy farms, with the threat of a machete through your head if you're ever tempted to steal? You could go into service on an Exchange ship or worse, a pirate vessel – El Tiburón has consorts who would like a smart young thing like you. I hear he's fond of boys too. Then again, they might chain you to a computer – ah, now, now he reacts. Is that a shudder I see? A little shiver up your spine? I can't say these sound like appealing options to me. But then again, I'm not Patagonian, so what would I know . . .'

Evil old bitch, he thinks. How does she always guess what he is thinking?

'Maybe I'll go to Alaska,' he says boldly.

The Alaskan gives no sign that this small hit has even dented her. She stares at him without blinking. Like a snake, he thinks, although he has never seen a snake. He has never been outside the city. He was born here, he was dumped here. The Alaskan knows that too.

'If you plan on going to Alaska, you had better learn your history,' she says. Always, these lectures, delivered in her pious instructional tone, as though she actually cares about him, when all she wants to do is show off how much she knows. Mig and Maria are her sole audience. What does Mig care about the Blackout? It was centuries ago, in another world, and not even his world, a world belonging to people like the Alaskan. Mig's concerns are straightforward: food and a place to sleep each night. He and his crew. Pilar.

Pilar, who is singing in the pit tonight. Pilar, who barely knows he exists.

Shift it, Maria. He can't be late.

'Well I remembered it, didn't I?' he says. 'I remembered the wars and the Neons and all that old stuff.'

'Remembering is not the same as knowing. If you went north of here, Mig, you would see things. Ruins. What remains of the great cities of the twenty-second century.'

A key turns in the door. Maria, about time! She shuffles in. A shy, stunted girl, Maria is terrified of the Alaskan. She is hampered with bags of groceries, her puny arms straining with the weight.

'You're late,' he tells her on the way out. Maria's eyes widen in fear. Mig regrets the words instantly, but he is desperate to escape the Alaskan's lascivious laments for the dead past and there is no time to take it back. As he closes the door he hears the Alaskan crooning.

'Is that my Maria? Come in, girl, come in here. I've been wondering where you've been.'

Another hot, restless evening in the city. But he's out. Away from the cloying cosiness of the Alaskan's rooms and down into the belly of the city.

Down where thieves tell the stories of the parrot and the condor to unsuspecting pedestrians, where workers await the slow shudder of the tram to take them home, the carriages packed full of humdrum faces glazed from another day on the outskirts, where their hands and eyes have worked like cogs in a watch. Not for him, the factories. Not such an afterlife.

Over the grey gleaming river where small punting boats pass. Wilting passengers sniff at a river breeze, and on the banks the city's jugglers ply their trade.

Past a shop where they sell personal radios with headphones, shiny lustrous things. He presses his nose to the glass, wanting. He has enough cash, but no, he needs to save; these peso in his pocket are his ticket out of here. Walk away.

Past the shops, past a school where they corral the kids who are counted into lessons.

Under the bridge where there was a stabbing last week. The dead girl oozed blood for twenty minutes without dying and no one touched her because someone said the word redfleur. Like magic, like a charm is the word redfleur. She died alone, which makes Mig uneasy when he walks past that wall now, as though her alone-so-alone spirit is still there pressed into the wall, like someone pinned a shadow there.

Down where the street kids flip and spin their scalps in the dirt and shoot words in their epic, warring, never-won never-finished battles. Who will find glory among the lowlings this week?

Mig is no wordsmith, but he knows people. That's his power: to listen. To translate the city into the Alaskan's greedy ear. For this power, Mig has respect among the children of the streets.

The old warehouse, the only place he has ever known as home, squats in a row of dilapidated buildings. It's a filthy-looking place, boarded up, bits of the structure crumbling, the paint long since peeled and grasses growing out the brickwork. To get in you have to squeeze behind the rotting graffitied boards and climb through a window on the ground floor. Inside is a high, echoey space that drips incessantly when it rains and heats to sweltering through the summer months. The warehouse is split over two levels. The kids live on the upper level, so if there's a raid they can get out over the roof.

The floor is covered in droppings from the birds that chitter in the rafters above. In daytime the place is full of the sound of their flapping wings, darting in and out of broken windows. If you want to piss, you go out into the street, but you can still smell the ammonia. The people inside smell, their blankets and solar wraps and sleeping bags smell, but Mig no longer notices it, if he ever did. He only remembers when the Alaskan screws up her nose in a put-on show of disgust – nothing truly disgusts her. She's undisgustable.

Mig checks behind him before entering the warehouse through the usual window. It isn't much, but it is a kind of home, this place, for kids that have no home. Their numbers have varied over the years. Some get lucky, get out. Others have been here forever. They are almost adults, though they try to stay like kids, to make themselves look small. They don't want to move on. One day they will have to. Kids can slip by, kids can keep this place secret and safe. Adults attract attention. Mig doesn't like to think about what will happen when he becomes an adult. It's not so distant now, when it used to seem a lifetime away. That's why he started the stash.

Today he counts fifteen bodies, bunched into small groups, the loners curled up with their faces to the walls. He knows all their faces. Most of them run errands for him, from time to time. He hands over the Alaskan's cash. It buys them hot meals. He tries to do it fair, a kind of rota so no one loses out, though some of them you couldn't trust to trail a Tarkie.

The rest of them are next door in the pit, where Mig goes now.

Tonight's pit billing lists Pilar, *Pilar y el Loro* as she must be known, but currently the kids are sitting round clicking and egging a disorganized wrestling match. Mig ignores it and looks directly for a sharp little highlands kid called Ri. Easy to spot, he has a face like a lizard that's all peeling from the pox. He sheds skin on you, this kid, drips and flecks of skin, shrivelled like scales; Mig has learned to stand clear when he talks to Ri. There's nothing infectious, or you'd know, but still you look at the boy and you think, spirits and angels, who wants to look like that?

'Hey, Ri. Ri, get over here.'

The boy comes over and Mig holds up a hand: not too close. The boy stares up at him from under his peeling eyelids. It's kind of fascinating and creepy at the same time. That's how reptiles are. That's how they've survived when the others, the wolves and the jaguars, are gone.

'I need to know about Fuego,' says Mig. 'Something's going down at the harbour.'

'Who wants to know?'

'I do.'

'Who really wants to know?'

'Who do you think? You going to do it or not?'

The boy sneezes. Flakes of skin fall from his upper lip and drift down to the floor.

'How much?' says Ri. His voice is nasal and expressionless. Mig wonders if the pox got his vocal cords too, if parts of Ri are shedding on the inside as well as the outside. Perhaps Ri's voice will disappear and then other bits of him until eventually Ri collapses in upon himself like a waterlogged box.

'It's the cash when you come back with information, isn't it?'

'Yeah.'

'So go.'

Ri scuttles off. It's a relief to see the back of him, and yet Mig knows he'll be thinking about Ri, which walls he'll be climbing, which windows he'll be leaning on to eavesdrop. The younger boy is like a shadow inside of Mig. He knows, strangely, that if anything happened to Ri it would stay with him forever. He would be haunted.

It is not only street kids in here tonight; others have snuck in too, people who've heard about the underground sensation that is Pilar. People with homes and families. It's not good for them to come here. They draw attention. It makes Mig feel bristling and defensive.

The wrestling match ends with one girl bleeding heavily from a torn ear. Next up is some kid with a trained lizard. The lizard stands on its back legs and dances. Mig's seen it before: a cute act, but nobody cares today. They are all here for Pilar.

In another corner, a group of younger kids are paying no attention to the pit. They're sat in a circle, facing inwards.

Mig is aware of their voices moving against him, rustlings, like soft hairs. He moves closer to make out what they are saying.

A girl with a round, comical face, a clown face, dominates the group. She has stripes painted on her cheeks like a desert tribesgirl, or are they scars?

She speaks in a low, mystical voice. 'The jaguar comes down from the sky and stalks the streets. If the jaguar passes you, you can feel his fur and his hot breath. It goes right through you. His eyes are on fire. His feet are mountains and each fur on his tail is a dried-up river. If the jaguar looks at you . . .'

A shudder goes through the group and Mig feels a coldness under his arms.

'. . . then you will die for definite within three months,' says the girl. 'The jaguar chooses his souls carefully. He picks each soul, and after they're dead he scoops them up and takes them back up into the sky, and he makes them warriors in his war.'

More talk of war, thinks Mig.

'I've seen the jaguar,' whispers a small boy.

'So've I.'

'And me.'

'Did he look at you?'

The small boy shakes his head, terrified.

'Then you're safe,' says the clown-girl, with authority.

A stir from the onlookers. Pilar is on her way.

Mig listens to the chant: El Loro, El Loro. Slapped skin, popped cheek, whistle click huff. Part of it is a front, a way to make the non-streets, the counted ones with families and homes, know their place. The sound gets into his ears and then it works into his chest, the rhythm, the lilt of it. El Loro, El Loro. The first word short and then the lo long and drawn out. El Lo-ro, El Lo-ro.

Here is Pilar, swaggering into the pit. She has decorated her hair with bright dyed feathers, so many of them it's hard to tell where the hair ends and the feathers begin.

'All right?' she shouts, throwing her arms wide.

She waggles her tongue at them, showing off the metal bolt that she is alleged to have stuck through it herself. Mig's heard things about Pilar. He looks at her waggling holed tongue and thinks they are probably true.

Pilar glares at the crowd. She does her first set, voice and body percussion, all angry, and mostly shouting. The non-streets look uncomfortable. This isn't what they have heard about. But the sharp filth that comes out of her mouth sounds angelic to Mig. His heart stops for a minute, watching his beloved.

After a few songs, someone calls, 'Do a fado one, Pilar.'

Pilar looks pissed-off, then relents. She sits on the edge of the pit. She picks up her guitar and starts to play. When her voice cuts over the guitar the room falls silent. Even the kids in the corner shut up. Mig nods in satisfaction. *Now you get it, you morons.*

Pilar's voice flows into every crevasse of the room. The comical parrot is gone now. Her voice is all longing. A lump in the throat, a sadness you didn't know was a part of you. She sings in Portuguese. She sings of loves and opportunities lost, fate's inescapable grip upon your soul, the endless sea which takes you on journeys so long and eventful that when you return, those you knew no longer recognize your face, and look upon you as a stranger. She sings: You can leave a place and promise to come back but you must remember. What you left is not what you return to.

When Pilar sings it is as if her body disappears and she becomes all mouth, all voice, like a conduit for something not present in the room. But Mig sees. Mig sees the muscles move in her throat and the lungfuls of air she draws down into her chest. He sees the melancholy in her eyes through the feathers and the hair, and wonders if she is sad for herself or if the song is the sadness of others.

At the end of the set she stands up without a word and makes to leave. She is instantly mobbed.

Mig loiters. Everyone wants to talk to Pilar, but now that Pilar is done she doesn't care about the adulation. The non-streets, the counted ones, they all want to touch her. Now she's chatting with some flash kid who looks like he's from as far from here as you could get before the enclaves. He's not a street kid, or if he is he's a high-class thief, that much is evident from his clothes. He's cooking up some fat story, his attitude all relaxed and his voice butter soft so Pilar has to lean in to hear what he's saying. Pilar looks interested, for the first time since she stepped out the ring. Her body is angled towards Flash kid's. She's nodding and fiddling with that tongue stud of hers, clacking it against her teeth. Flash kid has a smirk. He's trying to hide it but Mig can see plain as day. He is riveted with jealousy.

Flash kid says something to Pilar and Pilar laughs, long and low, throwing back her head. Then she picks up her guitar case and they go outside together.

Mig is swamped with the desire to go after them and punch Flash kid in the face repeatedly. He imagines the moment where his fist – miraculously larger and tougher and stronger – is coming towards Flash kid, and Flash kid realizes what's about to happen to him, and in the slowed-down moments before his fist lands, the smirk vanishes from Flash kid's face. And then Mig's fist connects with a *thunk* – no, a *crack* – and Flash kid flies through the air.

He wanders aimlessly about the floor of the pit, going from group to group, looking for something to occupy his head, cards or dice or whatever, but all he can think about is Flash kid and Pilar, Flash kid and Pilar, and wonder what they're doing, if she's letting him kiss her, and touch her, or showing him her pierced tongue.

He ducks out into the street. Best head back to the Alaskan, score some supper, let her know he's got people on the case of the Fuego lockdown. Best not loiter in the streets. When the night comes down those who are safe sit in bubbles of music and light, on the higher levels, away from the streets. The larger the light, the larger the sanctuary. The lights in the warehouse are small.

It's a worry, that people are coming to see Pilar. He can't pretend it isn't. Soon she'll have to find other venues. It won't be safe for the kids.

He sees the glowing end of a cigarette, and hears a spasm of coughing.

It's Pilar, smoking and hacking. She's alone.

Mig hesitates.

'Hey.'

Pilar glares at him.

'What?'

'Nothing.' He shrugs. 'Just saying hi.'

Pilar draws on the cigarette and coughs again. He can't remember seeing her smoke before. Maybe that's why she is coughing.

'Nice show,' he says.

'It wasn't my best. It was average.'

'Sounded good to me. But what do I know?'

She looks at him suddenly, right on. The force of her gaze is like a lamp, bright and fierce enough to blow the night away.

'You know a lot, from what I heard.' She coughs again and makes a phlegmy sound in her throat; really she doesn't care.

A flicker of suspicion settles into certainty. It was Flash kid who gave Pilar the cigarettes. Maybe, he thinks with a spark of hope, that's why she was nice to him. He notices one of her feathers has fallen to the ground. He picks it up for her.

'Keep it,' says Pilar grandly. 'There's plenty more of them.'

Mig tucks the feather carefully into his pocket.

'You want to go for a walk?' says Pilar.

'A walk?'

'Yeah, you know, a walk, a wander, a stroll. A walk.'

'Sure.'

Pilar stubs out the cigarette. She peels herself away from the wall and sets off at a slouching pace. She always walks this way, folding in on herself. It was this walk that made Mig think when he first saw her that she wasn't really angry, only sad underneath.

The streets at night are chill, furtive, full of shadows and planned deeds that may or may not come to pass. He has no choice but to walk them but it is never without unease. Tonight, though, is different. With Pilar at his side, the night is pushed away. He becomes invincible. Perhaps she's only with him because he showed up – perhaps she's still thinking about the other kid – Flash kid – but Mig doesn't care. He is just happy to be with her.

They walk through the district where prostitutes pose in windows and lean out from balconies, their hands soft and draping, their faces bored. A tram horn blows. They pause while the half-full tram clatters past, and Mig sees the vague reflections of his face and Pilar's face in its windows, side by side. They cross the tram-tracks and walk on, to a district where the second level is busy with rowdy night-time drinkers and the streets below are busy with waiting rickshaw drivers and expectant thieves. Pilar weaves her way through, ignoring all of them.

While they are walking he says, 'Where'd you learn to sing like that?'

'Like what?'

'Like the fado.'

Pilar uses her guitar case to push a way through the crowds.

'My papa found a musical pod in one of the old cities. That was his job, he'd go to the old cities and find things that were buried, and sell them to the pedlars or the caravan. They like those things up north, or sometimes people would buy them for a museum or whatever. Anyway, he got the pod working and one of the things on it was this woman who sang fado. I couldn't understand all of it until I learned the Portuguese but I knew it was special. It just . . . you know, it felt right. It felt like me.'

'Have you still got it? The pod?'

Pilar hesitates.

'You don't have to say,' says Mig quickly. He feels slightly stunned. He has never heard Pilar speak so much in one go.

'I do have it. Don't tell anyone, though. They might think I was cheating.'

Mig thinks of the Alaskan's instructions. 'It's not cheating,' he says. 'It's learning.'

'Whatever it is, that pod's the only thing I got in the world that belonged to my papa. Anyway, I can't use it now. There's no more juice in it.'

'How'd you come to be on the streets, anyway?'

'Mama died in an accident in the poppy factory. I don't remember but that's what my papa told me. And then he got the jinn, and died too. Ironic, isn't it? What about you?'

'My ma couldn't look after me. So she lost me.'

He realizes they are on an inevitable course for the bridge where the girl died. He doesn't want to pass it, but he can't choose another route without an obvious diversion, and to mention it seems even worse. They keep walking. When they come to the bridge he feels it, the dead girl's spirit lodged there still, and he senses her large, dead, sorrowful eyes upon him as they pass under it, and her hands tug at him with cold air as though to try and regain some of the warm life from their two bodies.

When they are safe on the other side Pilar says, 'There was a girl there.'

He says, 'I know,' and instantly feels better, knowing that she felt it too.

'The little kids say when someone dies the jaguar's taken them.'

'Yeah, I heard them say that too.'

'They make up all kinds of shit.'

'You don't believe in the jaguar then,' he says with a laugh, like it's a joke.

Pilar says, 'No,' but too quickly.

They both fall silent. Something comes to him: the pilot's last words in that messy street scene with the infected Señorita Xiomara, the woman who throws people into the swallowing sands up north.

'There's something I want to show you,' says Pilar.

'All right.'

He would follow her anywhere. He suspects she knows that, already, but it doesn't bother him.

Pilar leads him through the city, taking cuts and bypasses he has not seen before, and Mig thought he knew all the routes. Her trust is at once touching and thrilling. He loves this about the city. You think you know the place and one day, just like that, it shows you a side you've never seen before.

'Where are we going?' he asks, knowing she won't answer, teasing her a little.

'Secret,' says Pilar mysteriously.

Mig grins to himself. She might be taking different routes but he can tell the general direction of where they are heading: winding through the Brazilian quarter, out towards the university campus where Mig likes to sit sometimes and listen to the students arguing. He is astonished by how much they can argue over things which, to him, seem either incomprehensible or perfectly obvious. Mig and Pilar pass through the campus, silent now in the night.

They reach the plaza in the centre of town where the silver tram lines converge on the approach to grand Station Sabado. As Pilar skips across the tracks, a tram horn blares at them, and Mig feels the rush of the tram cars passing at his back.

'Come on.'

Pilar walks confidently through the main entrance to the station. The lights under the glass and steel canopy are blinding, even at this hour, and it is only now that Mig hesitates. The station is full of late-night commuters, women's high heels clicking in small groups and the men suave in their evening shirts. A tram unloads a new cargo of raucous, drunken bodies. Enforcers work their way through the station, systematically kicking out beggars and tramps. There are no homeless here. The lights are too bright. The lights will seek out the stink of the street. Mig feels horrifyingly visible. He wants to cringe under them but Pilar strolls through the place like she owns it, right past a scowling enforcer with a baton at his waist, a ticket officer and a cleaner moving a mop in slow circles over the floor tracked with footprints. Pilar opens a service door marked 'No Entry' and slips through. Mig does not dare to glance back as he follows. The door shuts behind him with a foreboding clang.

He finds himself in a concrete stairwell. Pilar is ascending.

'Come on.'

Higher up, the stairs are covered in bird shit and he can hear claws scrabbling where they have made their nests. At the top of the stairwell, Pilar jimmies open a panel, gives him the guitar case to hold and levers herself up through the hole. He passes up the guitar. Her hand drops down.

'I'm fine.'

He scrambles up, insulted by the suggestion he might need help, but forgets it when he climbs out the hatch and sees the view. They have come out onto the roof of Station Sabado. The city is spread out below, softened in its night-time dressing. A tram exits the station and rolls across the plaza and into the weave of the city streets. Couples stroll across the criss-crossing plaza lines, heading home, swerving away from the ejected beggars.

Pilar is crouched a few metres away, looking for a moment like some kind of statue, a hunched, wingless angel, a peculiar guardian for the city. He likes that idea. Pilar watching over them.

She takes out a pocket radio.

'You get the best signal up here.'

She switches on the radio. Music leaps out, bright and clear. Pilar leans back, the radio resting on her stomach. Her face in the gloom is beautiful, her expression content.

Mig recognizes the little jingle as one song fades into another.

'Good choice,' he says.

Pilar nods. 'This is the only one worth listening to.'

Mig agrees, but he loves the radio in all its variations. It is the oldest and most constant thing in his life. Wherever you go in Cataveiro, you can hear the radio. You can creep close to an apartment window or simply stand in the street and listen to the competing stations of the vendors. If you have a favourite station, you can follow it around the city all day, tracing the morning show, the afternoon show and the night show through their different listeners. Mig likes to mix it up. He likes the chatting in the morning, the yawning presenters exchanging banter and insulting one another. In the afternoon he catches the news reports – useful to the Alaskan. To Mig they are stories from another planet, places he has never been to, things he will never see, like the ocean, the shipping reports with their peculiar words and sullen tone. But at night, he is all about the music. He likes it all: big brash music to throw your limbs about to, or quiet, shy music that sneaks up on you like Pilar's hunched walk. Once or twice he has fallen asleep on balconies in the lull of some late-night tune, and woken in the morning to the irritated tones of its owner evicting him.

Pilar is looking at him strangely.

'If you tell anyone about this place, I'll kill you.'

'I won't tell.'

'Good.'

'How'd you get past all the enforcers, anyway?'

'They've got better things to do than worry about me. And they like my songs. Some of them.'

They listen to the radio in comfortable silence. Pilar sings the odd line, not full singing, not fado, a sort of whisper, half-notes and syllables. It sounds like starlight, like Pilar is whispering to the stars that grow brighter and more defined as the city lights go out, and one city shuts down, leaving only time for a single breath, a brief intake of air, before the other city, the city of the nocturnes, begins to venture out from the cracks.

It makes Mig think about all those places he doesn't know. The world beyond Cataveiro. A funny thought occurs to him: he wonders if, in some of those faraway places the Alaskan likes to scorn, there are people like him and Pilar, perhaps listening to the radio, perhaps wondering about his city, and his country. The idea is at once thrilling and alarming. He wants to share it with Pilar, but he is afraid she would mock him.

Instead he asks, 'Did you know there's a war on?'

Pilar steadies the radio. 'What, like the guerrillas?'

'No, a bigger war. Like a secret war.'

'Between who?'

'Antarctica and the north.'

'Who told you that?'

'The Alaskan.'

'She's touched.' Pilar taps her skull pointedly.

'She knows things, though. Don't you think it's strange, to be in a war no one knows about?'

'I think she's spinning stories. I think she went mad when she left Alaska. Why did she leave, anyway? Why would a northerner come here? It doesn't add up.'

He thinks about the Alaskan. Her cold black eyes. What she is.

It was Maria who told him. Maria wouldn't lie. After she told him, he knew why Maria was always scared. He didn't blame her.

'I don't know,' he says. 'But I think she was important there.'

He looks at Pilar, her head tipped back, her eyes half closed. 'What would you say if I said I was going to Alaska?' He tries to gauge her reaction.

'Like tomorrow?'

'No, not tomorrow. But some day.'

'I don't know. Don't they have all that robotics shit up there? Neon stuff?'

'I don't know. That's what people say. I want to see for myself.'

'Nothing stopping you.'

'Don't you want to get out of the city?'

Pilar shrugs. 'Might not like my singing up north.'

'Why'd you choose the parrot anyway? Teachings say the parrot—'

'—ate all the world's voices till it lost its own. I know. That's one version. But there's another version that's better.'

'What's that?'

Pilar's lips curve in a secret smile and the edges of her eyes crinkle. A feather has fallen down over one eyebrow, giving her a roguish look. 'Maybe I'll tell you . . . one day. Do you want to share a cigarette?'

Mig nods. Pilar lights the cigarette carefully. She draws on it and exhales a few times, then passes him the end. She leans back, sighing.

'Gives you a lift, doesn't it? Hey, don't listen to all the shit that old witch tells you. You've got to think of the day. That's all there is, the day. Like this music and those stars up there. This is a good one. This is one to keep and wrap up inside you. Else you got nothing.'

Mig lies on his back, like she is. He watches the stars forge into hard, shiny diamonds. Despite the night-time chill, Pilar's words and the nicotine give him a warm, spaced-out feeling deep in his stomach. He thinks about his secret stash of peso and his plan to buy Pilar a way out. Perhaps it isn't such a fantasy. She says there are days she keeps and this one, this one with him in it, is one of them. He wants to ask her why she brought him here, him and not any of the others, but there is only one answer he wants to hear. If it's anything else, it will spoil it all. So he keeps quiet, listening to Pilar's breathing and the whistle of a wind sneaking about the rooftops. He cannot say it aloud so he thinks to himself: I love you, Pilar.

22 ¦

Station Cataveiro babbles in the background. When Taeo first arrived in Patagonia, the sound drove him to distraction. So many airwaves, jammed with loose chatter, music and propaganda, the escapades of pirates at once celebrated and denounced. The broadcasts slide into one another without announcement; it is impossible to distinguish what is truth and what is fiction. In Cataveiro, every home in the vicinity is hooked onto a different wavelength with the volume cranked up, and they ripple over and under one another, burbling through the day and the night, thrumming in the walls. Taeo hears voices when he is trying to sleep and voices when he wakes. He longs for a moment of silence.

He has to get used to it, else he will go mad. But between the dialects and the speed they gabble, he almost misses her name.

He thinks it is the hourly news report. It might be, it might not be. Two men are discussing an accomplice of the pirate El Tiburón, who has recently been captured.

His accomplice, that is, listeners, or should we say her accomplice? But right now we need to tell you about the fugitive Ramona Callejas. Who hasn't heard about the pilot, the lucky one they call her, the one who carries the hummingbird with her . . .

Ramona Callejas, clear as water. Taeo listens with increasing alarm. Ramona is wanted in Cataveiro. She was here in Cataveiro just recently, a week ago, or was it longer? Look for her picture in the posters. There is a reward, from someone named Señorita Xiomara, whose name the broadcaster pronounces with an air of reverential importance. Xiomara almost died; the pilot was involved. Then they are talking about something else, guerrilla movements in the north-west, and there are no more clues as to the pilot's fate.

Taeo flicks rapidly through the radio stations, straining for the combination of those few syllables again. He gets weather reports, music, agriculture, more music.

Of the pilot, nothing.

Why did she stop here? What the hell was she doing? Now she is wanted, hunted, just like himself and Vikram. Whatever she has done, it has put all three of them in danger. She carries the holoma. If she still has it. He tries to reconstruct her face, her expression as she took the device. He believed her when she promised she would go directly to Panama. Despite her fear, or perhaps because of it, he trusted her.

Now he doesn't know.

'Everything all right?'

Vikram hovers in the doorway. Taeo is kneeling on the floor, holding the radio up, right against his ear.

'Yes. I thought I heard something – about Fuego. But it was nothing.'

'I'm listening to another station,' says Vikram. 'If I hear anything, I'll tell you.'

'You don't understand the dialect.'

'I'm learning,' says Vikram. 'I have nothing else to do.'

He leaves the room abruptly. Taeo puts the radio back. He is in a precarious position, now more than ever if his message north has been delayed. Vikram will go. At some point he will walk out and leave, and there will be nothing Taeo can do to stop him. He cannot keep the other man here by force. His hold over Vikram is weakening with every day they spend in the city, waiting for Taeo to find the Antarcticans, as he promised he would.

A good three weeks on foot: those were the words of the fisherman who ferried them to the mainland for a hefty fee. Three weeks without storms, that is. Get caught in a storm out in the open . . . The fisherman said no more, but the twist of his mouth made it clear what he thought of their chances. There must be transport, Taeo pressed. He could not wait three weeks. The fisherman shrugged. There's the farm trucks. Maybe they'll take you. And the army. He looked at them, knowingly. Maybe they won't. And there's others who'll like your money, but maybe you'll avoid them, if you want to keep all of your fingers.

The farmland of Patagonia was all open. There were no greenhouses or biodomes and there was little cover. At first their journey was uneventful. The farms were intensive islands, production hubs amid long stretches of cultivated land. Taeo and Vikram were able to pay for food and shelter overnight, and the farmers took the money and did not question them. The people with which they stayed were poor, sometimes very poor. They wore face masks in front of strangers. Their children had never been vaccinated. Some of them had the jinn.

As they progressed north, following the ridges of overgrown highways now used only by farm workers or the army, the climate grew hotter and drier. When they could they begged or bribed for a lift, travelling wedged between crates of produce in the back of a truck, watching the land recede, kilometre after kilometre swallowed up in the truck's solitary, jolting wake. The harvest changed. They passed old anti-aircraft towers, installed to protect Patagonia's most important export. There was nothing to suggest whether the towers were manned or empty.

When he decided that flight to Cataveiro was their only option, Taeo had not thought about the poppies. It had not occurred to him that the route would take them deep into poppy country, field after field of flower heads, tall and resplendent on their stems. Sometimes in the distance they saw the careful hands of a family at work, children scoring the ripening pods to produce a thin trickle of latex that would harden in the sun, the children watching them with a strange detached curiosity, interested and not interested, wondering and not wondering. He had forgotten that traversing this country would be dangerous, that there would be farmers with machetes in their belts, sometimes soldiers too, and the soldiers would have guns. He had not thought about how those bright bobbing petals would make him feel. That his chest would go tight with a terrible longing. He would find it difficult to breathe. The headaches would take him in sudden, fierce bursts so that there were times he could barely see, and would have to hold his hand in front of his face to shield his eyes from the open sky.

He had not thought about Vikram, who stared at the flowers the way Taeo's children stared at the ocean the first time he took them to the beach. Vikram, who wanted to pick the flowers, to examine the petals and the delicate stamen, touch them and smell them, marvelling that the land he had believed poisoned could produce such a beautiful thing. Vikram wondered about the children they saw and the farmers with machetes that ran at them, shouting, brandishing their shining blades. Once a woman hurled a machete in their direction. The blade buried itself in the ground no more than a few metres from where they stood, and then they ran.

The question from Vikram was always why.

Why are they guarding the flowers?

Why are they chasing us away?

Why are there no greenhouses?

It was a strange thing to explain, while in the back of his mind was nothing but the pulse of his addiction.

It was the first time Taeo had acknowledged it to himself: an addiction. In the poppy fields he could no longer deny it. There was a relief in the admission, even if it were only to himself. He was having visions. Once his craving was so great he got up in the middle of the night, first checking Vikram was asleep, and he went and lay among the rustling flowers. He took one of the pods and tucked it into his pocket, not to use, just to hold there, like a charm, an amulet, just in case. The sky was clear overhead and a thousand stars looked down on him. He could not remember the last time he had lain and looked at the stars. As he gazed up they seemed to descend towards him, surrounding him on all sides, cocooning him in their silvery light. He closed his eyes and felt Shri, lying beside him. She took his hand and whispered.

You're very far away, she said. *Come back soon.*

But then he imagined he heard another sound: a purposeful movement through the flowers, the calculated stealth of a farmer coming to hunt the trespassers like prey. He crawled from the fields in a state of terror to collapse shivering on the ground.

Where did you go?

Vikram, awake.

Nowhere, he said. I went nowhere.

The pod was a hard nub in his pocket. In the morning he clenched his teeth and hurled it from him, as far as he could throw.

While they walked he thought often of the villagers who had taken his stash in exchange for Vikram. He imagined them lighting it, releasing its potent smoke. He imagined the dreams they might have, of jaguars and strange northern things, burning beaches and the people of the sea city who turned to mermaids and hurled themselves into the sea. Or whatever it was they dreamed of while high. But he could not say to the man beside him: these flowers bought you, although he thought it in his own head regularly, sometimes bitterly, when he caught Vikram standing on the edge of the fields gazing at the flowers as if in a dream.

He had to explain the function of the flowers to Vikram. They adjusted their route, skirting the edges of the guarded farms, making their way along the scrubby hills that bordered the farmland.

Vikram said it was like the manta trade in Osiris. Occasionally he would reveal a small detail such as this, and Taeo gathered them eagerly, knowing they might be of use to the Republic when he finally returned and made his report.

He asked about the manta. Vikram said it was a narcotic that was smoked. From a sea plant, he thought, he wasn't sure. It had a strong smell and produced hallucinations.

There was little to do on the journey other than talk to one another, but Vikram had little to say and Taeo was tortured by his visions, so he continued teaching Vikram a few words of Spanish. By the time the farmland gave way to the small settlements and factories that marked the city's approach, Vikram had mastered simple phrases. He said he liked the foreign words. He said people had not kept their languages in Osiris.

Sometimes Taeo caught himself looking at Vikram, and as the only question Vikram had was *why*, the question Taeo had about Vikram was always the same.

What are you?

What are you what are you what are you?

Now they are holed up in the city, venturing out only to acquire essentials. Is it possible to hate a space after only a few hours? Practically, there is nothing wrong with the rooms he found. In the Brazilian quarter, they are cheap, very cheap. Taeo has enough cash to cover them for a few weeks, and the landlord is the ask-no-questions type, a resolve strengthened by a substantial tip. Across the hallway is a self-proclaimed high-class brothel whose madame declares herself the soul of discretion, if only for her clients. Another screen to hide behind. The rooms themselves are ugly but clean. There is plumbing and a fridge. They are up on the fifth floor. The shutters close tightly so no one can see in. Providing Vikram keeps his head down and stays indoors, no one will ever know the Osirian has been in the city.

Despite all of these advantages, the rooms have an overwhelmingly depressing air. Resentment has seeped into every nook and cranny: his resentment, Vikram's resentment, the resentment of those who came before them and left, perhaps abruptly, perhaps violently. There are suspicious stains on the underside of his mattress, stains he does not mention to Vikram. He did not ask the landlord about the previous occupants. Now he doesn't want to know.

They pass the hours. Vikram, sat by the radio, listening for words that Taeo has taught him, piecing together a world from half-comprehended sentences. Taeo, dreaming of opium, dreaming of Antarctica, dreaming of Shri, dreaming of home.

Home which is suddenly that much further away because the pilot, the fucking pilot, has caused an incident.

He has been comforting himself that this will not be for long. All he had to do was find a fellow Antarctican agent. Then they could get out. His people wouldn't let him down, not this time. Not when he has Vikram.

And now the pilot's name is on the fucking radio.

What by all the ice in Antarctica were you thinking, Ramona Callejas? Didn't I fix your plane? Didn't you say you would go straight to Panama? Now what do I do?

Taeo is convinced there is at least one Antarctican agent in the city, more likely several. He spent yesterday tramping over Cataveiro with his one remaining holoma, surreptitiously activating it in different locations, and waiting for a response. Not a flicker of life came back. There are no holomas in the city, or his holoma is somehow blocked, or the signal does not work here.

He tells Vikram that today will be the day: he will find the agents. Vikram looks at him without expression but Taeo senses his disbelief.

'We'd have more luck searching together,' says Vikram.

Taeo feels panicked at the mere idea.

'No. We agreed, it's too dangerous. The villagers are bound to have given your description. Half of Patagonia will be looking for you.'

'They know what you look like as well.'

'I speak the language. And I know who I'm looking for. Besides, they can't arrest an Antarctican.'

He holds Vikram's gaze, worried that the other man will call his bluff. He feels like a jailer.

But the Osirian says only, 'You should ask the beggars,' and shuts the door to his room. Fleetingly, the thought crosses Taeo's mind that Vikram is just playing along, then he discards it. He can't afford to give in to paranoia. Vikram knows this is for his own safety.

Taeo returns to the hot, languid streets. It is a strange world, this city, always in ascent or descent. Something is forever catching your eye: a child scrambling up a ladder, an invalid being lowered in a sling in a building without lifts. He watches furtively from behind his sunglasses.

First he tries the vendors. Every time he is offered something, on a tray or from an open hatch, he asks, 'I need to find someone, who do I go to to find someone?'

The reaction is invariably the same. They refuse to acknowledge him, hastily foisting their wares on to some other sorry bastard. Taeo can sense the circle around him again.

He tries the vendors. He tries the humitas sellers and the grain sellers and the cloth sellers. He tries the buskers. He tries the beggars, as Vikram said. He tries the acolytes in the Houses of the Nazca. With each approach he makes, he is aware of the flimsiness of his cover. Another avenue closed, another witness to remember his face. He needs to find the person who knows. There is always someone who knows. He is skimming the surface of the city, and there is a whole other city underneath the one he sees, but he cannot find a way in.

Shadows lengthen. The afternoon is vanishing before his eyes. He sits on a flight of steps leading up to a public building, neither knowing nor caring what it might be. On the other side of the steps a juggler is plying the street crowd. Taeo follows the movement of her hands, the red-and-white batons revolving in patterns whose logic is accidental or premeditated, he doesn't know which, and he thinks that the course of his own life now appears similarly inexplicable, even to himself. The juggler drops a baton and gives a rueful, yet knowing smile. Taeo cannot tell if it is part of the act.

He watches people walking past. Citizens of a non-nation. A gamine boy with a shaved head. A girl wearing a wide-brimmed hat, something of the outback about her; he can picture her in Antarctica, measuring ice melt. A child carrying a pocket radio, the unit swinging from her hand, mouthing the words to the issuing song. Are they happy, are they unhappy? How many lives does this city hold? Fifty thousand? A hundred?

He feels weary thinking about it. He has never considered Vosti Settlement in such stark terms. Vosti just is, and it is only here, where he feels so far removed, that he has these thoughts.

The boy is watching him from across the street.

It's a scruffy, ill-kempt boy, in his early teens. The boy meets Taeo's eyes quite deliberately, and then turns and starts to walk away.

The boy leads him through the streets, down narrow alleys and through hidden courtyards, over and under bridges. They cross the tramlines one way and cross them again another. He quickly loses all sense of location. The boy darts in and out of view and he begins to wonder if he is chasing someone actually there, but he is lost and it is too late to stop. At last the boy scurries down a reeking backstreet. He pulls down the ladder to a metal fire escape, and begins to climb.

Taeo follows gingerly, first the ladder, then up the steps. The boy's shoes make no noise. Taeo feels loud and clumsy. He will never get used to these precarious constructions. He follows the boy up to the very top, where the boy wedges open a window and climbs through. Taeo hesitates, then does the same.

He is standing inside the reception room of a small apartment. An unfurnished space. The walls painted off-white and empty. The front door, presumably leading to the interior stairwell of the building, is kept shut with three heavy bolts.

On the other side of the room, a screen hangs over an open archway. Printed with birds and jaguars, it is the sort of thing that is foisted upon out-of-towners: culture bought cheap. He hears a querulous voice from within.

'Yes, Mig, bring him in.'

The boy reappears through the screen and says, 'She'll see you now.'

Taeo hovers, uncertain.

'Who?'

'The Alaskan,' says the boy, impatiently. 'Don't keep her waiting.'

A Boreal.

He has never met a Boreal before.

He pushes through the screen. An old woman is lying in a bed, surrounded by radios.

Taeo is not sure exactly what he expected in those brief anticipatory seconds. Someone plump and healthy, perhaps marked with robotics (the worst propaganda he has seen shows them sprouting with wires). Not this angular, faded creature propped against the wall. The Alaskan's face is lined like a piece of ceramic containing a hundred hairline fractures. She has the darkest eyes of anyone he has ever known. Strangely so. Not quite human.

The Alaskan leans over and switches off a boxy radio, the antenna of which protrudes out of the window.

'I understand you've been looking for me,' she says.

'I've been looking for someone. I don't know if it's you or not.'

'You've been looking for me. And raising quite a stir while you're doing it. Mig says he's never seen anyone so indiscreet.'

Taeo glances behind him, just in time to catch the boy's head swiftly withdrawing through the screen.

'You're not a spy, that's for certain,' says the Alaskan. Her eyes travel over him. The eyes of a collector, he thinks. 'Have a seat,' she says, pointing to a chair. Taeo removes a radio and sits, warily. The heat up here is intense; he is already sweating from the climb, and now he can feel it pooling in his armpits. Afternoon light streams through the windows in concentrated beams, hiding nothing, not the sling hanging over the bed, not the Alaskan's mottled hands, or the slight hump of her legs under a plain brown cover. The Alaskan wants to be seen.

Her windows have no shutters. He glances at the smeared, slightly grimy panes, wondering. Is that bufferglass? If so, it is a subtle, but a strong statement. The Alaskan has means, and she has connections.

She sees him looking and smiles. He realizes it does not matter if the windows are made of bufferglass or not; the fact that he has considered it is enough.

'There isn't always time for discretion,' he says. 'I know nobody here, and I need answers quickly. My method seems to have worked.'

'Too well,' she says. 'Mig was tailing you for most of the day.'

'Then Mig might have presented himself a few hours earlier.'

'He might,' she says. 'But he is trained to observe.'

'Who are you?'

'Didn't you hear what the boy said? I'm the Alaskan. That's what they call me, anyway.'

The Alaskan inhales, a hollow sucking sound that reminds Taeo of spring slush underfoot. Her body spasms. For a moment he is concerned, then he realizes she is laughing.

'Do you have a real name?' he asks.

'Not any more,' she says. Her gaze settles upon him. There is a strange satisfaction in being looked at, really seen, after all this time.

'What about in Alaska?'

She says nothing.

'I'm not from here either,' he says.

'Yes. I can hear that. Your accent is unmistakeable.'

Something in her tone offends him. Mockery? She is Alaskan. A Boreal. But her Spanish has no discernible accent. He experiences a sudden, overwhelming desire to know what she knows. Everything she has ever experienced – he wants to know it and feel it for himself. If the Alaskan's memories were a pool, he would wallow in them.

'Is it true the Boreal States have reintroduced scapular chips?'

She does the silent laugh. Another long, wet inhalation.

'The first question is always the same question. Even from you.'

It takes Taeo a moment to register that she has switched effortlessly to Portuguese.

'What do you mean, even from me?'

'Don't you consider yourself a notch above these Patagonians? Better educated? All the Antarcticans I have met are proud.'

'And how many Antarcticans have you met, exactly?'

She shrugs.

'I've never been north of the belt,' he says.

'Mmm.'

'And it's rare that Boreals venture south, never mind staying here. You can understand why I might be interested.'

'Mmm. You've never been anywhere except Antarctica, have you, Taeo Ybanez?'

Taeo goes cold. The Alaskan's eyes gleam with swift triumph as she continues.

'Taeo Ybanez, Brazilian-Antarctican engineer, partnered, a father, previously exiled at the Facility in Tierra del Fuego under pretence of being a botanist and now appeared, mysteriously or fortuitously, depending upon your viewpoint, here in Cataveiro. Have I got anything wrong? Do correct me if I have. I like to know I've got all the facts.'

With each word she utters he seems to fall further backwards. There is nothing beneath him. There is nothing to break the fall. The air is rushing against his back.

'I listen to the radio,' says the Alaskan. Taeo suppresses a shudder. Despite her declaimer, he cannot discard the notion that she might be wired up, that the Boreals have invented telepathy, or dug up who knows what from the vaults of the knowledge banks. Suddenly he understands the pilot's reaction to the holoma.

'But you were not very hard to trace,' the Alaskan adds. 'And you won't be hard to trace at all, if you keep this up. We must do better, Taeo.'

'What do you want from me?' he manages.

'I think the question is, what do you want from me.'

'No,' he says. His mouth is very dry. 'Let's be honest, at least. Your . . . messenger, found me, and brought me here. You have a reason.'

The Alaskan grasps the sling above her and pulls herself up into a more upright position, displaying a strength and agility that surprises him.

'Mig, the tea,' she calls sharply.

The boy appears silently. He places a steaming cup on a saucer at her elbow and disappears again. The Alaskan stirs syrup into the tea and for a while the only sound is the rasping of the spoon against the ceramic. She makes no move to offer him a drink.

'The greatest currency in this country is information,' she says. 'There is a war on, a silent war, but a war nonetheless. You and I both know that. Patagonia is a porous membrane wedged between two aggressors. This city is a hotbed of spies. So it is useful to me to know that you, an Antarctican, are here. At this stage, I have no intention of doing anything with that information. But it's my currency, and I don't mind telling you that, either.' She smiles over the edge of the teacup. 'I like to give people a fighting chance, especially when I think they might possess some intelligence. Now tell me what you want.'

Taeo's head is whirling.

She's dangerous. She's informing me, outright, that she is dangerous. But what choice do I have? She knows I've got nothing. She knows. She knows.

'I'm looking for someone in the Antarctican network.'

The Alaskan slurps at her tea. He can smell the syrup in it.

'Tricky to find. They're all bluffs and doubles, the Antarcticans. Suspicious types. Never use the radio.'

'But you could find them.'

'It's possible.'

'It's a matter of urgency.'

'Urgency to whom?'

'To everyone this side of the belt,' he says. 'You said I'm an exile. If you know my name then there's no point in me denying it. But I'm not blind either. This is no palace you're living in and clearly you get along by your wits. There's a reason you're not in Alaska any more.'

He leans forwards a little, watching her face closely.

'In fact, I'd be willing to bet that you were cast out too.'

The Alaskan's gaze does not falter. But neither does she deny the accusation.

She says, 'I wouldn't choose to live in Alaska now. We lost a lot of assets in the year of the Great Storm, and the economy never really recovered. Expensive assets, too. There were the arks. There was the sea city. What a lot of investment lost.'

All at once they are back where they were, playing games. But this second shock is more manageable after the Alaskan's earlier reveal. Taeo is able to keep a hold of his composure.

'We all know what happened to the sea city,' he says.

'Yes. The Osiris project was a visionary idea. It is most unfortunate what . . . happened.'

'I imagine the north must regret that investment now.' It is a long time since he spoke to anyone who was so well informed. He is almost beginning to enjoy himself. 'Now that it's gone.'

The old woman looks at him steadily.

'I've heard a rumour that the sea city is still out there.'

Taeo forces himself to breathe normally.

'How strange. I haven't heard that rumour.'

The Alaskan's dark eyes are shrewd.

'Rumours come and go over the years,' she says. 'Like fashion. I have heard many. I have heard the ones where the citizens of Osiris live as angels taken up by ancient gods, only their wings are fins like the flying fish of old. I have heard the rumours that they were whisked away to the underworld of their city's name. I have even heard that they are devils, forced to dine upon their own kind, living as cannibals on seaweed and human flesh. Cannibals. Ferocious indeed. And of course, I have heard that one of their number landed upon Patagonian shores but a few weeks ago, be he angel, devil, ghost or cannibal.'

She sets the teacup aside. Her smile blooms slowly.

'But you have not heard that rumour,' she says.

'No,' says Taeo. 'I have not.'

Her black eyes meet his. For a moment he imagines he can hear the whirring of her brain in motion, as though she is powered by clockwork. He wonders what on earth she did to get herself banished from Alaska.

The Alaskan uses a slender pole to switch on the radio in the window.

'Ah. The shipping news. I enjoy the shipping news. Don't you?'

'It has its uses.'

'Come back tomorrow,' she says. 'We'll see if we can find your agent.'

23

More often than he feels he ought to be, Mig is amazed by the stupidity of adults, even – especially – when they believe themselves at their most intelligent. The Tarkie is an exemplar of this particular type, and his belief of being better and smarter than the Patagonians makes it all the worse for him. He enjoyed tangling with the Alaskan. Mig could see it. He can tell when two people are trying to outsmart one another, even when he does not know exactly how they are doing it – but he could also see where the power lay. The Alaskan was toying. She had that gleam in her eyes, the one Mig has seen and been on the bad end of before now.

The Tarkie does not know who the Alaskan is. And he doesn't know what she is either. Mig shudders. He could tell the Tarkie some things. Perhaps the Tarkie would be less sure of himself if he knew the Alaskan keeps a list of her debtors, and has methods of dealing with those who renege on their bonds.

Nor does the Tarkie know he is being followed, even though he keeps glancing over his shoulder and taking sudden evasive actions through narrow streets, which inevitably leads to him losing his way and having to ask for directions. Mig cannot blame him so much for his poor skills of deduction. Mig is one of the best trackers on the streets and, although the Tarkie's paranoia is making his job more difficult, it is by no means making it impossible. He trails the Tarkie right back to Avenue Lorado in the red light district, which is home to the notorious Madame Bijou's brothel.

Mig sighs. He can see what the Tarkie thinks he is doing, but really there is no such thing as hiding in plain sight. There is hiding well, and hiding badly. If the Tarkie really knew the city, he would know that Bijou gets raided regularly, because Bijou's main game is not the girls, or the boys, it's gambling. The Tarkie would have been better off taking up an apartment in some filthy tenement block full of croc addicts.

The Tarkie goes up into the stairwell. Mig waits at the bottom and listens to his footsteps. He counts five floors. He pads silently upstairs. The Tarkie is living in the place right opposite Bijou's, where Old Man Guido was murdered just a few weeks back. That was a sad business. Guido was one for the stories and the tequila, not a bad man, though dangerous when provoked, mad and raging dangerous, not cold and sinister dangerous like the Alaskan. Guido is ashes now.

Mig puts his ear to the door. He hears low voices. Two speakers. Both male. There is someone else in the apartment, just as the Alaskan thought.

The Alaskan believes it is an Osirian, a man from the lost sea city. But that is not possible because everyone knows what happened in the lost city fifty years ago: all the Osirians went mad and killed themselves on a chosen day, leaping one by one into the ocean, and there they drowned. He told the Alaskan this, and the Alaskan laughed as though it were a joke. She said: That's a new one, Mig. Let's see if our friend is a fish, shall we? She laughed so hard she dropped her tea. Cleaning up her mess, Mig thought that he would not be so surprised if the Osirian (if he really is an Osirian) turned out to have scales.

Footsteps creak across the apartment. One of the men is pacing up and down, still talking quietly, but the creaking obscures the words.

Mig goes back down to the street and camps on a doorstep behind a vendor's stall a few doors down and watches Madame Bijou's customers sneak into the stairwell, some bold, some furtive. It is easy to work out which are the windows of the Tarkie's apartment. The shutters are closed. Mig waits, watching and listening to the radio for several hours, but there is no movement, not even a twitch of the shutters. The Tarkie does not come out again.

Once more Mig creeps up the stairwell and knocks on Madame Bijou's door. A girl answers. Scrawny with exploding spots and greasy spikes of hair, clearly not the immense bulk of Bijou herself.

'I want to see Madame Bijou,' says Mig.

'Bit young aren't you? Go home to your mama.'

Mig scowls.

'I'm not here for the girls. I want to see Bijou.'

'Fuck off.'

The girl shuts the door. Mig wants to shout *fuck you too* through the door, but he can't risk the Tarkie hearing his voice.

He listens again at the Tarkie's door, but this time there are no discernible voices, only the radio tuned to Station Cataveiro. He retreats.

People come home. The counted children emptying out of their schools, the factory workers and the data drones, their faces tired and lined. They go into their homes. Some of them gather in the bar at the end of the street. An enforcer walks through, slapping her baton against her leg. In the summer heat the enforcers are like crazed rats, spoiling for someone to bite. Mig has seen shins splintered with a baton just like that. He ducks into the next street and waits for the enforcer to pass before he returns. Munching on an empanada, he thinks about Pilar. He wonders where she is and what she is doing. He imagines her singing, the huge voice and the moody face. He imagines her on the roof of Station Sabado, perched among the birds with feathers falling out of her hair. He still has that green one in his pocket. His parrot girl. He imagines taking off her jumper, then her T-shirt.

The light slowly fades. Dusk creeps through the street. If lights come on behind the shutters of the fifth-floor apartment, he does not see them. Who is in there? Who is the Tarkie hiding?

Mig knows what it is to hide. He knows what it is to want to stay hidden. There is a part of him that does not want to give away the Tarkie's secret.

But the Alaskan pays, and Mig's funds must grow. It's his and Pilar's future.

24 ¦

'**Y**ou are not dead then,' says the Alaskan humorously. The woman who is perched like a jewelled beetle on the edge of the opposite chair, not quite willing to commit her full arse to its dubious surface, does not laugh. She is not the laughing kind. It is one of the reasons the Alaskan enjoys manipulating her.

'As you see, I am well,' says the woman. Her famously high, girlish voice is slightly muffled behind a designer mouth and nose mask. It does not sound like the voice of a woman who pushes people into ravines, but the Alaskan does not doubt that Xiomara is capable of such an act, nor does she underestimate her intelligence, as so many do.

'Certainly, you don't have any signs of redfleur that I can see. Your skin's still on for a start. Unless that's the reason for those gloves.'

'You are crude,' says Señorita Xiomara.

The Alaskan chuckles.

'In my own den, I am what I am. Honoured by your presence, in this case. What do you want? Come on now, out with it.'

Xiomara smoothes out a wrinkle in one white elbow-length glove. They are gloves, the Alaskan can tell, that keep the skin cool. Northern tech. The Alaskan used to own materials like those. She remembers the feel of the sheer fabric: at once weightless and protective. It made you feel invincible. The saliva is gathering under her tongue just thinking about it. Yes, she used to have things. Now she has a trunk full of grubby Patagonian peso under the bed, cash stained with other people's messy lives and transactions.

'I want the one who offended me,' says Xiomara.

'Ah, the pilot. Elusive, that one. Played you at your own game, did she?'

Xiomara's voice becomes shrill. 'She infected me!'

'Then don't come any nearer. My immune system is a puny thing.' The Alaskan hacks wetly, not bothering to reach for a tissue. Señorita Xiomara's nose shifts under the mask.

'Remember who you are talking to, Alaskan.'

'With that length of hair, could I forget?'

'Tell me now. What do you know about the pilot?'

The Alaskan shrugs. 'Not so much. She first appears on the map here in Cataveiro, a garage apprentice fixing cars. Cars like yours, I imagine. Maybe she even shined up your car, Xiomara, there's a thought, isn't it? Callejas's hands all over your pretty engine? Later on, let's see, she finds the aeroplane, somewhere in the desert, so the story goes. Now she freelances for the government. Maps what's left outside the habitable zone.'

'It is true she is a cartographer?' Xiomara's tone is incredulous.

'Mapping is a useful exercise, as far as it goes. I'm fond of maps, myself. And you're rather short on them in this country. But you're right. Doubtless she is useful in other ways too.'

'And it is the del Torres plane?'

'Is there more than one?'

'No.'

'Then you are safe enough to bet on del Torres. Who is del Torres?'

'The plane belonged to the del Torres family, they preserved it when others were destroyed. Del Torres herself was insane, a lunatic. No loss to the world. Where did the pilot come from?'

'Do I look like an oracle to you? I don't know. Mig! Where's that pilot from, what does the radio tell you?'

'Highlands,' comes the boy's voice from the next room.

'There you go. Mig says she is from the highlands, one of those small villages that scrape out a living up there. I've never been but I wouldn't recommend it as a holiday destination. Or if you do go, pack your malaria pills.'

Señorita Xiomara's brow creases. 'What are her weaknesses?'

'I don't know her personally, Xiomara. I could find out more, but that would require facilities, obviously.'

'Whatever it takes.'

Mig's voice sounds thinly from the next room. 'You should be careful. She's the lucky one.'

Xiomara tilts her head enquiringly. 'What was that?'

'Ignore him,' says the Alaskan. 'He's full of absurd superstitions. Here, have a nougat.'

She rattles the tray of sweets under Xiomara's masked nose.

'You shouldn't mock so easily, Alaskan. What do you mean, boy?'

The Alaskan is irritated by the interruption. She scratches at an insect bite on her arm. 'Tell her, Mig, if you must.'

The boy talks through the screen. 'She's lucky, is all. That's what people say. She has the spider's luck. It was spiders who led her to the plane, two hundred of them. It was in the desert. Before she came there was nothing there alive and when she arrived the spiders appeared. They showed her the way.'

The Alaskan and Xiomara wait, but nothing more is forthcoming.

'Interesting,' says Xiomara.

'Don't tell me you believe in these ridiculous stories?'

'I think luck is a curious concept, Alaskan, very curious. I would not expect one of your . . . kind to understand. There are those who might say I was unlucky my parents died. Others might say I was lucky, for I survived.' Xiomara's voice hardens. 'Lucky or not, I want the pilot, and I want her alive. Sooner or later, everyone's luck runs out. Hers will too.'

'And what are you planning to do with her, when you find her?'

'I have not yet decided.' Xiomara sits in deep reflection for a few moments, doubtless imagining the tortures she will inflict on Ramona Callejas when she gets her hands on the pilot. Two visitors in as many days – the Alaskan should count herself lucky. It is lucky, she supposes, that Xiomara came the day after the Antarctican, that there was not some unfortunate collision. The Alaskan feels a greedy hunger when she thinks about the Antarctican. He is her secret. No one else is having him – not unless the price is right, anyway.

Now that he is coming back, she will have to keep a sentry. Xiomara has a bad habit of turning up uninvited. She never gives warning, such is her terror of being assassinated. The Alaskan has occasionally toyed with the idea of having Xiomara assassinated herself, if only to see the diplomatic mess that would unravel. For now, though, Xiomara is too interesting an opponent to remove, and the book of debt is waiting.

Through the wall, the Alaskan hears a quiz show on her neighbour's radio. She listens out for the questions with one ear, answering them one by one in her head.

'You know that my parents died of redfleur,' says Xiomara quietly. 'For three days they lay in our house dying, and the only people who saw them were doctors in hazard masks and suits. I could tell they were terrified. I was not allowed to see them, of course. But I could smell it. I could smell the blood and the rotting flesh. One of the nurses came out with a bucket each day and each day I wondered what part of my parents it might contain.'

'You think too much on it,' says the Alaskan. 'Keep a gun or a syringe on yourself. If you get infected, do it quick. Make sure your bodyguards are loyal enough that they'll kill you before they kill themselves. That's my best advice.'

Señorita Xiomara gazes at her. With her perfect oval face it is the gaze of a robot, but a robot who has a secret life in the moments its owner turns away. The salt woman's brown eyes are accented with soft purple shadow; the rise of her cheekbones is artfully highlighted in blusher. The mask, in hiding the lower half of her face, only serves to accentuate the beauty of what is on display. It is not often the Alaskan sees anyone so well made-up. Looking at Xiomara makes her feel mournful for her younger self. She was radiant once. She was adored.

'There have been new cases,' Xiomara says.

'I've heard.'

'Six months ago the government found bodies near the archipelago. An entire village of bodies. The rumours say only one girl survived. That was the first.'

The Alaskan squeezes the insect bite until it produces a perfect bead of pus. 'You only have to shake a hand. It's no surprise the entire village succumbed.'

Xiomara ignores her.

'Two months ago, I heard of a poppy farm whose workforce were wiped out within days. And only three weeks past, a remote case, further north, but most certainly redfleur.' Xiomara pauses. 'The army have investigated, of course, and all the quarantines are in place, but I am highly concerned. I want you to be alert to any more cases. If necessary, I must evacuate. I cannot put myself at risk. The plants would suffer.'

'I don't doubt it,' says the Alaskan, looking at Xiomara's long, luscious sweep of treated hair. It reminds her of a girl . . . what was the name? Ah, she's forgotten. A girl from Veerdeland, with old Scandinavian blood. A girl whose hair the Alaskan once wrapped herself in like a silk veil. She knows perfectly well, as does the woman herself, that Xiomara has nothing to do with the day-to-day running of the desalination plants whose water supplements so much of the city.

Xiomara smiles prettily.

'I brought you a gift. One of those street vendors was offering them – really quite a bargain, my bodyguards tell me.'

With the contrived gesture of a magician, Xiomara produces a hand-held plastic fan with a miserly solar wrap. She thrusts it before her.

'To hold off the heat.'

'Thank you,' says the Alaskan. She manages to mask her anger as Xiomara zips up her handbag, rises, smooths her northern gloves and her northern dress, and rustles through the screen. Only when the door to the apartment has shut behind her does the Alaskan feel the heat of rage rising to her face.

A gift. A gift! This cheap tawdry thing! She flicks the switch. A whisper of warm air moves against her face. The Alaskan hurls the fan across the room. It clatters against the wall and drops to the floor. It does not break. That it does not break further incenses the Alaskan.

'That woman insults me, Mig!'

'Yes, señora.'

'She cannot think beyond her own paltry empire. She has no true ambition, only more wealth, the illusion of power, as if there is any true power to be had in this country. You know it's that woman's fault we are in this shithole. It's her who keeps me out of the enclaves. There's enough cash under this bed to purchase a river view and enough energy for you to take a hot shower every day, but they block me at every turn.' The Alaskan scrapes viciously at the insect bite. It starts to bleed. She smears the blood over the bedsheets. 'If she really knew who I had been—'

'Who were you, señora?' asks the boy dutifully.

'I was . . . someone.'

She thinks longingly of cool Arctic seasons. Every year the Alaskan dreads the onset of summer. Even in the relatively temperate climes of Patagonia, the city heats to the point of combustion. The Alaskan sweats into her bedsheets and wakes each morning with a pounding head. Sometimes she cuts her painkillers with opium, but it makes her mind lurch in a way that is both pleasant and unpleasant, like masochistic sex. Northerners like to punish the freaks. Sometimes in those days she would be overcome with recklessness and tell her lovers the truth in the middle of fucking, just to see what would happen. It was rarely good but there was a moment of giddying power in the telling.

She examines the smear of blood on the sheets. Something for Maria to wash later.

'What do we know about the pilot?'

'What I said. That's all.'

The Alaskan remembers something. 'Did you send that telegram? The first posters?'

'No, señora. You said don't send it.'

'Send it now. See what you can find out. Report only to me. I don't want you to have any dealings with that despicable woman. Understand me? No more.'

Mig nods but looks uneasy.

'Yes, señora. I mean no, señora.'

'Go. Go now. Get out.'

'Yes, señora.'

'Yes, señora, yes, señora,' mutters the Alaskan. This is what she is reduced to. Yes, señora.

Xiomara's desire is not limited to vengeance, the Alaskan is well aware of that. Xiomara wants the plane. And the more the Alaskan thinks about it, the more she begins to wonder. She has been in Cataveiro a long time. Perhaps it is time to move on. Perhaps Xiomara's tawdry barbs are a sign.

The Alaskan is wasted here among the damned. She can see exactly how Patagonia's future will pan out, clear as a knife shells peas. If the rumours about the sea city are true, and it seems likely given Mig's evidence, then her countrymen will come south. It is the perfect excuse. There will be a battle. A full-scale Boreal-Antarctican war. Someone will weaponize redfleur and make a fat profit. Patagonia will be squeezed in the middle until the country falls into a second Blackout. The survivors will go north or south, or regress to primeval status. Plants and insects will choke the continent. It will be a living dead zone.

The Alaskan needs new challenges.

She has never seen Antarctica.

25

aeo gazes at the contents of the shop's first aisle. Soap, toothpaste, mouth-and-nose masks, cheap painkiller patches – he takes a packet. Strange that the contents of a shelf can say so much, and so little. The packaging of the goods is plain, marked with the spider glyph that denotes government-issue produce. He hesitates, then puts two face masks into his basket. The next aisle offers potatoes and quinoa, dried packet soup, imported grain. Alaskan grain. Antarctican rice – the expensive stuff – is at the back of the store. Taeo is not sure he can afford Antarctican rice, but he craves it.

At home they each had their own method, but despite Shri's antipathy for cooking it was her way that prevailed in the end; she would not give up until he seceded. An announcement in the store makes him jump, but then he realizes it is Shri speaking, offering her instructions in a slightly distorted voice. First soak the rice. A few drops of oil – no, not that much. Cloves, cinnamon, cardamom. Let it cook through its own steam.

Taeo can see it: the bowl on the table full of the hot fluffy lozenges. The rice in Cataveiro is extortionate, and he has no idea how long he is going to be here, and even if he had limitless cash there is no stove to cook it on. He carries his life on his back, like the pilot said he should, and what he has found is that his life is small. As small as a box of rice. He stares at the shelves and upon the shelves, the boxes and tins and glass jars that contain the ingredients for the preservation of life, and he notices a hole in one of the boxes. As he stands there, staring, a small insect crawls out from the hole and along the shelf.

The burst of vertigo catches him unaware. He puts his hand to his temples, startled by the giddiness. His vision fades at the edges. That's weird. What he sees tunnels to the slow motion of the bug as it traverses the shelf, its tiny feelers probing the air ahead.

'Do you mind, I need—'

A woman manoeuvres herself in front of him. When he steps back, Taeo feels a wash of nausea, and for a moment he thinks he might actually faint.

The sick feeling fades. His vision clears.

He is standing in the aisle of the store, clutching a basket containing two masks and a packet of painkillers. The woman gives him an odd look. She skirts around him. Around the circle that goes with him everywhere. One thing he does not need to pack.

He puts some things in the basket, hardly caring what they are, just wanting to get out of the airless shop. He pays and walks out into the sunlight. It is mid-afternoon and already the temperatures are soaring. This morning he visited the Alaskan for a second time. Once again they talked. Once again in circles. Once again she intimated the things she knew, the many things. But when he pressed her on progress with the Antarcticans, he received nothing but a canny smile.

I told you, it takes time. They're careful, your lot. Very careful. Don't leave clues.

But you do think—

Oh yes. It's only a matter of time.

He trusts her less today and he barely trusted her yesterday. He cannot be sure he is doing the right thing. If she doesn't come through, what will they do then? Could he commandeer a Patagonian boat, take Vikram home himself? The only other option is to return to Fuego and throw himself upon Ivra's mercy, and he cannot bear the idea of having gone through all this for nothing.

He cannot remember ever having so little faith in his own judgement. All his life he has been decisive and confident. If a decision was right, it was right. If it was wrong, let it be wrong and take the consequences. The important thing was that the decision was taken, in love and work and everything in between. Now he wavers over the tiniest action. Every thought, every word he utters is subject to dozens of minute deliberations.

If you say this . . .
If you don't say this . . .
He'll trust you . . .
He won't trust you . . .
He doesn't trust you anyway . . .
You can't trust her . . .
You don't know what she knows . . .
And now you've said that . . .

Cataveiro is chipping away at the core of who he is, and he hates the city for it. You ask a Patagonian the history of their city and they'll spin you tales until your head is dizzy, but the truth is, the city's name is only one letter away from the Portuguese word for captivity. That is the only story Taeo needs to know.

When he climbs the stairs to the rooms (he cannot think of them as his rooms, or their rooms, they are simply the rooms) he hears voices. There is a burst of low laughter, friendly, conspiratorial. Is it coming from the fifth floor? It sounds like Vikram's voice. He is sure of it. He climbs faster. Vikram should know not to—

At the top of the building, a girl is sitting on the threshold of Madame Bijou's. He has seen her a couple of times, a funny-looking thing with acne and protruding eyes that give her an expression of permanent surprise. She is smoking a cigarette and nattering into a handheld radio. The voice coming out of it is male. When the girl sees Taeo she stops talking and waits until he has gone into the rooms before resuming her conversation.

The girl's secrecy instantly lowers his mood, as does the confirmation of his own paranoia. He takes the shopping inside. The door to the room where Vikram sleeps is closed, and he finds himself relieved. It is easier not to face the Osirian. A twinge of by now habitual guilt accompanies the thought. It wasn't meant to be like this. They should have been on a ship by now. A pardon for him and a fresh start for Vikram. Instead, the lies he has told seem bigger and more impossible to retract with each passing day. He feels transparent, as though Vikram might see through him at any moment. But even if he wanted to, how could he tell the truth now?

Taeo unpacks the bags slowly. Most of what he has bought can be prepared by pouring boiling water over it. Packets of powdered nutrition. Fuel rather than food.

The door to Vikram's room is closed.

Suddenly anxious, Taeo knocks on the door.

'Hello?'

There is no answer. He eases the handle quietly and pushes the door ajar. Inside no lights are on; other than a sliver of daylight through the shutters, the room is entirely dark. Taeo has to open the door further to make out the figure of Vikram – it *is* Vikram – lying on the bed.

His heart rate evens again. He is about to close the door when Vikram stirs.

'You're back.'

'Did I wake you up?'

'No. I was just hoping the dark might help.'

'Help what?'

Vikram rolls slowly to sitting and swings his legs over the bed. He kneads the heel of his hand into his forehead. His face is screwed up in frustration or pain.

'It's these fucking headaches.'

'You're getting headaches?'

'I've been getting them, I don't know, ever since the shipwreck. I thought it was because I was dehydrated, but I'm fine now. My leg's good, I'm eating enough, everything's fine apart from being cooped up in this fucking place, so why am I still getting them? And why are they getting worse? This isn't right, it isn't *me*.'

Vikram leans his head into his palms, kneading ferociously.

'If I could just get a drink of tea. I know I'd feel better.'

Tea. The simplicity of the request relieves Taeo; tea he can deal with.

'You should have said. We can get tea. I'll go back out now, if that helps.'

'Can you get coral tea?'

'Coral, what's that? An – Osiris thing?' He still feels nervous saying the city's name, even in private.

'Maybe. I don't know. I don't know where it came from. I don't know, I never went to a tea factory. I just need it.'

'Is it made from coral?'

'No, it's the colour, the colour, not the stuff.' Vikram looks up at him agitatedly. He almost looks like he might cry. 'You can't get it here, can you?'

There is something uncomfortably familiar about Vikram's gestures. His tone of voice, the tremor of desperation. His hands clenched into fists. For a moment, Taeo has the surreal sensation of looking into a mirror, seeing himself as he must have appeared to others. It is not a pleasant experience. On the contrary, it makes him want to run, as fast as he can, away from this room and everything in it and anyone who might ever see him again.

He pulls himself together.

'How often did you drink this coral tea?'

'Every day. At least, when I was in the city it was every day. Less before that, on the other side. In the west, what we had wasn't as good. You cut it with rum, you know, when it's cold. When I used to go out with the work parties . . . But everyone drank it.'

The mumbled words seem to cost Vikram a great effort.

'And on the boat? You had it on the boat?'

'Yes, we had supplies. Some we lost.'

'Is it just the headaches? Is there anything else?'

'Like what?'

'You said you needed the tea.'

'I do, I know it'll fix me.'

'So you're thinking about it a lot. All the time.'

'I suppose so. I know it'll help, so yes, I'm thinking about it. I'm thinking about anything that'll help, I don't care what it is.'

'There's quite a simple explanation,' says Taeo.

'What's that then?'

'You're addicted.'

Vikram laughs. The movement makes him wince. 'To tea?'

'You're getting the cravings, the rebound headaches. It's obvious. Whatever it was you were drinking in Osiris, it's highly addictive.'

Vikram frowns. 'I'm not sure. Isn't that a bit far-fetched? Coral tea? Seriously? I mean just because you—' He breaks off, but Taeo can finish the sentence for himself.

'Trust me,' he says. 'I know what I'm talking about.'

It is Vikram's turn to regard him for a long time. Suddenly, Taeo's heart is beating fast. The walls feel very close. He is acutely aware of how thick the air sits. The infernal heat. Why does it matter if this man, this stranger, knows him for what he is? But it does matter. It matters because Vikram is the way back. And it matters, he realizes, because he cares about this man's opinion.

'The poppy fields,' says Vikram.

He does not need to say anything else. Taeo can see Vikram's growing comprehension as the final pieces slot into place. He is surprised by the relief, how large it is, how shaky and abruptly vulnerable he feels.

'Do you want a glass of water?' he asks. Vikram nods.

Taeo goes to the fridge and gets two glasses. The fridge is their single luxury, a luxury he appreciates more than ever now, as he gulps down mouthfuls of the cold water. He can feel the coolness tracing a line from his throat down to his stomach.

He turns to Vikram. 'Can I show you something?'

'Sure.'

Taeo retrieves the holoma from his room. 'This is an Antarctican device.'

Vikram nods, an expression of curiosity replacing his earlier agitation. Unlike the Patagonians, the sight of the machine does not appear to disturb the Osirian. Taeo activates the holoma and pulls up Shri in stasis. Her hologram shimmers between them.

'This is my partner.'

'She's very beautiful.'

Shri is frowning a little. Taeo used to think it meant she was cross about something, but in fact it is her perpetual expression of greeting for the universe: Hello, what are you, how are you?

'When I came here,' he begins, 'I'd lost everything. Shri . . . well, she may never forgive me. My children are on the other side of the Southern Ocean, being told by everyone they know that I'm a traitor. People are vicious. The ones you'd never guess are the worst, the ones you thought were your friends. Shri and the kids had to go and live with my cousin in some back-ice mining town, miles from anywhere. Anyway, when I got here, I had one thing. I was rich.' He laughs bitterly. 'Antarctican currency is worth a lot in this country. The opium was . . . too easy.'

Vikram studies the hologram. 'Your partner. Shri. She's alive?'

'Yes, she's alive. And she hates me.'

'Then you haven't lost everything.'

'I left her a disgraced citizen and I'll return to her an addict, if she'll ever have me back.'

'You've got to stop feeling sorry for yourself,' says Vikram.

'What?'

Vikram repeats each word, slowly, as if talking to an imbecile. 'You've got to stop feeling sorry for yourself.'

Taeo stares at the younger man, unable to mask his indignation. 'Who the fuck—'

'I mean it,' says Vikram. 'You want to get better, right? You want to get home? So start fighting. You've got someone to go back to. So fight for them.'

Vikram is leaning forwards now, his eyes, those intense brown eyes, blazing with a passion Taeo has not seen before.

'The friends I grew up with are dead,' he says. 'The woman that I loved is dead. So don't talk to me about having lost everything. Your family are safe. You have Shri. You have your children. And now you've got me.'

The words are a shock. This is the closest Vikram has come to admitting he knows Taeo's game. And he hasn't finished.

'Fortunately for you, I want to go to Antarctica. I want a new life. So from now on, if it's no addictive coral tea for me, and I doubt we're going to find any in Cataveiro, then it's no opium for you. Deal?'

Taeo feels dazed. It's as if he has been struck a blow to the head. 'All right,' he manages. 'Deal.'

But as soon as he has spoken, the cravings start. The thought of the smoke, the sweet oblivion . . .

Stop it. Stop it now. You've got to stop or it's going to get you for good.

'Tell me about Shri,' says Vikram. 'And will you turn that thing off? I don't want to offend you, but it's freaking me out having her in the room with us.'

Taeo laughs. The laugh surprises him, and after a moment, Vikram laughs too.

'All right.' He wraps the holoma carefully in its cloth. 'Shri. Well, she's – she's fierce.' That is the first word that comes to his mind. Fierce about life, fierce about love. Like the sun at the close of winter, with all its heat and potency and wonder. 'She's strong. Intelligent. Not just smart – she understands people, you know. What they're about. You'll meet her, when we get to Antarctica.'

'I'd like that.'

'I met her at First Light. It's a festival we have, at the end of winter. People in the streets, dancing . . . It's special. She went against her family to be there. And to be with me.'

That interests Vikram.

'Her family don't like you?'

'She has Indian heritage. I'm Brazilian. I mean, not any more, but those roots go deep, for some people. We have different languages of the home. Her family would have preferred her to stay in her own community. But sometimes I wonder . . . I don't know.'

'Wonder what?'

'If it was something more than that.' Taeo shrugs. 'It seemed too easy an excuse for them. Who knows, perhaps I'll never know.'

'My city was divided too. The other side, the City side, that was the original Osiris. In the west, where I grew up, we had – well, we had nothing. But I lived on the City side, for a while. I got across the border.'

'What were you, an activist?'

Vikram grins. 'Something like that.'

He remembers Vikram's talk of *underwater*.

'Is that why they put you in jail?'

'Yeah. Twice.'

'I don't suppose it was an easy task.'

The Osirian shakes his head. 'No. But someone had to do it. I was told that, a long time ago. Sometimes there's no one to do a thing but you. I suppose I always tried to live up to that. I don't know if I succeeded.'

'The woman you loved. What was her name?'

A muscle works in Vikram's throat. When he speaks, his voice is gruff and stifled. 'She was called Adelaide.'

'She must have been glad to have known you.'

'She was an idiot,' says Vikram angrily. 'She got herself killed. It was so fucking typical of her, to do that.'

'It wasn't your fault.'

'It was my fault. It was both of us. We were both stupid.' His voice grows quieter. 'Sometimes I wish I'd died in there too. I did think about it, you know. Afterwards. More than once. But where I come from, that's not what you do.'

Vikram falls silent. Taeo can sense the depths of his grief: so vast, so achingly empty. To imagine Shri dead is to imagine the world tearing open beneath his feet; it is cataclysmic. Unthinkable. The Osirian is right. He still has her. He still has the children. Most importantly, he has a chance to win Shri back. He pictures them now. Early evening. The light is long and steady over the ice fields behind Nyari Town. They'll be eating together. Kadi directing the feeding of Nisha because she takes after her mother, that one. That gives him a pang because he always loved preparing the family meal, with all the small squabbles and triumphs of the day that emerged over eating. The sense of togetherness.

Vikram stirs from his contemplation.

'So what do we do next?'

Taeo speaks firmly. 'I'll go back to the Alaskan tomorrow. I'll get information out of her. She knows more than she's saying. I can't believe she doesn't have Antarctican connections.'

A decision. A decision that is firm and solid; he can examine it from all angles and know that it is right.

And something else. He has made a friend; his first in this foreign country.

In his sleep that night, Taeo dreams of the smoke. The perfect, rising helix coil, the wisps of silvery white in the dark room, his body suspended, cocooned in it. He dreams that the smoke lifts him into the sky and carries him gently home. It drops him in their bedroom where the blue lights of Vosti glow through the crack in the curtains, and Shri is by his side. She whispers: I love you, I forgive you. They have both become the smoke, wrapped in the ecstasy of their reunification. When he wakes, the dream is so perfect there are tears on his face that he did not know he had cried.

A new day. A new identity.

The first thing he does when he gets up is to take the pipe and the lighters and all the paraphernalia he has kept and stuff them into a bag. He'll throw it when he leaves the building.

He dresses carefully for his appointment with the Alaskan. For the first time in weeks he shaves, watching his jawline emerge from the stubble, surprised by the transformation offered by this simple act. He has grown accustomed to a wild, flustered appearance. Red veins mark his corneas, and there are new, deeper lines around the eyes and lips, but there too is the man he recognizes: the engineer he used to be. This is a man who knows about diamond and yttrium and the energy of the future. A father, and a partner.

Today will be the day. Today, he will get what they need.

26 ¦

Carla's niece is a slip of a girl, a dreamer, the kind of child you cannot help but fear is too fragile for life's rough hand. She is nervous and frightened. Carla encourages her gently.

'Come on, pet. Tell Ramona what you saw.'

Ramona crouches so she is on the same level as the child.

'Anything you can remember, any little detail, will help me.'

Slowly, holding her impatience in check, she extracts Gabi's story. The girl was on her way uphill, 'to see old Inés'. She was instructed to check on Inés and if she needed it, collect water from the tank. 'Because, you know, it's heavy, and Carla said she shouldn't strain herself with the—' she glances nervously at Carla but the woman nods: you can say it '—the jinn.'

She saw the first raider approaching the shack from higher up the mountain. It wasn't one of their people. Gabi knew that right away. She knew she had to hide. She dropped down to the ground and watched from between the grasses.

The first raider was a woman. She looked like a Patagonian but not like a Patagonian. She was sunburned, but under it her skin was pale. She was very tall and she wore clothes that were the same colour as the dry scrub, as if she were one of those lizards who sit motionless for hours, not noticed by anyone, because their scales look like everything around them.

The woman moved like a reptile too, quiet and creeping, in a way that scared Gabi and made her certain she was up to no good. Then she saw the others. There were two men, converging on the shack. Gabi was too terrified to move.

The raiders did not strike immediately. They waited for a long time, Gabi was not sure how long, but at least thirty minutes. In that time Gabi did not dare to move. Her bladder was bursting. She was scared she would pee and the sound would be enough to alert them. At last she saw Inés come out of the house. Inés saw the first raider but she didn't look scared, said Gabi. She looked angry. She shouted something. Gabi thought it was, 'What do you want?'

Inés turned to go back inside and as she did there was a soft sound, *phutt*, like that, and something struck her. She looked down. Gabi saw a thing, something metal, shiny, *robotic*, sticking out of Inés's stomach. Inés fell to the ground.

The raider woman walked towards Inés. Gabi held both hands over her mouth so she would not scream. The woman knelt and looked at her lying there, helpless, making no sound. Gabi was sure she was going to kill her. Then the raider tested her weight. She hoisted the old woman over her shoulder and walked away, the other raiders following behind her, one watching their backs until they disappeared out of sight.

At the end of her story, the girl whispers, 'What are you going to do?'

'I'm going to hunt them down. I'm going to get her back.'

'Are they cannibals?'

'Don't be silly, Gabi,' says Carla, but her voice is fearful, and Ramona wonders what other ideas have been terrorizing Félix's people.

'No,' she says. Carla looks at her. She repeats it, firmly, 'No. They aren't cannibals.'

'Then what are they?'

'They're northerners.'

The night-vision goggles. The paralysing dart. It is Boreal tech, and Boreal or not, the raiders are working for northerners. Of that she is certain.

But what do they want with the highlanders?

Carla has little more to tell. They had sent a tracking party, but as with the villagers who disappeared in the storm, they found nothing. Carla is distraught.

'I've let you down, Ro. I said I'd look after her and I've failed.'

Ramona hugs her tightly.

'You haven't failed. You haven't let me down. I'm going to find her. I promise.'

She has one last question for Carla.

'Félix doesn't know?'

Carla shakes her head. Ramona takes Carla's face in her hands. She can feel the roughness of Carla's skin, lined and mottled from a lifetime under the baking sun.

'Please, if you hear from him, don't say anything. He'll only worry.'

From the sliding city she flies the short distance east to the coast. The plane is not handling as smoothly as it should. The unsettling whining noise is back. Whatever the Antarctican did, it was a temporary fix, or not a fix at all. She feels almost paralysed with frustration when she thinks of the ludicrous route she has taken: all the way down from the Nazca Desert to the archipelago and back up again, when if she had only known about the jinn she would have crossed the continent directly.

Perhaps then she would have been ahead of the raiders. She could have protected her mother.

Or they would have taken you too.

That is what Carla said, but Ramona cannot bring herself to believe it. She could have done something. Now all she can do is guess. She is pursuing a ghost.

There is one more functioning desalination plant on the east coast between here and Panama, an independent, so she need not worry about Xiomara's influence. Félix's ship will also need to stop there, and there is a chance that their paths will intersect. She wants to see him; at the same time she dreads a meeting which will force her to lie.

The windshield absorbs the sun, building heat inside the cockpit. Ramona drains another water bottle. She watches the shadow of the plane flitting over the terrain beneath her, and as always when she flies this way, she remembers the long journey by foot made from the sliding city to Cataveiro. She remembers sucking water from huge cacti, the slimy texture of the flesh they chewed on for sustenance.

From above, this territory looks harmless. The land is patterned with swirling stripes where mudslides have crashed through, now pretty to behold. Disintegrating buildings look like a child's toys strewn across the floor. You cannot hear the sound of rockfall, or the dull implosion of another roof caving in. Out of habit, Ramona takes out her master map, comparing map to ground, pencilling in the slight alterations she notices to the landscape. The precision and focus of the exercise calms her. For a few precious minutes she can lose herself in calculations.

The plane judders alarmingly. One by one Ramona checks her instruments. Everything reads as it should. The battery is three-quarters full and charging cleanly, so what is causing that noise? She touches the instrument panel. *Colibrí* cannot let her down now.

'Come on, *Colibrí*. It's not that far now. This is easy.'

As they draw nearer to the coast, she spies the lead line of a water pipe. A recurrent glint catches her eye: sunlight on water gushing from a break. The sight makes her hot with fury. All that precious water sucked up by the thirsty ground, never reaching the small villages tucked in the lee of the mountains who will be dependent on this supply. Pipe breaks are more often sabotage than accident. Guerrillas, seeking a tactical advantage.

Or raiders, she thinks with a chill.

Another hour's flying brings the ocean into view. She descends and heads a short distance out to sea, scanning in both directions for sign of the fleet, but the sea is empty. Returning inland, she makes another awkward landing, a rocking, skidding manoeuvre that flips the contents of her stomach.

What if the plane gives out before you find Inés?

No. That cannot happen. Not to Ramona, not with her luck. She has not one, but three missions now. She has to find her mother. And when that is done, she has to find the Antarcticans and give them Taeo's message. Taeo promised they would help her to get the medicine she needs for Inés.

An uneasy thought crosses her mind. What if the message had something to do with these raids on the villages?

No, that is ridiculous. Why would Antarctica be mixed up in something like this?

Still the thought lingers, unpleasantly.

The workers at the desalination plant are not aware of the break in the pipe. Ramona draws a map and marks the location. A team of them take out a repair truck.

Ramona exchanges news with a group of workers. She tells them that the pirate El Tiburón has been spotted near Fuego but not yet caught, but his associate is on trial soon, perhaps this week, and the city of Cataveiro is embroiled in another quarrel with the government over taxes. They tell her the pedlars report a new dispute between the Solar Corporation and the Boreal States. The Boreals say they own the patents to greenhouse technology. The Corporation claim they are using new, innovative agricultural techniques. The workers tell her, uneasily, that there are rumours of a new outbreak of redfleur. Even up north, they are worried, and it is spreading south.

'I've heard that too,' she says. They stand for a moment in unhappy conference.

She asks if the ships have passed. They say only one. Not the *Aires*.

Late, she comments.

They agree. It is late. It happens sometimes. Pirates, or storms.

Ramona cannot afford to wait. She'll have to miss Félix.

Before she leaves she asks the plant manager if she has heard of raiders taking people from the villages. The woman is concerned.

'We've heard nothing here. But we don't have much contact with the south – only the radio, and travellers like you.'

'It's in the highlands,' she says. 'They're kidnapping people – vulnerable people. I think they're northerners.'

The plant manager looks perplexed. 'I've heard of money kidnappings – but taking people from the villages? That's new.'

'You should warn your staff. If any of them have families . . .'

'I will do. Thanks for the heads-up.'

Ramona pays for her water and returns to the plane. She is in the cockpit, pulling on her parachute, when she spies the man hastening towards her in the rear viewfinder. It is one of the plant workers, dressed in plain coveralls. The man comes up to the cockpit. He glances quickly behind him.

'I heard you speaking to the manager.'

Ramona tightens the parachute straps. 'Yes?'

'I— About the people.'

'What can you tell me?'

The man hesitates.

'What you said – about them being taken – it's true. Nobody dares talk about it but everyone knows it's going on. Northern raiders have been coming down the past couple of years, further south each time. They take people to the Exchange. One of the ships picks them up – I don't know which one – but that's what I heard.'

Again, he checks the space behind him. 'That's all I know.'

Ramona grips his arm. 'Thank you. Thank you so much.'

'Did they get one of yours?'

'They took my mother.'

'Oh. God. I'm so sorry. I hope you find her.'

Ramona smiles grimly. 'That's where I'm going now.'

The man strokes the plane's nose with wistful fingers. 'Good luck.'

'Do you know why? Why they would want people?'

The man shakes his head.

'If it's northerners, I don't want to. But you'll find them. I've heard the stories about you. Your aeroplane is beautiful. I've always thought the hummingbird was lucky.'

What lies north of here is unchartered. Ramona has never flown into the Amazon Desert. She has only the stories of the pedlars who came to the sliding city when she was a child: tales of sandstorms as huge as a mountain and mirages that dissolve before your eyes.

She flies north between the highlands and the Espinhaço mountain range, their bald peaks rising and receding starkly, as if it is they who are moving while she remains static. The sky is clear, her vision perfect, but mountain flying is strange and sometimes disorientating. She feels that now. A sense of not-rightness, as though the world has tilted and with it her perceptions. She pushes the plane, propelled by fear, shutting her ears to the protesting engine and letting the battery drop below seventy per cent.

On the edge of the desert she spies a camp of traders with their carts and desert motorcycles, and spirals softly down to intersect them. They look up as the plane approaches. It is a bad sign if they can hear the aircraft from the ground. She ignores that too.

She opens the hatch, moving slowly, with more than her habitual caution, the gun ready at her waistband. The traders are a camp of twelve or so, men and women, dressed in desert clothes. As she jumps down from the aircraft she recognizes one or two faces from previous encounters and relaxes a little. The traders know who she is, but exchanges are cautious until she talks to the leader of the caravan. They confirm they are both Panama bound, and he invites her to join the overnight camp.

After that, everyone wants to see the plane. Ramona gives them the superficial tour, batting away playfully probing questions with a smile and a laugh. She never lets anyone have more than a cursory glance at the instrument panel. When they are satisfied, she locks the hatch and asks to take a look at their motorcycles. She admires the robust desert riders, and they stand about in the evening light talking about engines and rudimentary mechanics, sharing tips and tales of the storms they have suffered, each a little more incredible than the last, in the way of travellers north of the habitable zone, until supper is ready.

Ramona has always felt an affinity with these itinerants. She feels it more strongly than ever now, knowing there is no turning back. The emptiness of the land ahead is a pulse in her head, its beat at once a call and a warning. The salty winds and cool oceans of the archipelago lie thousands of kilometres to the south, perhaps out of reach for good. Regardless of what goes down in Panama, Señorita Xiomara has put a price on Ramona's head. That alone is enough to sever her connection with the government; Lygia will never trust her again, and for that Ramona cannot blame her. She has made her choice.

A part of her life is over. Now she has reason to be glad that she has never, in all the years of mapping, disclosed the location of the sliding city.

The traders heat packet soup and potatoes on a small portable stove. Over supper, the party exchange stories. Ramona eats quickly, grateful for the warmth of the food and the steaming, bitter tea brewed by the cook as the land temperature cools; an opportunity to sit and listen, without thinking. Then someone asks how she got the plane.

'That's a long story,' she replies. But they insist.

'Must be a good story.'

'Or make it a good one.'

A ripple of laughter around the camp. They nod encouragingly. Tell us, go on. We want to hear it. Did the spiders show you, like they say? Ramona hides her reluctance. To refuse would be a discourtesy after they have shown her hospitality. The least she can offer them is a tale.

'Well, it starts in Cataveiro. I know, all the best ones do. I was doing my apprenticeship in a garage, cleaning the army trucks, and the cars owned by rich folk from the enclaves. Sometimes people waited around while I cleaned, and they talked about this and that, the way people do. There was a woman from the south who wore a pendant with the Nazca spider. She had a beautiful voice, and a beautiful car, and I always took particular care while I was cleaning it. Yes, I had favourites.'

They laugh again.

'She could tell that I liked the car. She asked me if I'd like to have one of my own one day, and I said yes, of course. Well, who wouldn't?'

There are appreciative nods around the circle. She cannot help glancing towards the silver-winged plane. Its cells are charging up the battery as it glows in the last of the sunlight.

'She asked me why. I told her that if I owned a machine like hers I would go places where people didn't usually go. I'd explore the wetlands and the stormlands. I said I would make maps, like those I'd made of Cataveiro already. That interested her. She told me there was a better machine than a car to do that, so she had heard.'

'Was it hers?' asks a round-faced young man.

'No. But she knew a story about the plane, which I'll tell to you now. It was the last of its kind, she said. It had disappeared with its owner, half a century ago in the year of the storm, you know the one, when the sea city disappeared.'

Murmurs of assent. She hears the soft whine of a desert wind and the cook adjusts the windbreaker around the stove.

'The owner's name was Violeta del Torres. Her family owned a number of prominent radio stations, and they had money. The plane had been preserved and passed down from generation to generation, but it was like an object in a museum, never used. Until Violeta. She decided she was going to make it fly. She was a reckless character. She loved the power of flying. It became . . .' Ramona thinks. 'I suppose you could say it was a kind of addiction for her. She liked to fly through storms. The more catastrophic the storm, the greater the lure. Her family despaired. Not only were her escapades illegal, they were convinced she would kill herself. They tried everything to stop her – reason, entreaties, even threatening to lock her away. In the end she took the plane and cut all contact with them.'

Ramona's audience is rapt.

'That was the last they saw of her?'

'She was witnessed flying out towards the Atacama Desert, at the head of a storm. No one knew why she went. Some say she had the jinn. Some say her mind was stolen by the winds. No one ever found her, alive or dead. They assumed she had crashed in some uninhabited place, perhaps out to sea. But the woman at the garage told me, del Torres's aeroplane is out there somewhere. And I knew then that I had to look for it. I can't explain – but I knew it was out there.'

'And you found it.'

'Yes, I found it.' She lets the pause drag out a little. 'It took me a long time, but I found it.'

'How?'

Ramona glances around the camp. A woman stretches out on a sleeping bag, her head propped on her hand. A man watches her over the rim of his tea mug.

'I spent all my savings on an old solarcycle. It took me three weeks to get it fit for travel. I hitched a ride with the army as far as the mountains and after that it was me and the bike. I had provisions for three weeks, no more. I went all over the Atacama Desert. Of the few travellers I met, none had heard of the plane. Days passed. I began to doubt the woman's story. I was almost ready to give up, convinced that Violeta must have crashed into the sea after all. I had only two days left of supplies. And that was when the spiders appeared.

'I spotted the first one scuttling past my foot. It joined another, and another, and then I realized there were hundreds of them, all running in one direction. A river of spiders. They were the first living creatures

I had seen in the desert. When I put my hand in the way of their path they ran around it and carried on. They had a purpose, I thought. I left the bike where it was and I followed them. Why? I don't know. It didn't feel like a choice. I walked for over an hour. I was thinking, how do they live here, where there isn't even a fly? Where have they come from? After a while I could see the old telescope array, away to the right, where I'd already searched and found nothing. And then the spiders disappeared into a hole in the ground.'

She waits.

'And?'

'And I looked up, and there it was. The aeroplane. Its body was the colour of the desert, it blended almost perfectly into the background.'

'That's the truth?'

She smiles mysteriously.

'The truth is whatever you believe.'

The woman on the sleeping bag sits up.

'What about Violeta del Torres? Did you find her?'

Ramona pictures the site. The long shadows of the derelict telescope array fell across the plane, perched on the desert floor as though it had alighted there only moments before, with the hatch jammed halfway open. Inside was the fragile skeleton of Violeta del Torres, her skull dipped towards her sternum. Clothes still swaddled the human remains, sculpted and stiffened by the winds that swept through the barren desert. She remembers gently removing the body from the cockpit, and the way it disintegrated in her hands, as though Violeta had held together only long enough to be discovered, before she could disappear completely. She remembers lying in the desert that night with the unearthly clarity of the heavens opening above her and wondering if this was the last thing Violeta del Torres had witnessed, and if so, if perhaps her life had ended well.

She remembers drawing the lines of the hummingbird in the sand where the molecules of Violeta had dissipated, vowing: I will keep the secret of your grave.

'No,' she says. 'I never found her.'

'It's a great mystery,' says the eldest of the group. Ramona feels his gaze upon her, thoughtful and intelligent. 'You were meant to find the plane, it seems.'

'I like to think it found me. But I had to make a deal with the government.' She grimaces. 'Give me sanction to fly, I said, and I'll make you maps. I'll find out what's left in the habitable zone. Funnily enough, they weren't so difficult to persuade . . .'

'And you're headed now to Panama?'

'Yes. To the Exchange.'

'We'll be following you,' says the older man.

Ramona hesitates. She does not want to bring bad feeling to the camp, but it would be foolish not to use the knowledge of these travellers.

'Someone I know was taken, from a village in the highlands, by northern raiders, but that's all I know. Have you heard anything?'

The atmosphere around the camp is suddenly charged. Conversations cease abruptly. One member of the group gets up and strides away, disappearing into the gathering darkness outside the camp.

The older man says quietly, 'You are not the only one to have lost someone. We don't speak of it. There is nothing we can tell you. Perhaps we will learn more in Panama.'

'I'm sorry to upset anyone,' she says. 'But if we have information between us, we should share it.'

'There is none,' he says firmly, and to her annoyance, she understands the conversation to be closed. She listens to others take their turn to talk, but now she finds it impossible to concentrate.

As the sun disappears, the company draw closer together. A flask of sweetened rum is passed around. The alcohol makes Ramona drowsy. Voices rise and fall in quiet rhythm, faces are softened by the glow from the stove and the torches they have placed in the ground. Her tiredness is strong now. She wants to sleep; the faster the night is over, the sooner she can be on her way.

Then she hears the word north.

'A few years ago, before I joined you, one of my old group split in Panama. No word to where he was going but we all knew. He'd talked about north before. He became obsessed. He had these mad ideas of stowing away on a Boreal ship.'

'We've all heard of someone who's gone north,' says another. 'And I tell you, the one thing's the same for all – they don't come back.'

'I knew a boy who did.'

'How d'you know he ever got there?'

'Said so. He'd seen things.'

'He said so?'

The man's tone is sceptical, but he cannot quite conceal his curiosity. Looking around the circle, Ramona sees the same intrigue in each of the travellers' faces. They know that the story will be exaggeration at best, but they have to hear it. The north is its own drug. The woman speaking, stretched out on her sleeping bag, knows this. She takes her time before replying, catching each pair of eyes around the circle, tiny spots of torchlight reflected in the centres of her pupils.

'The people up there aren't like us. They're each hooked up to a web of robotics. They've got machines that sit between their shoulder blades.' The woman gestures, twisting her arm behind her back. 'And this web is alive. It can decide things, with or without them agreeing. And it makes them live for hundreds of years, whether they want to or not. It can fix when they're sick, see.'

'That's a load of shit,' mutters one of the party.

Another says, 'What about the jinn, Cristina? Does it destroy the jinn too?'

Ramona feels a shiver run down her spine. She draws her coat more tightly around her. She can feel the cold now, a deep chill in her hands and feet, and on her bare face.

Cristina shakes her head. 'They don't have the jinn. And another thing this boy said. He said their eyes are weird from the web. It turns them black, like lava stone. Or maybe they're born with eyes like that, he couldn't tell. Then again, he had been talking to a nirvana, so he was probably mesmerized.'

A flutter of agitation runs through the camp. A nirvana? Why would he – how was there – are they – common, up there?

'More than you'd think. They keep their heads down. Boreal law protects them, but it makes no odds. If they're found out, they might as well kill themselves. Lots of them do.'

'What's a nirvana?'

Everyone turns to look at the speaker, the youngest member of the group. The others are incredulous. You don't know? They're freaks, they're – not natural. Ramona says nothing, but she feels the collective terror of the camp. Nirvanas are an old dark dread, like witches or ghosts, to be evoked on a night such as this when anything could come out of the shadows. Ramona has never met one. She is not sure if she believes they truly exist.

The old man, Aris, says, 'When the Blackout virus killed millions, there were a few, very few, who survived. The virus altered them. It rewired their brains. Nirvanas are their descendants. It is said they can read minds, among other things.'

There is a protracted pause while the company digests this. The conversation picks up again.

'This boy you met, Cristina. I don't believe he ever went north. People that go Boreal never come back. Never.'

'He escaped, didn't he. He was captured. They were going to cut him up and experiment on him, but he managed to get away.'

'That's what they do with the people they take. Experiment on them.'

Suddenly, Ramona's heart is racing very fast.

'You don't know that,' she says. 'You don't know that's what they do.'

Aris interjects quickly. 'Hearsay and rumour, that's all. The truth is, we don't know what the Boreal States do or don't have, because they do not wish us to find out. They are secretive. They will keep their Neon technology from the Corporation and Antarctica at all cost, locked up in the knowledge banks, as they have done ever since the Blackout.'

'You say they have Neon technology, Aris. What if it's something different – something new?'

'Neon or new is irrelevant,' he replies. 'Whatever it is, we don't want it here.'

'Fucking right. They can keep their robotics.'

'Now think about it,' says Aris. 'Have you ever seen a Boreal crewman with wires? With eyes like lava stone? No. They look like us.'

The us is inclusive, and Ramona understands it to be not only Patagonians, but what they are, and what she is: traveller, or outlaw; those who flee before a wind they do not understand but know must be kept behind them at all times.

Cristina grumbles. 'You ruin all the fun, Aris.'

'You can rely on me for that,' he replies.

Ramona's attention is drawn inexorably to the old man. His skin is weathered and wrinkled, his white hair and beard are sparse, but he sits very erect, without stooping. And his eyes – his eyes she recognizes. They are the same eyes of the pedlar as she saw him for the first time in the sliding city. That man must be long dead, but they hold the same truths: a long life, witness to joy and horror in equal measure, although Ramona did not understand this dichotomy back then. She only saw the road.

Aris notices Ramona's attention. 'If the night is still young, then I have a story too.'

He glances around the company, but Ramona imagines that his eyes flick deliberately in her direction.

'I want to tell you about my ancestor,' he says. 'Who remembered the fires and passed her story down to her children, until my mother told it to me.'

A silence has descended upon the party. Ramona becomes aware once again of the night breeze, sweeping across the desert, ruffling the stunted bushes at its border. Insects hum as they flit through the night air. Aris begins to speak.

'When my ancestor was a girl, she lived by the jungle. Her village was in one of the last pieces of rainforest, and every day, she woke to the voices of animals. Strange, curious-shaped creatures that we can no longer imagine. She heard monkeys and birds and frogs. She would go into the jungle and collect fruits where they had fallen, and there were some that were edible and there were some that would kill you. There were flowers red as sunset over the sea, and there was water, drops as big as your fist, dripping from the leaves. But my ancestor noticed, as she got older, that the jungle was growing quieter.'

Aris's voice is very soft, and Ramona leans forwards to catch his words. At times his breathing is laboured, and he pauses to recover it, but no one interrupts as he continues.

'Of course, from their village, no one could imagine what was coming from the other side. Year by year, walls of flames swallowed up another stronghold of trees. Animals ran from it. Birds – paradise birds, they used to call them, and perhaps they were worshipped – exploded in the air. When the fires passed they left stumps of trees and carpets of ash. The land smoked for days.'

Aris pauses, gazing into the stove fire, as though he is seeing its terrible predecessors sweeping through the ancient jungle. A few of the party are nodding, and Ramona too recognizes this tale: it is a familiar one, relayed by many storytellers, with many different twists. But somehow it never grows old.

'My ancestor knew none of this. She only knew that every year, the stream from where the villagers took their water grew thinner. From time to time, she would see a red bloom above the jungle. My ancestor liked to watch the skies on nights like these, not knowing what they heralded.'

Unconsciously, the company draws closer together. A woman brings her legs to her chest and inches forwards. Another leans his elbows on his knees.

'Soon people began to appear out of the forest. They spoke of other villages, razed to the ground. Don't stay, they warned. This place is cursed. But my ancestor did stay, although the stream was now the barest of trickles, and the animals were all but silent, and people kept coming out of the jungle with eyes that saw waking flames and would do for all the remaining days of their lives.

'One day, my ancestor awoke early with prickles running from the top of her head to the soles of her feet. She went outside. The horizon was red. Thousands of birds flew overhead, making the air even darker so that now the whole world looked like a lake of blood. In the distance she heard a roaring noise. And then a magical thing happened.'

The word *magic* ripples at Ramona's back. This is the part she has been waiting for.

'From between the trees came a huge cat. My ancestor stood very still, facing it. It was as tall as her. Its fur looked like some rich Boreal material. On the gold were black rosettes. When it opened its mouth she saw its teeth. The cat could have bitten off her arm in a single mouthful.

'The cat looked at my ancestor. She looked at the cat. Then the cat turned and leaped away. Now my ancestor could identify the sound of approaching fire, and other noises too – crashes as trees tumbled to the ground. The village was awake, gathering possessions and preparing to flee. But my ancestor could not leave, not yet. She was in a trance. She stayed, watching the cat until it disappeared.'

There is a long silence before someone speaks. 'It was the jaguar.'

'It was the last jaguar,' says Aris. 'Three days later, my ancestor, whose village had burned to ashes, caught up with a band of vagabonds. The vagabonds were kind to her, for everyone had witnessed the burning of the last piece of jungle, and there was a sombre air in the country. So they offered the travellers stew and water. Only later did my ancestor see the skin of the cat, stripped and stretched out to dry, and she met again the eyes of the jaguar. But this time, the eyes were empty.'

Aris lets his words hang, but the gravitas is broken by a flurry of responses.

'No, that's not how it ends. The jaguar was captured and taken south by the Tarkies.'

'I never heard that.'

'It's true. They froze it into an iceberg.'

The circle is alive again, as each person puts forward their version of the jaguar's fate. He bounded to the ocean and turned into surf; he ran to the Nazca Desert and imprinted himself in the ground; he was captured by the Solar Corporation agents; by a salt mogul and bought by the Xiomaras; by pirates and bartered for in Tasmania; El Tiburón carries him on his boat, preserved in a diamond case.

As she listens to the theories, Ramona feels an old irritation creeping over her. She has heard this story many times, and it is always the same outcome. The jaguar is always dead. It seems to her that the story of the jaguar is indicative of a greater malady: a resignation to the fate of the continent, despite all the restoration laws; a covert agreement that this is how it was always destined to be. It is exactly this kind of unthinking acceptance that caused the majority of Brazil's population to decamp to Antarctica, and has produced a civilization of people like Taeo. And look where that has led us, she thinks, angrily remembering the state of the plane.

'What if the jaguar survived?' she asks.

They all turn to look at her.

'What?'

'What if the jaguar was taken north, or if it escaped, or its cells were cloned and a new jaguar was made . . .'

Their faces are sceptical.

Someone says, 'For sure, there are those who say he's still running about somewhere.' But Ramona knows it is said as an appeasement, and she finds herself further annoyed.

The old man, Aris, glances around the circle. The gathered faces are sleepy now, reddened by the last glow of the fire. Aris is not looking at Ramona, but she feels as though his next words are spoken directly to her.

'By the time I was born, sands had covered the scars left by the jungle's burning. They are there now, those dunes. Tomorrow, we will begin our journey across them. So I have for you a warning. A million tiny lives are buried there, and they say that anyone who tries to cross the desert without the utmost precautions shall lose their life too. They shall die with visions of paradise birds in their eyes, and their body shall dry laid out under the sun while the ghost of the jaguar walks across it with his tailbone swishing in the sand.'

The traders offer Ramona the shelter of a tent but she declines. While they are setting out bedrolls, she catches the man who walked away when she mentioned the raiders.

'I lost someone. You did too. We should talk.'

He turns away.

'I've nothing to talk about.'

'What's your plan in Panama? You must have ideas. We could team up.'

'I said, I've nothing to talk about. Now leave me alone.'

Ramona puts her hand on his arm. 'But that's crazy, you must know something, I know something, we've a far better chance of finding our people if we share our stories—'

'Leave it!' He shakes her off aggressively. Their encounter has drawn attention. Others glare at Ramona. Aris is watching her. She walks away, bewildered by the man's reaction. Why wouldn't he want to exchange information? It makes no sense.

She sleeps in the plane, wrapped in her bedroll in the hold in her usual spot, half-alert, her gun at her hip ready to grab. She rises before any of the camp. She leaves the plane only to urinate, crouching in the sand, the desert dark and cool on the boundary of the twenty degree line.

She is gone before anyone is awake, and as the sun comes up, she watches the birth of the desert around her, an immeasurable landscape, hushed and long abandoned.

27 ¦

It happens early in the morning. Mig is with Pilar in the stairwell of Station Sabado where they sheltered last night from the rooftop winds. He wakes, and at once feels something strange about the day, not heat or cold, or the pressure of a brewing storm, or even the ominous quiet that descends before a guerrilla invasion. For a few minutes he lies there, worrying at the coarse new hairs on his legs and puzzling over the odd sensation, and then he realizes. The radios have gone quiet.

Pilar is curled up, half of her head buried within her coat collar and her hands gripping the lapels as though someone might try to wrestle it from her. Mig nudges her with his foot.

'Hey. Hey, wake up. Listen!'

Her eyes unscrunch groggily. 'It's early, kid, fuck off—'

'Listen!'

She yawns. 'You just woke me right in the middle of this crazy dream—'

'Pilar, the radio.'

She peers suspiciously above the collar of her coat, blinking, and cracks her neck to first one side, then the other.

'You turn it off?'

'No. There's no broadcast.'

He holds up her radio, which is hissing static. Pilar's eyes narrow. She grabs the radio and shakes it, turns it upside-down and every which way.

'Fucking thing's broken. I knew it was a con—'

'No, it's not just here, there's nothing anywhere – listen.'

They climb out onto the roof, straining for any sound. Suddenly Mig is conscious of noises he would never usually notice – the trill of small birds alighted on the dome, his breathing, Pilar's breathing, the sound of her swallowing. But of people, he hears nothing. It is as if there has been some massive terminal incident, leaving him and Pilar the only survivors in a devastated world. He feels fear, but it is laced with a peculiar excitement. What has happened?

Pilar gets to her feet and walks across the roof with slow, deliberate steps that sound infinitely loud. She cups her hands around her mouth.

'Helloooo!'

The howl goes up into the air and dissipates and all is still again. Pilar pulls a face of clownish surprise.

The sound of static issues abruptly from Pilar's radio, making both of them jump. They laugh nervously.

'Loser.'

'Twat.'

Pilar hits the radio and fiddles with the tuner until the sound resolves into speech.

'. . . quarter of the city. Quarantine is enforced until further notice. We advise those who can to stay at home. All citizens are instructed to wear emergency masks. No one will enter or leave the city without permission. This is a broadcast for all residents of the city of Cataveiro. An outbreak of redfleur has been identified in the southern quarter of the city. Quarantine is enforced . . .'

Pilar stands and stretches her arms high above her head. She holds the pose, poised on the tips of her toes, like an angel at dawn. Mig senses no fear from her. But she must remember the last outbreak: it was five years ago. He was one of the younger ones then, but he remembers it. And he's scared now. Not for himself. For Pilar.

'Well,' says Pilar. 'That shit's just gone and ruined my day.'

The Alaskan was awake when the radios went black, and she is awake when the broadcasts resume. Station Cataveiro is the first. Others follow as she twists the dials, netting the radios sat on chairs and shelves and depositing them on the covers around her legs until she is surrounded by radios, each broadcasting a different wavelength. First come the subsidiary stations, then the independents, then the singly operated outfits, picking up and rebroadcasting the same message, over and over. Quarantine! There hasn't been a quarantine in five years. Over three thousand died in the last big outbreak of redfleur; they were fast, but not fast enough.

After a while there are other messages, supportive and subversive, and then there are doctors and scientists, someone from Tierra del Fuego urging the city not to panic, to stay safe and in the home. She leaves all of the radios on. The cacophony of voices brings a shiver of excitement to her aching bones.

Don't go out unless you have to. A stern government official.

Wear a mouth-mask. A researcher with a mellifluous, reassuring voice.

'Ha!'

The Alaskan snorts aloud at that. As if a mask would help anyone with redfleur. She twists her awkward body and feels under her mattress where the gun is and yanks it out and checks it is loaded: yes it is. She places it under her pillow. Then she waits.

And listens.

And waits.

The hours, the light slides by. She hears panicked banging about in the apartment next door. The streets below are busy at first, shrill gossip and exclamations interspersing the broadcasts from all the radios around her legs, who's-dead and who's-sick and whose-doctor-is-best and where's-your-mask-I-told-you-not-to-come-out-without-your-mask, as though there were any point in talking, as though there were any point in anything but finding the poor infected bastards and shooting them and then burning the corpses to ash.

Mourn them later. That is the stance the city's enforcers must take. You cannot firefight redfleur: you eradicate it, or lose the population. It is that simple.

The heat intensifies. The Alaskan's mouth is parched. Her tongue feels like paper in her mouth. The water jug by her bed is almost empty. She will not resort to dragging herself across the floor. Someone will come.

By midday the street has fallen silent. Occasionally she hears a single set of hurried footsteps passing by. She keeps the radios turned up loud. The broadcasters continue to chitter. Now they are full of eyewitness accounts and journalists interviewing the families of redfleur victims. It is the same story. My-sister my-brother my-mother my-bedridden-grandmother – she switches that station off – my-friend my-lover my-daughter I-knew-someone I-knew-someone and the redfleur took them and this is how it went.

The story is the same. The ending is the same. They died. They died badly, in agony. The Alaskan will not allow herself such an ending. She has suffered enough indignity for one lifetime.

She takes the gun from under her pillow and looks at it. She feels its heft. She points it at her temple, then fits the barrel against the roof of her mouth, above her tongue, tasting the sour metal. That is the most effective way. She leaves the gun out on the bed, her saliva drying on the barrel.

She waits. Mid-afternoon. The jug is dry.

Mig does not come until past three o'clock and by then the Alaskan is angry, very angry.

'Where have you been?'

He shrugs. His eyes slide away from hers, sly. He has a secret, this one, something he is keeping from her. The Alaskan doesn't like secrets, not when they do not belong to her. She'll worm it out of him.

'Where have you been, eh? I've been sat here all morning waiting for you to show your worthless face!'

Wordlessly, Mig picks up the jug. He refills it, returns and pours her a glass of water. She sees him notice the gun. She has to hold herself back not to slurp the liquid down and ease her swollen tongue.

'I had to check on the kids,' says Mig. 'Ri and the others.'

Kids, says the boy. As if he's not one of them. Forgetting his place, he is.

'And what of me, stuck here with legs that don't work, waiting for you to enlighten me? Am I supposed to die of thirst?'

The boy shuffles. 'Where's Maria?'

'Maria's not going to come with that death message all over the radio, is she? Why would Maria come? Cowardly. Disloyal, she is. Disloyal. You're not going to be disloyal, are you, Mig?'

'No,' he mumbles.

'What was that?'

'No, all right? I'm here, aren't I? Didn't I come?'

Mig's face is flushed and sweaty. The Alaskan relents.

'You did, Mig. You did. And don't think I don't appreciate it. You'll be well rewarded.' She moves a radio and pats the bed. 'Sit here. There's work to be done. We need to know who is dead. Who's stayed and who's gone. Is Xiomara still in town, or has she scarpered? Because, Mig, it's times like these when the power can shift.'

'They're moving people out,' he says. 'Testing them and telling them to go to the country.'

'Moving people, are they? The military has moved in, I'll wager. They'd better be in by now. Do you know how fast redfleur can travel, Mig? Have you seen what it does?'

The Alaskan's brain is powering. She can feel the shift, like a gear in a motorcycle. She used to love a motorcycle. The wind on her face and the thrum of the engine. The speed. The Scandinavian girl sat behind her, clinging to her waist. Up through the gears. One moment her thoughts are following the usual patterns, racing along their natural highways, the next it is as if she has lifted above the network of intersecting pathways and tramlines and river routes and Nazca lines and she sees each of them at the same time, with complete clarity. The Alaskan does not know if this is a result of her freak ancestry or just a fluke of genetic code, but when it happens, she feels a girlish thrill, an awareness of her own power and intellect that is intoxicating. The city reveals itself like a map before her. The players take their places upon it: Mig, Xiomara, the Antarctican, the hiding Osirian, the chemist, the government agents, and Alejandro Herrera, the ambitious mayor's apprentice who came for Mig's telegram. What is each of them thinking, deciding? Who will make the first move?

Taeo is shocked at the speed at which it happens. The broadcast. The rush to the shops as everyone in the district buys as much as they can carry, wheeling home trolleys stacked with tottering piles of tins and bottles of fluids. How quickly he finds himself prepared to fight for his share. Outside the store a small girl plucks one of his precious purchases straight out of the bag. Taeo shouts but she is already twisting away. Other thieves are waiting, expertly assessing the panicked shoppers, slicing open bags with pocket knives so the contents spill to the floor. Taeo hurries back, clutching his purchases to his chest. An evacuation official is shepherding the children of several families out of the building. Each child has a single bag. One clings to a floppy stuffed dog. Their faces are frightened and defiant, stained with tears. Climbing the five flights of the apartment block, Taeo hears the sound of running water as residents throughout the building fill their buckets and sinks in anticipation of cuts to the water supply.

The shops close. The street falls quiet. The radio issues nervous reports of zones where the disease has struck. Districts are named: a park, a street. Nothing is certain. Nothing is confirmed. By early

278 / E. J. SWIFT

evening, army trucks are taking regular patrols through the streets, and Taeo curses himself for not making a move before.

When he opens the shutters to see the street below, it is dimly lit and appears deserted.

Vikram taps his shoulder.

'Let me see.'

He moves aside to let the other man look out. Vikram stands silently. Watchfully.

'Can you see anyone?'

'No.'

'Nor could I.'

'You said before that redfleur never reached Antarctica, didn't you?'

Taeo peers past Vikram. The building opposite is dark except for the occasional sliver of light through the shutters. He cannot tell if anyone else is doing what they are doing. 'It's one of the reasons the Republic maintains an isolation policy. Too many northern plagues.'

'I never heard of anyone in Osiris having it either.'

'You wouldn't have. The superstrain only emerged around forty years ago – it was probably created by the northerners, knowing them.'

'You think they created it?'

'I'd put nothing past the Boreals.'

He hears the sound of an engine. A minute later an army-marked truck drives through the street below. The soldiers sat up top are wearing masks and full hazard suits. The white suits look like shrouds. The sight sends a chill through Taeo.

'I have to go out,' he says. 'I want to find out if the city is blocked. There must be a way out. We should get out while we can. If there's an epidemic—'

'You know I don't want to spend a day more than I have to in this place,' says Vikram. 'But we haven't found any of your Antarcticans, and how are we going to get out of this country until we do?'

'They must have lifted the lockdown on the harbour by now. There'll be an Antarctican boat. I'm sure of it.'

'You don't know that. We have no idea what's going on inside the city, never mind outside of it.'

'They're evacuating children. That means it's serious. Vikram, you've never seen someone with redfleur. It's a horrific way to die.'

'Is there a good way?'

'What?'

'I've seen a lot of people die. I've never seen anyone die in a good way.'

'I wouldn't wish redfleur on a Boreal. It's messy and incredibly painful. Your relatives won't recognize your face when you're dead. Is that horrific enough? Fucking hell.'

Vikram's face is expressionless.

'Anyway, quite apart from the actual danger of infection, even if we do escape an epidemic, we'd be put in isolation for months before Antarctica would let us in. I really think it's best to pretend we've never been here.'

Vikram shrugs. 'Then check it out. Just watch yourself out there. Or take me with you, if you want to stay safe.'

'No,' he says quickly. *If Vikram's lost, then everything's lost.* 'No, we can't risk you being caught. And one of us needs to stay with the radio.'

'Then why are you even pretending to ask me?'

Taeo opens his mouth to react and realizes there is no point. If Vikram was planning an exit, he would have gone a long time ago. For better or worse, he has placed his fortunes in Taeo's hands.

The building, usually clamorous with gossiping neighbours and children shrieking and running up and down stairs, is eerily quiet. When Taeo steps out into the street he feels its emptiness acutely, as though in that short stride he has crossed aeons of space and time to the surface of another planet, one strange and unfamiliar.

Mig has three checks to make. First is the enclaves, where Señorita Xiomara lives. The gates to the enclaves are shut and everything within silent. Some of the cars are gone. Not all. There are soldiers with guns, patrolling the perimeters. She's still in the city then, for now. One of the soldiers sees him. He shouts. Mig sprints away, the click of the soldier's gun loud in his ears.

Second: the heart of the city, a lesser street where the creepy old chemist brews his potions. The chemist's frantic customers of the morning are long gone. The shop is closed, the lights off. Is he still there, down in his basement? The Alaskan has a suspicion that if the chemist stays, it means something. Mig wonders if she thinks the chemist has a cure for redfleur, which would be a miracle, so Mig does not believe it, but still he wonders.

The third and final check is the Tarkie and his prisoner. Then he can find Pilar. He is worried about Pilar. She does not care for the quarantine, or the curfew, which starts around now, not that anyone is out. Doors and shutters are closed tight to the empty streets as Mig hurries on his way. He can barely hear the radios, as if the city is afraid that too much noise might provoke an onslaught of redfleur symptoms. Enforcers wearing full-face masks pop up on every corner, the young ones twitchy, the veterans hard-faced, all of them itching for trouble. Mig has only seen the city like this once before. It makes him nervous. There were things that happened – the last time. There was that gang who took the heads of Born Again Mayans, or those they believed to be Born Agains. Another group invaded a House of the Nazca. They sacrificed an acolyte; his screams could be heard in the next district.

People turn when death is close. You can't trust what they say and you can't trust what they don't say.

When he reaches the Tarkie's block Mig feels more relief than he would care to admit. He is almost at the top of the stairs when he hears voices in the corridor. Madame Bijou? No, but definitely a female voice, possibly that mouthy girl who answered the door to him once. And a male, speaking in Spanish, but badly, with a distinctive accent. Not the Tarkie.

Mig freezes.

Is it him, the other, the one the Alaskan wants? Is it the Osirian?

He creeps up a few more steps.

They are talking about the quarantine. The man is asking the girl questions and saying yes, yes, and once, slower please, as she responds. The girl says business is bad, no one has come, but Bijou will not close. They are all scared – what if a customer comes, a rabid one, infects them all? They'll be dead in hours. Or what if the gamblers decide they want quick cash? What if they raid the place and kill everyone? They'll be dead even quicker then.

Mig smells cigarette smoke. What should he do? This is his chance to see the man. But to see him, he exposes himself. He presses against the stairwell wall. The stone is cool on his bare shoulders. He *wants* to see the man. He wants to see if he has scales, like the stories say, or gills. Curiosity is burning a hole inside him.

The man asks, how do you get infected? Is it through blood?

Stupid question, thinks Mig. She'll know he's not a Patagonian.

Yes, blood, says the girl. She doesn't seem bothered by the question; perhaps she already knows about the man? Or touching, she says. Or spit. Snot, if you sneeze. Or tears. It's true you can die from the tears of a dead one. Once they're infected, you can't touch them. That's why they're burned.

What about the symptoms? asks the man.

Well, says the girl. It's the rash that comes first. But that's the tricky thing, because, you know, it might be heat rash or a mozzie bite gone bad or whatever. The redfleur looks a bit like flower petals, but not always. When it spreads all over your body and gets gooey, that's when you know it's bad. Then you start sicking up blood. Then everything inside you folds up and hours later you're dead. That's how fast it is, by the hummingbird.

A long exhalation and a whiff of smoke.

I hope it doesn't come here then, says the man.

Mig hears the sound of a cigarette being ground against the floor.

The pair are winding up their conversation. Now, now is the moment!

He pads up the final steps, certain of not being heard.

The door to Madame Bijou's closes. As the door opposite pushes shut, he catches the briefest glimpse of a man's face in profile: dark hair, brown skin, a nose that has been broken. If he has scales, they are not on his face.

When Mig puts his ear to the door there is only the radio. For a few minutes he sits with his back to the door, wondering, listening.

Who are you in there? Who are you that the Alaskan wants so badly? Who is it that doesn't know about the redfleur?

The army has set up manned barricades at each of the major roads leading out of the city. The soldiers are armed and suited up. Taeo sees only one attempt at escape. A man approaches the barricade. He is told to go home. It's past curfew. He retreats, then makes a run for the barrier. A soldier levels her gun and calmly shoots the man in the leg. The man drops with a shout. He lies there, yelling and clutching his leg. Eventually someone drags him into the back of a truck and drives back into the city.

By the time he has seen the last barrier, Taeo is exhausted, and it is long past curfew. The atmosphere of the streets has changed. There is barely any light, but he senses he is not the only one out. He notices forced doors and shutters pried up; shops have been raided, a chemist's window is smashed and its shelves almost entirely cleared. A child – a little girl – is looting through packets of pills scattered on the floor. She picks up one, frowns at it, discards it, chooses another. Her shoes crunch on the broken glass with each shift in position. When Taeo passes she looks up instinctively, and remains frozen until he has gone.

As the night deepens he hears unidentified shouts and the sound of things being smashed. He cannot tell if they are very close or several blocks away, and hurries back through the streets that have become surprisingly familiar in such a short space of time. When they arrived he could not imagine knowing the place. Its people and customs made it seem larger and stranger than it actually is. Now the city's smallness is its downfall. He can see how quickly, how immediately, the population could be eviscerated in a single sweep of plague. He and Vikram have to get out. They should pack their things tonight. He thinks of Vikram's blank face and his insistence that there is no such thing as a good death and a sudden fear strikes him that did not occur before.

What if Vikram *wants* to die? What if he's given up, like Taeo almost had?

He walks faster.

He is five streets away from Avenue Lorado when he hears the mob. First the angry shouts, then an advancing light, a strong orange glow that defeats the wispy luminescence of the few functioning street lamps. Firelight. Taeo runs to the end of the street. *Right or left?* The shouts seem to come from all sides. He chooses right, hoping to avoid whatever is coming his way, but he hasn't gone far when he hears voices again, nearer now, perhaps on the next street. He ducks down an alley and runs into a huddle of three dark figures. A hand grasps for his shoulder. He backs out as fast as he can.

Shit. The mob has turned onto this street. They are at least twenty strong. Some of them hold blazing torches, others grip batons or cudgels.

The only way out is to go up. Now he sees the sense of the ladders; they're not a convenience, they're an escape. He reaches for the nearest rung and climbs. Hand over hand, feet slipping, toes curling in his shoes until he rolls over a balcony rail. He hears soft breathing and knows at once he is not the only one on the balcony, but the faceless shape at the other end does not move. He or she is also watching the scene below.

The mob advances. There are men and women among them. Young and old. They are driving before them a hunched, stumbling figure.

They are shouting as one.

Out! Out! Out!

The chant goes through Taeo like a series of shocks, turning his insides to fluids. The mob's victim lurches down the street. Taeo realizes it is a woman. Her hair is grey. She doesn't seem able to walk properly, or in a straight line, but falters a few paces at a time, occasionally prodded forwards by a jab from one of the jeering mob's weapons. In the glow of the torches Taeo can see she is bleeding. There is blood on her face, and her arms and clothes, although Taeo cannot tell if it is from a beating, or if the woman is a victim of redfleur. His hands clench in fury. There is nothing he can do.

The voice from the other end of the balcony whispers softly, 'That's old Elena.'

'Does she have redfleur?'

'She didn't before. Maybe now. She belongs to the jaguar now.'

Taeo is confused. 'To who?'

Out! Out! Out!

The chant grows louder. As the mob passes beneath them, Taeo sees the face of the balcony's other occupant in the light of the flames. It is a small boy, scarred by the pox, his skin still peeling. Taeo sees again the other child, the girl, rooting through boxes of pills. For a moment he is paralysed by the hellish vision of his own children transported into these Patagonian bodies. He looks at the boy and sees his son Sasha in the physical space before him. Sasha's skin is peeling from his face and he stares at Taeo with mute, pleading eyes. The vision is so strong that Taeo reaches out a trembling hand. He has to wipe away the pox, or wipe Sasha from the other child, whichever it is, he can't tell, but those eyes are staring at him, frightened now, begging for help or mercy . . .

The sound of screeching tyres pulls him back to the street. For a moment Taeo is drenched in sweat, not knowing where he is. An army truck rounds the corner and careers towards the mob, coming to a halt ten paces from the victim, only metres from where Taeo and the boy are frozen. The mob pauses, their torches wavering. Three soldiers in hazard suits leap from the truck. They throw a sheet over the old woman and scoop her up as if she is weightless. They throw her carelessly into the open back of the truck. Inside, Taeo glimpses several other sheeted, body-sized humps.

A soldier shouts at the mob to get back home. The mob jeers. The soldier waves a rifle threateningly. Several in the mob turn, seemingly ready to disperse and go their separate ways. But one does not. He stands his ground, staring defiantly at the soldiers. In a sudden swift motion he throws his torch into the back of the truck.

The reaction is instant. The soldiers open fire. Taeo ducks down and holds his head, his heart rate trebling in his chest. Through his hands and the cracks in the balcony he sees the mob scatter, screaming. Several drop in the street and don't get up. The sheet over the old woman has caught fire and flames leap from the back of the truck. The soldiers let loose another round of bullets. They jump back up, swearing. As the truck races away, Taeo can see flailing figures, wreathed in flames, as the redfleur victims try to escape the burning sheets that constrict them. He hears agonized screams until they fade into the distance.

Moans drift up from the street. Taeo is shaking all over. His bowels feel loose, his stomach nauseous. A smell of burning lingers on the air.

'Where do they take them?' he whispers.

The boy sniffs and wipes his nose with his wrist. 'No one knows. It happened before. They took them. Like this.'

'When?'

'Go now. You don't belong here.'

The child's eyes are on Taeo. He climbs over the balcony and descends slowly, wondering how many of these little ledges are occupied by other children, sleeping under the open skies, observing the acts of terror in the streets below.

He passes two bodies in the street. One is still alive.

'Help . . . help me . . .'

A hand on the ground crawls towards him. Taeo cringes away, mute with horror. Would the mob have killed the old woman? Will she burn to death in the back of that truck? Did she really have redfleur, or was the attack just an excuse for someone's personal vendetta?

His bladder is pressing on his abdomen and he feels so little control over his own body he has to stop and urinate in the street. He cannot shake the image of his children dropped into this lawless city. The army is in control for now, but their numbers are not large. Ivra always used to say that guerrilla groups were only waiting for an opportunity to raid Cataveiro.

What if there's a coup? What if they really can't get out? He can't rely on the Alaskan now. For all he knows, the redfleur has got her too.

He is walking on autopilot, dazed and shaken. Avenue Lorado is just around the corner when he sees the glimmering light from below street level. A teenager in ragged clothing squats on the doorstep.

'Croc? O?'

'No, I—'

'Dark night, señor. Dark things happening. Come in, señor, we'll look after you, just step down here.'

'No really, I don't want—'

'Are you sure, señor? You look troubled. Why not forget your troubles for a time . . .'

'I'll . . . yes, I . . .'

The teenager runs down the steps. The door opens. The kid beckons. Taeo stares at her helplessly. There is light down there. Light and people, people who unlike Vikram will not look at him as if he is a jailer, will not care who he is and what he has done. He finds himself walking down the short flight of steps. When he steps inside the scent of opium assaults him and he stands, quite stupefied, unable to move of his own will. It is a parlour, not unlike the one in Fuego where he first discovered opium, a little dingier, a little seedier. He doesn't care. It could be anything. Someone takes his coat and steers him to a couch and lies him back. They bring the pipe. A narrow-faced woman says a price, not cheap, not cheap at all. He nods, already anticipating the hit. She wants cash first. Fine, fine, have it. Have whatever you want, just let me at the fucking pipe. He reaches for his wallet.

His pocket is empty. He checks the other side, panicking. Nothing. His wallet is gone.

'Fuck!'

'There is a problem?' She speaks sharply; he spoke too loud.

'My money . . . it was this kid, it must have been, he took my money . . . I'll pay you after, I'll come back tomorrow and pay you, I swear.'

She shakes her head.

'No money, no pipe.'

Before he stepped inside Taeo might have been able to walk away. Now he is desperate. He can smell the opium, but he cannot quite inhale it. He can see the other addicts stretched out on their couches, already lost in states of private bliss, their worries drifting away with the smoke that cradles them, their bodies relaxed and replete. He has to have it. He has to get to where they are.

'I swear I'll pay you, please . . . I . . .'

The lines around the woman's mouth tighten. She says payment is in advance. If he can't pay, he has to leave.

He looks at the pipe, *his pipe*, laid out on the couch.

'I have – I have information. I can give you a name – an address – there are people who would pay very well to know what I know—'

'Get out.'

Two men appear out of nowhere, one at each of his arms.

'No – no, listen!'

The smokers are oblivious to his shouts as he is manhandled from the den. They drag him up the steps and shove him roughly into the street. He lands awkwardly on hands and knees.

'Shut up or we'll make you shut up,' says a voice. 'This is no night for making a scene.'

He hears the door shut. The teenager's soft voice.

'That's a shame, señor, another time, señor . . .'

Taeo is trembling all over. For a minute he stays as he is, on all fours, his eyes closed against the world, the strange, other world, the side of the city he has found a way into, now when it is too late. Slowly he gets to his feet. No street lamps. It is almost pitch black. There are no stars. He hears a rumble overhead. A light rain begins to fall, fine at first, but growing in strength, until it is lashing against his face and his scraped palms. He stands there, feeling the water soak through his clothes.

He promised he would protect Vikram. He even told himself he had made a friend. They have shared their weaknesses and shaken hands on a pact, and all it took was this one instance of temptation to prove that Taeo's word is worthless. He almost betrayed Vikram. He was ready to give away everything.

A wave of self-loathing swamps him.

'Move on, señor, you can't stay here. Soldiers'll be coming, every hour they are, every hour they come this way,' whispers the teenager. The kid squats where she was, shielded from the rain by the lip of the balcony above, arms wrapped around her shins.

Taeo can sense the malice leaking from the place. How long has that den been there, waiting to be found, waiting until he was most vulnerable?

'Señor,' insists the teenager.

'Yes, I – I'm going.'

Mig searches everywhere. He goes to all of Pilar's usual haunts: Station Sabado, the garden of the city museum, the eastern House of the Nazca, the radio tower. She isn't there. He tries the balcony where she sleeps if it's raining, the one where the occupants sometimes leave out food for her. She isn't there. The streets are bad; there are people out with torches, people who want to burn things. Sirens wail in the distance. He ends up back at the warehouse. He checks twice, three times before slipping through the gap in the corrugated metal. The mood in the warehouse is tense and quiet. Suddenly the warehouse does not seem like a safe place. The kids are curled up in their separate corners, trying to sleep. He feels the nervousness. What if the soldiers find us? What if the redfleur finds us? What if someone snitches?

He wants to reassure the little ones. He should be stopping to comfort them, like the older ones did for him, last time, but he can't stop. He goes from sleeper to sleeper.

Pilar? Have you seen Pilar?

It's the girl who knows. The girl who told the tale of the jaguar. Her round clown face is furrowed in half-sleep.

'She's singing. Downtown. Secret party, enclaves end. Ri scored some cash. They all went. Only me, I didn't.'

'Where?'

She tells him the address. She clutches his hand. Her eyes are huge.

'You shouldn't go. It's bad out. The jaguar's roaming.'

Mig says, 'I don't believe in the jaguar and neither should you.'

As he leaves the warehouse it is starting to rain.

A beetle makes its way around the edge of the wall. Taeo watches its slow progress, the hard, shiny carapace shell, the spindly, scurrying legs. The beetle is a nuisance here, but in Antarctica it is a small miracle. Does the tiny creature know where it is going? Or is it exposed in the open, blind and uncertain, making its best guess for cover? He has changed his clothes but he is shivering. He cradles the mug of hot coffee that Vikram made him, Vikram who is now sitting opposite him, a concerned expression occupying his features, Vikram who he made a pact with, Vikram who he came so close to betraying.

He is overwhelmed with the knowledge of his own mistakes. It is all he can think of: the lies he has told to Vikram. The inescapable lies.

Rain splatters on the shutters. On the roof, a bathtub overflows. He imagines the rivulets of water diverging and running every which way, like the strands of his life he has lost a hold of, every one. Now is the time for confession.

He takes a long, shaky breath. He cannot look Vikram in the face, so he looks at the dark swirling surface of the coffee with its faint oiliness.

'I lied to you before. On the island. On Fuego.'

There is a pause. He stares at the coffee.

Vikram says, 'I know you did.'

'Then why did you come with me if—'

'What else was I supposed to do? Everyone has an agenda. If it wasn't you it would have been someone else. So I threw in my lot with you. I could tell you were smart. I guessed you would know things, useful things. If now's the time for the truth, I'm ready for it.'

'I barely know where to start.'

A creak as Vikram settles back in his chair.

'Just tell me. There's a storm out there and we're barricaded into the city. We're not going anywhere.'

He thinks of Antarctican maps. The Boreal States stretched around the edges of the northern hemisphere. The huge continent at the centre of the map, half covered in ice. The gulf of desert that girdles the earth.

'There is a war that no one speaks of between south and north,' he says. 'No one can speak against it because it doesn't exist. Not in words. But it's there. It's under the surface of everything. And where you come from is a part of it, whether you like that or not.'

Taeo hesitates, but he has come too far now.

'Antarctica has been monitoring your city from afar ever since the Great Storm.'

A brief silence. Taeo's nervousness increases.

'What do you mean, monitoring?'

'I mean, the Republic has always known about Osiris. When everyone else believed the city was destroyed, we knew the truth.'

Taeo can sense Vikram staring at him. He can feel the intensity of the other man's gaze. He wraps his hands tightly around the mug, trying to control the shakiness in his hands. He has to finish.

'We knew – the Republic knew – the city had gone into hiding, so—'

'You knew.' Vikram's voice is sharp with accusation.

Taeo forces himself to look up. 'Yes.'

'You knew – for fifty years. My entire life, you're saying Antarctica knew?'

'The Republic had to keep the secret—'

Vikram's punch catches him squarely in the face. Taeo is completely unprepared for the attack. A hot scald burns over one hand. He hears the coffee mug break. Then he is sprawled on the floor, an explosion of pain behind his right eye, blinking lights filling his vision. Vikram is on top of him, pummelling with his fists. The blows land erratically before Taeo manages to twist and throw a wild punch of his own. He catches Vikram below the ribs. Vikram falls to his side, caught off balance. Taeo scrambles away. He staggers to his feet just after Vikram. They circle one another warily. Taeo hears shouting and moments pass before he realizes it is he who is shouting, in Portuguese, with no will or control over what is coming out of his mouth.

'Why did you have to show up here now? Why couldn't you stay in your fucking sea city? You fucking idiot. Do you have any idea what will happen if the north finds out about you? What will happen to all of us? You think the Republic kept this secret for a laugh? Just to spite you? Fucking hell!'

The other man has a hold of his shoulders. He is shaking Taeo violently and screaming back. Taeo tastes blood in his mouth.

'You left us there? You knew we were out there and you left half the city to starve and drown when your fucking country could have taken us in? You lying fuck, you're no better than a skad. My friends died! They didn't have to die. None of them had to die. Adelaide didn't have to die!'

Taeo feels himself shoved violently away. He staggers back. When he puts out his hands to break his fall he feels another small pool of pain. He has cut himself on a shard of the broken coffee mug. He stays where he has fallen, exhausted, incapable of further defence, a trickle of blood working its way over his hand. Vikram is leaning with his forehead against the wall, eyes closed, breathing heavily. Taeo waits, numbly, for Vikram to relaunch his attack. The other man does not move and after a while Taeo asks, 'What are you waiting for? You might as well finish it off.'

Vikram says, 'I hope you die of redfleur.'

Taeo winces. His right eye throbs relentlessly. He can feel his face swelling up, closing off one half of his vision, liquid oozing from between the distorted flesh. His body is a sea of pain.

He thinks of the opium den, just a couple of streets away, its inhabitants drifting on the raft of the drug. He would do many things for a hit. Unconscionable things. He wants to weep.

The rain intrudes on the silence of the room. If he closes his eyes, Taeo can imagine it is Antarctican rain. If Vikram is about to kill him, there are worse things to have as a final memory.

But Shri is there too, standing in the rain, her arms folded, her hair wet. Are you going to give up this easily? she says. On me? On the children? Talk your way out of it.

Taeo gathers his last resources.

'The decision was made a long time ago, before either of us was born,' he says.

Vikram turns away from the wall. This is it, thinks Taeo. This is the end. He waits for the inevitable, but nothing happens. When he opens his one good eye Vikram has slumped to the floor where he was stood. A bruise is forming on his cheek and blood trickles from the corner of his mouth.

'I'm sorry I lied,' Taeo says. 'But I'm Antarctican, and whatever they've done to me, I love my country. My family . . . I have to protect them. I don't think you feel that – about Osiris.'

'You're right,' says Vikram. 'I don't. And you told me you were exiled because you were working on some military programme you didn't agree with. You said your colleague betrayed you. So it sounds like you're not that interested in protecting your country after all. Or was that all lies too?'

'No, some of it . . . There is a military programme. I spoke out against it. It was my decision. I went public. That's why they sent me here. But you have to understand, that decision, I spent years . . . I didn't know what to do or who to speak to . . . I was good at what I did. I was starting something new, something no one had done before. All my research, I had to hand it over. Even now, I don't know if it was the right thing. And then you appeared. Like some kind of cosmic joke.'

He laughs raggedly, but it hurts too much and he has to hold himself still. Silence falls between them. The rain drums relentlessly on the roof. A truck swishes through the waterlogged road in the street below. When Vikram begins to speak his voice is low and trancelike, as if he is speaking to himself.

'It's Osiris too,' he says. 'We only escaped because we'd been secretly armed. Linus Rechnov supplied us. He'd found out about Whitefly. Operation Whitefly, they called it. A plan to keep the city secret. His family were part of it. He knew – I knew – there would be a fight. The others didn't believe me until it happened. Half of them died right out, the night after we left. We couldn't give them a proper send-off, we had nothing to burn them with. We had to drop them in the ocean and leave them to sink.'

A trickle of blood works its way down Vikram's jaw and neck. He makes no effort to wipe it away.

'We weren't supposed to leave Osiris,' he says.

Taeo probes his throbbing lip experimentally with his tongue and discovers a split. A fresh influx of pain sears through him. He speaks awkwardly.

'There's so much I need to tell you. One day, Antarctica will be the wealthiest nation in the world. The land is so vast. Under the ice – we can only start to imagine. Untouched resources. We're discovering precious materials. Strains of diamond. Rare metals for electronics – stuff the Neons were mad for, and the Boreals pay well for them. Gas and oil. And that's not all. As the ice melts, we'll be able to recreate the kind of world that hasn't been seen in hundreds of years. Already it's beginning. There'll be beaches. White sand. We'll plant forests. New coral reefs. We'll import animal DNA. Grow plants from seed banks. Antarctica will be . . . a paradise.' He pauses, swamped by another wave of sickening pain. 'I won't . . . live to see that. It's going to take hundreds of years. But the Republic will make it happen, and maybe my descendants will live to see the day.'

'Paradise,' says Vikram. The word is hard and angry.

'One day . . .'

'Keep talking.'

'Only one thing could stop it. The war. Between south and north. It's always been there, behind the scenes, since the first colonies set up on Antarctica. You understand what I'm saying, don't you? We'll build this paradise, and everyone will want it. The Boreal States. The Solar Corporation. All of them.'

'And Osiris?' says Vikram.

'Osiris was another move in the war. It was made out to be – a philanthropic exercise. A new utopia for a broken world. After the Blackout, something was needed. But it was a Boreal thing. The Osiris Knowledge Bank poured funding into it. Everyone knew the real reason the city was built, but nobody could ever say. Your city is a military base. It's a stepping stone for the north to invade us, whenever they feel fit.'

Taeo touches his head gingerly, and feels the stickiness of blood.

'Why Osiris? Why couldn't they use Patagonia?'

'Setting up a base here would directly contravene the Nuuk Treaty. Nothing is ever said outright, it's all chasing shadows. That was the thing about Osiris – it was the perfect cover. Until the year of the Great Storm. That must have been a blessing for the Republic. I can imagine how it happened. Your city seemed to disappear, but that couldn't be right. There was still energy output. There were still ships appearing on Antarctican radars. It can't have taken long to find out the truth. And since then . . . well, the Republic has been happy to maintain Osiris's myth.'

Something flickers in Vikram's face with his last sentence. 'A myth,' he repeats softly. 'Yes. Like the Tellers, I can see how they worked. I can see it now. But you're forgetting something. Osiris doesn't belong to the Boreal States. Osiris is independent. Nobody has any right to it.'

'Do you think that would stop the Boreal States? You think those countries would give a shit about the independence of a single city?'

'Osiris would defend itself,' says Vikram, but uncertainly now. Watching the other man through his one good eye, Taeo feels a weight of sorrow and guilt descending. He has done this to Vikram, to someone he considered a friend. Someone would have, some day, but it has proved Taeo's responsibility, and Taeo's load to carry. Vikram, who thought he had the measure of a world he had never believed existed in the first place, now finds that beneath it there is a network of hollow caves.

He speaks gently. 'I'm sorry, Vikram. If the world finds out Osiris exists, your city wouldn't stand a chance. The problem with Osiris is it means too much, to too many different players. For the Boreal States, it's the platform they made to spy on us. To Antarctica, it's a Boreal outpost which we've ignored for fifty years precisely to keep the north from our back door. It would be a symbol of hope for some – those isolated civilizations left in Tasmania and the far south of India. The Solar Corporation is something else again – for them it's leverage, a way to toy with south and north – and the Corporation has a stake in Osiris too. An energy stake. And for the people in any of those nations, your city is something else. It's stories to scare children, rumours and fantasies. A dream.'

The speech exhausts him. He wants to lie down and smoke and never wake again.

Vikram says, 'You haven't said what it means for Patagonia.'

'The discovery of Osiris would be a nightmare for this country. Patagonia is just another victim of the war. It's a trading station. They don't want the Boreal States here any more than we do.'

'And you want to take me to Antarctica to keep the secret.'

Taeo bows his head. 'Yes.'

'How do I know they won't just kill me when we get there? If I'm that important?'

'That wouldn't happen.'

'How do you know?'

'I wouldn't let it.'

Vikram shakes his head. 'You're an exile. What leverage could you have?'

'There would be no point. Besides, people are curious. People would want to know about Osiris. They'll want information.'

He thinks of Kadi and Sasha with their holobooks. He imagines them listening to tales of the sea city, their faces rapt, spellbound in the glow of the bluish night lights.

Vikram gets to his feet and walks painstakingly across the floor. He opens the shutter. The rain is louder. Strains of guitar trickle through from Madame Bijou's night-time radio. From elsewhere, a late-night report on the redfleur outbreak, low and urgent.

'I should tell you something about Osiris,' says Vikram. 'Because there are things you don't understand too. And the thing is, however hard you try to stop it, people like me are going to appear. And keep appearing. I might be the first but I won't be the last.' He pauses, watching the rain. 'You probably can't imagine how it feels, to live believing there's no one else out there. Thinking this is your world and none other exists. Knowing what the edges are, the boundaries . . . the border.' He peers out, looking down into the street below. The overhead light is on and, instinctively, Taeo wants to stop Vikram showing his face, but the power has shifted. It is all too late.

'I spent my entire life wondering.' Vikram's voice is quieter now, withdrawn, as though Taeo is no longer present. 'Not knowing, not quite believing, but sometimes, in a dream, you sense something, or you feel something, and you think, perhaps there could be . . . And then you wake up, and you know it couldn't, and yet there's always this doubt, this lingering, nagging doubt. Sometimes I thought I was going mad. Now I know I'm not. I wasn't. I wasn't mad to think like that. Knowing. Being certain. It changes you. It's changed me. Maybe I only realized it now.'

He turns to face Taeo squarely. There is a light in his eyes, something surprised, almost evangelical in its fervour, that takes Taeo aback and makes him feel at once sad and relieved. As though he has been absolved.

'There are lots of people like me in Osiris,' says Vikram. 'I won't be the last. Your Republic will have to deal with that.'

He moves, awkwardly but with sudden purpose. He goes into the next room and comes out, pulling on a waterproof jacket. Taeo watches, powerless.

'What are you doing?'

'I'm going out,' says Vikram. 'I need to clear my head. I won't be long.'

'But the quarantine . . .'

'I'll be fine,' says Vikram. 'I can look after myself. Stay here. I'll be back in a couple of hours.'

The door clicks shut behind him. Taeo lies back where he is. There is no part of him that does not hurt. He wonders where Vikram is going and what he is planning to do. He wonders if Vikram will ever forgive him, and wishes now he had said something more. *I'll make it up to you.* Something like that. But what do words mean anyway? He made promises to Vikram, but he made promises to Shri too, and did not keep them. I'll never leave you, he said. And she said, I know, I know you won't. I know *you.*

298 / E. J. SWIFT

There is a ringing in his ears and the rain drums through it. They play a futile battle in the centre of his head. He wonders, if he imagines the effects of opium, if it is possible to trick his body into feeling them. He closes his eyes, and the world is mercifully dark.

PART THREE
EL CINTURÓN / THE BELT

28 ¦

She has never been this far north before. The Amazon Desert surrounds her on every side, stretching away as far as she can see. It has a strange, bleak, unspeakable beauty. Striations of ochre and soft gold merge into burnt orange and umber. She is mesmerized by the shape of the undulating dunes, the way shadows dapple the peaks and troughs. The shadow of the plane skims over the sand, there, then gone, then there again, and there is a part of her that cannot quite believe the scene is real, as though she too is skipping in and out of existence, and which side she will land upon has not yet been determined.

At first, in the outer reaches of the desert, she sees the remains of cities half submerged in sand. Further in, towards the basin, there are strange, twisted shapes: the burned carcasses of trees still standing. And then there is only sand. With the plane on autopilot, she maps what she can, a cairn of rock here, the sweep of an old river bed there. Rough sketches, notes and measurements. She is cutting across the centre of the desert. It is the fastest route to Panama, and she has no time to lose.

Somewhere in the upper half of the continent, the raiders are making their way north. If they plan to make the Exchange, they must have transport. She suspects they are taking the eastern coastal route, but she cannot be sure, and so her plan is to make it to Panama ahead of them, and wait.

Rescue Inés, find medicine, take her mother home.

Where is Inés now? Are the raiders hurting their prisoners, or cajoling them? Is Inés in the back of a truck, every bouncing motion jolting her jinn-ridden body as they navigate the crumbling highways? Are they travelling by ship? Have they bribed a member of the fleet or a pirate vessel and locked Inés in a cabin, dizzy and nauseous as the ship braves the waves of the Atlantic?

She doesn't know.

Inés could be anywhere between the Highlands and Panama and she doesn't know where and the not knowing takes up the hot, dry space in the cockpit, and the whole of the canopy of the sky around them, and the vast plains of the desert below. Even though there is nothing there, she is scanning every ripple of the sand, as if the desert might reveal Inés at the edge of her vision, a fierce, tiny figure, striking out alone.

As the day wears on, the heat in the cabin intensifies. Her back and thighs against the seat are soaked with sweat and every movement becomes an effort. Her feet swell and throb. She considers landing and resting over midday, but presses on. Best to make as few landings as possible, with the plane in this state. At first the whining was just a small, persistent sound, like an insect veering suddenly close to the ear. But it has got steadily worse, until it is as bad as it was when she left the Nazca Desert, before the Antarctican fixed *Colibrí*.

If he fixed *Colibrí*. That seems increasingly doubtful now. She puts on a set of headphones to block out the noise. There is no radio signal, so there is no sound. She sings loudly to herself. Old Nazca songs, familiar as her hands. The parrot who ate the voices of every living thing, the hummingbird who stole the winds . . .

She tries to picture the landscape of Aris's stories, the jungle with its dripping canopies and chattering creatures. It feels important, to be able to picture it. But all she sees is sand. The sand is so majestical, so absolute, it is impossible to visualize anything but what is here.

For the first time she finds herself seriously considering the Antarctican's offhand suggestion that she might find work in the south. He is right. To map the ice continent would be a challenge, the greatest challenge she could accept. It would be a joy. She imagines a land where there is always water, where rivers form at the ice frontier and there are no ocean dead zones; where there are fish and green grass grows in the lush fields. She imagines towns full of people who use robotics for all things as if it were a second skin. She imagines taking Inés there. She could bargain for that. Inés would be safe. Inés would have good medical care. And old age. A comfortable one.

Inés would never go.

Movement catches her eye on the desert floor below. At first she thinks it is a trick of the light. But the movement is linear, and steady. It's a vehicle, she realizes. A truck painted in desert colours.

A truck.

The man at the plant said a ship, but what if he's wrong . . .

She circles back, dropping lower, wanting a better view, and as she does the whining noise increases even through her headphones. The plane banks violently, tilting far further than she intended. She is staring at the sky with the world falling away below.

She kicks the pedals and hauls the plane back, but they are moving away from the truck now, heading in the opposite direction. She can feel that something is terribly, terribly wrong. Banking to make another turn could be fatal. But she is off course now.

Then they lose height. The plane starts to shake. There is a crash as something comes loose in the hold and starts to shunt back and forth. Ramona's stomach leaps with the sudden steep drop in altitude. She stares at the instrument panel. The altimeter needle swings rapidly to the left. Two thousand metres. Fifteen hundred. The pressure in her ears is horrendous. She wrestles with the controls.

'Come on, *Colibrí*! Come on now! Fuck!'

The plane is plummeting and she knows she is going to crash.

The hum of the engine magnifies into something colossal, screeching in her ears and all around her. The plane shakes so violently she feels like all her bones are going to break. It begins to spin. Sky, dunes, sky, dunes. They are in free fall.

Out, get out!

She checks her parachute straps. One solid strike on the ejector when the sky is where it should be. The plane will survive the crash. It will. Time to save herself. She hits the ejector. Nothing happens. She hits it again, punching with increasing desperation.

'No, no, no!'

The plane nose-dives. Land careers towards her. In the last few seconds she hangs on to the yoke with grim desperation, trying to wrench back some level of control. The plane is completely unresponsive.

She wraps her arms around her head and braces for impact.

Rolling crests of pain. There is something wet sliding over her face, across her chin and down her neck.

She opens her eyes.

It is dark. The instrument panel has gone dead. The windshield is entirely blocked with sand. Ramona is tipped forwards, the safety harness holding her into her seat and pressing into her shoulders. Her left shoulder has dislocated from the socket. Blood drips from a head wound. Her ribs scream when she breathes.

She puts out her right arm to brace herself against the panel and releases the harness, then shrugs painfully out of the parachute. She tries opening the cockpit hatch but it has jammed. She has no idea how much sand is weighing it down. She's going to have to get out through the hold. She feels for her pack; it's fallen out of the passenger seat. The pack is heavy and she'll need her good arm. She hooks it over one foot.

Gingerly, every movement revealing a fresh root of pain, she hauls herself up through the back of the plane, dragging the pack behind her. Her ribs and shoulder are agony. The hold door sticks and she is scared she won't get out, that they are entirely buried in sand, but then it releases. The desert light temporarily blinds her. She blinks away tears. She slithers out onto the sand and stumbles away.

She staggers fifty metres and collapses, lying on her back, trying to breathe as shallowly as possible. She fishes in the pack and retrieves a water bottle. She presses it to her lips, taking small sips, holding them in her mouth and letting each precious drop slide down her throat.

The sky overhead is infinite blue, the sand a dry, baking amber. Squinting, she can see a long furrow scattered with debris, where the plane skidded on its belly before plunging into the side of a dune.

Lucky, she thinks. Lucky again. If you call this luck.

Her mother's voice echoes in her head.

Ramona, Ramona, Ramona.

Always you try to fix things.

And some things, they cannot be fixed.

When she is certain she can stand it, she bites down on the piece of rubber she gave the girl in the highlands, bites down hard, and snaps her dislocated shoulder back into its socket. The tears that stream down her face feel like treachery. She cannot afford to lose water through tears.

She opens her pack and takes out the contents one by one, laying them on the sand. Water bottles. Canned fruit and vegetables and protein slips. Malaria pills. A sunhat. The emergency medical kit.

She straps up her shoulder as best she can without assistance. Her ribs are burning. She lifts her T-shirt and runs fingers lightly over the bones. Nothing broken, but almost certainly cracked.

Next she pulls out a light tarpaulin to deflect the sun. She unfolds the tarpaulin and sits underneath it like a tent, grateful for the semblance of shade.

What else? A mapping book and pencils. A flare. A combination knife. A gun. What use is a gun in the desert? Unless the truck . . .

The truck is gone, raiders or not. Forget about the truck.

The Antarctican's holoma has also survived the crash. She stares at it with hatred. Of course their Neon technology would crawl through unscathed, of course it would.

She looks at the meagre little pile of belongings. Under strict rationing, there is enough food and drink to last her for a week. There are more rations in the hold of the plane, but she isn't sure how much she will be able to carry with cracked ribs and a shoulder that won't take any weight. How many days' walk to get out of the desert? A week? A fortnight?

She lies on her back under the tarpaulin. Her breath hisses against its pale cover. She can hear the minute skittering of grains of sand in the hint of a wind that brushes against her face. She closes her eyes but the light remains intense through her eyelids, the veins within the skin glowing red like the lines on a map. She pulls the sunhat over her eyes to shut out the light.

The heat. The midday desert heat.

The pain catches her and pulls her up into some distant place. She drifts away.

She wakes parched and stiff. The sun is low in the sky. Time to get moving. She opens a can of tofu and eats the sticky mess inside. Each swallow hurts.

She climbs painfully back into the plane and tries to get the engine going. Nothing. Not even a flicker of power. She disconnects the batteries and takes a few more rations from the hold. There is no more she can do. Not alone, not in the desert. She will have to abandon the plane. She stares at *Colibrí*'s long wings, the hummingbird glyph that runs the length of the fuselage. The solar cells draw down power but there is nowhere for it to go. She remembers the bones of Violeta del Torres, her neck broken, the remains of her body slowly crumbling.

'I'm coming back,' she speaks aloud, to make it more certain, but she does not sound certain. '*Colibrí*, I'm coming back.'

There's nothing for it: she is already weak and she might as well make the most of the cool night. She rearranges her pack with the heaviest items at the bottom. When she eases her shoulders into it the weight is too much for her sore ribs. She ropes the pack to her waist so that she can drag it behind her like a sledge. Loaded up like this, she is able to walk.

She sets out north across the dunes, following the compass and the path of the sun. Even this late in the day, she can feel the heat rising off the land. She thinks of the pedlar's stories. Aris's warning. She will have to travel at dusk and start anew before dawn. At night, too, the heat will drop away and she is going to be very cold. She tries not to think of the sandstorms . . .

Her progress is slow. The sand is hard to walk on, even if she were without injury, and despite her best efforts, the pack is a terrible strain. Several times she slips and falls, shouting aloud with the pain. Her shadow marches beside her, elongated then shortened as the shape of the sand alters.

The sun sets in an infernal blaze, and night falls almost at once. When it is too dark to see, Ramona wraps herself in the tarpaulin and lies flat, watching the stars come out one by one, very sharp and clear, as they were in that other desert, a long time ago.

She thought the desert would be silent, but it is full of whispers. The sand shifts like a living thing. Spirits of the jungle, she thinks uneasily. Here in the desert basin, the jaguar is abroad, with his tailbone swishing in the sand. In another world monkeys are climbing the ghosts of trees and birds of paradise are singing unearthly songs as they spiral on a slip of air.

It turns very cold. She buries herself in the sand, seeking warmth. She thinks of her mother, and wants to cry, but stops herself. Instead she imagines Inés speaking. *What did you expect, eh? You and that aeroplane, unnatural it is. Such a one as this I have raised and now she is surprised – now she wonders, how is it that I am alone in the desert days and days from anyone and anything? I tell you how it is, Ramona. This is the Neon end – what comes of meddling. I told you this aeroplane is no good. But you will try and fix things.*

But I was trying to find you, Ma . . .

Eh, always an answer, always an answer, she has. My lucky one.

She sleeps uneasily and wakes in pain.

On the second day she finds the bed of a river and follows it north-west. She walks along the fissured yellow earth and the piles of silt woven into ridges, like fingers winding through dust. The riverbed is at once hard and soft beneath her feet, sometimes crumbling where she steps, sometimes sinking her whole body as though it will drag her down into the depths of the earth's core.

She sees, on the opposite shore where the bank rises steeply, a serpentine breakage in the sand. As Ramona moves closer she sees that the long curve is sectioned into small hillocks, and that the hillocks are bones, the vertebrae of some long-dead animal. She squats beside it. The sand is hot under her hand when she brushes it away. The bones are yellowish, smoothed to glass. She brushes away at the dirt, gradually exposing a long tail, ribs and four blunt legs. Further up, bits of bobbled skin still cling to the vertebrae, but when she touches them they disintegrate in her fingers, just like Violeta del Torres. All we are, she thinks. The skull is elongated, and the jaw holds an impressive array of teeth. A caiman.

She uncovers the rest of the skeleton. When the whole animal is clear, she sits back on her heels, marvelling at the sheer engineering of the thing, trying to imagine how it must have moved in the water. The bones shine in the sunlight. The light dances among them and the shadows cast by the legs and spine, as though it can lend the animal a second life. The heat is a fierce beam on the back of her neck. Time to move on.

She needs to find cover before the midday heat becomes too

punishing to move. The land slopes away red and charred. The weave of the river is the only marking in miles. She could find shade under an outcrop of rocks, perhaps, and sit with the lizards. Their scampering company is one of few survivors she has seen among this desolate land with its half-buried ossuaries.

She cannot remember how long she has been walking. The pack drags behind her, a dead weight. The old break in her thigh bone is coming back to haunt her; she should have known it would. She is starting to limp. Hours have passed. Days and nights have passed. She can barely imagine a time before the desert. The food is gone. Her tongue lies in her mouth like a sponge, sucking up every scrap of moisture. There is a foul taste when she swallows.

She talks to her mother regularly now. Inés walks just behind her, but whenever Ramona turns and tries to see her, she disappears.

She tries to explain about *Colibrí*. She wants her ma to understand.

The thing is, you see the world differently from above.

Different? Ha. I see what I see and I know what I see.

No. I mean . . . you see how things fit together. You can see where people were, and where they are now. You can see a story.

I don't need to go into the air to see a story. I've got stories coming out my ears.

But you've got no one to talk to. You're mean to Carla, and you frighten away little Gabi. Where do you get your stories from?

All over the place. The lizards. The lizards tell me.

You're being silly.

I suppose it's the birds who talk to you, do they? Up there? In your Neon flying machine?

It's not just the thing, Mama, it's the use *of the thing.*

The sun beats down on her head. Through her blood. Its light pulses with her heartbeat. The world throbs as though the sand itself is alive.

Strange things come out of holes in the ground. Crawling things, scuttling things. Eyeless shadows grown bodies and wings. The horizon shimmers. Blue lakes materialize and vanish. An approaching motorcycle turns into the trunk of a lone, long-dead tree. A voice tells Ramona to take her eyes away, not to look, and not to believe. But the voice is small and tremulous. Ramona looks again. She sees it, at last.

A city. A city of living, breathing gold.

Panama.

'The Exchange.' Her throat, parched and swollen, produces no sound. 'It's the Exchange!'

She looks down at her shuffling feet. So slow. At this rate, it will take days to reach the city, and days she does not have. Her water is almost gone.

'Come on,' she orders herself. 'Faster. Faster!'

She trudges on, buoyant now with hope. People are ahead. *You see, Ma. I told you so! I told you I'd make it.* She looks to the city. But now the horizon is bare and blue. Uncomprehending, she scans its length, turning, gazing in every direction.

Where has it gone? *Where has it gone?*

Tears fill her eyes. She blinks. They trickle down her face, a scant two drops. She reaches with her tongue to capture their moisture. The salt stings her lips. She keeps walking. It's there, somewhere. Just in hiding. Spots decorate her vision, like stars coming out at night, slowly crystallizing. Then they vanish; it becomes entirely dark. Night has descended quickly tonight. Today. The night in the day. She is upside-down. *Colibrí* is hanging in the sky. Remarkable. She feels the darkness envelop her as she topples sideways.

I'm sorry, Ma. I did try, you know.

Inés's hand fastens around hers. She can feel how thin her mother's fingers have become.

I'll bury you with Camilo and Paola.

At the end of the veranda?

Yes, my lucky one. In the ground. That's what we were made for.

All right, Ma. I'm ready now.

Consciousness slips away from Ramona. Her heart begins to slow. Her breath rattles, and the wind blows reddish sand over her face.

Breathe in, breathe out. The rhythm of the world. Breathe in, breathe out.

Breathe in—

29 ⁝

Vikram runs down the five flights of stairs, quickly and silently, without hesitation. He has had plenty of time to memorize the stairs: where they creak, where they are robust.

What to do?

Outside the rain continues to fall thick and steady. Each drop is a minor explosion against the ground (the ground! Even now, every time he puts a foot outside he is unable to suppress a leap of amazement). Water gathers in pools, runs off in minor diversions that rush down the streets. The rain patters against the light waterproof material of his jacket, soaking his hair. He starts to walk. Does it matter which way?

What to do?

He can hear the rain clattering into the bathtubs and buckets left out on the balconies, the stream of water being siphoned indoors into sinks. The Patagonians are conservationists; this much he has learned. A people both careful and reckless.

Careful and reckless.

Stay or go?

What to do?

*

He walks. Head down, purposeful. It is about faking it. Making it look like you belong, even when you don't. Especially when you don't. Taeo, who before he came to Patagonia must always have belonged, has never had to learn that.

Taeo.

Did he ever trust him, really? The Antarctican's explanations were always too suave, even when his honesty was evident. Vikram has known enough people capable of true evil to believe Taeo did not mean him any harm; nonetheless, it is easy to do harm without intent. He should know. He has kept secrets that do not belong to him. No, the real shock is the magnitude of the revelation.

Taeo knew. All along, Taeo knew. But Taeo is only the beginning of an infinitely long chain. He is the tip. It's as if Vikram has plucked a strand of kelp from the surface of the ocean, only to discover that the strand willows down under the water, spiralling deeper and deeper and deeper, evolving into some obscene, ever-expanding farm on the seabed.

Antarctica.

The war between south and north.

He has never thought of his city as small before.

All he wanted was to forget. *Erase the past. The past will trap you.* This he knows; this he has learned, the hard way. And throughout the journey from Osiris, the battle with the skadi boats, the days adrift on the open ocean, the terrible storms, his thoughts were simple. *Just get through it. Stay alive. Make it to land, if land exists. And if it doesn't, you'll die a free man.* A better fate than many he has faced.

Some of the crew died in the initial skadi attack the night after they departed: shot, or lost overboard. Those that survived were left in shock. They had not expected to be attacked. They did not know what Vikram knew, about Whitefly, even though most of them were Linus's people. Or they knew, but could not believe it, until it happened. They could not imagine that a place they had known all their lives, a place they called home, could turn on them so maliciously, and without remorse.

But Vikram knew Osiris, knew its nature and the people in it. He did not want to be Linus's ally any longer. Yes, it was Linus who got him out the tower and onto the expedition boat, giving him the promise of land. A new life, this time for real. But it was also Linus who got him into the tower in the first place. He is done with Linus and Linus's fucked-up schemes.

Just make it to land, if land exists.

It does exist. And there are people. There are cities like Cataveiro and strange countries to the north and the south that he has only ever heard named in history. There are fields full of flowers. There are guanacos. There are mountains and rivers. There is grass you can feel on bare feet, earth you can walk on – and you do not wake to find it was a dream, although often in the past few weeks he has felt as though his dreams are unfolding around him, opening into dimensions that can barely be trusted, despite the evidence of his senses. What makes it real: it is not a paradise. There is disease and quarantine but there is hope here too, because the people here know the world is larger than their place within it.

Now he knows things even Linus, who knew all about Operation Whitefly, did not know.

Antarctica.

The war.

The truth about Osiris.

What to do?

The city in quarantine is silent under the rain. It offers no answers, no obvious solutions. He has wandered some distance, into a part of the city he has not previously explored. In the last couple of weeks Vikram has been careful, going out only when he is sure Taeo will be absent some time. He has been reckless, risking talking to strangers with his fledgling Spanish, aware that they may have seen his face on a poster. Careful and reckless. Patagonian.

He crosses tram lines, but there are no trams. Most lights are off or turned down low. The bars are closed. Once he hears the rumble of a truck and he ducks into a doorway.

He notices two hunched figures ahead. They are too small to be adults. He follows the kids – the only people he has seen out on the street so far. They move furtively, skirting close to the buildings. Once they glance up to check the name of a street. They turn into a little alleyway which opens up into a small square, shielded from the street.

He hears music. At first he thinks it must be the radio, but then he realizes it is coming from a building within the square. Raucous piano playing, and voices, and clapping. It is so long since he has been among people socializing, people celebrating, even if all they are celebrating is having made it through another day. There is something Osirian about such a celebration. He catches sight of the kids running down a flight of steps and sees a glimmer of light from below street level. He follows. The door is just ajar. He peers through the gap and sees the crowd, gathered around a tiny stage with just enough room for a piano.

On the piano top is a single red rose.

Memory paralyses him. In an instant, Vikram is transported back to the Rose Soirée, less than a year ago, in the City. He can see the languorous figure of Adelaide Mystik leaning against the piano in her dark scarlet dress, surrounded by fawning acolytes. The scent of roses is everywhere, thick and sweet and cloying. You can't escape it.

For a moment it is difficult to breathe.

Some mornings, in that ephemeral time between sleep and full consciousness, he can picture a world where she is still alive. In this world she is in hiding, biding her time, or perhaps even happy with her lot, glad to be alive. He can picture her in his old room in the west, with ice frozen over the window, her red hair covering her face for added warmth. He can picture her breath misting in the cold air. At first he tried to exorcize these half-dreams, but now he clings to them, drawing the fantasy out. Soon enough the moment comes where he is awake, and he knows, without question, that Adelaide is dead.

The rose is there. The piano is there. They are real, solid things. A young man is perched on the stool, riffing on the black and white keys. People. Just people. People drinking and talking. Spanish. A language new and old. He understands snippets of conversation. It is warm inside. The room invites him.

He pushes the door open and slips through. People adjust to make room for him. People are laughing and smiling, clinking glasses. They do not look like the city is in quarantine. They do not look like the city is plagued by redfleur, or in the middle of a war.

He looks about for the kids he followed, but cannot spot them.

The pianist finishes with a flourish, stands and bows. Applause. He exits. A woman comes onstage. She raises her voice, speaking over the chattering crowd.

'And now, we have a brand-new act. She's never played the circuit before, but I can promise you, she's something special. And don't forget, we're broadcasting, so please keep your voices down. Now, for the very first time, please welcome to the stage *Pilar y el Loro!*'

El loro, he thinks. The parrot. An animal of the Nazca, like the girl from Bijou's told him.

Pilar y el Loro does not appear. The stage remains empty. The curator stands, her arm held wide for a few moments in a welcoming gesture, then she drops it. She goes to the side of the stage. There is some whispering and murmuring. Then a thin, angry-faced girl with green feathers in her hair and a guitar across her body steps out. She squints and points up at the lights. The curator gestures and the lights dip. The curator gets the girl a stool but she remains standing, fidgeting, very small and very angry-looking. Very scared, Vikram can tell. All his life he has known people like that girl.

She plucks a few notes on the guitar and starts to sing.

As he listens, Vikram feels a strange, tingling sensation filling the room. The chatter drops away. Drinks are cradled, the glassware hushed, the room falls still. In a dizzying moment, Vikram understands that something special is happening here tonight. This girl, *Pilar y el Loro*, has the most beautiful voice he has ever heard, perhaps anyone in the room has ever heard. The hairs are raised on the back of his neck.

He sees his choice then. He sees it very clearly.

There is the new world. These people, this country. He could make his way here, maybe even be happy. He can see a life for himself. Perhaps in this city, perhaps out in the landscapes they have walked through, the valleys of flowers that drive Taeo mad, the mountains where he saw the guanaco. He is smart enough, resourceful enough. He could make his ground dreams into a reality he trusts.

But there is the place he comes from. The place he cannot escape, however far he runs. He understands that too, listening to the voice of *Pilar y el Loro*, which speaks to him as song follows after song: waves and salt and kelp and red hair and green eyes and hot battered squid and roses and ghosts. The place he vowed never to go back to. The place where Adelaide's body drifts, somewhere beneath the waves. The place that is imprinted on him.

Osiris.

All those souls, living in secrecy. The westerners and the Citizens. The one thing they share is their ignorance.

He knows then that there is no choice.

When the girl has done her set, he'll go back to the rooms, get his stuff, find a way past the quarantine barriers. He'll go back to Osiris, and Taeo can make his choice: stay here, or come with him.

The girl stops, breaking off mid-lyric. She is standing in front of the stool, one hand gripped very hard against the edge, as if to hold her up. Her skin is blotched and she is sweating all over. She starts to sway.

30 ¦

The address that clown-face girl gave Mig is some swanky off-street place full of wankers who have decided to party because they think it's the end of the world. But there is Pilar, up on the stage. Looking and sounding like the real thing. She is going to be on the radio. She is going to be incredible. Everyone in the room is holding their breath because of her, including him. Mig feels awash with emotion. It frightens him, the hugeness of what he feels: relief that he has found her, terror that she will be snatched into the plump arms of the rich, and at the same time he is riding on a great swell of pride and love. Pilar is from his block. His warehouse. Maybe one day she will let him say she's his girl. He imagines stepping up to the stage and kissing her, showing everyone that: Mig and Pilar, they're the ones to watch. They're a unit. She has the words and he has the spaces around the words. Together, they are unbeatable.

He won't go up to her, not here. Pilar wouldn't allow it.

But he'll wait. And later, when these drunken idiots have all gone back to their homes, then he will find her.

Pilar stops singing in the middle of a song. Mig waits. He has heard this one before. It's a favourite of his, one of her fado ones with lots of verses, and she is only halfway through. Has she changed her mind? Seconds pass – five seconds, ten seconds. The crowd waits sympathetically. Mig can feel them silently urging her on. The curator hovers at the edge of the stage. Pilar's lips are moving. There's a pulse in her throat. From what he can see it looks like she's trying to sing but nothing is coming out. Has Pilar lost her voice? She can't have lost her nerve.

Something is wrong. Mig's heart constricts. He tries to push through the crowd but they keep him back with jostling elbows. *Pilar. Pilar, what is it?*

The curator is offering Pilar a glass of water. She takes it and drinks the entirety of its contents in one go. When she hands back the empty glass, Mig sees a thin line of blood running from the corner of her mouth. She clutches her stomach. She spasms. Her head jerks forwards and she vomits a rush of watery blood all over herself and everyone in front of her.

Screams fill the room. The crowd back away, wiping dementedly at their faces, arms, any inch of exposed skin. The curator has been sprayed. Spots of blood stand out clear on her bare throat and her face. She stares at Pilar in shock. Pilar is focused on the ground, the blood that's come out of her. She moans and holds her stomach.

'She's sick. Get away from her, she's sick—'

'It's redfleur, it's redfleur!'

'Let me out, let me out of here!'

Something clicks in the curator's face. Mig can see the influx of terror in her eyes. The curator leaps off the stage and starts to fight her way through the crowd, which screams and parts before her.

Pilar staggers about the stage. Her face is full of confusion and fear, so much fear. Mig has never seen her look like that. He watches, trapped by the mass exodus and unable to move from the side of the room. He wants to go and put his arms around her and say he'll look after her, but he can't – he can't. He can't do anything.

The audience trips over one another in its haste to get out of the single narrow exit to the building. Mig sees a girl fall, feet stepping on her, not seeing the girl or not caring. He hears yells amid the screams.

'Get an ambulance!'

'Call the enforcers!'

His heart sinks.

A hand tugs at his. He looks down, sees the scaly hand, sees Ri's face, not scared, no expression because Ri never has any expression. He is saying, 'Mig, we got to go. Mig, we got to go.'

'I'll follow you.'

Another tug.

'The enforcers,' says Ri, insistently.

'I'll follow.'

Ri disappears. And then all at once the room, with its low-lit stage, is deserted. The bartenders and the audience are gone. There is no one left inside except Pilar, collapsed in a puddle of her own bloody vomit, shuddering over her guitar, and Mig, standing a few metres away. For a moment he believes it is a terrible dream. Pilar's eyes open. They meet his.

Recognition.

He can smell the ripe tang of blood.

He is aware of the commotion outside, the shouts and one girl shrieking like a lunatic, but gradually that too fades away, or at least he cannot hear it. There's only him and Pilar, Pilar's brown eyes on his, wide and terrified.

She whispers, 'You should go.'

'I can't leave you here.'

'It's the redfleur.'

'You don't know that.'

'Yeah I do. And if it isn't, they'll shoot me anyway. Contagion law, isn't it.'

Mig thinks of the girl under the bridge and he knows that Pilar is right.

She says again, 'You should go.'

'You could try and escape. Go down into the sewers. They wouldn't come after you there.'

'My insides feel like they're eating themselves. Not just my stomach. It's like there's teeth everywhere. Fuck it hurts.'

'Pilar—'

'I felt kind of weird this morning. I had cramps in my stomach. I thought, don't be so pathetic. You're El Loro. *El Loro*. Ha ha. Hey, if you won't go you could come a bit closer. Just a bit. Don't touch the blood.'

He steps closer, avoiding the spatters of red on the floor, the contagious smears where shoes have skidded on her blood. Carefully, he climbs onto the stage.

'You twat, what are you—'

'Shut up,' says Mig. He crouches, as close to her as he can get without touching anything.

'You're stupid as hell.'

'I love you.'

Pilar starts to cry. Tears stream down her face and snot is coming out her nose. There's even blood in the snot.

'Why d'you say that, you stupid—'

She coughs, a horrible sound, like there are claws scraping around inside her throat. She clamps her hands over her mouth, turning away from him, leaning into the floor.

'Because it's true. I always have, ever since I've known you. I know you've never noticed me much, but that's how it is.'

'I did notice you, course I did.'

'I've been saving up. I've almost got enough for us to get out of Cataveiro. We can go anywhere you want. I don't care. You can choose. Somewhere better than here.'

She smiles. White teeth show through the red blood. He knows this is how he'll remember her. Not with feathers stuck in her hair, but helpless, like this, when her life – and his future – is collapsing around him.

'Mig, I want to say something to you – you got to be careful with that woman, the one you work for. You know what she is – what they say about her—' The coughs start again. Her eyes widen in pain. Is this the end? It can't so be soon, so sudden. He reaches out a hand but she cringes away.

'No! Not you too. The army will be here any second. You've got to go. Go on, get out of here.'

He looks at her frightened face. Pilar, his girl, his beloved. He can't touch her. Can't hug her goodbye or hold her hand. He can hear sounds from outside, and now he realizes they were there all along. She's right. The army is coming.

Pilar closes her eyes. Later, Mig will believe that this was to make it easier for him.

'Bye, Pilar,' he whispers.

He slips into the wings of the stage. Hesitates.

'Go,' she says. He ducks behind the stage and finds the back way out and a fire escape. He gets up high off the streets, expecting the shout of a soldier at any moment, and doesn't stop until he reaches the roof.

The situation in the street is bad. The curator is crashing about in terror, trying to grab anyone who hasn't fled. Mig sees the army trucks arrive. The hazard suits. The masks. The breathing apparatus. The ground is slippery in the rain. They throw a sheet over the curator. She shrieks and fights it but they throw her into the truck and he sees her feet in their high heels kicking. The soldiers don't stop there. He can hear other trucks in the vicinity. They have cordoned off the entire area. They grab whoever is nearby, whoever the curator might have touched. There is fighting, screaming, running. Mig sees a face that looks familiar and hears a yell, 'No, not me!'

The words are not Spanish, they are Boreal words he has seen in the Alaskan's book. He remembers where he saw the face before, the briefest glimpse, in profile. Where the Antarctican lives. The other man.

The suits go inside. They go inside for Pilar. They bring her out. Her body hangs motionless in their arms under the sheet. They throw her in the back of the van and drive off. Soldiers cordon off the area, putting up a white tent with a sign:

Contagion Zone. Do Not Enter.

It takes maybe three minutes.

Mig is not the only one to have come this way. He can see a group of the little kids, the ones that always huddle together. Ri is there. Faces he knows, wet with rain. They look at him sorrowfully and their whispers brush over him like flies.

She saw the jaguar.

Last night.

The jaguar looked at her.

Last night, in the street.

The jaguar.

31

Flashes of red, of gold. Bright dots on blackness.

She is swaying, shifting from side to side.

She hears breathing. A scrape into the throat, a rasp back out again. Is it hers? Can it be hers? Surely she must be dead.

But if she is dead then she does not know where she is. She does not believe in an afterlife.

Flashes of red, of gold. Bright dots on blackness.

She is swaying. She is being carried. Her face is covered and she cannot see.

Faint sounds: a hoarse voice murmuring, a grunt of effort. The deadening impact of boots on sand.

Under the palm of her hand, she feels the soft fur of the jaguar. Padding alongside, his powerful shoulders shifting. She smells meat on his breath.

Teeth, sharp, against her fingers. A long jaw smoothed by a million grains of sand. The caiman's skeleton twists into being before her and it dances. Its spine rattles and its bones knock against one another. The caiman says: Here we are. If we give you your life then you will belong to us. And the desert will have you for always . . .

Flashes of red, of gold. Bright dots on blackness.

When Ramona wakes, she remains still for a long time, not certain if she is alive or dead. She is lying on her back in a low bed. On the other side of the room is a window with the shutters closed. Chinks of light shine through the slats and fall in bars across the room. Ramona is dressed in unfamiliar clothing. Something loose and pale. Her boots have been removed and her feet are bare.

She wriggles her toes. Presses her feet together, one on top of the other. Her toenails are hard and faintly yellowed. They need cutting. She can see the scars of blisters on her feet, a patch of newer skin growing through. There is a reddish tinge to the skin of her lower calves and she thinks of the sand, the blood-coloured desert. Her feet ache.

She is aware, at the edge of her mind, of a weight of things that have passed which she is unable to recall. They press uneasily against her.

Cautiously, she feels her ribcage. Still painful, but she can bear it. Opening the robe-like folds of her clothing, she sees that someone has bandaged her body. She pulls the clothing back.

It is not cool but it is almost cool. She looks at the ceiling, where the long blades of a fan are turning slowly, and wonders where she is and what the roof is made of. Turning her head, she sees a pitcher of water has been left at her side. At once she is aware of a huge thirst. She tries to sit and exclaims at the pain.

A door opens, allowing a blast of light and heat into the room. The figure who enters is female. She shuts the door and it is almost dark and almost cool again.

'You are awake,' says the visitor. 'We are glad to see it.'

Ramona tries to speak and finds that she has no voice.

'Lie still,' says the woman. 'You're not recovered yet.'

She comes to sit at Ramona's side. She dips a sponge into the water pitcher and presses it against Ramona's mouth, squeezing the sponge so that the drops trickle steadily out. The water tastes pure and sweet. It tastes good. It tastes real. The woman squeezes the sponge several times until Ramona's tongue feels a little looser.

'Who are you? Where am I?'

'I am Yamila. This is the Exchange Point. You were carried in from the desert by travellers. They brought you here, to my clinic, and I treated you.'

'Thank you.'

'There is nothing to thank. At the Exchange, everything is a trade. What we do for you, you will do the measure of for us. That is how it is here.'

'Still, I have to thank you. And the people who brought me here. I'd be dead . . .'

'It's true,' says Yamila. 'You are a lucky one.'

She looks at Ramona. Her expression is impenetrable. Now that Ramona's eyes have adjusted to the low light, she sees that the woman is small and spare. She has neat, very regular features, only marked by a triangle of small moles in the hollow beneath one eye. She is dressed in the same robe-like attire as Ramona and her hair curls tightly to her head.

'Are you a northerner?' Ramona asks.

'Here we are not one thing or the other. Not south, not north. This is the belt. Panama is not like other places. In Panama, there must be balance. That is the only price. You should sleep some more. Tomorrow, you may rise.'

Ramona struggles to sit up.

'Wait – you don't understand, there are things—'

The woman pushes her back, using the tips of her fingers against Ramona's good shoulder. Ramona senses a lean, powerful strength behind the simple gesture.

'Tomorrow. Tomorrow the balance will be right. You cannot bring your body to such a low and expect to raise it within the day.'

'In the desert, I had a pack – some things—'

'The pack is here. Now sleep.'

Ramona does not believe she can sleep any longer, but the sweetness of the water is on her lips and tongue. It is only as a surge of tiredness washes over her that she is aware it is not water alone she has been given. The Panama woman slips from the room, and closes the door on Ramona and daylight.

When she next wakes, the pitcher of water is full and there is a note beside it. It reads:

Welcome to Panama.

Her ribs still ache but the sharp pain has gone; she is able to sit up. She pours a glass of water, sniffs it cautiously, then sips. She drinks more deeply, sating her thirst.

There is no sign of Yamila. Ramona goes to the door and listens. Despite the generosity of her rescuers she is wary; she is a stranger here. All she knows of this place is the fleeting impressions Félix has given her over the years, all of them imbued with the chaotic franticness of the Exchange. She opens the shutters a few inches and light floods the room. She opens them further, blinking.

A strong saline breeze whips against her face. The building she is in overlooks a large town which slopes down to a bay lined with docks. Its buildings are low, no more than three storeys, painted white with tended gardens on their roofs. She sees no tramlines or traffic. The town backs onto the desert.

From here, Ramona can distinguish the heads of motionless cranes against the horizon, the tall curve of the sea walls that shield the town, the warehouses and the trucks and the rows of containers. Beyond the docks and the bay, the Atlantic stretches east, a deep shade of aquamarine.

There are ships in the bay, but none of them have docked. Ramona screws up her eyes against the blazing light, struggling to recognize any of the vessels, but she realizes quickly that they are larger than any Patagonian vessel. The fleet she is looking at is that of the Boreal States.

Ramona feels a swell of rage. She embraces it, allows herself to feel the full extent of the revenge she will enact. Rage is good. Rage will keep her centred.

Who are you and what do you want with my mother?

There is little sign of human life. The position of the sun puts the time at midday. She decides the population must be sheltering inside.

Time for her to explore.

She fills one of her water bottles from the pitcher and exits the room, finding herself in a corridor with other rooms leading off it. She heads downstairs and out through the reception of the clinic. There is no one else about.

She walks down through the drowsy town. A cyclist passes her and she hears music drifting from the odd window, but all the shops are closed. Ramona is not in good shape. Her muscles ache and the brush of the white robes is sore against sunburned skin. Walking, she can feel the pain in her ribs. But she is determined to get to the docks.

Signs near the bay point to a desalination plant down the coast. The road leading away looks well maintained, like everything else: this is a prosperous place. Adjacent to the docks are several huge glass domes, the like of which she has never seen before. That's Boreal, she thinks. The hairs rise on her arms despite the heat.

At the docks she finds a single man dozing in the shade of a large container. He is wearing the same loose white attire as she, tinged ochre in colour by the sands. When she says hello he starts visibly, his eyes glaring through the bronze of his sunshades.

He says something in Boreal English.

'Español?' she asks.

He switches easily.

'It's the midday. Who creeps about in the midday?'

'I didn't mean to disturb you,' she says. 'I was hoping you could help me.'

His eyebrows knit.

'You're not from Panama.'

'No.'

'A southerner.'

'That's right.'

'What do you have?'

'What do you mean?'

'You're in Panama, so you must have something. That's how it is here. I'm a truck driver. When the fleets come I drive containers from one ship to another. In my truck. What do you have?'

'I was rescued from the desert. I didn't come here to trade. I came looking for something.'

'You were rescued?' A new curiosity in his voice. 'From the desert?'

'Travellers brought me here. A woman looked after me.'

The truck driver offers her a grizzled smile. 'Then you must have something, whether you know it or not. We would have let you die, otherwise.'

His voice is quite flat. She believes him.

'Your town has harsh rules,' she replies evenly.

He shrugs. 'It's a harsh world. This is Panama. This here bay was the entrance to a canal once, the greatest canal the world ever knew. Now the reservoirs are gone and there's a desert. Times change. We're not one thing and we're not another. Everything has a price. You'll find out yours soon enough, I'm sure.'

The truck driver tips his hat over his head and leans back against the crate, closing his eyes behind the shades.

'That's all very well, but can't you help me, just a little? Seeing as I know nothing about the town or its ways? If this is the Exchange Point, then when is the Exchange? I haven't missed it? Tell me that, at least.'

'See for yourself – the Boreals are here. The Patagonian ships are late, but that's Patagonians for you. They'll be here. Eventually. If it's the Exchange you've come for, you're just in time.'

He glances at the sun's position in the sky.

'People'll wake up in a couple of hours. Preparations are beginning.

Make yourself useful, you might earn what you're looking for. Or are you hoping to jump north?'

'People do that?'

'They might try.'

'I'm looking for information.'

And medicine, she thinks, but she does not tell him that. She needs to activate the holoma and find the Antarcticans; Taeo promised they would find her medicine. Maybe they'll even help her to find Inés, if Taeo's message is that important.

She wants to ask the truck driver about the crates he takes from one ship to the next. *What goes onto those ships? Are there people? Do you look? Do you know? Is this the first time or have there been others, before my mother?* But it's too early; she cannot risk drawing attention to herself so soon. She needs to use the chaos of the Exchange to cover her tracks.

'Again, you've come to the right place. But prices are high and those who can buy are few. Think about what you can offer, lady. And leave me to my nap.'

She leaves the truck driver and walks a little way along the sea walls, surveying the Boreal ships. They are heavyweight steel vessels. The Alaskan ships are blocked in blue and red, those from Veerdeland are blue and gold, and the Sino-Siberian vessels have bright yellow and white stripes. Even from a distance, Ramona can tell that these ships are the product of wealth.

She does not see a single soul on deck. The silent presence of the ships gives her a peculiar feeling. The Boreal ships are a statement. This is the might of the north: look at it, admire and respect it. Do not question it.

She looks back at the strange, hushed town. Who lives here, in a place that is neither one thing nor another? Traders? Spies? Is the Antarctican agent in one of those houses? When and from where will the raiders appear?

The unbroken heat of the day, the hypnotic blue of the sea, are making her faint. She takes shelter in the shade, suddenly fighting for breath. When the worst of the heat has passed, she returns to Yamila's clinic.

It is only then that she discovers the holoma is gone.

'You did not think you would be looked after for nothing, did you?' says Yamila. Her dark eyes regard Ramona calmly. She displays no sign of remorse.

'You stole from me!'

The thought of someone going through her belongings disgusts her. It is the worst kind of betrayal. She imagines Yamila's hands lifting each object, scrutinizing them, assigning values to the small things that make up Ramona's life. It makes her sick to the core.

'Where is it? What the fuck did you do with it?'

'It has been sold,' says Yamila. 'It paid for your treatment, after you were brought here half-dead from the desert. It paid for your hospitality. It paid for your life, which you'd do well to remember. Panama is a market, and everything has—'

'A value, yes, everything has a fucking value, you've said it a hundred times already. Guess what, that had a value to me. And in my country, stealing is a crime.'

Yamila shrugs. 'In my country, not paying your dues is a crime.'

The complete lack of contrition only fuels Ramona's rage. She clenches her fists at her sides. She is afraid she might hit the other woman, and she would, without regret, in any other circumstances. She grits her teeth to keep her voice down.

'You have to get it back. I was entrusted with that thing. It's not a toy. It is not something you can take from me. It's not even mine.'

'There is no way I can recover it,' says Yamila.

'What do you mean there's no way? At least tell me where it's gone, and give me the chance to get it back myself. Don't you understand? Don't you realize what you've done?'

Only then does she see a spark of warning in her host's eyes.

'My understanding is clear. It is you who do not comprehend our laws. I have saved your life and you have paid for it. There will be no further discussion on this subject.'

'I can't stay here. I'll find somewhere else.'

'Do what you like, although it would be foolish. Your hospitality is covered to the end of the Exchange. After that—' Yamila shrugs '—it does not bother me what you do.'

'Fuck you. I'm not staying in a place where my stuff is stolen.'

Ramona is trembling with fury as she walks out. She curses herself for trusting the other woman's altruism. She'll sleep on the streets, she doesn't care. She'll sleep by the docks and keep watch for the raiders, guarding her own stuff while she's at it. Fuck Yamila. Fuck Panama. Who knows what was in that holoma, the Antarctican who broke her plane was so cagey about it, and now it's in the hands of who knows, the highest bidder no doubt, ripe for the north and exploitation by the Boreals.

She is humiliated. She has never lost a package. Never, in almost fourteen years of flying, and there have been enough people who have entrusted her with their goods, their children even. She has let Taeo down. Maybe he let her down first but maybe she was a fool to put her faith in the hands of an addict.

She is afraid now she will make another error, another misjudgement, when the stakes are so high. She has to focus. What's lost is lost. It's all about her mother now. But the Antarcticans could have helped her. *Fuck.*

By the time she has walked as far as the docks, her ribs are throbbing with pain from the weight of her pack. She knows she has massively overdone it. It is mid-afternoon and the town is slowly rising from its siesta. She finds a corner in a quiet bar overlooking the docks, where it is possible to eavesdrop on the conversations of the dock workers. She drinks a beer and listens, trying to ignore the pain in her chest.

Talk of the Patagonian fleet.

Late as usual.

Talk of the rota.

I'm sick of operating that fucking crane.

Talk of the Boreals.

If they'd dock now, we could get half the work done today.

There is no mention of stolen people.

But there wouldn't be, would there.

That evening there is a storm. She watches the rain and asks the bartender to recommend a cheap place to stay overlooking the docks. He directs her down the street. She hurries the short distance, white Panama robes swishing at her ankles. The rain is already coming down heavily. The room available is not cheap but she takes it.

The owner of the hotel locks down the windows of her house and goes underground. She says that all the people of the town do the same. Their cellars are watertight, and in the event of flooding, a network of tunnels leads out into the desert.

Ramona elects to stay upstairs. She pries open a shutter and watches the storm thundering over the bay. Sheet lightning illuminates the Boreal ships rolling on huge, white-foamed waves. She can hear the rumbling clouds, the rain beating on the roof. She can see the waves surging against the sea walls.

Not one place and not another.

In what kind of place is Inés now?

Over breakfast, the hotelier asks if Ramona will stay for another night. Ramona says she will see. The hotelier warns her the town is filling up. A fresh wave of travellers and traders will arrive today and Ramona would do well to book now, before prices go up. That is how it is at the Exchange. Everything has a price.

As the hotelier speaks she is swiping through text and images in the flat weave of a square of cloth. Ramona leans over to look.

'Is that Boreal?'

'It's mine, so it doesn't matter if it was once Boreal or a product of the Solar Corporation.'

'Is that another rule?'

The owner smiles secretively. Ramona thinks, I don't trust their smiles. Any of them.

'Is this place networked?'

'That's an old-fashioned word. We're wired, if that's what you mean.' She looks at Ramona with open curiosity. 'You southerners are funny. What brings you to Panama, if not the north?'

'I'm looking for someone.'

'And?'

'That's it.'

'There's always an and,' says the hotelier. 'People like to say they're doing something for someone else, but the truth is, no action is altruistic. We understand this, in Panama. It's what the new age has brought us. Everything is commerce. Ask yourself why you wish to go north.'

'I don't want to go north.'

The woman nods as though she has proved a point.

What is it with these people?

The woman's words are like a spore, and having brushed against Ramona, it releases a miasma of doubts.

I won't let you, I won't let you make me believe I wanted this, I did not want this, I do not want to go north.

'I'm here to find someone,' she says firmly.

The hotelier is right. Over the next few days there is a steady trickle of travellers into the town. Some have travelled on foot, some with llamas, others with battered old trucks and motorcycles. Ramona spends as much time as the heat allows at the harbour, keeping the clothes from the clinic so she can blend in, and watching for any sign of the raiders. She asks questions and watches the faces of those she interrogates, hoping for clues. She looks for Aris's party but does not see them, and she starts to worry. How many people are here, how can she possibly notice them all?

And still the Boreal ships wait quietly and imperious while the Patagonian ships do not come.

It is midday siesta when the shout goes up. She hears one voice, then another joins in, and another, until the town is ringing with the cry.

'The Exchange! The Exchange is here!'

After days of protracted somnolence, the town is coming alive. People are leaning out of their windows and spilling into the streets. Bicycles and motorcycles stream ahead. Ramona does not hesitate; she joins the throng hurrying excitedly towards the seafront.

At the docks the tall heads of cranes rear into view, swinging elegantly above the ships. Some have already docked; others move ponderously into the bay. Lined up side by side, the Boreal fleet is a huge, imposing sight. The Patagonian ships are smaller, lighter, built for swift runs and dodging pirates. Already the harbour is swarming. Hulls open up, ramps are raised and lowered, crates are shunted down and the muscled arms of stevedores glisten with sweat as they lift and carry. It is as if she has been transported to an entirely different place.

Some containers, those of pre-arranged business contracts and regular exchanges, are driven directly from one ship to another. Deposits of Antarctican yttrium and dysprosium and the Patagonian poppy harvest are headed north. Shipments of Alaskan grain will travel to the south. Other merchandises are dragged to the nearest square, in minutes transformed to a bustling marketplace. The Exchange is more than business. It is a festivity. But Ramona's initial excitement quickly fades. There are so many crates, so many ships. The sight is overwhelming. A transfer could be going on right under her nose, and she would never know it.

She is standing in the marketplace, feeling lost and disorientated, not knowing what will be her next step, when she hears a voice calling her name. A familiar voice.

'Ramona! Hey, Ramona!'

It is Félix. Right there on the other side of the marketplace. His face caught between astonishment and laughter. Her heart leaps. They fight their way across the stalls towards one another. She collapses into his embrace; his arms wrap tight around her until she yelps.

'What's the matter?'

'Cracked ribs.'

'It's always something with you, isn't it? What by all the Nazca are you doing in Panama?'

They walk along the docks to where they can climb the steps to the sea wall and talk in private. Félix points out the *Aires*. Ramona tells him most of her story. She tells him about the jinn, and the medicine, but not about the raiders. She cannot quite bear to tell him that. She knows Félix: he will either try and help or try to stop her. Either could be disastrous.

'You look well,' she says. He does look well. He has always had a good physique, muscular from the physical work of the ship, and his hair has grown out a little from its close shave. She likes it; she runs her fingers through it.

'You do too,' he says.

'You're lying. I look a state. I was almost dead when they found me in the desert. You can't come back to life that soon.'

'No, you do,' he insists. 'Maybe it's this place.' He squints at the sky. 'There's something about the light.'

'It's because we're on the border. The very edge of the south.'

'The edge of the north too.'

They sit watching the sun glinting on the waves. All the oceans of the world, swirling about the continents, meet at this line. The wind carries the chorus of the Exchange: traders and loaders, contracts legal and illegal.

'What happened to the plane?'

'It's in the desert, somewhere.'

'Can it be fixed?'

'I don't know. Maybe Raoul – maybe even I can. But I'd need to find it . . .'

'You found it before.'

'That was luck.'

'You're lucky.'

'But luck runs out. Maybe someone else will find it and take it.'

'This isn't like you, to be so defeatist.'

She stares at him miserably. 'Félix, the plane is my entire life. What do I do now? How can I travel?' She would never have said she cared about her possessions before now, before they had been taken from her.

'You will find it,' he says. 'And you'll find medicine too. I'll help. I'll ask. We'll get this cure for Inés.'

She leans over and kisses him. He responds, his hands on her back drawing her closer. The smell of him and the smell of salt. She feels that familiar surge of tenderness and desire. There is a helplessness in it, but a certainty too. She has known Félix almost all her life; he is the closest thing to a soulmate she will ever have. They pull apart. Félix is smiling. She thinks, life is easy for him, and it always will be. She does not begrudge him that. But she feels the gap between them.

'Stay with me tonight?' he asks.

'On the ship?'

'We can take a room in the town.'

'Yes. Let's do that. Somewhere overlooking the docks.'

She rests her head against his shoulder.

'Why were you delayed, anyway?'

'Fuego was in lockdown. It was strange, actually.' He turns to face her. 'Maybe you've heard something.'

'About a lockdown? No, nothing. What happened? Not redfleur?'

'No – although, did you hear about Cataveiro?'

'Not the redfleur?'

He nods.

'Shit.'

'Yeah. They're in quarantine.' For a moment they sit in silence, knowing there is nothing to say, before Félix continues. 'We'd already departed Fuego, but half the fleet was there when it all kicked off, and they got held up. A telegram came up the coast; we had to wait for them to catch up. Fuego wasn't letting anyone in or out.'

She frowns. 'But why?'

'Pirates was the line we were fed. But the rumours were there was a shipwreck down the coast. And not just any shipwreck.'

'Antarctica?'

Félix's voice drops to a whisper. 'Not even. A boat from the sea city.'

She stares.

'You know, the one they called Osiris,' Félix adds, as if any clarification were needed. 'But it couldn't be, could it? I mean, the city was destroyed. Fifty years ago, it was all destroyed. Boats went there, they never came back, there was nothing.'

She tries to say something but all she is capable of is a slack-faced *oh*. Félix mistakes her shock for incredulity. He keeps talking. It can't be, it couldn't possibly be. But why would anyone say such a thing? Who would make up a rumour like that? What did they mean by it? While Félix wonders aloud it is as if a series of events are slotting into place before Ramona's eyes. The Antarctican, Taeo. His sudden, desperate message, the timing of which never quite added up, and yet she had never really questioned it, wondering, but not wanting to know more. She remembers his insistence that she fly a direct route to Panama. His fumbling for cash: take this. Whatever you need.

The holoma.

The holoma that was stolen from her.

You must have something of value, said the truck driver. Otherwise, we would have let you die.

'Félix,' she says. 'I think it's true.'

She thinks, how odd and unpredictable are the ways of the world. The lost city. The lost city is not lost. A revelation that, at another time, might consume her thoughts completely, and yet now all she can do is push it to the back of her mind, along with the fate of Cataveiro. After she has found her mother, she could try and track down an Antarctican agent and tell them what she suspects the holoma contained – but until then, this is somebody else's problem.

Through the afternoon she patrols the harbour relentlessly, but at no point does she see a transfer of people from a Patagonian ship to a northern one, or even people going on board a Boreal ship. They'll move them at night, she thinks. This is secret cargo. They'll take no risks; they'll cover their tracks. And there is no possible way she can watch the entire fleet in the dead of night.

She has to find out which ship her mother is on, and which ship she is being taken to.

There are ten Patagonian ships. Félix's ship, the *Aires*, is the only one she can absolutely discount. Of the others, the *Bogotá* is a renowned pirate hunter, and the least likely to be shepherding human cargo. She has had past dealings with the *Rio*'s captain, a young and impetuous character, but fiercely patriotic. That leaves seven ships to search which might have brought the prisoners, and the Boreal destination ship could be any of them.

All manner of people are here, but they have one thing in common. They are hunters. They are looking for something: a spare part, a geotech seed or a rare frog for a private collection. Information.

Ramona goes to the harbourmaster's offices, a two-storey premises in a row of secure warehouses. Outside the cranes are swinging into action as cartons are deposited onto the docks, then taken to temporary warehouses for logging before being trucked down to their destination ship, or up to the market for less formal distribution. Any one of those cartons might hold people.

Pushing aside her fears, she puts on her best swagger and strolls into the offices.

'Hey, who do I talk to here about an unlogged package?'

The clerk looks up at her, bored.

'What's your registration number?'

'I don't have one, that's the thing. I've been sent all this way to pick up a package and all I know is it isn't logged.'

He smirks.

'Sounds like blacklist dealings to me.'

'There's nothing blacklist about it. I just get told where to go and what to do. Seven years I've been hauling cargo and I never had to drive this far north before. Just do a girl a favour and give me a glance at the log register, would you?'

He hands her a slate. 'Everything's named and numbered. No missing packages.'

She scrolls dizzily through the logs. The numbers blink on the screen: fucking robotics, she can't escape it. She is looking for something. She doesn't yet know what. A glitch. An anomaly. If people are going north who shouldn't be, someone has to feed them. Bodies have to be accounted for.

'How many crew members on each ship?'

He pulls up numbers on the slate, too quickly for her to see.

'Look, it's all right here. You people need to get computerized. Seriously.'

'We don't like machines,' she says automatically.

'It's fucking medieval, that's all I'm saying. Do you know how long it takes trying to equate credit with cash? And now I've got to find everything for you and it's taking up my time . . .'

'You're taking up your time slurring my culture,' she says sharply, too sharply for her previous, laid-back persona. He gives her a look.

'I don't have to help you, lady.'

'I'm just doing my job, same as you.'

'Here. Look. Read. That's all the crews.'

She bites down a retort. 'Thanks.'

She checks the numbers of the Boreal ships, and then she navigates painstakingly through the slate to find the scheduled water intake for each ship. There is nothing to suggest provision for additional passengers, on any of the ships.

Félix is already waiting at the docks where they arranged earlier. She can tell at once that something is wrong. Félix's emotions are written into his body, and the way he is standing betrays his agitation now. She hurries towards him.

'What is it, what's wrong?'

He glances quickly about, then grabs her hand.

'Come on.'

'I thought we were going to eat here?' There are plenty of cafes and restaurants on the front, and she wants to maintain her surveillance of the ships, but Félix is leading her away from the docks, heading back into the town.

'Seriously, what's up?'

He shakes his head: not here. She knows she won't get anything out of him while he is in this state – it is rare for Félix to act so alarmist. She follows him through the town's backstreets. Félix approaches and rejects several locations before settling upon a gloomy brasserie with barely any customers, where he orders two beers and brings them to a dark corner. The beers are served straight from the fridge. Ramona presses the glass to her cheek, savouring its coolness against her skin.

'You'd better tell me what's going on.'

'You're on the radio.'

'What?'

'You're on the radio! They're saying you're wanted, Xiomara's after you. There's a reward and everything. Shit, Ramona, you need to get out of Panama before someone recognizes you.'

It is only in the silence that follows that she realizes why he has brought them to this particular place. There is no radio here. The brasserie's music originates from a jukebox in the corner, playing melancholy old songs.

'What exactly does the radio say?'

Félix shifts nervously. She puts a hand on his knee.

'Stop jittering. Tell me what you heard.'

He drops his voice. 'I heard Xiomara is offering a reward for anyone who captures the pilot Ramona Callejas. They said your name, your exact name. They said you're wanted in Cataveiro. How did you even get to that woman? You must have really pissed her off.'

She remembers Xiomara's face. Her final screaming words. The red rash all over her neck. On the other side of the desert, as far from Cataveiro as she could get without going north of the belt, she feels suddenly exposed.

'I did.'

Félix takes a gulp of beer. 'You should leave now.'

'How can I leave? I don't have any transport.'

'I've thought about it. We'll hole you up on the ship until we leave. But we'll have to do it at night, when it's quiet. And I can't tell any of the crew, not even the captain. They're good people but we can't trust anyone. I can bring everything you need, it won't be long, just until the Exchange closes and then we'll be on our way.'

'Félix, I can't leave, I can't hide on your ship!'

'It's the only way. You've got to stay out of sight.'

'I can't do that.'

'I know what you're thinking. You're thinking about the medicine. I'll get it. I'll get it for you, Ramona, I promise. Shit, I shouldn't even say your name in here. We don't know who's listening.'

'Shut up and listen to me a minute, will you? There's a reason I can't leave.'

'The medicine, I know, I—'

'My ma was taken by raiders.'

The fuzzy sound of the jukebox drops into the silence. A singer who was popular twenty, maybe thirty years ago. An old song.

Félix is staring at her, uncomprehending. 'Inés?'

Now Ramona is whispering.

'Taken. By northerners. They've been kidnapping people from the villages on the east coast, and bringing them to Panama. That's all I know.'

'They took Inés?'

'Yes.'

'And you didn't tell me?'

He is hurt, she can tell. Angry, too. He tries to swallow it.

'You should have told me.'

'I didn't want you to get caught up in it.'

'That's my people there too.'

'I know. I know. But Carla's fine. It was Gabi who saw – she saw them take my ma.'

'Fuck.' He squeezes her hand. 'Fuck. What do we do?'

For a moment she feels the panic rising. The Exchange is short and she has so little time. This is why I didn't tell him, she thinks. Because to say it aloud makes it real. Her eyes are wet. She can't cry now, not here. She's made it all this way. And she can't waste time away from the docks, letting desolation swamp her. She needs to be there, on guard, watching . . .

She wipes the tears impatiently from her cheeks.

'Ramona.' Félix pulls her into a careful hug. She leans against him, not caring that it hurts. 'We'll find her. We'll look together. Tell me everything.'

She tells him about the village in the mountains, what Gabi saw, about the worker at the desalination plant. She sees Félix's anger growing as she explains that the stolen people are brought north by ship, a Patagonian ship; he shakes his head in disbelief. It is a relief, in the end, to share the burden. So many fears, unspoken until now. What do the northerners want with Inés? What are they planning to do with her? Félix says not to think about that.

They finish the beers. Félix suggests a plan. It's the stevedores, he says, who know what goes on a ship and what comes off. Those are the people they need to target. They can divide the names up between them, and while they're at it, they can ask about the medicine. He'll do that. It will draw less attention to Ramona.

They begin their rounds the next day. Ramona is on edge, jumping at every unexpected movement. It takes an immense effort to get up and leave the room they are staying in. For all she knows, Yamila, who knew where she came from, has already sold the story to the Panama authorities. Her only hope is that the chaos of the Exchange will maintain her cover.

Outside, the day is even hotter. She can feel her skin tightening under the sun. Her feet sweat in their sandals as she clops through the dusty streets. To the south of the town, she can see the distant swirls of sand devils in the desert. There is something strangely alluring about the sight. She remembers the jaguar, the moment she believed herself dead. The desert has marked me, she thinks. But I don't yet know how and by how much.

In her pockets she has a list of names, provided by Félix. He has given her the ones who have been in their jobs the shortest times. He says they are more likely to talk.

The stevedores are all busy with the transfer of goods. She catches one on his break and offers to buy him a beer. He refuses, but says he'll take a can. She worries it was a mistake, to offer alcohol – will he think she is trying to bribe him? She asks about unlogged packages. The stevedore is adamant. Nothing gets through without being checked off on the register. What about the black market, she asks. Everyone knows there's a secondary trade. If there is, he says, it's nothing to do with what goes on here, under his nose. Is she implying he's not doing his job?

She fares no better with the other names. Some are willing to chat, some are not, but on one point they are all agreed: nothing gets through the net. Halfway through the afternoon she feels eyes on the back of her neck and turns uneasily to find someone is watching her: the truck driver she met on her first day in Panama. She meets his gaze, suddenly suspicious. What was he doing down at the harbour in the heat of day, when the rest of the town was dozing?

'Found what you're looking for?' asks the driver.

She shakes her head. 'Not yet. Care to help me?'

'You've been asking a lot of questions, it seems.'

'You don't get answers without questions.'

He smiles. She cannot tell the meaning of the smile. She begins to feel a creeping paranoia, a prevailing sense of dread pressing down on her with the impossible equatorial heat. Are they all in on it?

The last name on the list. Ramona is exhausted. She gets someone to point him out to her, and watches him stacking crates for a while before she approaches. He's the youngest of the workers she has spoken to, not quite grown into his body, with large hands and feet, lacking the rhythm of the more experienced stevedores. A light spread of acne still covers his cheeks.

'You got a minute, kid?'

He straightens, surprised.

'What's that?'

'You got a minute?'

'A minute, I guess.' He lifts his hat and wipes sweat from his forehead.

Ramona points at the crates. 'That's normally my job. Except the boat I drive's a lot smaller than those ships.'

'Yeah?'

'Yeah. I've never been this far north before either. You?'

'No further than this.'

'Ever thought about it?'

'Fuck no.'

'You're a southerner like me, from your accent.'

'That's right.'

'Where are you from?'

He names a small town south of Cataveiro.

'I know the region. Good people.'

'They are. But hey, I'm not supposed to be standing round chatting. This is my first year on the Exchange, you know. I don't want to make mistakes.'

'And I wouldn't want to distract you, believe me. I've got a boss too. I know what they're like. That's why I was hoping you could help me out.' She pauses. He doesn't say yes, but he doesn't say no either. 'Some of the people in this town, they aren't so friendly, you know? There's no doing anyone a favour. Not how my mama brought me up.'

'I guess they're not the most talkative bunch,' the young stevedore acknowledges. 'But they're all good guys.'

'I'm sure they are. Listen, all I want to know is, is there anything that slips through the books? I mean, I can tell you're all ridiculously efficient, but the Exchange is so huge, there must be the odd thing that isn't logged.'

'No, not really. It's all very efficient, like you said. Look, I've got this list, everything's got a number and a destination, every number's ticked off by us as soon as it comes off the ships. So nothing could get in or out the bay without us knowing, see?'

'So there's no fear of smuggling?'

'Harbourmaster runs a tight crew. What you asking about smuggling for? That talk'll get me into trouble, it will.' He sounds distinctly nervous now, and she wonders if it is just the new job as he claims, or something more. She smiles.

'I probably phrased it wrong. Like I said, I'm here for my boss. She's had some stuff go missing – nobody's fault at this end, I'm sure – and she's asked me to come up here and have a look around for myself, see where the loopholes are. That's all.'

He shakes his head firmly. 'I can't see how anything could get lost. All the crates are logged.'

'What about passengers?' she says idly.

He tugs nervously at the fine hairs on his chin.

'What about them? All crew, isn't it? Hardly any passengers cross the belt, I'm not sure there's even a single one this Exchange. Not any I know about.'

'Have you seen something?' she asks softly. 'Have you seen people?'

The stevedore's eyes dart around.

'No. No, I haven't seen anything.'

Ramona feels a shiver of certainty. She leans closer, not letting him evade her gaze.

'I'm looking for those people. They shouldn't be here. You know they shouldn't be here. So tell me what you saw.'

'Look, all it was, a few people changed ships in the middle of the night, no lights or nothing. And that's kind of strange. I only saw because I'd had a drink with one of the guys, and we were out late.'

'Did he see it too?'

He hesitates. 'He said he didn't see nothing. Maybe I imagined it. It was probably just shadows, is all. And I've got to get on with my job. I've been chatting to you way too long and you're making me say things I shouldn't.'

'I won't tell a soul. Which ship did they go to?'

He turns pointedly away.

'Which ship?' she presses.

'The *Polar Star*,' he mutters. 'Now leave me alone.'

'Thank you. I'll remember you helped me.'

She continues walking along the harbour front, trying to contain her nerves. When she reaches the *Polar Star* she stops and finds a spot where she can observe the ship discreetly. It is one of the smallest northern ships, with Alaskan markings. She knows all the ships by now, and the cargo it has been taking on board is suitably innocuous: deposits of Antarctican rare earth metals, exhausted solar batteries for refurbishing . . .

And people.

I'm here, Ma, she thinks fiercely. And I'm going to get you off there.

32

When the grave-watcher signs in for his shift, the fifteen or so glass units in the isolation ward are full again. He knows what that means. It means he's in for another night below.

He changes into his hazard suit, tucking everything in carefully so nothing is exposed. He takes a last gulp of clean air before he puts the mask over his face. He signs out his syringes. They have given him a larger consignment than yesterday. When he says thank you to the nurse she looks at him the way people do sometimes, as though he is something unnatural.

A truck has just come in. After the infected have been sedated, the grave-watcher helps the soldiers carry them down into the sealed basement where he relieves the other guy. It is getting full down here. The smell of death is ripe. He directs the soldiers to lay the new infected on the empty pallets, each of which has a preparatory body bag as an undersheet. The soldiers look spooked, probably because the place is also a mortuary – or was, and will be again, soon enough. You'd think they'd be used to death, but redfleur has that effect: it makes people want to run and hurl themselves into a river or off a cliff. The soldiers have to wait while the grave-watcher logs the new infected. Each case gets a number, an entry time and a date. On the other side, another number will be assigned. An exit time.

The soldiers are impatient: Aren't we done yet?

That's it, he says.

They can't get out quick enough. The basement door clangs shut and he is left in almost darkness with the infected, a case of syringes and a gun.

In the next four hours he does not see anyone except for a doctor who comes to take a blood sample from each of the infected. It is hot tonight, too hot to be here a minute longer than he has to be. The grave-watcher's feet swell up in his rubber boots and his filter mask itches his face. It feels as though his breath is coagulating in the narrow space between mask and mouth.

He remembers the heat from the last outbreak. That was summer, too. Five years ago. Three and a half thousand dead. The virus is smarter than humans. Every time they find a vaccine, another strain appears.

This job is well paid, but few would want it. Most of the infected are dead within hours of arrival, but some take a long time, gurgling on their own blood, breath rattling away in the almost darkness, moaning softly. Something of the dying must stick to him, because people in the city leave him alone. They veer around him in the street as if he is a rock in the middle of a river. The grave-watcher checks the time, although he doesn't need a watch; he can tell the hour true to the minute. One after five. Time for the hourly tag. He eases himself up from his chair, his plastic hazard suit crackling, and switches on his torch.

He prefers to remain in the dark, because in the dark you can only hear them. It's easier to cradle their heads if you can't see what's happened to their poor faces. But he needs some semblance of light for this bit. He flashes the light over the chamber. Eight souls, they brought in tonight.

He works along the line. The first is late stages, but still alive. Male, in his thirties, cheap clothes under the sheet, a dribble of blood-flecked saliva down his chin. The peeling is severe. His internal organs will be collapsing soon. The grave-watcher gives him a couple of hours.

He injects a squirt of heroin into the man's neck. It's the cheap, nasty stuff that would fell any addict in a matter of months, but it makes little difference to them; they only need it for a few hours. Three days is the longest anyone has lasted.

The man breathes a soft *aaaah* as the opiate hits.

'Easy, boy, easy now,' says the grave-watcher. Often he wonders why they don't just shoot the infected outright; everyone knows how it ends. And it got to that way, last time, because they were too many. But no, the monitoring must be done. Sometimes the grave-watcher eases them along.

The next one is dead. Cords of the neck rigid in a final contortion, eyelids stretched wide. One eye has imploded. That happens sometimes. The grave-watcher draws up the sides of the body bag and zips it tight. He hauls the corpse to the other end of the basement and puts a fresh bag on the pallet. The burners will be round in a couple of hours for the morning collection.

The girl is young, a teenager with clumps of feathers stuck in her hair. She's been here a couple of days now. Her clothes are covered in dry blood. It looked like she'd vomited up most of her insides on arrival. Still, she's hanging on. Strong, this one, but strength means nothing to the redfleur. It makes him sad to see them young. He tries not to linger with her. Quick shot and on.

'Help me.'

'I'm coming, boy. I'll be with you, never you worry.'

'Help me.'

The same voice again, faint and croaking, but surprisingly clear. They are not normally lucid, or if they are, he gets the heroin quick. You don't want to be aware of your last hours in this place. He gets a syringe ready.

A hand takes hold of the plastic leg of his suit. The grave-digger jumps and swears.

He swings the torch-light onto the next victim and gets the shock of his life.

A young man is lying there, between the girl he just injected, and another whose face he cannot see, curled on its side with the hands clawed in rigor mortis. He recognizes this man. He was brought in two days ago with the girl. He had all the signs: the bleeding, the vomiting. By yesterday the skin on his hands was beginning to peel. He should be dead by now.

But he is not dead. He is alive, sweating and shivering, and his face is clean, except for a few scabs – scabs! – forming on his cheeks. His eyes are open – swollen, but no blood – and he gazes imploringly at the grave-watcher.

'Help me,' he says. 'Help me get out of here.'

The grave-watcher is frightened. He glances at the long row of the infected. There is no question that they are redfleur victims. The man between them is infected. He must be infected.

'My name's Vikram,' says the young man. 'Please, help me.'

Enough. Names are bad. The grave-watcher does not want to hear names. He does not want to know who they are. He grabs his syringe and, before the man can protest, he injects him. The man's eyes fly wide in shock and protest. The grave-watcher wants to switch off his torch but he can't, he has to stand there watching until those dreadful eyes lose their focus and roll up. The man shudders and goes into that space they go, the last place before the end.

33

'Ramona, that ship isn't going anywhere.'

Late into the night, the docks are deserted and the lights are low. The ships and the silent cranes cast long shadows, making the docks a chequered, uncertain ground where it would be easy to creep about unnoticed, flitting between the rows of locked containers. The *Polar Star* rests between a large Alaskan ship and a smaller Siberian neighbour. A few lights glow from its upper decks. The ships groan faintly with the movement of the tide, and the night is full of unidentified sounds: taps, creaks and murmurs, the hiss of the sea.

Ramona's eyes are strained from hours of vigil at the window. It's so hot, and even stripped to her tank top and shorts with the window open wide to let in the sea breeze, she is sweating.

'What if they leave tonight?'

'There are two more days of the Exchange. They won't go anywhere without the rest of the fleet. That never happens. It would draw attention.'

'They could leave any time. I have to be ready.'

'Ready for what? To get arrested like you almost did today?'

'There's no police in Panama, Félix. They don't arrest people here.'

'No, they drive them out into the desert and leave them there.

That's how Panama deals with anyone who interrupts the Exchange. They let you die the slow way. Trust me, I've been coming here long enough to know this is a violent place, even if it doesn't look it.'

She sees something. Movement? No, just the shadow of a crane as it shifts in a gust of wind. She rubs her eyes. She is starting to imagine things.

'I had to ask questions. What else could I do?'

'I don't know – how about not talk to anyone related to the *Polar Star*?'

'It's my ma in there, Félix!'

'And I've told you what we should do. We should go to the harbourmaster and ask for an official search.'

'They won't find anything.'

The few crewmembers she managed to talk to gave nothing away. The *Polar Star*'s captain has not been witnessed off the ship since its arrival. Félix is right, she did draw attention to herself. But she has nothing to lose.

One thing she has learned today: the *Polar Star* has better security than any other in the fleet. Ordinary dock workers morph into security guards the moment you drift near the loading ramp. But there has to be a way on board . . .

'Tell me what you're thinking, Ro.'

She stares fixedly at the isolated lights of the ship.

I can't tell you, Félix. You can't come with me. And if it doesn't work out, someone has to stay behind to tell my story.

He says, 'You can't sit there all night.'

'I can. I have to.'

Félix comes to stand behind her and wraps his arms around her, careful not to squeeze her ribcage. He kisses her neck gently. His hands move over her hips, down to the bare skin of her legs and up, his fingers teasing at the hem of her shorts, then slipping inside. She thinks her mind is too busy for sex, but finds herself turning to kiss him, pushing him back towards the bed, surprised by the sudden leap of desire.

They are tender with one another, Félix attentive of her bruised body. He keeps saying, is this all right, it's not hurting you? No, she says, don't stop. She doesn't want to think. Only this, this feeling, here, now. She comes almost at once, and when he does, inside her, she has a moment of anxiety whether her contraceptive implant has expired, before she remembers she has another six months. Five? Six. Time is like sand, everywhere and nowhere. Félix shifts beneath her, and she lies against him with her head in the crook of his neck and he strokes her hair. She thinks, I must get that implant replaced, and then six months stretches out ahead of her, uneasily, and she wonders, where will I even be in six months?

'Do you feel any better?' murmurs Félix.

'Yes. My body does.'

'It's not hurting you? Your ribs?'

She shifts her head to his chest. 'I'm all right like this.'

Beneath the rise and fall of his chest the beat of his heart thuds against her ear, as loud in this moment as thunder. She listens to its deep beat, the clench and release, and she thinks how strange it is that a sound which is so powerful when heard in another she cannot hear in her own body. But they are suspended together in this rhythm, Ramona and the beat and the warmth of his skin against the side of her face, and she lies half-comatose, not asleep, yet not quite awake, her mind here and elsewhere, wishing she could draw out this moment.

She remembers the machine-checked heartbeat of the boy she took to the medical centre, whose veins now hold cells of her blood.

Knowing he is asleep, she murmurs, 'I love you, Félix.'

She leaves the room while Félix is still sleeping, careful not to wake him. It is not cool but more so than the draining heat of the day. A small crowd is gathered at the sea wall, pointing at something down in the water. Three large white seabirds spiral overhead, their long wings beating slowly in the morning air currents. The crowd has an air of consternation, shifting uneasily among themselves. A dock officer arrives and moves authoritatively to the waterfront. Ramona wriggles her way through.

On the other side of the sea wall, a body floats face down in the water. The figure is male, dressed in the practical clothing of the stevedores, a smudge of wiry hair, a dark clot of blood at the base of his skull. Ramona's stomach clenches. There is nothing to identify the man, but even before the dock officer uses a long pole to turn the body over, she knows.

The body in the water was, until yesterday, the dock's newest stevedore, and the only one to tell Ramona the truth.

The body in the water is a warning.

'Félix, it was horrible, he was just there, floating – what the fuck have I done—'

'Hey, hey Ro, it's not your fault—'

'Of course it's my fault, I spoke to him – I got him to tell me which ship it was. All yesterday when I was trying to get on-board, they must have known, and they killed him, Félix. They fucking killed him. Because of me—'

'Hey, none of that. Did you give the order? Did you tell them to kill him? We don't even know he was killed. It might have been an accident. He was new: he didn't know the docks like the others. He could have knocked his head, walking about in the dark.'

'The back of his head? He was killed. I know it.'

'You don't know that, and you don't know it was your fault. He talked to you – what if he talked to other people as well? We don't know what he was saying.'

'I know what you're trying to do, but there's no point in pretending, Félix. He's dead because of me. He's my soul to carry.'

Félix puts his hands on her shoulders.

'I'm worried about you,' he says.

'They can't get to me.'

'Whoever's behind this, they've got reach. If they just killed a stevedore—'

'That was a warning. Stop looking and go home, that's what it meant.'

Félix falls quiet and drops his gaze.

'What, you think that's what I should do? Just give up?'

'I didn't say that.'

'You were thinking it.'

'Well what are you going to do, Ramona? What if you can't rescue Inés? You should go direct to the harbourmaster. Report this. Tell him everything. Get him to act.'

'Don't you understand? They're all in on it. They have to be. That kid was the only one who didn't know he wasn't meant to talk – or at least, he didn't know what the consequences would be. The harbourmaster knows. I'm telling you, *he knows.*'

'I can't believe that. Say you suspect smuggling. Get them to search the *Polar Star*. I'll come with you.'

'What about the radio? The price on my head?'

'We'll say you're my sister.'

She is too frustrated to answer.

'Ramona?'

'All right, we can try.'

'You don't sound very convinced.'

'I'm not convinced. That ship will come out clean from any search, I can tell you that now.'

'I just want you to stay safe.'

'I know.' She is shaking. 'Whatever they want my ma for, it's nothing good. I keep imagining the most awful things . . .'

Félix wraps her in a hug and they stay like that, holding each other, until her shivers abate.

She tells the harbourmaster about Gabi. The man at the desalination plant. The dead stevedore. As she speaks, she watches his face intently.

The harbourmaster exhibits a professional concern, arms folded, nodding. With each stumbling word Ramona's courage ebbs away. Félix is talking now. There must be a search, he says. But everything in her gut is telling her: this isn't right.

The harbourmaster assures them he takes his responsibilities for the docks extremely seriously. He will inspect the ship himself, with a senior officer. Ramona asks if she can go with them. She already knows the answer, and it comes as no surprise when the harbourmaster shakes his head.

'That would be in breach of the Boreal trade agreement. Believe me, if there is anything amiss, we will find it.'

She exits the offices feeling lightheaded. She is frightened now, very frightened. She cannot shake the sense that she has played right into their hands, and she doesn't even know who *they* are, how many, how far their influence extends up the hierarchy of the Exchange.

Félix is pleased with the outcome.

'You see? I told you. They'll find Inés. And then they can drop the kidnapping bastards in the desert. Panama justice. If anyone deserves it, they do.'

She cannot bear his optimism.

'We've made a terrible mistake, Félix.'

'No, you did the right thing—'

'And they know us now. I've put you in danger too.'

'Don't worry about me. I'm crew. I'm protected.'

The inspection of the *Polar Star* finds nothing.

On the last night of the Exchange they sit up late, talking, with the shutters closed. Félix has a plan. In the morning he will round up the crews of all the Patagonian ships. He will tell them what has been happening. They will get on-board the Boreal ship, by force if necessary. They'll open every cabin and every container. They'll check for trapdoors, secret floors and double walls. The Boreals will not be able to stop them.

Ramona agrees listlessly; what else can they do? Félix says he doesn't want her to do anything stupid.

'Like what?'

'Like trying to get on the ship yourself.'

'No,' she says. 'You're right. I can't do this on my own. Not any more.'

It is only then that Félix gives her the package. It is a pack of individually wrapped skin patches, numbered one to thirty.

'What's this?'

'It's the medicine.'

'You got it?'

'Yes. I asked around. A guy on the docks – all the right people say he's the real thing. It's the one-month course, a patch a day. I've got to be straight with you, Ro. He said it's a rough treatment. Not everyone survives it.'

She stares at the innocuous little pack and starts to cry.

'Félix . . .'

'I got it a couple of days ago. But it didn't seem – I don't know – it seemed kind of wrong when we were still looking. But I wanted you to have it now. Before we go in. So you know there's hope for Inés.'

'What did it cost?'

The briefest hesitation before he says a price. A high price, and she suspects he has adjusted it to her benefit.

'I don't have enough,' she says. 'I can't pay you.'

'I do.' Félix taps his pocket. 'I don't have much, but I have some savings. The captain stood me it. She knows I can repay her back in Fuego.'

'I can't take this from you. What if you – what if Carla needed—'

'Shh.' He puts a finger on her lips. 'It's done, Ro. I've already paid.'

She feels something inside her break then.

'Félix, I can't—'

'You don't have to thank me,' he says. 'You know that.'

His smile says the rest. I love you, I have always loved you, I will do anything for you.

And it is only now, seeing that love in his face, that she knows why she lied about Inés before. Because she did not want to say goodbye. She had always assumed that if – when – they parted for the last time, neither of them would know. They would go their separate ways, spared the sorrow of goodbyes because they would not realize that it was goodbye. In this way, their last memories of one another would be happy.

She had not thought of the possibility that one of them would know the truth.

The truth is, she will not be getting up with Félix in the morning, and rousing the Patagonian crews, and storming the Boreal ship. By the time Félix wakes, if all goes to plan, she will already be on the ship. There is a fair chance that she will not be coming back. It is as though the belt, where the edge of the south meets the edge of the north, is where her luck runs out.

This is the last time. She feels it in her bones. But she cannot take this ignorance from Félix, even though her betrayal tomorrow, when he realizes she has gone, will be a terrible thing. She cannot take this last memory from him.

34 |

The grave-watcher sits on the steps, as far away from the infected
as possible. He cannot remember ever having felt afraid like this.
His mother used to describe seeing ghosts. She was religious,
and believed in reincarnation, and she believed that ghosts were souls
who had not managed to reincarnate, and they petrified her. He
always thought it silly but he feels that fear now.

There's another hour to go of his shift. He wishes his replacement
would come early and take over. The minutes crawl by. Every time he
raises the light a little to check the clock, he is afraid the man will be
awake, staring at him with that healing face. Who is he? What is he?
What if he's one of them from the north; what if there's robotics in him;
what if he's – the grave-watcher shudders now – a nirvana? Do they get
sick, nirvanas? Unnatural things they are, born of folk who should have
died and didn't. It makes your skin crawl just thinking of it.

Twice now he has hovered near the bell, wondering if he should call
a doctor, but each time something stops him. He is afraid that if he
makes the call, the man down there will do something.

Instead he puts his headphones on and flicks through the radio
channels, turning the volume up high. He wants something that
will distract him. It's all talk of the redfleur and the quarantine, like

he needs to hear it. Government promises, reassurance from the army: they have it all in hand. You haven't seen what's here, thinks the grave-watcher. And you've forgotten what's coming. I remember the last time. He switches to another channel. And then he finds it. The purest, saddest voice he's ever heard. *Pilar y el Loro*, says the broadcaster, at the end of the song. Recorded only the other night, at a secret gig. She's a homeless girl. A homeless singing sensation. She sings fado, explains the broadcaster. A voice for our times. Here's another, have a listen to this.

The grave-watcher listens, transfixed. His head empties. For a few minutes, it doesn't matter that he watches over the dying, and is reviled for it. It doesn't matter that he lives a solitary life, never quite sure how to speak to other people, wondering what is the right way to do it. It doesn't matter that his replacement is late. Alone with his headphones in this dark basement where no one comes and no one wants to believe exists, he listens to *Pilar y el Loro*. The broadcaster isn't exaggerating. She's something special all right. You can hear the tension in the room where she sings, the audience hanging on to every note.

Although he is facing the basement, the grave-watcher senses, rather than hears, the figure lurching to its feet.

His heart pounds. It hurts his chest, it's beating so bad. He clutches a hand to his sternum, scared he's going to have an attack. He can't bring himself to take off the headphones or turn the light on full. The figure is fumbling about in the darkness. Down there, where the dying are, there's someone who *isn't dying*.

He is coming towards the grave-watcher. Heading for the stairs. The grave-watcher can see him now, a darker shadow swelling against the dark basement. It's the man. He looms at the bottom of the stairs. The grave-watcher presses against the wall, terrified. For a moment he sees the man's features in the dim lights. The scabbed, brown cheeks. The red-rimmed, hallucinatory gaze. The man looks at the grave-watcher. The grave-watcher's lungs constrict.

His chest is on fire.

'Help me,' says the man.

The grave-watcher's limbs are frozen. All he can do is point to the card. The man takes it. He hears the man ascend the stairs in slow, awkward movements, one step at a time. He hears the card swipe and the beep of the lock releasing. He hears the door open. The card is thrown back, pattering down the stairs. The door shuts.

When his heart rate has slowed enough to move, the grave-watcher checks his records. Carefully, meticulously, he removes all evidence of the man who walked away.

He was never here.

The grave-watcher says it to himself, over and over. I never saw him, because he was never here.

At the end of his shift the burners come. They take away five bodies. He waits for the next intake of the infected, but none arrive. When he goes upstairs to scrub up and hand back his suit, they tell him the basement is no longer in use. There are too many now. It is an epidemic.

35 ¦

ikram is gone.

Twenty-four hours have passed since he left, and he has not returned. Another night has set in. The temperature has dropped, the stars have come out, the curfew trucks roll through the street once an hour and the redfleur death toll rises on the radio. Vikram is gone.

It is Taeo's fault. He can see it all quite clearly now. He should have been straight with the Osirian from the start. If he had only had courage enough to tell him the truth, to trust him and ask him to trust Taeo, they might have come to an agreement. Now he has told the truth and with it, the truth of all the lies, and now Vikram has gone.

Where he has gone, Taeo has no idea, but he no longer doubts Vikram's last words – the Osirian can look after himself. Perhaps he was only waiting for Taeo to break down. Perhaps he has been using Taeo as much as Taeo has been using him: gathering information, practising the foreign sounds of vowels and consonants until he believed himself equipped to get by alone. The more Taeo thinks about it, the clearer the case.

Vikram has run away. Perhaps he decided to strike out for Antarctica alone; perhaps he plans to head north; or just find a place to hole up in Patagonia; maybe he wants to go home, warn his people, tell them the truth. Whichever it is, he has decided he doesn't need Taeo.

The worst of it is, Taeo can't blame Vikram for acting that way. It is his fault. He brought Vikram to Cataveiro. From beginning to end this has been nothing but a farce. They should have stayed at Tierra del Fuego, waited out the harbour lockdown and jumped on the nearest Antarctican ship. Swum to it, if necessary. Instead he entrusted a holoma to a renegade pilot who is wanted for the attempted murder of a desalination mogul, and dragged the only physical proof of Osiris to a city terrorized by the world's deadliest disease, where he is now left – alone – barely able to walk, with nothing. And to think he used to consider himself an intelligent individual.

He remembers the boy. The one that works for the Alaskan. What is his name? Mig. He should go to the Alaskan, put her on the case. But no, he can't betray Vikram. Not even now. He should find Mig and speak to him directly. That is a plan. He needs a plan. He needs to do something, anything.

He raids the flat for whatever cash he can find, checking the floor, the drawers, under the beds. He pulls together a decent amount. He should feel angry about having his wallet stolen, but he no longer has the energy for it.

He nudges the shutters open and checks the streets below before heading out, but he can see no one. Day three – or is it four? – of the quarantine. After the riots and castings-out of those first nights, a nervous hush has descended over the city. He imagines others, opening their own shutters, peering down and seeing his figure limping down the street. Wondering where he is going. What he is up to.

By now he knows the way to the Alaskan's by heart. He sets out purposefully. His body is stiff and bruised and every step is a battle. It quickly becomes evident he will never make it as far as the Alaskan's. He sits on the nearest step, a looted pharmacy, kicking away the broken glass from the windows.

Directly across the street, the teenager squats on the steps that lead down to the opium den. Taeo looks at her. He begins to laugh. The laugh is infinitely painful; his one-eyed vision dances and for a moment he thinks he is going to black out. He wonders if Vikram broke some of his ribs.

The teenager's chin lifts a fraction as Taeo shuffles across the road. Her eyes lock onto Taeo's battered face.

'You got money today, señor? You want croc? O? She's got new stuff in . . .'

The teenager's eyes are strangely imploring.

'How can she,' says Taeo, 'when nothing's getting in or out the city?'

'You think that, señor, you think that; but there's ways, there's holes in the circle, there's places to slip in and out, there's routes, señor . . .'

Places to slip in and out. Places for Vikram to make his escape, alone, leaving Taeo to rot.

Suddenly he is overwhelmed with rage. Whatever his intentions were at the start, he tried to help Vikram. He could have killed him right there in the cave in Fuego and rid the Republic of a problem. He could have. But he didn't. He chose to help the other man. He kept him safe. They had a pact. And this is how Vikram thanks him: by running off on his own, abandoning Taeo in a city full of disease.

He remembers Vikram's words.

I hope you die of redfleur.

'Señor, you want something? You should say so now, don't wait around like that, don't draw attention here—'

'Yes. Yes, I do. Take me in.'

The transaction is brief. He has no desire to linger in the opium den. The look in the proprietress's eyes is almost enough to deter him, but the scent of the opium is stronger.

Why fight it? Why pretend to be something you are not? Give in. You are an addict. This is all you have left.

He hands over the remainder of his currency. She gives him the croc. He can't afford the opium.

He unwraps the stuff with trembling hands and looks at it.

Don't be fucking stupid, this is the last thing you need.

He wraps it back up. Puts it down and goes into the other room and returns and takes it out again. The teenager lied. This isn't the good stuff – the pure stuff straight from the pods – but it's packed full of opiates and that's all that matters. He chucked out the pipe when they made the pact; how the hell is he going to do this? Something metal, a spoon. Just inhale it straight. But he hasn't got any fire. Fuck! He runs out, bangs on Madame Bijou's door. A girl lends him a lighter, asks no questions, but stares openly at his face and raises her eyebrows in a knowing arc. Her knowledge shames him but he doesn't care. All he wants now is the hit. He wants to be dead to the world.

Back to the apartment. His fingers tremble in anticipation as he preps the spoon and sets light to the stuff. Tiny translucent bubbles form out of the resin, swelling and imploding like primeval soup. He has missed this. The little rituals of the preparation. The magic of it.

He sits back and inhales. It feels like coming home.

The warmth that suffuses him is such a beautiful thing that he could almost cry, but he doesn't; he doesn't need to now.

He hunches over the spoon, takes another inhalation. He turns on the radio and finds a station playing gentle, ebbing music. Funny that he used to hate it so. Now he feels odd if it isn't there.

For a long time he is floating on the surface of the ocean. The waves rock him gently. He realizes he has reached the sea city. Pyramids rise before him, vast silver constructions that could only be the work of gods or aliens. Wet seaweed drips from their sloping walls, and clinging on are strange people who are not people. Taeo observes them curiously. Their throats flap; they have gills. Taeo touches his neck. He has them too. When he looks at his hands, they are webbed.

Slender fins rise from the Osirian spines. They look at him with round fish eyes. He should be afraid but he is not, because he knows this is Vikram's story, he has fallen into Vikram's story, and he will fall back out of it, soon enough.

The pain returns with sudden, shocking speed. He is sweating and shaking. He needs a second hit. But he will do it properly, with etiquette, the way he was shown in Fuego. Respect the O, they told him. He does respect it, or he respects whatever shit this is. Once again he goes through the ritual lighting. Inhale. Lie back. Inhale. The room shifts around him. His visions grow stranger. Now he sees that his hands are covered in scales. Something is walking up his leg, a weird hybrid animal, insectoid with fins. Its knobbly legs march steadily on, proceeding up his shin, onto his knee. It has hard black eyes. Pincers and fins. There are others, rows of them crawling up the walls of the room. How strange they are. How strange the world and the people in it, what strange things they do. It is strange that Vikram did not take any money. He only thinks it now. It is strange to run away with no money and no belongings. Perhaps Vikram did not run away after all. Perhaps he is coming back. He will have found a way out. They can go to Antarctica after all.

The finned insects are on the ceiling now. Their many eyes stare down at him, but he is not afraid. It's only a hallucination. There are things far worse to fear.

A voice, singing. He knows it is coming from the radio but it seems to come from someplace else entirely, an ethereal place, a fantastical place, like the very centre of the ice or up in the clouds where the pilot flies. Another song, the same voice again. All the insects on the ceiling are singing, their tiny mouths opening and closing in unison. They are the voice.

He inhales and falls back on the bed, his muscles lax, his body floating. This beautiful stuff. This beautiful stuff in this shitty country.

He remembers the holoma in his hand and squeezes it gently,

activating the machine. He brings up the projection of Shri and watches for a few moments, then pauses her. She hovers over him, her lips slightly parted, as if she might bend closer for a kiss. He reaches his arms towards her.

The angelic voice stops abruptly but the insects' mouths on the ceiling continue to move. They are talking gravely now. Their eyes are solemn. Taeo hears the words *crisis* and *epidemic* and the revelation comes to him that everyone in the city must be dead. He is the only one left. Dimly, he is aware that he should feel something – horror or grief – but the truth is he doesn't care. He doesn't care because he is high and because he is high Shri is in the room with him. The radio burbles. It is Shri's voice that is transmitting. The insects have it. They are playing: her heart to his heart on a never-ending loop.

36 ┊

The Alaskan is talking and Mig wishes more than anything that she would shut up and never speak again. The sound of her voice grates on him; it feels as though every word is a thumb pushed into an open wound. He doesn't want to hear. He doesn't want to know. He doesn't care about her agendas and schemes, he doesn't care about her money. All he wants is to find Pilar, or what is left of her.

He replays those moments over and over. Pilar's body, whisked away. The soldiers in their hazard suits. The truck. The Osirian man from the Tarkie's apartment.

'Are you listening, Mig?'

'Yes, señora.'

'What did I say?'

'You said—' he stops. He has no idea what she just said. He keeps his eyes down. He can feel the laser beam of the Alaskan's gaze upon him. You would have thought that the quarantine would slow her down, even frighten her – after all, he and Maria are the only help she has in the city, and Maria has not been seen since the outbreak – but the Alaskan seems to thrive upon the drama. She has at least ten radios tuned to different stations. She listens to them simultaneously, comparing the mounting figures of the epidemic, a few individual cases now stretching to tens and hundreds. Thousands will die by the time it is over. That is what the radio says. And something else: guerrilla forces are gathering on the outskirts of the city. Redfleur does not deter them. The army is nervous.

'Go on,' says the Alaskan. 'Tell me.'

'I wasn't listening.'

'What did you say?'

'I wasn't listening.'

He keeps his eyes down, waiting for the tirade. When it does not come, he dares to glance up. The Alaskan's eyes are upon him. She looks very calm and very cold. The kind of cold so severe it burns you. Concentrate, he thinks. Keep the witch happy. With her contacts, she is his best chance of finding where Pilar was taken.

'Did I ever tell you,' asks the Alaskan, 'about the time the guerrillas came to kidnap me?'

'No.' Mig racks his brains – did she tell him? For insurance he adds, 'I don't think so.'

'They came here,' says the Alaskan. 'It was during the coup of oh-six, before the government took back power in oh-eight. They came to this room, where you and I are sitting right now. They broke the door down, waving their guns about. They knew about my legs, so they brought a sling. A sling, I say! They expected to carry me out all rolled up like a cigar.'

Mig knows what is expected of him. 'What did you do?'

'I said to them: You know who I am. One of them spat at me. Another began breaking things. Small things at first, then my radios. "The northerner," they said. "We've heard all about you. The time's come to pay." "Oh," I said. "I have money. A lot of money. It's in a trunk under this bed. It would make all of you rich, but you won't take it." I could see the greed in their eyes. Pirates, the lot of them. They would have robbed me and kidnapped me without a flicker of remorse. They'd try and make someone pay for me – who I can't imagine – but they didn't have the capacity to think ahead like that. And then, when that failed, they would probably kill me.'

The Alaskan twists the dial on a radio and tilts her head, listening.

'You are probably too young to know such a feeling. But I saw my final days played out before me. I saw what they had planned. I saw my own death.'

He tries to imagine a life without Pilar in it. He can't.

She'll make it through, he thinks. She'll be the one to survive the redfleur.

'So did you kill them?'

It seems the only logical conclusion to the story.

'No,' says the Alaskan. 'I said to them, "You know who I am. But do you know who my ancestors are?" They played along, like you do, Mig. "Why would we care?" "Because," said I, "they survived the Blackout. Both of them."'

What she is.

Now Mig is unable to look away. Maria told him, of course, and now he knows the Alaskan knows Maria told him, in fact that was probably why she told Maria in the first place. But he has never heard it from the Alaskan herself.

He feels the cold of her black eyes, until every part of him, skin, blood, his internal organs, is chilled. Words run through his head.

Freak, mutant, witch.

Nirvana.

'Of course they knew, as you know, Mig, what "survived" means.' Now the Alaskan's voice holds a note of vicious triumph. 'They dropped the sling. Backed away. "Freak!" they shouted. All the usual, mindless insults. But they wouldn't touch me. Or rob me. Not a nirvana. Not that.'

She is breathing very quickly, her chest rising and falling, her nostrils flared.

'They left very quickly after that. Because, as you know, we are not people.'

Her fingers tremor, a quick spasm against the bedsheets. He cannot mistake the bitterness in her voice, but she has told him this for a reason.

Do not underestimate me. Do not cross me.

If he could feel anything, he would not dare to ask the next question. But Pilar is gone, and all he feels is dull inside.

'Is that why you left the north?'

The Alaskan's gaze is suddenly cleared of expression. The shift is terrifying. He senses a searing rage concealed behind the soft cheeks and jowls, a rage that makes him shiver. He remembers the chemist. The poisons.

'The north is no longer my concern. My concern is the plan which you were not listening to, and which you will listen to now. Do you understand me?'

'Yes, señora,' he whispers.

'There is a man coming. You have seen him before. He came for the telegram. His name is Alejandro Herrera. I wish for you to take him to the Antarctican's residence.'

'Who is he?'

'It doesn't matter who he is. What matters is that there are several people who are interested in what – or rather, who – we believe the Antarctican is hiding, and now is the time to exploit our knowledge. So firstly you will take this contact, Alejandro. You will check that Taeo Ybanez and his mysterious friend are in the building and you will fetch Alejandro. After that, others will come. Xiomara's people will be primed to trail you. And a team of city enforcers will be following them. Your role is to check the coast is clear, take Alejandro upstairs, and then get out. Do you understand?'

'Yes, señora. Take Alejandro and then get out. I understand.'

She continues to hold his gaze.

'Who's capturing them?'

'The enforcers, Mig. And then we will bail out the Antarctican, and then he will be in our debt, just like the others. And that will be a job well done.'

'And what about the one from the sea city? What happens to him?'

The Alaskan shrugs. 'His fate doesn't concern us. I've been thinking, Mig. I know how you look at me. You look and you see a decrepit, bedridden old woman. An evil woman, even, if you believe in evil as a force. Perhaps you do. Maria believes in a jaguar in the sky so why wouldn't you believe in evil? They broke my spine, you know. You didn't know. Yes, they broke it. I was twenty-six. A group of rabid children heard the word nirvana and decided they would teach me a lesson for what I was. They weren't so different to you. They'd been to school but it hadn't made them less ignorant. I doubt they could have told me the history of the anthropocene.

'It's one of the reasons I have enjoyed this city. You can choose your story here. You can choose what you wish to be, and what you wish to believe. But when it comes to nirvanas, there is only one story. And Cataveiro is running out, Mig. Time is running out for your country. The future is Antarctica. It's time for me to head south. You should think about it. I could use someone resourceful like you.'

Mig stares at her. He has no idea what to say, or what she wants him to say.

'Ah yes. You wanted to know about the Osirian. Well, once the sea city is discovered, it will be destroyed, one way or another. I have no further interest in who Taeo Ybanez is hiding. I could play with this man, yes, I could sell him to the Boreals. But the time and investment are too great, and I have plans to make. For all I care, they can kill him.'

He waits. Nothing more is forthcoming. For once, the Alaskan appears to have exhausted herself.

'Yes, señora,' he says.

'Now get the hell out.'

He goes.

37 ┇

Always carry your life with you.

That was the advice Ramona offered the Antarctican, flippantly enough, little realizing it would soon be truer than she might care to think. Their conversation on the roof of the Facility seems like a long time ago, but when she counts the days, barely four weeks have passed. She has her life with her now. Her pack is wedged between her knees; within it are supplies of food and water, her toolkit, a knife, a torch. The medicine. She clutches the straps of the pack tightly. She is in total darkness, but she doesn't want to waste the battery on the torch now. She'll need it, once she's on-board.

She can hear the machinery of the docks, at once loud and muffled. She can hear directions being shouted.

When the crane engages with the roof of the container, the reverberation goes right through its metal walls. She feels a primitive fear as the container is lifted from the dock floor and swung up into the air and across, the boxes of papaver tea shifting around her. The truck driver promised she would be unhurt by the brief ride.

Everything has a price, including bribery. The truck driver was happy to take the night-vision goggles. No doubt they will serve him well.

Perhaps he knew who she was. Perhaps when the container sets down on the ship there will be someone waiting on the other side, to open the door and shine a light in her face. Perhaps they will be Xiomara's agents. Perhaps they will be the harbourmaster's officers, ready to take her out and drop her in the desert, where this time there will be no return. Perhaps it will be the raiders themselves, pleased to have another victim, and she will be reunited with her mother sooner than she expected.

Or perhaps the driver saw her as just another southerner desperate to see the shining north. A woman whose life is so wretched she is prepared to endure incarceration and starvation to stow away in the hold of a Boreal ship; risk discovery, risk capture, risk her life. She is not the first and she will not be the last to go north this way. There always had to be an enabler.

The container swings down and lands with a sickening thud. A flare of pain shoots through Ramona's ribs. Once again she feels the urge to turn on a light.

Not yet.

She thinks of Félix, lying in the bed where she left him. The clench and release of his heart, a little slower, as he dreams the sinuous dreams of the poppy flower, lost in the labyrinth of sleep until he is woken, groggy and confused, at midday. A fellow crewmember shaking his shoulders: You're late, we're leaving!

By then it will be too late. By then the Boreal fleet will be edging away from the docks, and Ramona will be switching on her torch and shining it on the cubic interior of the one-and-a-half metre container.

Don't hate me too much, Félix. You'd have done the same to save me.

Ma, I'm here. I'm with you. I'm coming.

38 |

The door is unlocked but there is no evidence of forced entry: the first sign that something is wrong. Vikram enters cautiously, avoiding the sections of the floor that make a noise. He smells it first. A faint but cloying scent that lingers in the apartment. Stale air and vomit. The smell is sweetish, like burnt honey.

He finds Taeo lying on his back on the bed, a dark-haired woman leaning over him, one arm slightly raised, her face arrested. Vikram backs away, startled. Seconds pass before he realizes the woman is not moving. She will never move. She is frozen. The woman is Shri, Taeo's partner, and she is a hologram.

Vikram edges closer, trying to ignore the staring eyes of the shimmering three-dimensional projection. Taeo's one open eye is glazed and prominent, a green bauble. His mouth is slack and a trail of vomit and saliva has congealed on his chin. The light falling through the window makes the damp interior of his mouth glisten, and catches the saliva, as well as the dull gleam of a spoon scorched to black at Taeo's side. The radio is hissing static. Vikram leans over to switch it off. The silence is sudden and intense.

In this room the smell is stronger. Vikram's head swims. He feels sweat collecting on his forehead, sliding down his face and neck and getting into his eyes. He wipes it away roughly, knocking a fresh scab from his cheek.

He takes Taeo's pulse, but he already knows he is dead. His skin is cold and hard. Dead for at least a day, probably. It looks like he choked on his own vomit. Vikram tries to close the eye that is open but the flesh has already set. The bruises inflicted by Vikram are a permanent fixture now. He hadn't realized he had done so much damage. He hadn't meant to – he'd just been so angry . . .

The room feels shaky and shifting, as though he is suddenly stood on the decking around an Osirian tower after so many days on land. On the table beside Taeo is a lighter and what is left of the drug, a tiny nub of something black and waxy. Taeo's hand is wrapped around the holoma. Vikram has to walk through the frozen woman to get to it. He feels a tingling sensation all over his body as he is immersed in her image. He squeezes Taeo's cold, stiff hand around the holoma, as he observed him do once before. After a few seconds, the woman vanishes, and the room seems even quieter.

Vikram prises the holoma from Taeo's hand. It weighs less than he thought it would.

Visions of familiar faces appear and recede before him. Mikkeli. Eirik. Nils. Drake. Adelaide.

Taeo.

He leaves the room and closes the door. He cannot bear to be with the staring eye of the corpse a moment longer.

Walking about the apartment, he has a sense of extreme unreality. Everything that has happened in the last few days feels like a hallucinatory experience, and his disorientation is intensified by the stuff pumped into his veins in that hellish basement. He changes his clothes, fumbling with zips, falling over himself when he pulls on his trousers. He raids the apartment for anything of use, stopping and clutching at the furniture when sudden rushes of nausea take him by surprise. He finds a few coins, but most of the money has gone. Taeo must have used it to buy the drugs that killed him. Vikram loads packets of food into a backpack. He fills two bottles with stale water from the sink. He hesitates and goes back into Taeo's room. Avoiding looking at Taeo's body, he roots through the Antarctican's bags. He has had ample time to check Taeo's belongings; the Osirian gun is what he is looking for. After all this time the power will have leaked out of it, but he puts the gun in the backpack too. Intimidation alone might save his life.

Lastly he brings a blanket from the room where he slept for two weeks and covers Taeo's body with it. He flushes the drugs and kicks the spoon under the bed.

In the doorway he hesitates again. It feels as though he should say something, apologize, but the silence is too wide, too heavy, and he doesn't have the right words, and if he did they would be sucked into it.

He thinks about saying goodbye to the girl next door who helped him with his Spanish while Taeo was out visiting the Alaskan. No. Best leave no trace. He picks up his bag and steps out into the corridor.

A boy is standing there. A skinny boy, with a look in his eyes of unbearable sorrow. A boy who is strangely familiar, although Vikram cannot think where he would have seen him before. The boy stares at Vikram, a similar, confused recognition spreading over his face.

'You're the other one,' says the boy. 'The one from the sea city.'

Vikram realizes then. There is only one person who could know about his presence in the city. The Alaskan, and the Alaskan's accomplices. She uses children, Taeo told him. Homeless children. He had seen a girl and a boy.

'Mig,' he says.

The boy nods, cautiously.

'You don't have scales.'

'No.'

The boy looks past Vikram into the room.

'Taeo is dead. He—' Vikram does not know the Spanish word for overdosed '—he died. He is in there.'

The boy is staring at him openly now, at his face, and the scars on his cheeks.

'I saw you,' he says. 'I saw you, where she was singing. The soldiers took you.'

'They believed I was sick.'

'Where did they take you?' says Mig, urgently. 'Where?'

'It's a way from here. The other side of the city.'

Mig glances down the stairwell. 'They're down there. They're waiting for me to say it's clear.'

'Who's down there?'

'I don't know. Soldiers. Government people. Xiomara's people. Maybe all of them. I don't know who she told. She's a witch. She's a nirvana. She wants the Tarkie.'

'The Alaskan?'

The boy nods. He darts another nervous look back.

'Mig. Is there another way out?'

The boy hesitates. Vikram watches him weighing up his options. He can see the boy's impulses grappling in his face: his fear of the Alaskan, of the place where Vikram was taken, a great loss, a need to act.

'Yes,' he says. 'There's another way.'

'Show me.'

'You have to take me to the place. To Pilar.'

'Pilar?'

The boy swallows. 'She's the one who sings.'

The girl on the stage. The girl who sings. Vikram looks at Mig and he understands.

'I'll take you there, and you'll get me out of the city. Deal?'

The boy reaches for Vikram's hand. He leads him to the end of the corridor, tugging, making Vikram move faster. Vikram fights the dizziness clouding his head. Mig opens a door onto a fire escape.

'The roof,' says the boy. 'Now.'

*

The morning sun glints off solar panels and fractures Vikram's vision, but it doesn't slow down Mig. Following the boy over the roofs, he has the incongruous sense of tracking a younger version of himself. Mig moves swiftly and certainly, as at home up here winding in and out of the bathtubs and twitching radio antennae as Vikram ever was on the raft racks of Osiris. The kid knows his city. In momentary pauses, Vikram glimpses the streets below and sees that Cataveiro has been segmented. Areas of contamination are cordoned off by army barricades. White hazard tents pop up on street corners and red sheets draped from windows mark the redfleur zones. He asks Mig, has this happened before? Yes, says the boy, and it will come back again. The redfleur always comes back. Vikram knows the words should frighten him, but instead he finds them oddly comforting; the knowledge that redfleur has come and gone; that this is not an end but the end of one time that only marks the beginning of another.

He watches the ground ahead of him, and he runs.

05/ 12/ 2417

INTEL MEMO URGENT

FM   SPECIAL UNIT ATRAK / GRAHAM STATION 6
TO   DEP CIVIL SECURITY HQ / HOME SECURITY CHIEF MAXIL QYN
INFO   CIVIL SECURITY REPUBLIC OF ANTARCTICA PRIORITY HIGH

SUBJECT: MONITORING OF THE SOUTH ATLANTIC OCEAN CITY OSIRIS
(INTERNATIONAL STATUS: DESTROYED)

REF: OS17532

Classified by: KARIS IO, CMR SPECIAL UNIT ATRAK (FM 04/05/2414)

On 05/12/2417 at the hour 22.09, a long-range radio signal was detected originating from the City of Osiris. The signal is transmitting a
distress call addressed to all land nations within range.

Cmr Karis Io requests an emergency briefing with the home security chief.

EPILOGUE

In the city of Cataveiro there was a man who survived the redfleur. He was a man from nowhere. He was a man without a name, although some say that he had scales like a fish, and could swim for hours underwater without coming up for air. The redfleur had him, and the redfleur let him go. Who can say, listeners, why some are spared? The man lived. He walked out of the city, awake and breathing, amazed to find himself alive. Afraid? Yes, perhaps he was afraid, at least a little. Giving death the slip has that effect, and this was not the first incidence of the man escaping a horrible fate. For a time after the epidemic he was seen in places – south of the city, and around the archipelago. Places where there was water. Here and there he would appear where he had not been seen before. And then, just like that, he was gone.

You're listening to Station Cataveiro, and it's a quarter to midnight. So sit back, relax, and take a sip of that cachaça. We have a tale or two for you.

ACKNOWLEDGEMENTS

I'm immensely grateful to the friends who have supported me through the past eighteen months, making the road to Cataveiro and the transition to life in publication that much lighter. Particular mention must go to my sister, Kim, for critiquing the drafts I wouldn't dare show anyone else; to my parents, for always being there, and for understanding when I've been a hopeless correspondent; to M-P for those late nights talking through tricksy narrative issues; to John for supporting me through all the seen and unforeseen challenges of the writing life; to Chris and Nina for their friendship, advice, and inspiration; to Lavie for helping me find my feet in the hitherto mysterious world of SFF; to my editorial gurus Michael Rowley and Emily Yau for their insight, patience and invaluable work on the book; to the team at Del Rey UK for putting *Cataveiro* out into the world: a thousand thank yous.